TWICE THE ACTION!
TWICE THE ADVENTURE!
TWO PONY SOLDIERS NOVELS IN ONE LOW-PRICED VOLUME!

SLAUGHTER AT BUFFALO CREEK

During a Comanche uprising, the frontier was awash with the blood of innocent settlers. But the Indians didn't know what they were in for when they killed Captain Colt Harding's wife and son and kidnapped his daughter. Because Harding wouldn't stop pursuing them until he had rescued his daughter—and killed the savages who had murdered his wife and son.

COMANCHE MASSACRE

A ragtag group of misfits, the Pony Soldiers weren't much to look at. But when Indians were on the warpath, they were the best protection anyone on the frontier could hope for. So when the Comanches had had enough of white men cheating them and started an all-out war, the pioneers knew that nothing could save them from certain death—except the Pony Soldiers.

SLAUGHTER AT BUFFALO CREEK

Bowers watched the painted Indians charging forward. When they were within four hundred yards he gave the order to fire, and a dozen rifles barked. Two Indian horses went down. He saw one brave wounded, but the attackers drove forward. On some unseen signal they parted and half went each way as they began circling the line of four wagons.

Only three or four of the Indians had rifles, Bowers decided. But that only made them more deadly—they had to get in close to use their arrows and lances . . .

COMANCHE MASSACRE

Sgt. Casemore led the brave with his pistol and hit him in the side. The Comanche went down and tried to get up once, then flopped down and didn't move.

Everyone was screaming and shooting. Sgt. Casemore figured it would be a miracle if at least two of the troop were not killed by friendly fire. He rushed from one tipi to the next. Most were deathly silent.

He came out of one and looked back at the Indian he had shot on the run. The brave was not there. The savage must have been faking his wound. He was gone . . . .

Also in the PONY SOLDIERS series:

PONY SOLDIERS

SLAUGHTER AT BUFFALO CREEK/
COMANCHE MASSACRE

Chet Cunningham

LEISURE BOOKS   NEW YORK CITY

A LEISURE BOOK®

AUGUST 1990

Published by

Dorchester Publishing Co., Inc.
276 Fifth Avenue
New York, NY 10001

SLAUGHTER AT BUFFALO CREEK

1

Corporal Alf Lewton stared at the rolling plains around him and shook his head.

"Know what I know, Sarge, and *I sure as hell felt them savages*. They watching us, I still say so, and it's a raiding party sure as hell. We should find a spot we can defend and ride out a patrol."

Sergeant Bill Bowers sent a long stream of tobacco juice squirting into the Texas sage. He had been with the Troop since it was formed back in fifty-five. There wan't much in the way of soldering and fighting he hadn't seen, including the Comanche.

"Alf, you don't shoot a Comanche until you see the little bastard. Half the time you never see them. You damn well won't see them until they want you to. So we keep moving. If we pull up here, we'll be a day late getting into Fort Comfort and the old man will raise all bloody hell."

Corporal Lewton slouched lower in his saddle where he sat the army black. He looked at his anchors, the three big Pittsburgh supply wagons, each with five thousand pounds of supplies. Then there was the real problem, the fourth rig, a covered wagon that held the most precious cargo, the wife and two small children of Captain Colt Harding, the fort's commanding officer.

Fort Comfort wasn't exactly a hardship post, but damn few women had elected to come into the wilds of Western Texas. It was the last fort before the country turned into the raw and unmapped Comanche hunting grounds.

Alf wanted to light his pipe but he didn't. It was hot enough already and not yet ten o'clock in the morning. He shaded his hand over his gray campaign hat with the low crown and wide brim. It did a lot to keep the sun out of his eyes. He stared at the small sandstone ridge to their right.

True he had not seen any Comanches. He had not even seen smoke there. No Indian smoke signals. He'd heard about them but never actually spotted any. Damn, he wished they were out of this long narrow valley. That is if you can have a valley without any hills. The country was so damn flat it gave him the shakes. He was a Tennessee mountain man himself, and damn proud of it.

Alf loved riding with the Cavalry, the famous Second Cavalry, the sharpest, most highly decorated outfit in the whole damn U.S. Army! Corporal Lewton looked at the ridge of sandstone again, then went back to the head of the small supply train where he rode the point of a fifteen man Cavalry escort.

Eight members of the escort detail were ahead of the rigs, the rest along the sides and a rear guard.

Alf would be damn glad to get in two more good days of travel and arrive at the gates of Fort Comfort. It was called a Fort but was not the headquarters of a regiment. It was more of an outpost over a hundred and twenty miles west of Austin.

Inside the rocking, jolting covered wagon, Milly Harding was trying to read a story to her two children. Little Sadie was just past her fourth birthday. Captain Colt Harding, her father, tried not to show it, but he plainly favored the shy little beauty. She had long blond hair and sparkling blue eyes, a mischievous grin and a laugh that won everyone's heart in a minute. She looked up at her mother now.

"Why is it so hot? Why are we bouncing so much? Mommie, why did we have to leave St. Louis?" The questions were softly spoken, laced with a smile of confusion.

Milly had answered the same questions a dozen times on the long trip, most of it done on the more comfortable stage coaches. Now she smiled and pushed back her own long blond hair that Colt wouldn't let her cut. She had washed her hair last night and was too tired to put it up properly. Now it swung around her shoulders and half way down her back.

She watched Sadie with eyes that matched the child's intense blue ones and smiled.

"We're going because Daddy wanted us to! Isn't that wonderful! A lot of places Daddy has to work aren't nice enough for sweet little girls and jumping jack boys to stay. But Fort Comfort is the best one so far. And we'll be there in just two more days!"

"I liked it back home," Sadie said shyly. Then she shrugged. "I know I'll like it at our new house too. Won't I, Mommie?"

"Yes you will, Sadie. Fort Comfort is your new home. You'll love living there."

Yale, seven now and the big brother and man-of-the-family when Daddy was away, launched his own worry.

"I sure won't have many kids to play with. Didn't you say there were only two other officers' families there?"

"Yes, Yale, but we don't know how many children they have. Remember the Johnsons? They have twelve little ones."

Yale tried to spin a top on a board but the top, made from a wooden spool for thread, kept falling off the side.

"I hope they both have twelve kids. If not I'm gonna play with the enlisted kids. Maybe I can play with some Indians!"

"Yale Harding, you will not. Indians are savages. That is no way to talk. I'm sure there will be plenty of playmates. Anyway, you'll be able to take riding lessons. Your father promised."

Yale twisted his face, nodded and concentrated on the top.

Milly watched him a moment, he was so like his father, single minded, determined . . . yes, stubborn, a good strong Harding stubborn steak that was evident in both her children. She looked back at Sadie, her beautiful little daughter, and her last child, the doctor had told her.

Sadie was such a love. She seldom complained, almost never got into mischief or trouble, and was as pretty as a picture in her little calico dress and blue ribbons in her long blonde hair. Milly was so thankful to have a sweet little girl. She was the luckiest woman alive! She hugged both her children.

"Now, where were we in the story? Yes, the old fox was in the garden waiting to see if the chicken coop would be closed tightly that night by Farmer Brown."

Milly heard a whoop outside. Yale scrambled over

the mattress laid in the bottom of the wagon to the tailgate and looked out the round opening made by the canvas top.

"Something is happening!" Yale called.

Milly walked on her knees to the back of the wagon and pushed her head outside.

The wagon had stopped. The Cavalrymen were shouting. She saw the soldier escort milling around Sergeant Bowers. He looked to the west, and when Milly stared that way she gasped and pushed her hand to her mouth.

Coming down the small rise a quarter of a mile away were at least twenty screaming, shouting Indian braves. She had never seen an Indian before, but these must be Indians, and they were coming to attack the wagons!

Bowers barked orders, dismounting the Pony Soldiers, spotting them behind the wagons. Their breech loading, single shot rifles loaded and ready to fire.

The Comanches came at the supply train in their traditional attack method, a sweeping V with the best war chief riding on the point of the V, his war shield held up as powerful medicine to ward off the roundeyes' bullets.

The Cavalry mounts were tied to wagon wheels and the blue shirted troopers lay behind the wheels to fire at the coming charge. Some of the recruits snapped shots at the raiders.

"Hold your fire!" Bowers bellowed. "Wait until the bastards get within good range, damnit!"

Bowers wished his men had been issued the Spencer repeating rifle like some of the troops had. The seven shot, lever operated weapons, could hold off an attack. His men had a variety of single shot breech loaders and even some muzzle loaders left over from the Civil War.

"God damn, forgot about the civilians!" Bowers yelped and charged to the covered wagon with the passengers and barked in the back opening.

"Mrs. Harding. You lay down low as you can get and keep your kids down. Pile anything you have round you that will stop bullets. Stay in the wagon and keep that pistol handy. Then you better start praying!"

He saw the startled look on the woman's face as she poked her head out of the opening. Then he was gone, diving under her wagon, unlimbering his Gallager breech loading carbine. It was a .52 caliber but the range was no more than 500 yards. He had to wait to fire to be sure the hostiles were in range of all the carbines his men had.

Bowers watched the painted heathens charging forward. When they were within four hundred yards he gave the order to five, and a dozen rifles barked. Two Indian horses went down. He saw one brave wounded, but the attackers drove forward. On some unseen signal they parted and half went each way as they began circling the line of four wagons.

Only three or four of the Indians had rifles, Bowers decided. But that only made them more deadly—they had to get in close to use their arrows and lances. The sergeant had seen Comanches attacking before, and he was always amazed by their horsemanship. They rode so they were almost entirely hidden on the far side of their charging ponies. They shot their arrows and rifles from under the belly of the horses! There was nothing to shoot at except the Indian pony, which Bowers did now and brought one down.

The Comanche riding the mount rolled away, his bow and arrows held in his right hand. A moment later he vanished behind a small bush, but Bowers knew the savage would be crawling forward still on the attack.

The Indians' circle came closer and closer, sometimes at less than fifty yards, but still there was little to shoot at except the ponies. Some of the Cavalrymen didn't want to kill the mounts. Horses were precious to them.

When the Comanches made their first circle, the troopers had moved between the wagon wheels, where they had some protection from both sides.

The first time the Comanches circled also brought the death of six army horses. The Indians knew if the Pony Soldiers were on foot they would be easier to run down and kill.

Bowers bellowed over the firing for the men to shoot the horses out from under the Comanches, but still few did. The horse was almost sacred to the newer recruits, and Bowers had six of them on this escort duty.

Bowers felt the thud of the arrow but no pain in his back as a lucky shot arrow slanted between the wooden wagon wheel spokes behind him and plunged into his flesh. Funny that it didn't hurt, must be a slanting blow he decided. Bowers tried to lift his carbine to aim it, but his hand wouldn't move.

"God damn!" Bowers screeched. He couldn't move either arm. He tried to sit up only to find that he couldn't move his legs. Christ! The arrow must have hit his spinal column! He was paralyzed! Only his eyes would move and he could talk.

"Lewton, get over here!" Bowers bellowed. A lull in the firing let his voice reach out to the corporal who dashed from the second wagon and slid in beside his superior.

"Yeah, Sarge?"

"I'm hit, can't move!"

Alf Lewton looked at the arrow in Bower's back and swore.

"I can't touch it, Sarge. It's deep in your spine. You stay right there. We'll get rid of these damn Comanches and we'll put you in the wagon."

Just as Corporal Lewton said the words, a .52 caliber bullet from Walking White Eagle's rifle slammed through the Pony Soldier's left eye, killing him instantly, dumping him half over Bowers.

The firing diminished. Troopers called to each other as they used up the sixty rounds they carried for their rifles and carbines. Pistols began to fire when the rifles ran dry.

Inside the last wagon, Milly Harding lay on top of her two children, tears of fright and worry streaming down her face as she listened to the fight rage outside. She heard the rifles firing less and less. She could not look outside. Already three arrows had slapped through the canvas top.

The troopers would defeat them, she was sure. Indians were well known to strike and pull back, to strike again and if the defense was too strong, they would pick up their dead and wounded and move to an easier target. It was talked about all the time by the officers' wives who had men fighting the Indians.

These Comanches were savages and cowards and fought only when they had surprise and three times as many Indians as Cavalrymen.

Another arrow sliced through the canvas and tore into her left arm. Milly screamed. The arrowhead pierced her upper arm, missed the bone and came out the far side.

Little Sadie began to cry.

Yale squirmed from under his mother and looked at the blood on his mother's arm. The point had gone all the way through with the bloody metal tip sticking in the mattress. Milly shuddered, a soft weeping from the sudden pain flooded from her.

Yale's eyes went wide for a moment, then he swallowed hard. He took both hands and without a word broke off the feather end of the long shaft. Milly choked down a scream when the shaft moved in her flesh.

Yale lifted her arm, grasping the arrow just above the point and suddenly jerked the arrow shaft through the bloody wound and free. Milly screeched in pain, then covered her mouth, tears welling as she tried to control the agony.

"It will be fine now, Mother," Yale said. "I heard Father talking about how to do this," he said solemnly. Then he tied his kerchief around the wound to stop the bleeding.

Milly looked at him with wonder. "Thank you, darling." She shivered, beat down the pain and then pulled her precious children to her. They lay down, pushing as low as they could get and piled bags and boxes on top of them.

Outside under one of the big Pittsburgh freight wagons, Private Templeton fired his Gallager and then pushed a new Poultney foil cartridge in and aimed again. Just before he fired, he saw an Indian break from the pack and ride straight for him. Templeton tried to change his aim, but he was too late.

The fourteen-foot lance the warrior threw from twenty feet away, shot from his hand, flew between the wagon wheel spokes and drove through Private Templeton's throat. He jolted backward, his last shot going wild as he died.

Under the next freight wagon Private Zedicher screamed at his buddy six feet away. "Zeek, you got any more .52 caliber rounds!"

Zeek couldn't reply. He lay as if he were firing his pistol, but a Comanche arrow still quivered where it had driven six inches into Zeek's forehead.

Zedicher saw Zeek's head clearly then, bellowed in rage and jumped up from under the wagon and ran for his horse. It was one of two U.S. Cavalry blacks still standing.

A riderless Indian pony raced toward him. Zedicher waved his pistol at it, but the animal came on. Zedicher couldn't understand it. Then at the last second he saw the buckskin fringed legging showing where an Indian's foot was wedged under the wide rawhide surcingle around the horse.

In a second and a half the Comanche brave lifted up, leaned over his charging pony's back and his knife sliced Private Zedicher's throat from one side to the other. Zedicher died before he fell to the prairie grass.

The brave wheeled, rode upright looking for more yellow legs. He saw only two still firing, and both were about to be cut to pieces by his brothers. The brave rode back, slid off the back of the pony to the body of the yellow-leg-who-ran-away.

Fox Paw made two quick cuts around the Pony Soldier's head, then popped off the short hair. He tucked the scalp under his horsehair belt, then vaulted on his mount and rode toward the last wagon with the tall cover.

There would be much loot to claim and he wanted to be the first in the richest looking wagon.

He leaped from his horse to the wagon's wooden side and sliced the thin canvas with his knife, tearing it back.

Milly Harding lifted the revolver when she saw the savage leap on the wagon. She aimed the heavy six-gun and when the Comanche's face peered through the rent in the wagon cover, she fired. The bullet went wide. She closed her eyes and fired again and the brave slammed backward off the wagon.

Walking White Eagle spun his pony around when he saw Fox Paw fly off the covered wagon. Blood gushed from his shoulder. The last of the Pony Soldiers was down. White Eagle touched his knees to his borrowed war pony and raced up to the rear opening of the last prairie schooner.

In a graceful leap, the Indian went through the covered wagon's small rear opening and came up with his knife in his hand and pressed it against the throat of a white woman. She had no warning, no time to lift the heavy six-gun. White Eagle knocked the pistol from her hand as his knife pushed her back on the mattress.

The two children scuttered to the far end of the wagon and wailed in terror. White Eagle picked up the pistol, it was one of the fires-many-times weapons. He put it in the rawhide band that circled his waist, then caught the woman's long blonde hair and pulled her toward the rear canvas opening.

He threw the woman outside for the braves and turned back toward the children. The boy screamed at him in fury and charged at White Eagle with a pocket knife. White Eagle let the boy come, then suddenly held out his own knife with a six-inch blade. Yale Harding could not stop. He screamed as he staggered and fell on the knife. It penetrated his chest and his heart, killing him instantly.

White Eagle pushed the small boy away without looking at him again and wiped his blade on the boy's clothes. The boy child was too old to train properly.

He walked over the carefully packed household goods to the small girl who screamed in gasping, wide-eyed terror.

He picked her up and held her under one arm as he sorted through the goods in the wagon. He found ribbons, a dozen different kinds that he took for his wives, then a long streamer of cloth as wide as his arm. He wrapped the cloth around his torso, took the pistol and a rifle he had found and leaped to the ground.

The white girl was still under his arm, struggling and kicking. He slapped her gently, and she stopped screaming.

Fox Paw had bound up his shoulder wound and had claimed the blonde roundeye woman. He had stripped her clothes off until she was naked, then staked her hands to the ground and spread eagled her legs, tying them to stakes driven in the ground.

With great ceremony he removed his breechclout and dropped between the woman's white thighs. She screeched at him, calling him every vile name she could remember. He slapped her, then twisted her breasts until she screamed in agony.

He drove into her quickly, grunting and panting as three braves stood watching.

The other braves looted the freight wagons. They turned out to be army supply rigs loaded with food and material for the fort. There were many hundred pound sacks of beans, flour, sugar, potatoes, new uniforms, small axes and thousands of items for the Fort Sutter's store.

White Eagle quickly looked at the goods in the wagon. They were three days ride from the safety of the upper Brazos River. They had come far into Texas this time raiding. With any good medicine they could drive one of the wagons closer to their camp. At once he rejected the plan. No brave would drive a wagon, that was woman's work.

A new plan came quickly, it would work. He looked at the stacks of uniforms the braves were throwing around. He caught one pair of blue pants. By cutting the legs off he could use them for winter leggings. He found two more pair and tied them to his mount.

The squalling child under his arm bit his shoulder. He whacked her with the back of his hand. He had forgotten about her. Quickly he tied her hands and feet together with rawhide, then stretched her across his back like a blanket roll and tied a wide rawhide thong from her hands to her feet across his chest. She would be secure there and leave both his hands free for looting.

When he got back to the big covered wagon, the braves had thrown out everything, even the mattress. Two more braves had taken their turn with the white captive, laughing and joking about her blonde muff of crotch hair.

Fox Paw made certain that everyone understood she was his captive and he had claimed her. White Eagle shrugged. It was the way of the People. She would be a difficult slave, but with good training she might do. Even the roundeyes had slaves. He never thought twice about taking slaves or captives or killing hostages. It was simply the way of the People.

White Eagle kicked through the goods from the wagon. He had no need for dresses or clothes. His women would enjoy the ribbons and the cloth he found. He uncovered a copper kettle. It would be good for boiling stew, he tied it to the horse's surcingle and kept looking.

From a small chest he found a round mirror with

silver on the handle and a picture on the back. He put it in the kettle and tied it securely.

Also in the chest White Eagle discovered a leather bag filled with cartridges for the revolver. There were over a hundred of them. He smiled as he took them. The fires-many-times small weapon would help make the Comanche as well armed as the Pony Soldiers. Every Pony Soldier had one.

He ran from one of the blue shirted soldiers to the next, picking up the revolvers. Soon he had found them all! It was the best loot he could imagine! He stripped the pistol rounds from the men's pouches and pockets until he had more than he could carry. He filled the copper pot with them, and motioned to Thunder Dog to collect the long guns.

All would be tied securely on a mule to be taken back to the lodges. Soon there was a contest among the braves to find the rifles and carbines, and to locate as much ammunition as they could. They checked each wagon, but there was no more ammunition.

White Eagle called a small council and the senior warriors stood to one side with their war ponies.

In quick order they decided what must be done. The Pony Soldiers' beans, flour and potatoes would be taken. One of the young boys who had been herding the horses was sent to bring back twenty of the mules they had stolen.

The hundred pound sacks of beans, potatoes and flour were tied on the mules. Two sacks of coffee beans were discovered and a great shout went up. Many of the braves had grown to like coffee. All of the food would be distributed when they got back to their camp.

An hour later, the raiding party was ready to move. Fox Paw stood over the white woman. He had satisfied himself three times with her. More than a dozen braves had emptied their loins in her and pushed themselves back in their breechclouts.

Fox Paw decided the white woman would be more bother than good as a slave. She had fainted several times as the braves used her. She was weak. Now she screamed at him, lunged upward until she pulled free one stake holding her hand. She raked broken fingernails down Fox Paw's chest drawing blood.

Fox Paw swung his knife, slicing her breast. She screamed and fell back to the ground. Her eyes pleaded with him. Fox Paw shrugged, and swung his sharp knife again, slitting her throat. As she died, he took her scalp. Fox Paw let out a Comanche war cry as the long blonde hair and scalp made a popping noise as it came free. He tied the blonde hair on his lance, and lifted it high.

Every Pony Soldier had been scalped. They had been sliced and cut, mutilated so they could not fight well in the afterlife.

White Eagle made one final check of the wagons. They had left the sacks of sugar, they had no need for them. He had found a strong wooden box, but when he opened it he discovered only worthless yellow discs. They were squaw's clay, too soft to be any good for hunting arrow tips or scrapers. He took three of them, placing them in a leather pouch on his wide leather surcingle. Perhaps Always Smiling would like them.

With a whoop and a shout they rode away with half a dozen army mounts and mules that had survived the attack.

They formed a strange looking war party. Every brave wore some item of clothing from the wagons. Two had on Pony Soldier blue shirts. Several had put on the Cavalrymen's broad brimmed hats with the chin straps.

Half the war lances held fluttering strips of cloth and freshly taken scalps. One sported a pair of woman's drawers. The warriors shouted and sang as they drove the pack mules across the dry Texas landscape toward a small valley just beyond the sandstone ridge.

There they picked up more than four hundred horses and mules they had stolen on their Texas raids, and began herding the animals west and north toward their lodges high on the headwaters of the mighty Brazos River. The Comanche were safe there.

The small roundeye girl slung across White Eagle's back cried again but White Eagle paid no attention to her. She was safe, she could not get away, and in three days he would give her to Cries In The Morning. She had no children and she had asked him to watch for a small girl to adopt.

White Eagle and his warriors rode toward their camp with happy hearts. It had been a productive raid with many horses stolen. They had not been attacked by any other tribe, had not lost a man, and only four had been wounded by the Pony Soldiers.

The Kwahari Comanches soon would be safely out of the lands penetrated by the roundeyes and back to their wilderness camp where they would always be safe.

2

"Five Goddamned days overdue!" Captain Colt Harding thundered at his adjutant. "Five days in that wilderness! That means damn big trouble out here!" The big Cavalryman scoured his hand over his bearded face and slammed his palm down hard on the desk top.

His face showed an angry flush on his cheeks not covered by a dark, close-trimmed beard and his eyes showered his adjutant across his desk with sparks of fury.

"We sent Sergeant Bowers, an old hand with the troop and with the Comanches. He took his fourteen men on a two day ride to meet the wagon train."

Captain Harding swung to the map on the wall of Western Texas. His hand stabbed at Fort Comfort on the White River west of Austin a hundred and twenty miles.

"The escort left us here and were to ride sixty miles to the old Indian Springs camp for the meeting. Then at twelve miles a day, the wagons

23

should have been back here in five days. Seven days overall."

"Yes sir, but those big Pittsburgh freight rigs can have troubles," First Lieutenant John Riddle said. "Sir, have you ever tried to change a wheel with five thousand pounds of freight pressing it into the sand?"

Captain Harding gave no indication that he had heard.

"It's been twelve days. They are five days overdue." He stood, a man of just over six feet, taller than most men, lean, well muscled and in the best physical condition of his life.

"Call out Troop A, full field gear and rations for five days. No wagons. Issue every man a hundred and twenty rounds. Lieutenant Riddle, I'll lead the patrol. We'll leave in an hour, that'll be at four P.M. You'll remain here in command."

"Yes sir." Lieutenant Riddle gave his commander one last look, then went out the door, through the First Sergeant's office and onto the parade ground.

Damn curious, but five days delay out there was not all that unusual, especially for those bastard Pittsburgh freight wagons. He'd done enough supply runs battling the freighters when he was a second lieutenant to last him the rest of his life.

He gave the order to Lieutenant Oliver, CO of A company and Sergeant Casemore, who was with him. They scurried off to get the troops into action.

Riddle looked over the layout of Fort Comfort. It was anything but comfortable. The fort was still being built. After a year it was a little over three quarters finished.

Adobe. It was sturdy, long lasting, but smelled, and it took too long to form the bricks and let them dry in the sun. But when it was done, Fort Comfort would last for a hundred years, long after it was needed he was sure the way the settlers were crowding and pushing each other West all the time.

He heard the whistles shrilling and knew the men were being informed of the patrol. There would be a full company out, ninety-five men and animals. They had nearly an hour to get ready to ride. No small band of Comanches would surprise this patrol.

For the first time, Lieutenant Riddle let his thoughts go to what might have happened to the supply train. The goods were not all that important. But every man on the post knew that the captain's wife and two children were on that supply train. If any harm had come to them, the captain would blow the Comanche world apart, one way or the other, with or without official orders.

Even now Captain Harding was splitting his troops in half. Not that they expected any attacks on the fort by the Comanche. The hostiles were still in the raid and retreat mode. But they could change that at any time, join forces with other tribes of hostiles and overwhelm most of the forts along the frontier.

As the cabins, ranches and whites moved farther and farther into the sacred, long-time Comanche hunting grounds, the Indians would probably alter their attacks.

Riddle stood outside the door of the fort's headquarters office. He could hear the men getting ready across the square in the enlisted men's quarters. Fort Comfort would be in the form of a large square when completed. Three of the sides were done, built of tough, durable native Texas mud-clay and straw bricks the Texans called adobe.

The bricks were made in wooden forms twelve by eighteen inches long and four inches thick. They were laid up with adobe mortar in a wall two feet thick that would reject a five inch cannon ball.

Inside the walls were one foot thick with timbers spanning the 24-foot wide rooms. Each side of the square was a little over three hundred feet long. The roofs consisted of tarpaper over the log beams, a foot thick layer of soil on top of the paper and that covered with native sod. The outside wall was usually three feet higher than the roof to afford the troopers a parapet to fire over if they needed to.

Only one corner of the fort quad remained to be done. It would house the future sutter's store, the tack room, and fort smithy, as well as the inside stables. Now the mounts were in the paddock with a sturdy four strand barbed wire fence just in back of where the stables would be, and along the rear of the dependents and guests quarters area.

The captain's orderly came running from the commander's office and hurried to the paddock to ready the captain's horse. He was back quickly, with the big black saddled, the shoes checked, blanket roll in place and the captain's Spencer 7-shot repeater rifle in the boot.

Riddle wished he could get the Spencers for all of his men. They had seven different makes of rifles in the troop. From the old Gallager .52 caliber carbines, to the officers' Spencers, to the Sharps single shot .50 caliber rifle. The Sharps were far too long to be carried on a horse, but they had to use what they had.

At least Riddle had made sure that as many men in each squad had the same caliber and make of weapon as possible. This meant they could share ammunition if needed.

Captain Harding stomped out of his office.

"Ready?" he demanded. His square cut face was

set in a scowl. heavy brows shading his brown eyes that were guarded but angry at the same time. He wore his battered patrol hat that had an arrow slice through the crown and a bullet hole in the brim. A non-issue gunbelt circled his hips and held two Colt .44's with ivory grips. Just in front of the left pistol hung a 12-inch Bowie fighting knife.

"No sir, the men have twenty minutes yet. You did want Lieutenant Oliver to go with you?"

Captain Harding nodded. "I hope someday before I die we get a full complement of officers on this post. We're still short four?"

"Three, Captain. Doctor Jenkins came in last month."

"Yes." Captain Harding stared to the east a moment, then looked back at Riddle. "Keep the usual guards out, no patrols, no wood gathering, all civilians kept inside the walls. We'll force march to the rendezvous if we have to go that far."

He turned away. "Riddle, I . . . I have a bad feeling about this patrol. There's a good chance . . ." He stopped and looked away again. "If we find any evidence of hostiles, we'll pool our provisions, send a tracking squad after them and return for supplies before we follow in force."

"Yes sir," Riddle said. A chill hit him and he caught the mood the captain was in. He expected the worst. If a wandering party of Comanche had raided the wagon train, or had it pinned down, it would lead to a tremendous confrontation with the hostiles—sooner or later.

If Mrs. Harding was touched or harmed, there would be old Billy Hell to pay in spades.

Captain Harding went back into the office that was adjacent to his quarters. For a long time he looked at a picture of his wife on the dresser. He slipped the tintype from the frame and put it in his blouse pocket, then went back to his office. For a moment he read a communication that had come by messenger from the Military Division of the Missouri in Chicago. He started to read it but put it down.

Nothing mattered now. No orders, no Division demands, no pleas from the settlers. He had to make sure that his wife and children were safe! The Army of the United States had guaranteed them safety!

So where were they?

He checked his pocket watch. One minute to four. He hurried out, saw his orderly with his mount at the step. The lad, Corporal Swenson, sat on his own mount with the double provision bags lashed to his saddle.

Captain Harding stepped into his leather, took a quick report from Oliver who had his men at parade front, and told him to follow.

Behind him Captain Harding heard the familiar orders of: by two's to the left, Hoooo! The ninety-five men swung in behind the captain and his orderly as they rode through the front gate and took the trail east toward Indian Springs.

The captain muttered a small prayer that he would find everyone safe, then he checked behind him as Oliver sent out three men as a scouting point and an outrider on each side.

Captain Harding had been over it again and again. Fifteen hours in the saddle would bring them to Indian Springs. He knew in his heart that they would not have to go that far.

They rode for three hours without stopping. Twelve miles, Captain Harding estimated. More than a day's journey for the heavy freight wagons, even along the easy trail through the Texas plains. He told Lieutenant Garland Oliver to give the men a ten minute break for a quick supper. Then they would ride again.

It was a little before ten that night that a lead scout rode back to the column. He went straight to the captain, his face still showing his shock and anger.

"We found the wagons sir," the private blurted. "A mile ahead. Indians I'm afraid sir! The savages are gone."

Harding spurred his big black forward, nearly unseated the private, brushed past him and charged down the dim trail eastward. Oliver looked at the scout.

"Anyone alive, Private?" he asked.

"No sir. All dead . . . and scalped."

"Bring up the troops at a walk, Sergeant Casemore," Oliver shouted, then touched his horse with his knees and pounded down the trail after his commander.

The full moon cast eerie shadows over the scene. Death lay everywhere. Horses hung dead by their reins still tied to the wagon wheels. The fifteen Cavalrymen lay where they had fallen, some under the wagons, some in the open.

Each one had been scalped and sliced with sharp knives. Lieutenant Oliver rode slowly around the scene trying to envision what had happened. When he found the captain's horse, the reins hung down. Colt Harding kelt on the ground behind the last wagon. A form on the ground beside him was still spread eagled and staked to the ground.

"My God!" Oliver whispered. The figure was a woman, naked, her throat slashed, one breast almost cut off. Gently Colt Harding cut the leather bindings that held her to the ground. He picked her up and put his arms around her and rocked back and forth.

Oliver didn't approach him. Instead he found the other two members of the patrol point and told them to build a fire away from the wagons. Then Oliver examined the freight rigs. All the mules pulling the rigs had been killed or stolen. They would need to send for teams. Half the goods were gone or ruined. still they would need to take all four rigs back to the fort.

He found the broken strong box in the second wagon. It had been smashed open and inside he caught the glint of freshly minted double eagles. His eyes widened. He had never seen so much money in his life. He guessed there was ten thousand dollars worth of gold in the box. He closed it and stood there a moment thinking what he could do with that much money.

The savages could have taken it.

He could bury the box, gold and all and come back . . .

He could bury the gold, leave the empty box, and let the army think the Comanches had taken the gold.

Oliver hesitated only a second. He was a man to grab any opportunity that came his way. He had maybe ten minutes before the rest of the troops arrived. He used a shovel from the wagon, found a rock outcropping and dug a foot deep hole. He emptied the box of gold double eagles into the hole, covered it and scattered leaves and grass over the spot, then carried the box back to the wagon.

He put the shovel on the wagon. In the morning, with the daylight, he would memorize the exact location of his own private gold mine!

When the troops arrived he ordered them to stay away from the wagons, set them to digging sixteen graves, field depth, three feet. The men groused, but went to work. Every fourth man was required to carry a short shovel.

He sent others to get the longer handled shovels off the wagons.

Oliver made sure Sergeant Casemore had the men working, then went back to the last wagon. Captain Harding had found some of his wife's clothing, and dressed her, forcing stiffening limbs into place. When she was properly covered, he searched the moonlit scene for his children.

In the last wagon he found Yale, and his scream stabbed through the silent Texas night like a dagger. The troops stopped talking and listened. Oliver walked slowly to the wagon and looked in.

In the moonlight streaming through the cut up wagon top he saw Harding kneeling on the bare wooden floor. He held his son in his arms. After several minutes he stood and carried the boy outside and placed him tenderly beside his mother.

Then he went from one of the Cavalrymen to another, checking them, finding each dead. He turned to Oliver who had followed him.

"Sir, we have graves being dug for the troopers."

Harding nodded. "Bury them tonight, you read one service for them all. Then I want every man over here to walk this area foot by foot. I can't find my baby girl, Sadie."

As he said it, Colt Harding sank to the ground, his head went to his hands and he sobbed.

Company A, Second Cavalry, searched a ten acre area around the massacre scene at Buffalo Creek. Nobody found any evidence of little Sadie. Neither did any of the Cavalrymen notice the spot where

Garland Oliver had buried the gold. At last the captain called a halt.

Nobody said out loud what he was thinking. If there was no body, the baby girl must be a captive. The Comanches liked to steal young boys and girls, adopt them into families and raise them as Comanches. It happened more often than any of them wanted to admit.

"Unhitch the dead mules from the covered wagons and drag them out of the way," Captain Harding ordered. "Find six horses you can hitch to it, and take it and most of the men back to the fort. Hold a service in the morning for Milly and Yale."

He stared at them in the moonlight. "Men, I want twenty volunteers, all blooded veterans, to go with me following the hostiles' tracks. We'll leave tonight."

He turned to Oliver. "Take four days rations from those men going back to the fort. Divide the rations among the twenty volunteers. That will give us rations enough for sixteen extra days, twenty-one days in all. We'll pursue the killers until we determine their location or direction of travel."

"Yes sir," Oliver said. "You'll start at sunup?"

"No, Lieutenant. You have an hour to find the volunteers, collect the rations and re-distribute them. We'll be moving out at midnight."

Oliver passed the orders. Sergeants took care of finding the volunteers. There was no shortage of them. Many of the soldiers from Company A knew the dead men.

Oliver reported to the captain who sat his horse looking at the grave sites.

"Sir, after the funeral, I'll return in the morning, with fresh men from B Company, with mules to bring the freight wagons to Fort Comfort. We could

32

leave a guard detail here to protect the Government property."

Captain Harding nodded. "Whatever you decide, Lieutenant."

Promptly at midnight the twenty men and Captain Harding rode away from the death scene. They walked their mounts through the moonlight a half mile to the west, then began a wide circle around the death scene to cut the Indians' trail. Their route took them over the sandstone ridge and down into the small valley beyond.

"They must have eighteen to twenty horses and mules to drive home, as well as any horses they stole on their raiding," Captain Harding said to Sergeant Casemore. The sergeant had been the first volunteer.

"Yes sir. They also could have a hundred head of stolen stock. If we can't find a trail like that in the moonlight, we should go back to Washington D.C. and stand guard duty on the pavement."

They rode side by side, ten yards apart in a troop front formation to sweep a two hundred yard path through the prairie. Halfway through the valley they found where the grass had been trampled and grazed by a large herd of stock or buffalo.

Casemore dismounted and studied the tracks by the light of a torch of burning grass.

"Horses all right, sir. Half of them at least are shod. Hoof prints all over the place. Now all we have to do is see which direction they move."

"West," Captain Harding said. "West into the Staked Plains. Three or four bands of Comanche bands live up there on the high plateau. We've chased them this direction before."

It took them a mile to work out the system. Casemore had been on night tracking trips before. He had found a coal oil lantern among the weapons before they left and had a trooper carry it just in case. Now he lit the lantern and rode ahead a hundred yards and held the light to make sure the tracks were still there.

In some places it was obvious where the large herd had to be driven and they would ride for half a mile before checking the tracks.

Here and there they could see what looked like a strip of land heading west that had been ploughed up by a thousand sharp hooves. Five hundred head of horses and mules would make an easy to follow trail, even at night.

As they moved steadily west, Casemore decided there were more like three hundred head of stock and Indians making the trip.

At times he dismounted and examined the tracks. Every time the blades of grass that had been bent flat to the earth by the hooves had been bruised and scratched, but now had risen back to nearly vertical.

That meant the Indians were at least twelve hours ahead of them. The horse droppings were cold, which told the sergeant about the same thing.

They stopped at three A.M. to brew coffee and chew on hardtack biscuits. The coffee was black, strong and scalding. Casemore realized that his captain had said very little since they started the tracking. He had never seen Captain Harding so remote, so detached, as if he were holding everything inside. It seemed that he couldn't start talking because he might never stop.

The shock of losing a family was terrible, especially when his wife had been naked and spread eagled and used by the savages before she was killed. Garland Oliver had seen the results of Comanche raids before.

They had stopped near a small creek that still had water and filled their individual canteens and the squad, gallon-sized, canvas water bottles.

Casemore studied his big pocket watch in the light of the fire. It had been twenty-eight minutes since they stopped. The captain had given them a half hour. Casemore walked over to where the captain and his orderly sat by their fire.

The orderly held up his hand, palm out. Casemore stopped. The orderly tiptoed away from the fire.

"He's sleeping, Sergeant. I don't think we should wake him."

Sergeant Casemore motioned the orderly back to the fire, and came up humming a song and kicking brush. The captain was awake when the sergeant arrived.

"Sir, this might be a good time to give the men four hours of sleep. We could sack out now and have reveille at 7:30. I think we'll do much better tomorrow with some shuteye now."

Captain Harding had been dreaming about the first time he ever saw his wife back in Connecticut. He shifted by the fire and nodded. "Yes, Sergeant. Order the men down. We'll sleep in until 8:30, then ride until dark."

"Yes sir."

They were out there, the savages, the monsters who had desecrated his wife and murdered his son, and stolen his baby daughter. Damn them! He would see them all in the sights of his rifle before he rested. Every damn one of them!

Corporal Swenson walked up with two blankets from the captain's roll. "Your blankets, sir. Shall I keep the fire going?"

"No need, Swenson, get some sleep. We'll have a hard day tomorrow."

Captain Harding lay down and watched the dying fire. Tomorrow they would push it to six miles an hour. Driving even two hundred horses meant the Comanches couldn't make more than three miles an hour at the most.

The raiders were twelve hours ahead . . . maybe thirty miles. A ten hour day at six miles an hour . . . If they could maintain it. He turned over on the hard ground but didn't feel it. Tears stung his eyes. He would never see Milly again, never hold her, never even touch her!

Captain Harding turned away from the fire and stared west. He had one purpose in life now, to avenge his wife and son's deaths and to find his daughter. Little Sadie. Poor, sweet little Sadie!

It took him an hour to fall asleep.

3

When White Eagle and his raiders were a mile from their camp on a small tributary of the far reaches of the Brazos River, they stopped and prepared to enter. White Eagle had sent one of the herder boys ahead to tell the People they were back. There would be preparations to make in camp as well.

It was tradition, it was a ritual, it was their culture, recalling the way the Comanche had lived for hundreds of years on the high and the low plains of Texas.

When the messenger arrived, the whole camp burst into an uproar. The woman and girls frantically put on their best dresses of chewed antelope and deerskin, those with the fancy trade beads and others with small bells. They greased their hair and combed and braided it and hurried to the far end of the camp where the riders would enter for the grand procession.

The warriors had donned their war paint and some painted their faces black. They tied the fresh scalps high on the end of their lances and attached streamers and ribbons stolen in the raids, and then followed behind Walking White Eagle as he walked the victorious warriors into camp. There were twenty warriors and almost three hundred horses and mules they had captured. The herd boys drove the heavily laden mules into the center of the camp, but nobody tried to unload them.

The women and girls sang songs of past victories and raids and ran to meet the warriors. Always Smiling, White Eagles' number one wife, carried a long, just peeled sapling that would be the scalp pole where the scalps would be tied for the dance later.

The warriors rode into camp with their lances held high, scalps dangling from them, including one with long blonde hair. Again some of the braves wore items of clothing taken in their raids. The People cheered and shouted as the lances with feathers and streamers were lifted again and again.

Some of the warriors held their shields with long black scalps tied to them. Four of the men were bandaged, but rode with great dignity through the camp of fifty lodges along the stream from one end to the other.

As they came back, each warrior turned off at his own lodge, and gave his wife his fourteen foot lance and shield. They were placed in the spot of honor just outside the door of the lodge. The shield was set on a tripod so it faced the afternoon sun. The long lance leaned against the tripod as well and the warrior's quiver of arrows hung beside it.

The fresh scalps would be quickly readied for the ceremony. Each would be delicately scraped and shaved to remove all of the flesh from inside the scalp skin. Then they would stretch the circle of the scalp over a freshly made willow hoop. Next came the sewing, working from east to south then west to north and back to east. It was the exact way they entered a lodge. The brave would oil the hair and comb it, then attach it to a pole where it would dry all day before it was hung with the older scalps on the freshly cut scalp pole.

The whole camp was alive with talk and joy and activity. Old men sat around in small groups in front of their lodges telling half forgotten tales of their exploits in their younger days. The daring and the feats increased with each telling.

The younger warriors rehearsed the stories of their own coups, acting them out and at times making ear-piercing screams and yells.

The women and girls dug out their best dresses of soft suede leather, and some quickly sewed on more rows of white elk's teeth as decorations. The shiny white teeth were stitched on so they would rattle together as the person walked or danced.

A dance area was cleared in front of White Eagle's lodge. His tipi was the tallest and largest in the whole camp. He needed three wives to take it down, pack it and bundle it on the travois every time they moved . . . which was often. His first wife was Always Smiling, a short stern woman who took life seriously and despite her name, seldom smiled. She was as kind as a newborn puppy, and the favorite of the whole camp. She had a dignity and understanding of the medicine bag befitting the chief's wife.

Prairie Flower, twenty-two winters, White Eagle's second wife, was taller and much fatter than Always Smiling. She was a calm person, eager to please, happy to be a chief's wife, and kept hoping to become pregnant again. She had one child, a girl of three. Prairie Flower was the best worker of the group.

Talks A Lot, White Eagle's third wife, was just sixteen, and six months pregnant. She was White Eagle's girl bride, and she had promised him three sons. Less than half of the women in White Eagle's band had children. It was a worry to him. The roundeyes bred like rats with as many as twelve children per house!

Talks A Lot did just that, chattering all the time. She worked alongside the other women, but found little ways to get out of the harder chores. Prairie Flower understood and did much of Talks A Lot's work.

Talks A Lot watched her husband as he sat in front of his lodge beside his shield and lance. Dozens of people came up to congratulate him on his victory, especially over the Pony Soldiers. He showed off his bounty, and gave presents to everyone who came.

He saved only the long yardage of cloth and the ribbons for his wives and the copper kettle. The rest, even his yellow striped blue cavalry pants legs, he gave away. It was his custom to give away all the horses and mules he captured. He had a herd of over a hundred now, and would not trade with the Comancheros until near fall.

He did not give away the rifles and carbines, or the pistols. They were placed in his lodge and would be awarded to braves for special deeds. As raid leader he had asked the men to gather up the rifles, and then claimed them as his own. He would use them to benefit the whole band. The pistols were his without question, and he would present them once he had selected the men to receive them, and trained them how to load and fire them.

The sacks of beans, flour and potatoes were parcelled out to lodges according to need. White Eagle paid special attention to lodges where widows had no one to support them.

The biggest curiosity of the visitors around White Eagle's lodge was the small roundeye girl who sat on White Eagle's lap. She had long blonde hair and eyes so blue they put the morning sky to shame.

She alternately cringed away from the hands that reached in to touch her and the feel of the Indian man who held her. She had cried at first, but now could cry no more. Her wrists and ankles hurt where she had been tied on the long ride.

They had ridden non-stop after they left the wagons. Twice they changed directions, twice they split into four groups and crisscrossed their trails so even a good Indian tracker would have trouble following them.

Sadie Harding wore the same little blue calico dress she had on when she was captured. The soft blue ribbons were still in her hair. Her long blonde locks were snarled and dirty.

After most of the visitors had left, one thin woman in a worn "best" dress with many rows of elks's teeth sewn on it, came up.

"You had a good raid, White Eagle," Cries In The Morning said. "Many horses and mules, and much of the food of the Pony Soldier. But your greatest prize is there on your knees."

White Eagle smiled. He had known this woman for as long as he could remember. She had one child who died of the great fever, and she needed someone to help her do the work.

"Cries In The Morning, here is my present for you. She has no name yet, but I might suggest one."

Tears showed in the woman's eyes. She could only

nod. The child was so beautiful! Like a spring flower in full bloom with her yellow petals and blue eyes.

"We shall call her Laughing Golden Hair. I can see the laughter in her eyes." Chief White Eagle stood and handed Sadie to Cries In The Morning. "I hope you and Running Wolf will want to adopt her."

Again Cries In The Morning nodded as she clutched the startled child to her bosom. It was too much to hope for! So many times she had believed that she was pregnant, but each time she was not. Now she would have a family for Running Wolf, who had chosen not to have another wife. Perhaps now he would feel proud enough to buy a young wife, a strong one with wide hips for easy child birthing!

Cries In The Morning mumbled her hurried thanks and rushed away, the small Laughing Golden Hair child in her arms. She hurried through the camp, nodding and smiling to the other women who looked with surprise and some jealousy to see that she had been given the golden hair.

Cries In The Morning entered her lodge, carefully walked to the left and went around the small fire that glowed in the center fire pit, and then sat on her pallet of buffalo robes and the fox fur and stared at her new child.

"You are so young and will soon forget your old ways and become one of the People," Cries In The Morning crooned. "I will grease your hair and braid it to keep it out of the way, and I will make you a small, proper dress of the finest chewed suede with hundreds of elk's teeth! You will have tiny moccasins all beaded and proper, and a small breechclout made exactly to your size, so your pale white body can slowly tan and turn brown like a pecan nut!"

Cries In The Morning knew the small one did not

understand one word of what she was saying. But the soft, gentle hands, her smile, and the clay pot of thick stew from the fire let her know she was going to be treated kindly.

Sadie Harding looked up at this strange woman, who was so thin she seemed about to blow over. She had on a funny looking dress with ugly white teeth on it, and her face was smudged and dirty over her dark brownish red skin. But she smiled. Sadie knew a smile.

"I hate you!" Sadie screeched. "I hate you and I want to go home. My home is Fort Comfort. I want to go there right now!" Sadie crossed her arms, put an angry scowl on her face and refused to eat any of the disgusting smelling food she was offered.

"I hate you and I'm hungry, and I want a cookie!"

Outside the tipi of White Eagle, preparations were continuing for the dance.

In White Eagle's lodge his wives had on their best suede dresses. They took out their favorite brass bracelets and slid them on their arms. Then they braided each other's hair and painted vermillion down the hair part. The last thing they did was to paint one another's faces, and the inside of their ears the same bright red.

Outside the drummers had begun their continual pounding and the singers were wailing and chanting out the traditional songs of the successful raid against the enemy, whether another tribe, the hated People Eaters or the roundeye. It was beginning to get dark outside.

At the dance site, a large council fire had been built in the cleared area. The members of the council sat in a semicircle around the crackling blaze. Each of the leaders of the band wore his robes over his shoulders even though it was still summertime warm.

The scalp pole with all of the new scalps had been planted solidly into the ground in front of them. Prominent was the long yellow hair scalp.

Cries In The Morning had brought Sadie to the dance, even though she wouldn't understand. It was a good time for her to see her first victory dance and hear tales of taking coups.

The dancers were in the open part now. They circled the scalp pole, then divided into two lines, one of men and one of women facing each other. They danced forward until they almost met, then worked backwards to the steady beat of the drums. The costumes and jewelry of the women rattled as they danced.

Then from out of the light of the fire there came a Comanche victory scream and the dancers stopped and crowded back.

Suddenly a rider galloped into the clearing and a warrior, Fox Paw, drove his fourteen-foot lance into a buffalo hide that had been spread out near the council.

The drums stopped and there was total silence around the leaping fire as Fox Paw told of his first coup and then of the taking of the white woman. After he had dramatized his coups, he dismounted and joined the other warriors near the council.

Before the People could start talking, another warrior raced in and gave his account of his coups on the raid.

Cries In The Morning held her new child on her lap where she sat at the edge of the firelight. She wanted the small one to see everything, so she would understand it.

"The braves are telling the council about how

brave they were in battle and on the raid against the Pony Soldiers. Later the council will sort out the claims and award the coups to each man. No warrior can get credit for more than two coups from any one enemy."

Cries In The Morning explained each of the steps as the warriors rode in, realizing that the small white child did not understand the words, but it was a beginning. It was like having a new baby who was four winters old, but could not speak yet or understand the language of the People.

Sadie looked at this strange woman and scowled.

"It's not so hard to understand, Laughing Golden Hair," Cries In The Morning explained. "It doesn't matter which warrior has the scalp. It shows much more bravery to strike a live enemy with a coup stick than to lift the scalp off a dead enemy. Of course one warrior might kill the enemy, but another brave can count coup on him as well, perhaps before he was dead. Battles are always confusing, but the council sorts it all out to determine who really earned the coups."

The tales of coup taking went on into the night until every brave had driven his lance into the buffalo skin and the tales were told. Then there was more dancing that went on for as long as any of the revelers could stand.

There was no stupid water in the Eagle Band camp. White Eagle had seen what the white man's fire water did to the Indians who drank it. Whenever they found whiskey or rum in their raiding, the kegs or casks were opened and drained or the bottles broken. No brave in the Eagle Band would violate the unwritten law of their leader.

Long before the last coup story had been told, Laughing Golden Hair had slumped asleep against the dry, sagging breasts of Cries In The Morning. She smiled softly, her eyes showing the great love she had built so fast for the small, helpless roundeye with the golden halo around her head. Cries In The Morning knew that she had a lifelong job of teaching the small golden one of the ways of the Comanche, so some day she could marry a great chief, and help lead their people.

Cries In The Morning carried her small charge tenderly as she went back to her lodge, entered and put Sadie down in the bed of buffalo robes and soft fox pelts, so she would have a thick mattress and stay warm during the cool of the evening.

Gold Eagle and the council worked out the conflicting coups and awarded them to the warriors. When that was done Walking White Eagle went to his lodge and put down the entrance flap so no one would come in. He was finished for the evening.

He dug out the three round pieces of squaw's clay from the small bag tied to his surcingle and gave one of them to each of his wives. Always Smilling looked at it, bit it and left tooth marks, she shrugged and thanked White Eagle, but he knew she would soon trade it to Prairie Flower for ribbon. Each of them received the ribbons he had saved and the long piece of cloth.

Prairie Flower smiled when he gave her the roundeye's gold double eagle. She began boring a hole in it with a sharpened piece of metal she was making for a lance point. Soon she had the hole and she threaded a tough piece of buffalo sinew through it to make a necklace.

Talks A Lot watched with nervous excitement as White Eagle came to her. When he gave her the coin she squealed in delight and stroked his chest showing her appreciation. She at once began bargaining with Prairie Flower.

White Eagle sat on a buffalo robe near the small fire, watching the twigs burn, turn to ash and then wither into nothing but hot air and smoke.

It was the way of all life, he thought. Here on Mother Earth for only a few years, then to die and wither and turn to dust and bones, while Mother Earth went on for many hundreds of winters. She watered her hair and trees, kept the berries and nuts growing and brought the buffalo in the thousands over the prairies to feed and clothe the People.

Now the whites, the roundeyes came. When he was a boy, the roundeyes stayed far to the east, away from Comanche hunting grounds. They seldom saw the white men. But now they came farther and farther into the land the People had shared with Mother Earth for hundred of winters.

Why couldn't the Pony Soldiers stay to the east, and out of the sacred lands of the Comanche? He shook his head. He would never understand the whites. Never.

He felt a need. Perhaps his medicine would be strong tonight and he could sire a son. He went to Prairie Flower where she lay in her robes near their small daughter. White Eagle's hand went under the buffalo robe and stroked her soft, small breasts. She sat up at once and welcomed him.

"Tonight I will make you a son," she whispered in his ear as they lay down under the robes. It was the dream they both longed for, but after three years it had not happened.

Perhaps tonight, he thought as he moved over her and she opened herself to him.

Early the next morning, just as the sun broke over the far flat horizon, White Eagle lifted from the robes, dressed quickly and walked to the upstream end of the camp where most of his horses and ponies were pastured.

Two sleepy herder boys who had been standing watch all night saw him and waved in greeting. Soon the daytime herders would come to watch the precious stock. A warrior's wealth was measured by the number of horses he could steal and how many wives he could afford.

White Eagle had lost his favorite war pony on the last raid. One of the Pony Soldiers had shot the fleet gray from under him, and he had scrambled to find another before the raid was over. White Eagle had screamed in rage when his war pony went down. To a Comanche warrior his war pony was his most prized and most important possession, far outstripping the value of his wives and children.

A warrior was nothing without a good war pony. A Comanche brave cheerfully and without thought loaned his wife to a friend. He could expect the favor in return. A warrior risked his life for his friends and brothers without a moment's hesitation.

But he would share or give his war pony to no man.

He would guard the life of his war pony over that of most of his friends and relatives. He would not let a good war pony slip from his hands, not unless he were mortally wounded.

But the Pony Soldiers had snatched Devil Wind away from him. Now he would have to train a second war pony. Every warrior had a second pony in training. But with White Eagle's second mount, there was much work to be done.

He called out to Flying Wind, then whistled. The two year old stallion whinnied and left the herd and trotted up to where White Eagle stood. At least that training had been completed. White Eagle rubbed the mount's head and ears, gave him a handful of grass that he especially liked and then steadied him while he put on a surcingle, this one a four inch wide band of braided strips of leather that circled Flying Wind's back and belly.

The pony stood still. He was used to the cinch, used to being ridden, but the exacting training for a war pony was far from over. A Comanche brave had to be able to ride without using his hands, which he kept for shooting his bow and rifle, and for attacking with his lance. The smallest pressure by the rider's knees, legs, feet had exact meanings the war pony must know and respond to instantly.

The best trained ponies told, with the movements of their ears, their riders of the approach of other riders and if they were friend or foe. The war pony, when properly trained, would put the best Western cutting quarter horse to shame. White Eagle sat on a ridge all day once watching the roundeye cowboys below working with the stock.

A war pony could have done the cutting job in half the time. The Texas cattle were plodding and slow compared to the shaggy buffalo which any war pony had to be able to outrun, outmaneuver and out think.

White Eagle knew Flying Wind had the ability, he was like his father in many ways. Now he mounted the young gray which had spots of black from his mother, and rode easily for five minutes. Then he headed across a small meadow at a gallop.

Flying Wind accepted the challenge and stopped only when White Eagle pulled back sharply on a braided hair hackamore and ground his toes into the horse's ribs at the same time.

He made the stop ten times, and the last time

Flying Wind stopped abruptly when only the toe pressure was applied.

White Eagle praised the big gray and went on to a new lesson. He charged straight at a two-foot thick maple tree. Six feet before he would have slammed into the tree, Flying Wind veered around it.

The second time White Eagle raced the war pony at the tree and touched him with his toes at the last moment and the big gray slid to a stop within inches of the tree. Three more times they did the same routine.,

The next time White Eagle touched his left knee to the mount's flank and pulled the hackamore to the right turning him around the tree on the right.

Over and over and over, White Eagle repeated the instruction, until Flying Wind would respond quickly and deliberately to the learned commands.

After two hours White Eagle rubbed down his mount with hands full of fresh grass, removing all sign of sweat and lather, then led him along the creek to drink and higher to a favorite spot filled with thistles that the horse loved.

Back at the pasture, he checked his other stock from Flying Wind's back, decided he would keep the next batch of horses and mules he stole so he would have a hundred for trading with the Comancheros, the Mexican traders who ventured far into the Comanche hunting grounds once a year loaded with many goods that the Indians wanted and could pay for with horses.

Back at the camp, White Eagle stopped at Cries In The Morning to see how the small child was doing. He knew that Running Wolf would show little interest in the child. That was woman's work. Besides, she was a roundeye and while he had agreed to adopt her, he would have rather had a child of his loins.

White Eagle saw the pair outside the lodge. Cries In The Morning was radiant. She sat with her metal scraper, working on a buffalo hide. Beside her, Laughing Golden Hair held a small scraper with both hands and tried to do the same work. Cries In The Morning laughed and helped her, giving approval when she did it right.

White Eagle watched for a few moments more, heard the woman patiently teaching the child words of the Comanche tongue. Yes, it would be all right. The small roundeye would soon learn the language, and grow and learn the ways of the People. In two years Laughing Golden Hair would be a Comanche forever.

4

The troops of the Second Cavalry rolled out of their blankets the next morning promptly at 8:30 to the sounds of the bugler's reveille. Sergeant Casemore wondered how far the notes of the trumpet would carry in the open country, a mile? five miles? It might be good not to use the bugle on routine calls on this patrol.

He made sure every man ate a hearty breakfast of coffee, beans and hardtack. It would be their last hot meal for some time, the sergeant guessed. He'd never seen the old man so angry, so silent, and deadly furious. There was going to be hell to pay, and Casemore was glad he was on Captain Harding's side.

He reported to the commander's small A style tent. It was the same size shelter the troopers used. The only difference was he slept in his alone. The bugler and the captain's orderly shared a second A tent nearby.

Captain Harding had finished his own hot beans

and coffee and was munching on some sweet rolls he had brought along. He had his shot-up campaign hat on. That always meant he was ready for battle.

"Sir, the patrol is ready to form up on your command," Casemore reported. "All men and mounts are present and accounted for." He saluted smartly. Captain Colt Harding, usually one for strict military courtesy, half saluted, half waved in response.

"Five minutes, Sergeant. Wished to hell we'd brought along some of those Tonkawa scouts. Put your best tracker out a half mile in front of us with two men in a connecting file. One man to ride sweep on each side at two hundred yards. We'll move out as soon as you get your assignments made."

"Yes sir!" Casemore said snapping another salute. He did a proper about face and trotted back to the troopers thirty yards down a slight slope.

Three hours later they were still making what Captain Harding figured was about five and a half miles an hour. He walked the troop most of the time, but gave the mounts a ground eating lope for ten minutes out of every hour.

The trackers had no trouble following the wide trail. They functioned more as forward scouts than trackers. The youngest recruit in the patrol could see the path the big herd of horses had cut through the short plains grasses.

At noon on the first day they found a spot where the herd had paused long enough to drink and graze for "about an hour" the trackers reported. Then the horses were split into eight groups and driven off in eight different directions. All the trails still headed generally north and west.

The scout, a civilian called Hatchet, waited for the main party at the division of the trails.

Harding took the report of the scout and stared at

the countryside for a moment. To the far north he could see the start of a few higher ridges.

"The Concho River up that way?" he asked. "A tributary to the Colorado?"

The scout nodded. "Another fifty, sixty miles, maybe more. Gets a little higher but not much."

The captain scowled. "Figures, this is Texas. We'll take a compass bearing of northwest, and follow whichever trail leads closest to that. This is some kind of trick, trying to confuse us. We hang together and we move fast. Lead scout, half mile ahead, otherwise same formation." The captain nodded at Sergeant Casemore who whipped his mount around and bellowed at the troops.

"Detail! By two's, left wheel into column! March!"

The troops moved out behind the captain and sergeant. They rode at a canter for half a mile, then dropped to a walk.

An hour later they left the small stream they had been near and the tracks broke across a broad stretch of flat prairie with nothing to be seen for miles except the shimmering heat of the day on the sparse dirt and sand.

Hatchet came back from the point.

"Sir, we just found two tracks joining this one, looks like they are coming back together for the final march."

Captain Harding set his jaw a little firmer. "How far behind them are we?"

"Can't understand it. We're losing ground, sir. Figure the hostiles are now more than eighteen hours ahead of us."

Harding took off his weathered campaign hat and wiped sweat from his forehead. He looked at Casemore.

"Why, Sergeant?"

"We're pushing big army mounts, sir, which are pampered and grain fed. Those Comanches got their war ponies under them, and on the run back to their lodges. They trade horses, I'd wager. Ride one for six months, then switch to a fresh one for six. They must have been riding steady for at least thirty-six hours to be that far ahead."

"It's possible to push their stock that hard?"

"Yes sir. Seen it done before. The Comanche use grass fed ponies, tough little animals that are sturdy and hardy. They'll ride them for six hours twice as fast as we can push ours. Happens."

"So we can't catch them?"

"Not a round-balled chance in hell, sir."

"But we can track them! We move out at our usual pace. They've got to stop sooner or later, and we've still got twenty days of rations. Let's move, Sergeant Casemore!"

"Yes sir!" Casemore wheeled his big black, barked orders and the column swung out again to the northwest. They found the added tracks and another mile on the whole herd seemed to be trampling down the prairie grass.

After ten more miles they came to a spot where the herd had grazed.

"Here about two hours," Hatchet, the scout, said. "Still sixteen hours out in front of us, at least."

There was no dinner break. The men ate in their saddles, groaning and grousing.

"Shut up, you assholes!" Casemore bellowed at them. "At least the Comanche aren't slicing your guts open the way they did that escort party. Consider yourselves lucky!"

They rode all afternoon.

By a little after 5:30 the scout came back reporting the first signs of water in more than five hours.

"Small crick, Sergeant, enough water to keep the horses happy. Probably a tributary to the Middle Concho. We're probably too far west to be hitting the southern branch."

When Casemore reported this to the captain, Harding grunted.

"We'll water everything well there, men and stock, then ride five more hours. We can't afford to let that trail get too cold."

At the stream, the men drank first, holding the horses back so they wouldn't roil the water.

Private Victor bellied down by the little stream and gathered a double handful of water to splash in his face. Before he could move, a water moccasin struck from where it lay next to a rotted branch in the stream.

Victor screamed and the trooper beside him brought the heel of his heavy black boot down on the reptile and smashed its head into a flat oozing mass.

"Marlin!" Victor screamed holding his arm. The venom had jetted into his wrist.

Corporal Adolph Marlin was the unofficial medic on marches. He worked with the battalion doctor when he was in the fort. Now he ran up and brought out a short medical knife.

He looked at the twin fang marks.

"Yep, a poisonous bite. Take just a minute." He sliced each of the marks with an "X," applied a small rubber suction cup, then drew out blood and the poison. He squirted the blood on the ground to be sure he had removed enough, then he put some alcohol on the cuts, bandaged them and slapped Victor on the shoulder.

"Good as new. Next time look around before you start drinking. If you'd laid down and stick out your neck, you could be damn near dead now. Hard to make incision cuts in your throat!"

Captain Colt Harding walked up and down a twenty yard stretch of the creek. He looked northwest. Always he watched that direction. He knew he would see nothing, but he also knew his tiny, beautiful, sweet and tender daughter of four years was still somewhere out there in that direction. She was a captive of the most savage, inhuman, terrible creatures that Colt Harding had ever seen.

He owed them more than they could ever pay. He would have his revenge for the deaths of his beloved Milly and his son Yale, and then he would recapture and free his daughter!

Or he would die trying.

He motioned to Swenson to bring his mount. He swung up and looked northwest again. The land rose slightly, not enough to notice, but it was lifting as they worked toward the Cap Rock Escarpment well north of them.

"If we can't catch them, Corporal, we can damn well track them. We'll find them. We have to find them!"

"Yes sir," Swenson said.

At sunset Hatchet was replaced by the second tracker who took the lantern and worked out a hundred yards at a time, unless he was sure where the herd might go by the landscape. It slowed their net gain, but it helped.

Half the time the troops sat on quiet horses while the tracker found the way.

At 10 P.M. by his pocket watch, Captain Harding gave the word to halt. They had come at last to the middle fork of the Concho River. Here it was no more than a small stream flowing through a wild and treeless land where shrubs and scrub growth dominated what little vegetation there was higher than the grass.

They camped there.

"No fires!" Sergeant Casemore warned each of the groups of men. "Cold food and then into the blankets. We'll be moving early in the morning."

Casemore suggested he take the bugler's mouthpiece to prevent any automatic response by the musician. Captain Harding agreed while the bugler snorted.

Casemore took the first watch with two other men. They would protect the camp until 2 A.M. when the next shift would come on and wake up the troopers at six in the morning.

It was a dry, quiet camp and Captain Harding sat by his saddle. He wondered how Sadie was this night? Was she warm enough? Did they feed her? She had been prone to colds and earaches. He hoped they took care of her.

Colt Harding had not the slightest doubt that he would find and rescue his daughter. A band of savages would be no match for a concentrated, carefully planned attack by even a twenty man patrol of U.S. Cavalrymen.

Holding that thought firmly in hand, Captain Harding went to sleep and did not dream.

Daylight came at five that morning.

Sergeant Casemore sent out the two trackers and a scout to check the trail for a mile, then to bring back a report. The scout was back before the men were roused. Hatchet looked troubled as Casemore saddled his mount.

"Damn Indians split up the herd again, Sarge. Looks like at least twenty groups going off in every damn direction of the compass. I don't know what the hell they're doing."

Casemore pushed the scout out of the way and slapped his mount so she'd let out a bellyful of air so he could cinch up the belly strap.

"They're trying to get home. I've seen them do this before. There just isn't any way to hide twelve hundred sets of hoof prints."

"What the hell you going to tell the captain?"

"Same thing I told you. Get back out there and tell your trackers to move upstream on the Concho River here and see what they find. If nothing after three miles, break it off and meet us back at the split up."

"It's a possibility."

"Damn right. Why come this far and backtrack? Not a Comanche. Now get moving."

Casemore watched Hatchet move out, then went to see the captain with a report of the latest developments.

By the time the patrol reached the next point where the Comanches had split the herd, the scouts were back from upriver on the Concho.

The scout, a big, rawboned Texan, said he knew every inch of every Texas county, grinned at Casemore.

"By damn! They're coming back together. Some of them must have gone up the river. Found several places they splashed out when they came to deep pools. How'en hell you know they was gonna do that, Casemore?"

"The only way to get twelve years experience fighting Comanches is to fight Comanches for twelve years. Any more stupid questions, Hatchet? Go tell the captain what you found."

The troops moved up to the new juncture point and found five or six trails merging. Then they vanished almost completely.

"Few traces here and there," Hatchet said, a frown in his voice. "Where'n hell them savages go?"

Casemore studied the terrain as the captain came up. Colt Harding looked over the juncture of two tributaries and the partially flooded, swampy area ahead of them. He walked his big black into the soupy wet land then back out. No prints showed.

"You could ride a whole division of Cavalry through here with eight pounders and never leave a track," Harding said. "The bastards are here somewhere. Position the patrol on a searching front and we'll sweep through this mire. Tell the men to watch out for quicksand."

The troopers were brought up in a long skirmish line, spaced five yards apart and they moved ahead at a walk. There was no quicksand, and little firm ground. A quarter of a mile across the large marshy area, they came back to hard earth and stopped.

The scouts found no sign of hoof prints or horse-shoe marks on the solid land.

Captain Harding sat on the small rise and looked at the rest of the swamp. It seemed like a half dried up lake that had flooded again, and now was in the process of drying up once more. He followed the contours of the dry land on both sides and slowly swung to the north.

On that end the swamp turned into a heavy woods that seemed to shroud an opening leading to a low ridge farther north. There should be some sort of a valley below the ridge. It was a perfect blind for a concealed opening. They could ride through the swamp, which would wipe out any evidence of passage, through the woods and into the valley.

He rode a dozen yards straight for the woods, motioned for Casemore to line up the troops and they moved toward the pecans and willows and other small hardwoods that clogged the far end of the swampy area.

They were within twenty yards of the screen of trees and brush when one of the troopers screeched in pain and grabbed his shoulder. An Indian arrow quivered there, the steel point slashing through his blouse and into his upper arm.

"First squad, one round into the brush ahead!" Captain Harding ordered. The first squad to his left brought up their weapons. "Fire!"

Eight weapons went off in a roar and leaves and twigs and some branches shivered as the rounds blasted into the woodland.

"Charge!" Harding bellowed and the twenty-three men raced full gallop at the trees, splashing water on each other as the horses surged through the marsh.

There were no more arrows from the woods. The captain was the first rider into the greenery. He slashed through brush and small trees and fifty feet into the growth it thinned to nothing and a small valley opened to a chattering stream dancing down a rocky bed.

A quarter of a mile up the short valley he spotted two Comanches kicking their horses as they raced around a slight bend in the opening and were gone.

There were no campfires here, no evidence that the band had camped here. This was their vanishing point, where they would confuse the stupid round-eyes and force them to go back to their fort.

Harding wanted to chase them, but he knew it was probably a trap to lure them into a crossfire of whistling arrows and point blank rifle fire. Not today, Comanche savages. He held up his hand and his men stopped as they came through the screen of trees.

He ordered them back into the trees for cover, then let Corporal Marlin treat Private Kelly's arrow wound. The metal point had penetrated flesh beyond the prongs but had not gone all the way through the upper arm.

Adolph looked at Kelly who sat on the bank of the stream. They didn't have time to use whiskey, and he had none of the new ether. He moved suddenly, bumping the shaft in Kelly's shoulder.

"Oh, God!" the wounded private roared, then passed out from the pain.

Captain Harding stood nearby watching.

"Sorry, Captain," Marlin said. "It's the only thing I can do. The arrowhead has to come out." He looked at the depth of the arrow. He had to push it on through or dig it out. He figured he'd do less damage digging it out. Marlin used the scalpel from his kit and cut the flesh on both sides of the points until he could pull the arrow back.

Blood spurted. Marlin swore, pushed a white towel over the bleeding and when he tugged the arrow out he bound the towel firmly around the wound. After it stopped bleeding he would try to pull the sides of the wound together so it would not scar so much.

He washed Kelly's face with cold water from the stream and he soon came around groaning with pain and swearing in three languages. He couldn't lift his arm. Marlin made a sling for him from a pair of kerchiefs, then helped him mount and they moved out of the trees, through the marshy area to hard ground.

Captain Harding found a draw where they could camp for the night. He had no thoughts of pushing after the hostiles. Not with only twenty men. He would return to the fort, prepare a proper force and come after the Comanche with a high precentage chance of raiding their camp and finding his daughter. Now they would rest, put out good security, and let their wounded men gain some strength.

They had a hot meal that evening and fires, and defied the Comanche to come for them. It was a quiet night.

The next morning they kicked into their saddles at 6:30 and moved at a steady four miles per hour, backtracking the trail, cutting across areas where they knew they could, and angling well around the site of the massacre. They could save half a day's travel by moving at a better angle toward the fort.

Three days later after an uneventful return march, they arrived within sight of Fort Comfort. Private Kelly had developed a low fever but had managed to sit his saddle without having to be tied on. He would go directly to the post surgeon's office.

First Lieutenant Riddle met them half a mile from the fort. He rode alongside a quiet Captain Harding.

"Nothing untoward happened during your absence, Captain Harding," Riddle reported. The funeral services were held as per your instructions."

"Thank you."

"Did you locate the hostiles, sir?"

"We tracked them, found their general site, and have returned to gather a force to face them down." They rode in silence for a time.

"Anything in the dispatch from San Antonio?"

"Nothing unusual. General Sheridan is talking about a new way to rid the west of the Indian. A way to end the Indian wars once and for all. It's quite unusual."

"Right now I have my own Indian war to fight," Captain Harding said. He looked into the distance, and they didn't talk for the rest of the ride into the fort.

They arrived in the afternoon, and it wasn't until the next morning that Riddle broke the bad news to Captain Harding.

"Sir, the bills of lading were found in the material from the wagons. There is some disturbing news."

"Disturbing, Riddle? I don't understand."

"One of the shipments listed was a wooden chest filled with eight thousand dollars worth of gold double eagle coins with the mint date of 1869 stamped on them."

"Yes? So what's your point?"

"A wooden chest was found that had a few gold fillings and gold dust in it, however there were no gold coins found. None whatsoever. There is eight thousand dollars in gold missing from the wagons."

Captain Colt Harding stared at his adjutant. "No mistake?"

"I'm afraid not. You know the Comanche, they call gold woman's clay because it's good for nothing but trinkets. Too soft for arrow points, axes or scrapers. The chances of the Indians stealing the gold are almost non-existent."

"Which leaves our greeting party, and the men who brought the wagons back to the fort. All members of my command."

"I'm sorry, Captain. That's the way it looks."

Captain Harding wanted to laugh. He had a real problem, and this insignificant item popped up and took on an inflated importance. They would find the gold. It would be much harder finding Sadie. He'd never find Milly or Yale again.

He slammed his palm down hard on his heavy desk and stood.

"All right. Write up your report. Lay it out

exactly as you see it. They'll want to know the exact items stolen or destroyed by the Comanche. Give them line and verse on it. And include the eight thousand dollars in missing gold. We'll let San Antonio bring the charges."

"Going to be bloody hell to pay, Captain," Riddle said.

This time Harding did laugh. "Lieutenant, I'm already making all the payments I can to hell. You handle it."

"The paperwork is all done along those lines. I've had a week. If I could have your authorizing signature?"

Captain Harding signed the papers made out with three copies and a rough for their own files.

"I'll send two couriers this evening, as soon as it's dark. The men will leave six hours apart. Each with identical dispatches. One of them should get through. They'll travel only by night until they are well out of Comanche country."

Captain Harding nodded. He stared out his window into the parade ground. "I'll be putting together a long range patrol, Lieutenant. I'll need a hundred men, provisions for thirty days, two supply wagons, and twenty extra horse. We're going to run these bastards to ground and bury them."

He looked up at a knowing stare on his adjutant's face.

"May I go along, sir?"

"No. You've got a fort to run. Get the wheels in motion to put together the force. How many of the Tonkawa Indian scouts do we have on post?"

"About twenty braves, sir."

"Good, I'll take them all. They hate the Comanches, love nothing better than to slice them up. Let's say three hundred rounds per trooper,

Riddle. And we'll take the Gatling gun. I want to show these hostiles that we mean business."

"Special order, sir, from Division?"

Captain Harding looked at his second in command for ten seconds without saying a word. They had been friends on this post for almost a year. They got drunk together every Saturday night. They were both married and their wives had been back east.

Colt Harding shook his head. "John, you know we don't have any special orders. We'll be working under standing orders about pursuit of hostiles where civilians or military personal are wounded or killed and civilian or army property is destroyed. It's good enough for General Sheridan, it's good enough for me. Any questions?"

"No, Colt, but I do have a suggestion. Get out of here before some major or light colonel comes flying in here from San Antonio looking for that damned eight thousand in gold!"

5

The men of A company's extended patrol had been back for a full day now. Captain Harding paced his office wishing he could get into the field tomorrow.

That wasn't possible. It took several days to get up the supplies, the plans, the personnel and the army's way of doing things to get a two month campaign mounted and ready for the trail.

That didn't make it any easier to handle. Last night at taps, Captain Harding had slipped out to the lonesome graves just beyond the fort where regulations dictated they had to be. There was no grass, no flowers, just two simple wooden crosses with the names painted on them. He had to make better arrangements.

At the common grave he had wept, not caring if anyone saw him. He had loved Milly so deeply, so completely, that he had never even looked at another woman. She was the foundation that kept him sane in this insane world.

He wept for Yale as well. A fine young boy who

never had a chance to grow up. That was the real tragedy. The Comanches probably figured he was too old to re-train as an Indian.

Lieutenant Riddle had powered ahead on preparations for the patrol. He was calling it that for the paperwork. There were dozens of details to run down. Rations alone was a problem with fifty headaches attached. There had to be more than beans and hardtack for two months in the field.

Captain Harding had set this morning as time to do a practice run with the Gatling gun. He called for his horse and rode out to the practice range just north of the camp. A smashed wagon had been set up as a target three hundred yards away.

When Lieutenant Oliver saw him coming, the Company A commander rode up and saluted.

"We're about to do our first live round firing practice on the Gatling gun, sir. Would you like to observe?"

"Yes," Harding said, barely holding in his impatience. Why else would he have ridden out here?

They rode to a point where a dozen enlisted men sat on the short plains grass. Oliver raised his arm and brought it down.

A hundred yards to the left a team of horses charged forward pulling a light caisson and a wheel mounted, ten barrel Gatling gun that bumped and jolted over the uneven ground. The driver of the gun rig rode the horse on the right. He wheeled it around in front of the officers so the trailing gun aimed at the target wagon. Two troopers raced up on their mounts, leaped off, unhitched the gun from the caisson and swung it around to aim directly at the target.

The Gatling gun was mounted on smaller wheeled

units than the artillery used, but they were the same type. There were a pair of horses that pulled each rig, which consisted of the wheel mounted gun, and a second detachable two wheel caisson with its mounted box used for equipment, cleaning gear and mainly ammunition.

When the double rig stopped, the gunners detached the rear unit, which was the gun itself, from the front half, dropped the trailing hitching mount and positioned the tongue to give the gun a firm foundation. Then the weapon was set to fire.

The gunners made minor adjustments, positioned the trailing leg of the cession, then adjusted the ammunition supply and the sergeant in charge held up his arm that he was ready to fire.

It was a ten barrel, crank operating Gatling that the manual said could blast out four hundred rounds a minute. Captain Harding knew that in practice it seldom fired half that many because of the barrels fouling by the deposits from the black powder. But even two hundred rounds a minute could be devastating.

Oliver brought his hand down and the sergeant on the gun turned the crank. Each time the ten rifle barrel cylinder turned to a new barrel, a round fired automatically. The faster the crank was turned, the faster the barrels rotated and the faster the weapon fired.

After a dozen rounds the sergeant stopped, adjusted the aim of the weapon and fired again. This time twenty rounds blasted into the side of the wagon and the troops on hand cheered.

The next cranking produced only ten shots when twenty should have come out.

Oliver signalled to cease fire, and rode up to the gun.

The gunners opened the assembly, quickly cleaned the clogged barrels and when ready they fired another twenty rounds.

"That's plenty of practice," Captain Harding barked. Then he shook his head. "No, I want the assistant gunner and the third man on the firing team to be able to operate the weapon as well as the gunnery sergeant. If the sergeant becomes a casualty, the other men must be able to fire. Both you other men practice firing twenty rounds. Move the weapon, re-aim and fire it. See to it, Lieutenant Oliver." The captain returned the officer's salute and then rode back to the fort.

On his desk he found notes from the only two officers' wives on the post. Each invited him to dinner, one that night, the other the next night. He sighed and stared at the wall map without seeing it. The women were only trying to compensate, to make his loss easier.

But he wasn't ready to be civil or polite, not yet. He had revenge in his heart first. When the bloody Comanche band was run to ground and every man slaughtered, only then would he feel clean enough to associate with respectable families. Only then would he be able to enjoy seeing a family together, while his own had been murdered and kidnapped.

He took a deep breath, beat down the grinding ache in his gut and wiped his hand across his eyes. Then he called in his clerk and orderly.

"Corporal Swenson, take my regards to Mrs. Edwards and to Mrs. Jenkins. I won't be able to accept their kind offers to dinner. Pressing work getting ready for the patrol. Say something nice. Thank you, Corporal."

Swenson watched the captain a moment, started to say something then nodded and retreated to his small office outside the door.

Captain Harding went back to the map on his wall and studied the trail from Fort Comfort north and west to the middle fork of the Brazos. He knew the trail, it was embedded in his brain. He estimated the days. With the wagons, at least six long days to the marshy area and the hidden canyon.

What he would do once he got to the canyon, he wasn't sure. A plan of action kept surging through his mind, but he couldn't formulate anything solid yet. He had to wait to see what his scouts reported.

This time he'd take the Indians, the Tonkawa. They hated the Comanche as much as he did. A good fight would help keep them happy.

He dug into his files and took out a paper he had written almost a year ago about how to settle the Indian question once and for all. It was war, and they should take a war stance. They could not chase all over a billion square miles hunting the renegades—and finding them only when they wanted to fight.

What the army had to do was strike at the Indian camps, at the very heart of the Indian way of life. The army had to wipe out the Indian villages, the base camps, the squaws and their tents and racks of drying meat, their winter food stores.

The Indians must be treated the same way they treated the whites, kill everyone at the villages, burn down and totally destroy everything they owned.

The way the Comanche had done at the wagon supply train!

Captain Harding took out the paper now and read it again. Yes, it was practical. It was the only way to defeat the threat to the white settlers. The army had to destroy the Indian's way of life so he could not function independently. So he had no time to raid or make war.

Captain Harding was going to demonstrate to the army exactly how his plan would work.

Just as soon as he found the band who had murdered his wife and son and captured his daughter.

Harding went out to talk to Riddle. The roster was complete. The men would be inspected the following morning, and with any luck they would have the supply lists worked out and organized in another day and a half.

"If all goes well, Colt, we should be able to have you on your way in three more days."

They looked at each other.

"Which means somebody could be here from Department Headquarters in San Antonio before we leave," Harding said, slapping his riding crop against the desk top.

"Possible. With almost a nine thousand dollar loss from that Indian raid, some major or light colonel is going to be busting his ass to get out here and make a name for himself."

Harding nodded. "Damnit to hell! See if you can squeeze another twenty-four hours out of that schedule."

"Already have, Colt. It's as tight as I can make it. I'm not sending you off half prepared or half supplied."

They stared at each other again, this time Riddle looked away first. "I've worked out the spread of troops, half from B company and half from A. They'll take their sergeants and officers: that's Lieutenant Oliver and Lieutenant Dan Edwards who used to be in charge of a platoon but was moved up to company commander when Captain Adamson was ordered to San Antonio."

"Edwards, yes, too young for the spot, but we don't have anyone else. It'll have to do. Now try and cut out at least twelve hours for me. I'm going to look at the stock."

On the other side of the fort, across the dusty parade ground in Officer Country, Garland Oliver entered his quarters. After the Gatling gun practice, Oliver had returned the weapon to the special locked cabinet in the weapons room, double locked it and took the keys to the adjutant's office. They were always kept there. He relieved his special detail on the gun and went back to his quarters.

Army standing orders called for the troops in all posts and forts to fall out for drills and "gunnery and horsemanship" practice once each day. It was an order that was almost universally ignored.

Commanders ordered drills and training whenever they thought it might help, often for disciplinary reasons. There was no chance to do even rudimentary target practice. The men in his company had not fired a round in practice during the past six months.

On some posts target practice was considered a waste of good ammunition and too expensive. Some commanders had been charged for the rounds that their men fired during target practice. Lieutenant Oliver had gone around this error in army judgment by giving his men on wood cutting details and on patrols a minimum of ten rounds of practice per patrol. It had helped his men become some of the best shots in the fort.

He was downright embarrassed however by the horsemanship of his men. Most had little or no riding experience when they joined the Cavalry. More than half of the men did well simply to sit their horses during the slow riding on a long march.

A flat out Cavalry charge would find six or eight out of his company actually falling off their mounts. When they got back from this patrol he would fall the men out every afternoon for horsemanship practice.

He took off his saber, dropped his campaign hat on his bunk and washed up in the bowl on the small washstand in his quarters. It was a bachelor's room, twenty-four feet wide as were all the rooms and quarters and shops and stores inside the three-foot thick outer walls. His room was only ten feet wide and had one narrow window looking out onto the parade grounds.

He dropped on his bunk and stared at the spot near the dividing wall and beside his washstand where he had secreted the gold.

Oliver grinned as he remembered how it worked out. Before his troops had left the massacre site of the supply train, he had found time in the darkness and general confusion, to dig up the gold and store it in his saddle bags and in his blanket roll. No one had seen him, he had made sure of that.

The trip back the next morning had been without incident. It had been slow due to the covered wagon carrying the two bodies. Once at the fort he carred his tack and blanket roll into his quarters and quickly stored the gold under the loose floor board where he usually kept a small cache of cash he had built up after being on this post for almost two years.

It had been a simple project to hide the gold, shake out his blankets and have his orderly take his saddlebags back to the tack room. He lay there dreaming how he would spend the money. Oliver was not even sure how much was there. He hadn't wanted to take the time to count it when he first got back.

There had been no marking on the wooden box. He had thought of putting a blanket over the window late some night, opening the floorboard and making a count. But he decided it was more enjoyable to guess how much was there.

He could resign from the army at any time. His compulsory time was up after West Point. But he should make captain within another year.

He snorted. There had to be five or six thousand dollars in the box. He had not seen the report by the adjutant about the loss. He thought of all the things he could do in San Francisco with six or seven thousand dollars!

He could open his own gambling palace and live like a king the rest of his life. He could have all the women he wanted! He could build a big house and become a respectable merchant! There were a thousand things he could do.

He finished the afternoon's inspection of the half of his troop that would be going on the patrol. They were in good shape. Now if they could only ride better. Supper in the officers' mess that evening was uninspired, bland and overcooked. He went back to his quarters, rejected Lt. Edwards' offer to play some cards, and settled down behind the small desk he had made from some packing boxes.

He had a list of nearly thirty projects he could do if there were ten thousand dollars in the cache. He worked over the list all evening, then tried to figure out how he could logically resign, without bringing suspicion on himself. He knew that there had been a report made about the missing gold. How long would it be before the Inspector General would send an investigator?

These and a dozen other questions bombarded

Oliver as he burned the list of projects over the top of his coal oil lamp chimney, and mashed the ashes in his waste basket.

It wouldn't be long, if he knew the army, before someone began asking questions.

He was in the clear. Nobody could have the slightest inkling that he had anything to do with the missing gold. He went to sleep with a smile on his face, dreaming already about owning his own gambling palace and saloon with six cribs upstairs for the most beautiful whores he could recruit in San Francisco, and all of them would have double-handful sized breasts!

Oliver came awake with a start.

Someone loomed over him.

He felt cold steel, sharp cold steel, pressing against his throat.

"Liuetenant, sir, you make one little sound, and I slit your throat from one ear to the other. That would give you 'bout twenty seconds to live. You want that . . . sir?"

"No! No, of course not," Oliver whispered. He was scratching through his memory for the voice. Then he had it.

Corporal Quentin Pendleton, a sneaky, rank happy little bastard.

"Pendleton, you better have a good reason for doing this, or I'll see you spend twenty years in a Federal prison."

"Got one, Lieutenant. Fact is I got me about eight thousand damn good reasons. I watched you back at the supply wagon train. Saw you open that wooden box, then bury the gold. Then I saw you hide the last of it in your blanket roll just before we went to sleep that night. Strange when we got here how you brought your saddlebags inside before you had them taken with your saddle over to the tack room."

The knife blade pressed harder.

"Hell, I should just do it right now, then find out where you put the gold. You got it here somewhere, all eight thousand dollars worth, right in your quarters. I'd have all night to look. Figure I could find it."

"No! No, don't use the knife. We can work out something, Corporal Pendleton."

"Yeah, like what, high and mighty?"

"Like a thousand dollars!"

The knife moved a fraction of an inch and Oliver felt the blade bite into his flesh and a trickle of blood seep down his neck.

"Dumb, Lieutentant. Shit ass dumb! Thought you officers were smart. Make it fifty/fifty and you got a deal. You make it that way and have it ready for me tomorrow, and I won't turn you in. I won't go to the captain tomorrow morning before breakfast and tell him who stole the gold."

Oliver felt sweat seep down his face and join the trickle of blood down his neck. He had to do this exactly right or he would die. He knew Pendleton, the man was absolutely amoral, who thought only of money. He was a poker player, a gambler, a drinker and he sold his wife for two dollars a throw.

"Yes. Yes, I think we can agree on that. Tomorrow. Now move the blade."

The blade left his throat, but at once the point touched his chest over his heart. Oliver lay perfectly still.

"This way, big shot officer," Pendleton brayed. "You have the gold in a small carpetbag for me tomorrow. You call me from the barracks and have me deliver it somewhere. I'll stop off at my quarters and dump out the gold and deliver the empty carpetbag. Sound good?"

"Yes, good. I'll make all the arrangements with you tomorrow morning." He swore softly. "Damn, I have wood detail tomorrow. I'll pick a squad of ten men to go cut wood. Why don't you volunteer to come along as the NCO. Then we can work out the rest of the details."

"What details?"

"About where to deliver the bag, what time, all of that."

Pendleton pulled away the knife. He stood up and backed away being careful not to silhouette himself against the window.

"Yeah, okay. I'm easy to get along with. You pay half and I don't remember seeing a damn thing at Buffalo Creek." He laughed softly and a moment later the door opened a crack, then swung wide and a shadow darted out and the door closed.

Lieutenant Oliver lay there a moment, got up and splashed alcohol and bay rum on his nicked throat, then lay down on his bunk and smiled. Tomorrow on the wood gathering detail they would go a little farther out than usual, farther into the edge of the Comanche hunting grounds.

The next morning Oliver had his detail of wood cutters with their wagons ready just after morning mess. They pulled out of the fort and found the small stream to the north and went along it westward. Most of the good sized trees had already but cut for wood near the fort, and now he worked almost five miles west along the creek to a good stand of cottonwoods and some other fair sized trees which Oliver did not have a name for.

Pendleton had volunteered for the detail as the NCO and he put the ten men to work falling, sawing and splitting the wood into usable size and loading it on the wagon. They worked all morning, had a short dinner break, and were nearly done when Oliver and Pendleton walked upstream to the west.

"It's all set then," Oliver said watching Pendleton. "A fifty/fifty split. Four thousand dollars for you. I'll have it in a blue and black carpet bag just before evening mass."

Pendleton frowned slightly. "This is too easy, Lieutenant. I figured you'd be harder to convince."

'What's to argue? You saw me take the gold, you figure I have it in my quarters. I don't have much bargaining power."

The corporal grinned and bent down and took a long drink from the clear stream. He laughed softly.

"Yeah, I think you're right, Oliver. I've got you over a damn big barrel, and no damn way you can squirm from it, and stay out of prison."

"There is one way, Pendleton," Oliver said.

"What in hell could it be?" Pendleton said looking up as he turned from the water to face his officer.

"This way, you treacherous little bastard!" Oliver said. He held his army issue Smith and Wesson .44 aimed at Pendleton's heart.

"Not a chance in hell you'd shoot me," Pendleton said.

Oliver snorted and shot him twice in the chest, the second round slamming through his heart blasting him into hell a little early. The devil will be pleased.

Oliver fired three more times into the brush. Reloaded and took off his new hat and fired one round through it, then ran back toward the wood cutters.

They had heard the shooting and met him about half way.

"Damned Comanches!" he bellowed at them. "Stay low, I think I drove them off. One of the hostiles had a rifle. They must have been on a long range hunt."

That afternoon when the wagons came into Fort Comfort with the wood, the first rig held the body of Corporal Quentin Pendleton, and tales of how the whole wood cutting crew had to drive them off. More than eighty rounds had been expended in the brisk engagement with two or more Comanche hunters.

Lieutenant Oliver made a complete report to Lieutenant Riddle, who passed it on to the fort commander. Captain Harding read it with a frown.

"I've never heard of the Comanches sending long range hunting parties out this far. What the hell were they hunting for? The buffalo are all in the other direction."

"Who knows what the Comanches are thinking, Captain? We've got Oliver's statement. I talked to four of the enlisted men on the party and they all agree in principle. Nobody but Oliver saw the hostiles, but that's not unusual. You know how sneaky they can be when they know you're around."

"I know." Captain Harding scowled for a moment. "Hold the report until we get back from the patrol. Has there been any trouble between Oliver and this Pendleton?"

"No record of it. I asked the men the same thing. Nobody in his company has ever heard of any bad blood there."

Harding threw up his hands. "Hell, sign it and send in the report as a battle casualty. He has a wife on base, right?"

"Yes. I notified her as soon as I found out. She'll probably be returning to the east. They don't have any children."

"Go ahead. I'll countersign it as a killed in action. Now, how are we coming along on this patrol? Can we be ready to leave at noon tomorrow?"

6

Little Sadie Harding sat on the lumpy old buffalo
robe on the funny looking sled. She couldn't understand why they were moving again. She knew they
were Indians, she knew that the thin woman who fed
her and held her and put her to sleep was trying to
be kind to her. She even understood three or four
words the small, thin woman had taught her. But
Sadie still wanted her mother. She wanted to go
home to the fort, wherever that was.

Cries In The Morning stood watching her small
daughter. Laughing Golden Hair's blue eyes were
filled with wonder and worry.

"I know you don't understand any of this, Small
Wonder," Cries In The Morning said gently. "But
soon you will, we will learn more words. We move a
lot, it is the way of the People. We have a large herd
of horses and mules and they must have forage. If
we stay too long in one place, they eat off all the hair
of Mother Earth and it dies."

Cries In The Morning finished folding the heavy

buffalo hides that had been carefully stitched together with strong buffalo sinew to form the tipi cover. She had a huge task every time they moved to take down the tipi, fold the cover, lash the tall poles onto the travois, and pack everything she and her husband Running Wolf owned. Most if it went in buffalo robes tied to the travois. Sometimes in the summer there were rawhide boxes they could use.

She had done it so many times that Cries In The Morning had packing down to a routine. She had to decide whether to tie Laughing Golden Hair on a pony, or to let her sit on the travois.

The tipis came down now all over the camp, as the Eagle Band prepared to move.

Walking White Eagle had heard how the Pony Soldiers had penetrated through the marsh and into the secret valley itself. He had sent two scouts to watch for the soldiers, and when they came back with the news of the discovery of the valley, the whole camp had been in an uproar.

But more scouts soon came reporting the Pony Soldiers did not push foward. There were only four handfuls of them and they held back, cared for an injured man, and then retraced their steps.

White Eagle sent scouts to track the Pony Soldiers until he was sure they were heading back to the army fort. He had worried about how clever the Pony Soldiers had been, how they had avoided the false trails and even figured out the marsh. This was no ordinary Pony Soldier who hunted them.

White Eagle decided that they would move on in a week. It was nearing time for the first hunt, when they would take as much meat as they could. It would be the first of three hunts to provide them with the needed food for the long winter to come.

They would move well to the north and west even toward the Staked Plains, but they would not go that far.

White Eagle looked around at the camp that had stretched along the stream for more than three long arrow shots. There were now over fifty tipis in his band. It seemed to keep growing with each passing day.

Some families came from War Kettle's band, unhappy with the way he was turning from the old ways. War Kettle had been to talk with the round-eyes twice, and both times came back with many gifts—but also with word that the whites wanted only peace with the Comanche. White Eagle knew the whites wanted peace—if the Comanche would do exactly as the white generals wanted them to!

White Eagle sat on his new war pony, Flying Wind. He had learned his lessons well, and in the upcoming hunt he would be able to prove his worth. If he could chase the thundering buffalo and race flank to flank with the huge marvelous beasts, then he would be a true hunting pony as well as a war pony.

Flying Wind would have his chance soon. They were headed for a new summer camp, farther north and west than ever before, but it seemed the only alternative to harassment by the Pony Soldiers. They seemed to be everywhere this summer.

The head of the Eagle band saw with satisfaction that the camp was packing up quickly. Sometimes they had to make fast moves, in case of a sudden attack by enemy tribes or even by the Pony Soldiers.

His wives had his large tipi down quickly and everything packed. Now they waited, each on her horse beside the two travois. They set a good example.

Packing was woman's work. All the warriors were mounted with bow and arrows, lance and shield, ready to defend the camp from any attack. Fighting was man's work, he must be ready at any moment all day and night to fight for the band.

A dozen young boys, eight to twelve summers, charged past him on their ponies, shouting and laughing. Moving was one of the best times for them. They got to herd the horses and mules, to race up and down the line of march. They were future warriors and now was the time they began to perfect their horsemanship, and to use their bows. Each boy had a bow made especially for him, according to his height.

The boys raced off, slashing through the dismantling camp, upsetting some yet unpacked racks for drying meat, scattering possessions and raising the angry glances of the women working hard at packing.

White Eagle signalled Always Smiling, and she moved forward, leading the pack horse hauling the first travois. They would lead the line of march as usual, as was befitting the leader's first wife. She would also be in place if anyone needed her and her deep and all encompassing medicine bag.

She had learned about the healing roots and berries and shrubs and herbs from her mother, who had been medicine woman for many, many winters with the Comanche. There had been so much to understand, but slowly Always Smiling became as good at working with roots and powders and barks and potions from the bag as her mother.

White Eagle left two scouts in the hidden valley just above the one the Pony Soldiers had found. They were to stay there for four days, then follow the band north and west, remaining four days behind the band as security. After a week they would come into the new camp.

White Eagle sat at the departing point from the second hidden valley. They would go over a small rise and into a plain so flat on many days the best eyes in the band could not see the other side. He had divided his band into six groups, and sent them off at angles to their line of travel.

He took the most direct route, but made loops and circles to confuse anyone following them. In his heart he knew that no amount of trail trickery could disguise such a large group. They had sixty travois, and more than a thousand horses, ponies and mules. The herd made a river across the virgin grasslands if kept together.

The small white girl riding a travois near the head of the column stared in wonder at the mass of people and horses. At first she had whimpered in fear, but Cries In The Morning came back and walked her pretty spotted pony beside the litter and said one word over and over.

"Toquet, toquet . . . toquet."

It was one of the few words of the People that Sadie Harding understood. It meant, "it is well," and when she heard the word, she could smile and nod. Cries In The Morning went back to the front of the travois and Talks A Lot came beside Sadie.

The young Indian girl talked and talked, but never once did she say *touquet,* and Sadie, known to the Indians now as Laughing Golden Hair, did not understand a word she said.

The rolling, rocking motion of the buffalo robe stretched between the poles, affected Sadie, and soon she nodded, then went to sleep.

Talks A Lot smiled, slipped off her pony and

worked the small white body deeply into the robes and packed supplies so she would not tumble out. Soon Talks A Lot would have a baby of her own, a son for the chief, a future chief of the Comanche! Talks A Lot vaulted back on her pony's back and watched over the small *yo-oh-hobt pa-pi*, the yellow hair. A small smile wreathed her face as she thought of the child and held one hand on her swelling belly.

Seven days they worked across the broad plain. Some days they traveled twenty miles, some only eight or ten. Each night they picked a campsite near water and good forage for the animals, but they did not pause to put up the tipis.

That evening the leaders of the band sat around a small council fire and talked. Each man gave his ideas about the hunt to come. Advance scouts had reported back that there were two large herds of buffalo grazing just over a small rise. The band was down wind of them so no Indian scent would carry that way.

White Eagle listened to the comments, then stood.

"What you say is important and we will do as we always have done. With the morning we will be working quickly into the herd and taking as many of Mother Earth's buffalo as possible. We will use bow and arrows with the large hunting points of steel, and we will use our lances. No rifles are to be fired. They will frighten the buffalo before we have killed enough to make a good hunting camp."

Some of the warriors grumbled but there was no real opposition. Since the wagon wheel raid, White Eagle had given out half of the rifles, and instructed each warrior carefully how to use the weapon. But they agreed on the noise. There would be at least one more traditional buffalo hunt.

All that evening and into the night the warriors readied their lances, sharpened arrow points, finished a spare bow just in case one was lost or broken. Fires burned late that night as the old men of the band told of their amazing exploits in hunting the hulking buffalo in days gone by.

Wears His Coat had the best tale, and several of the warriors paused around a fire to listen.

"We were well below the Colorado and surprised a herd of not more than a hundred head that had wandered off from the rest. They were moving back north when we hit them.

"Twenty-seven braves rode out of the grass and charged them. I had only four arrows that day, tipped with black flint and sharp.

"We stormed at them from three sides. The cows gave the alarm and they bellowed and stampeded directly at us. You don't turn a buffalo stampede. Instead we waited for them, got to the side and began shooting buffalo.

"In those days every bull was over two thousand pounds. Huge shaggy brutes that stood six feet high at the shoulder. When an old buff decides to go one way, nothing changes his mind. He keeps right on running through and over trees and rivers and sometimes cliffs.

"I rode up beside this one and he glared at me from his big eye and I shot my first arrow. It went in just behind his right shoulder, down and through his heart. He dropped like a rock in a still pond, and I went after another one."

The stories by the old men would continue until late in the night. They didn't have to get up early to go on the hunt.

No camp was set up here, they would rest and move on in the morning. The warriors would go on the hunt and the women and children and the horse herders would move up only when there was word that there had been buffalo killed and the hunting camp would then be moved close to the kill and everyone set to work.

Cries In The Morning held Laughing Golden Hair a moment more, then put her down on a thick buffalo robe and went back to the small cooking fire. She returned a moment later with two pointed sticks, each with a piece of roasted meat on it. She held one out to the small white girl who took it eagerly and bit through the slightly burned exterior to the delicious pink meat inside.

She decided it was rabbit or maybe deer meat. It didn't matter, she was hungry and the meat was roasted and done. She let the dripping grease fall on the ground. Sadie decided that she liked the outside camping best. The tipi was all right, but it usually smelled so strange.

For a minute she wondered if her father would ever come and take her home. It had been a long time since her mother had left. And where was Yale, her big brother?

Tears welled up in her soft blue eyes, and when Cries In The Morning saw them she tenderly brushed them away.

"*Hi, tai toquet,* hello friend, it's all right, "Cries In The Morning said, and gave Sadie the rest of the roast meat she was eating. Sadie took it, and stared at the strange smile on the dark, lined face.

"Thank you," Sadie said, and Cries In The Morning bobbed her head and went back to the fire to roast more of the venison.

When daylight came, thirty-five warriors and young boys, almost warriors, held their ponies in check at the edge of a small fringe of trees. Just beyond lay a natural grazing land and there the herd of less than a hundred buffalo had made its bedground. The cows and calves lay in the center, the bulls on the outer rim.

White Eagle and the other hunters were checking themselves and their equipment. He had chosen to ride bareback, so Flying Wind would have that much less weight to carry. He had reins twenty feet long that would trail his mount. Then if he got knocked off by the buffalo, he would have a chance to grab the trailing reins so Flying Wind could pull him free of the murderous bison hooves.

White Eagle wore only moccasins, his breechclout and his skinning knife on his belt. Now he took a coiled bowstring of sinew from between his legs where he had kept it warm and dry from the morning dampness.

Quickly he strung his bow. If the sinew was too dry it would break when he pulled the bow. When it became damp it stretched. Now it was just right.

He balanced his bow on his thighs and shifted the quiver so it extended over his left shoulder where he could reach for an arrow easily with his right hand. Eight arrows rested there, each with his special mark on them, a bright, wide band of red near the feathers.

It was his arrow "name." Anyone finding an arrow so marked would return it to its owner. Arrows, good ones used for hunting and war, were hard to make and valued highly.

The buffalo were wary. The big animals did not have exceptionally good eyesight, but their sense of smell was highly developed.

White Eagle chose five arrows and held them in his hand as he gripped his bow. He would ride without the use of his hands.

A moment later the wind shifted, drifting the human scent to the animals. A cow snorted noisily. A bull bellowed, then three cows got to their feet and gave some kind of a signal. In moments the herd would be stampeding across the open plains.

White Eagle gave the cry of the eagle and the warriors and riders charged forward. The herd had lifted to its feet and led by a huge bull well over six feet at the shoulders, pounded away from the pony riders.

No buffalo can outrun a Comanche hunting pony, and quickly the hunters closed on the trailing members of the herd. The calves were passed up, and two younger boys worked together on a big cow that weighed over a thousand pounds. They took turns shooting arrows into her from their galloping ponies. The third arrow found its mark and the cow bison stumbled, tripped and tumbled over and over on the grassy plains.

The boys whooped in delight and rushed after another target.

White Eagle urged Flying Wind faster as he closed in on the leader of the stampede, the huge buffalo with the heavy shoulder coat and bare rear quarters where his winter coat had been rubbed free.

White Eagle had an arrow notched and came up on the right side of the beast. He nudged Flying Wind closer to the big, charging animal until the horse was barely a bow length away. White Eagle aimed and fired the arrow in one smooth movement, hardly conscious of aiming, knowing where the arrow had to go and willing it to its target. The arrow drove into the soft area behind the heaving shoulder, passed through part of a lung and daggered through the bison's heart before the arrow tip emerged out the far side of the dying creature.

The big animal continued for ten more charging steps before his front legs collapsed and he went down in a long skid that broke both his front legs as he drove his twenty-four hundred pounds of weight against them.

White Eagle pulled to one side and viewed the hunt. He saw more than a dozen animals down, and warriors still in pursuit. He urged Flying Wind forward again, picked out a bull and nudged his hunting pony faster so they pulled up beside the heaving, snorting animal. The big bull never looked their way. He was the king of the prairie and nothing was going to stop him from running straight ahead if he chose to. His small brain had picked his direction and nothing would dissuade him.

The Comanche warrior changed his mind with another broad tipped arrow and cut through thick buffalo hair and hide and found a vital region sending the big animal into a stumbling, snorting demise.

White Eagle pulled up. He was half a mile away from the first kill. Far enough. He turned and counted the dead animals as he trotted back to the fisrt one. They had dispatched twenty-eight buffalo! It would be half enough to fill their winter rawhide boxes with pemmican and racks of dried jerky.

He sat on Flying Wind and patted his neck as the leader of the band saw his wives running forward with their knives. Soon the butchering would start, and the choicest bits of delicacies would be eaten raw.

Always Smiling sank to her knees beside the first bull that had barely stopped its death struggle and slit open his belly and thrust her arm into the body cavity hunting the liver. She found it and cut it free and held it up to the first warrior who came by.

The raw livers were reserved for the hunters.

She continued exploring the animal. She found yellow tallow from the bull's loins, and popped the soft mass into her mouth. For a moment she moaned in delight. Prairie Flower came up quickly and cut out some of the entrails and chewed on them with a look of total rapture on her thin face. It had been nearly a year since she had tasted anything so delicious.

Something Good cut out the big bull's heart and set it aside since it would be honored to encourage the buffalo to prosper and multiply.

When the delicacies were eaten, everyone pitched in to do the work of butchering the twenty-eight animals. They were skinned carefully, the robes would keep them warm this winter.

Quickly drying racks were set up. These racks were often five feet high and that wide, with hooks in rows to hold the strips of buffalo meat to be dried into jerky so it didn't spoil.

Everyone worked quickly. Usually it took five women and girls to cut up one animal and get the meat hung on drying racks. They all knew that any of the meat not set to drying before noon would be spoiled by the next day. Even the hunters and warriors stepped in and worked over the animals. This was their winter's food supply and butchering work was acceptable.

Usually the hunter's family butchered out the animal he had killed. It was a hard job. First the animal was turned on its side, then the belly split open and the heavy hide skinned up to the backbone on one side.

Next the meat was cut out and strips made for drying. When one side was done, ponies were used to turn the buffalo over to do the same thing on the other side.

The hunting camp had been set up among the fringe of trees near the small stream. Packhorses were used to haul the strips of meat back to the hunting camp where they were hung on the drying racks.

Almost every part of the buffalo was used by the Comanches. They got the sinews from along the spine, they scooped out the brains and saved them in a stomach liner. They would be used later in the tanning process.

Bladders would become medicine pouches, the bones would be made into shovels, splints, saddle trees, awls, scrapers and even ornaments. The bull's scrotum was cut off and became a rattle for some of the dances. Paunch liners from the buffalo's stomach became water bottles. Even the hooves and feet would be used for glue and rattles. The small, curved buffalo horns would become fireproof coal containers for fire starting on long trips, and for holding black powder.

Hair from the hides that were tanned would become stuffing in saddle pads and shields and pillows. Some of it would be braided and made into ropes and halters and surcingles and headdresses.

It was too early in the summer for prime hides. There would be more hunts later in the fall and even into December to get absolutely prime hides when the fur was thickest.

When the last piece of meat was hung on the racks, and the last brisket taken and wrapped in hide, and the last bit of the buffalo saved and measured for use, the weary band returned to the hunting camp.

They splashed themselves in the stream to wash

away the blood of the butchering. There would be a dance that night, a celebration of the good hunt, and the hunters would tell of their skill in taking down a two thousand pound beast with a single arrow.

Cries In The Morning had left Laughing Golden Hair in the hunting camp with friends as she went to the butchering. Now she reclaimed the small one and saw that she had fallen asleep. Cries In The Morning picked her up and rocked her on the way to her small and low lean-to, which they always made at hunting camp. It was quicker than putting up the tipis each time. Also it was summer and warm.

Cries In The Morning lay the golden child with the blue eyes down on her small raised bedstead among the softest robes she owned, and watched her for a moment. Truly she was a fortunate woman. She not only had a child, she had a wonder child, with golden hair and eyes the color of the morning sky. She smiled softly and brushed some of the yellow hair from the small girl's eyes.

7

Lieutenant John Riddle, adjutant of Fort Comfort and second in command stood beside Captain Colt Harding's desk. He had a strained, worried look and Harding shook his head.

"Not a chance you can talk me out of it, John. I'm going. I'm going to find those bastards and cut their balls off and stuff them down their throats, then I'm going to make them suffer the same way my Milly did. You can bank on it!"

"Orders," Riddle said slowly. "What orders are we operating under, in case somebody asks me?"

"Standing orders, John, the way I told you before. The commander of every fort or installation has wide latitude in the pursuit and punishment of hostiles who attack, kill, kidnap, either military or civilian personnel, or who destroy valuable government or civilian property. I'd say the Comanches did both, and I'm going after them."

Riddle stepped aside. He waved the captain to the door.

"Your patrol will be ready in an hour. You have enough salt pork, bacon, beans and hardtack for six weeks. That's as much as we can scrape up until the next supply train gets through. You told me to use my judgment on the supplies."

"I said two months, damnit!"

"The fort garrison will be on half rations for the last two weeks you're out as it is. Seemed fair to me. If you order me to, I'll increase the supplies on your wagon, and cut the fort troopers to half rations starting now."

Captain Harding kicked his desk with a well worn boot and swore under his breath.

"You know I won't ask you to do that. We'll be back in six weeks—or we'll live off the land, what there is to live off."

He marched to the door, opened it and without a glance behind him strode through the outer office to the small porch.

Corporal Swenson had his black waiting for him. Colt stepped into the saddle and saw Oliver bring the line of troopers to attention.

He rode to the center in front of the Cavalrymen lined up four deep and stood in his stirrups.

"Men! You know what we've lost. . . . fifteen good men and three civilians. We're going to pay back the Comanches in blood. It won't be easy and it won't be quick. Let's ride."

It was straight up noon.

Oliver ordered the men into a column of fours and they led out behind the commander. A lead Tonkawa scout rode just behind the captain. Oliver sent two Tonkawas ahead a half mile indicating a direction and a landmark. They would ride directly to the hidden valley.

The special patrol was set up as usual for an army

unit. Each trooper carried his carbine or rifle, one hundred and fifty rounds of ammunition, half a pup tent, three days rations of salt pork, hardtack, dry beans and coffee. He had one blanket, a rubber sheet as a ground cloth, one extra uniform and five pair of socks and low cut shoes. The Pony Soldiers had one other item that was indispensible, fifteen pounds of grain for their mounts.

With scouts out ahead, two man security details on each side and a four man rear guard, the unit moved out. Directly behind the column of fours came the Gatling gun and its caisson, then the supply wagon, and one empty wagon that would be used as an abulance if needed.

The column moved forward smartly for the first four miles, then they had a small stream to cross. It took an hour to get the two wagons through the stream. It was finally accomplished with six added horses with ropes pulling the heavy wagon through the soft bottom.

The Tonkawa scouts would not help push the wagons out of the stream. They said that Mother Earth did not like the wagons or she would not make them stuck. They should leave them where they were so not to make Mother Earth angry.

They made only eight miles before it was time to stop. Most days they had to start camp two hours before dark. The troops had chores to do.

Their horses came first. They set up picket lines for the horses and mules, then fed and watered each one.

Guards were set up on the camp perimeter, and a wood detail was ordered out to bring back enough wood for the cooking fires. In this location there was almost no wood available, so the detail gathered up gunny sacks full of buffalo chips and turned them over to the sergeant in charge.

This night the two man pup tents were set up in a straight line by squads. The men pounded in the stakes and sergeants lined them up. With that out of the way permission was given to start the evening meal.

On a long march the only hot meal of the day was at night. Since no cooks came along, each man had to do his own cooking. As was the case with most soldiers, they had discarded the official mess kit, a tin plate and a collapsible skillet, and instead carried a small solid skillet and a big tin cup from the sutter's supply.

Sergeant Casemore was an old hand at range cooking. He dug out a portion of salt pork and parboiled it in the skillet, then threw out the water and fried it in the skillet until it crackled.

Earlier he had roasted the raw coffee beans in the skillet and ground the cooked beans into powder with the help of a pair of rocks and his knife. Then he boiled his coffee in the big cup sitting on rocks at the edge of the small cooking fire.

Captain Harding had the luxury of a Sibley conical tent, with a folding cot from the supply wagon to sleep on. His orderly and the bugler slept just outside in their two man tent. Usually Corporal Swenson cooked for all the officers on the trip. Supplies were drawn from the supply wagon, but the food was the same as the men ate.

Sometimes they had dried fruits, raisins and condensed milk, but this trip there were no extras, and the officers had to settle for the same salt pork, hardtack and beans the men were issued.

After the meal the men were free to spend what leisure time they might have as they chose. There were always card games that went until dark, some singing, letter writing and talk. The usual chatter about the officers and complaints about the army were in full swing on this night when Sergeant Casemore made the rounds of his men.

Each company had kept its officers and sergeants together, so they could function as units. One of the privates saw his sergeant and called to him.

"Sarge, it true that we're going to keep riding until we track down that band of Comanches, no matter if it takes all summer?"

Casemore snorted. "Who the hell told you that, son? We're on a search patrol, try to find the hostiles if we can. If we can't we come back and try again. Captain Harding ain't crazy. He knows about how far we can go and still get back to the fort without eating our mules."

He paused and looked at the soldier, who wasn't much more than a year past eighteen.

"You ever et mule meat, boy? It's not much good. But it'll keep you alive. I'm proof of that. Two years ago coming back from a two month patrol we ran out of rations and killed a mule every third day and threw away what the critter was packing. Ate up eight mules that way but we got back to the fort without losing a man."

Casemore told the men they better be thinking about bedding down. First call would be coming early.

It did.

Life on the trail for the men began at 4:45 A.M. when the troopers rolled out of their blankets and dressed if they had taken off more than their boots.

Ten minutes later reveille and Stable Call sounded. They had five minutes to saddle their horses and harness the mules.

At five A.M. sharp mess call bugled across the

Texas plains. Now they had a half hour to fix and eat their morning meal, which usually was coffee and hardtack, and some dried fruit if they had any.

General call came at 5:30, when they struck the camp. It was the busiest, hectic time when they tore down the tents, packed their gear on their mounts and stored any equipment in the wagons.

At 5:45 it was Boots and Saddles, when the Cavalrymen mounted their horses.

Ten minutes later came Fall In, and the entire group assembled in marching order in a column of fours.

Promptly at six A.M., Captain Harding lifted his saber and swung it forward. Lieutenants shouted the marching order. Sergeants down the column repeated the orders, and the long line of blue shirted troopers moved out across the prairie of western Texas.

The Tonkawa scouts not in the lead, rode to one side, out of the line of march, but close by, continually amazed at the routines of the roundeyes, but happy to have their own ration of hardtack and salt pork.

Now, as often happened, Captain Harding gave the order that six of the Tonkawas should swing away from the line of march on a hunting expedition. They should bring back any game they could by use of their bows and arrows or carbines. Most of the Indians had learned to use the rifles well and often could shoot better than many of the poorly trained Cavalrymen.

Casemore gave the orders that were passed down to him. He picked out six of the Tonkawa scouts and told them what to do. They grinned and laughed. They were getting army pay for hunting! It seemed like child's play to them, and they eagerly surged away from the main party, indicating they would be back to the line by midday.

Captain Harding rode at the head of the company sized patrol. He had enough rounds for each man for a major campaign. He had brought a box of a hundred sticks of the new dynamite, and had figured out a special use for it.

Grenades and grenadiers had long been military terms, but the U.S. Cavalry had no small hand held bomb for its troops. He had devised such a weapon that was devastating, easy to produce and carry and while not totally reliable, could be counted on in six out of seven times.

He had experimented with the new stick dynamite until he had precisely what he wanted. He had cut the twelve inch stick of explosive in half and wired the halves together. Then he used sticky tape and large headed roofing nails, and taped the nails around the six inch sticks of explosive.

By careful planning he could bind fifty of the roofing nails to the dynamite bomb.

By inserting a six inch fuse with a blasting cap pushed into the powder, he had an easy to carry, easy to use and deadly hand bomb. When it detonated it sent inch long roofing nails blasting out in all directions like shrapnel. He hoped to be able to use the new bombs against the Comanches.

Before he left the fort, Captain Harding had a detail of men fashion fifty of the small hand bombs. The six inch fuse usually burned in thirty seconds. Fuse was rated to burn a foot a minute, but as with any new weapon there were problems. Some burned much faster, some slower.

He had experimented and soon cut the fuse length to three inches, so the bomb would explode in fifteen seconds. He was sure he would find ample use for the hand bombs.

The route was familiar and fairly level across the flatness of western Texas. They crossed the upper reaches of the Colorado of Texas and pushed on toward the middle fork of the Brazos.

The second day the hunters came back with a good sized deer, which they had dressed out and quartered. Every man had at least a small portion of fresh meat that night to cook. The Indians had eaten the heart and liver and most of the entrails raw as was their custom.

The fifth day they forded the central fork of the Brazos and worked toward the marsh and the hidden valley. Two miles from it, Captain Harding called a halt at a small bluff near water and forage. The troop camped with its back to the bluff for protection and rested.

Harding took reports from his scouts. They had found no hostiles in the first valley across the marsh. He ordered them to scout the next valley and come back with a report before dark.

Again the Tonkawas reported no sign of the hated Comanches. They had camped in the second valley for two or three weeks, the Tonkawas said, but had left in orderly fashion, evidently in small groups at a time and in various directions. There was no way to be sure which direction the main band was headed.

Harding went into his Sibley, sat on his folding canvas chair and looked at the picture of his wife. He had no picture at all of Yale or of Sadie.

He slammed his fist into his open palm. Damnit to hell! What an ordeal she was going through! Living with those savages, those butcherers.

He paced his tent, then went outside and walked a half mile up a small creek and threw rocks in the water. When he came back he had his plan. It was generally against army policy to send out Indian scouts alone, but in this case it was all he could do. He sent for the head Indian scout, called Big Ear.

The Tonkawa was about twenty-five years old, had a saber slash on one cheek and insisted on wearing an army officer shirt with corporal stripes on it. Nobody minded but the corporals, but they were not ready to challenge him in a knife fight.

Big Ear had picked up English quickly and now communicated effectively with some English words and signs.

"Take all of your scouts," Captain Harding told him. "You'll get three days rations. Ride down those trails. Do at least sixty miles a day. Many, many miles. Find out where the Comanches are heading."

At last Big Ear understood. He laughed softly. With three days army rations he could lead his raiding party on a two week spree! They could find some cabins and have a feast! But quickly he changed his mind. There were no settlers this far out, and the Pony Soldiers would shoot him if he did not obey his orders.

But it would be good to find the Comanche! He could smell the soup cooking now! Quickly he hurried to the place assigned to the Indians for the camp, and spoke to the warriors. They would leave as soon as they drew their rations. Each scout had a carbine and a hundred and sixty rounds of ammunition.

For three days Big Ear and his Tonkawas rode hard. They tracked the puny efforts of the Comanches to hide their trails. The members of the band came together and separated, crossed trails, back tracked and split up again and again, but always they rejoined and always they moved northwest.

They soon left the land of the Brazos and ventured deeper into West Texas, well out of their usual hunting and camping grounds. The fourth day Big Ear could see the looming presence of the cap rock escarpment to the west. They had penetrated all the way to the flat Texas plateau just below the Staked Plains!

The main party of the Comanche band had assembled now and with no more trickery angled directly for the Staked Plains. They hit a small river that seemed to run straight into the cap rock. An hour later Big Ear saw where the Comanche band vanished. They had either vaporized and blew away, or ridden in the creek where it sliced into a narrow gorge that knifed into the eight hundred foot high cliffs where the Staked Plains reared up out of the Texas landscape.

Big Ear and his scouts stared at the contradiction, then turned and rode back toward the Pony Soldiers' camp. For some reason the Comanches had retreated all the way to the Staked Plains. Big Ear was not sure how they climbed to the top of the barricade, but the stream must be the pathway.

His men were disappointed that they would not feast on Comanche soup, but he promised them that soon their hunger would be satisfied.

The Tonkawas had been gone seven days when they rode into the small camp near the bluff. Captain Harding had about decided they had deserted. He told his officers that he would give the savages twenty-four hours to return, then he would declare them deserters, and leave for the fort.

Big Ear rode in with two hours to spare. He and Private Escobar who understood some of the Indian lingo, sat down outside the captain's tent and talked for two hours with the captain, before the Fort

Commander understood fully what his scouts had found.

"The Staked Plains? They must be two hundred miles from here. Why the hell did the hostiles go way up there?"

Big Ear heard the question, and understood it, but he had no answer for the Pony Soldier captain. He felt as if they should smoke a pipe, but there was none. He indicated that was the end of his report. The captain waved him away and began pacing up and down in front of his Sibley tent.

"What the hell are those hostiles running that far for?" Colt Harding asked the harsh Texas plains. The soft chattering of the creek, and the whispers of the wind would not give him an answer.

The following morning at 4:45 First Call sounded from the bugler's lips and the troops swung into action. Promptly at 6:00 A.M. the men rode out, heading back for the fort. They made better time on the way back, and in four hard days rode near Fort Comfort just before sundown.

Lieutenant Riddle rode out to meet the patrol as soon as his lookouts reported the dust trail.

"That's about the size of it, Captain. His name is Major Zachery, he's from the Inspector General's staff in San Antonio Department of Texas headquarters. He's been interviewing the men involved in the gold problem. The rest of the loss he says is clearly the action of the Comanche.

"His one theme is that there is a one hundred percent chance that one of the men in our command stole the gold. Indians do not understand gold. It's too soft to make arrowheads or scrapers. He's got the whole fort on edge and the men are bitching and fighting among themselves."

"And he can't wait to get at the rest of the men

who were on the rescue detail?" Colt asked.

"Right. He's panting. Especially wants to talk to you and to Lieutenant Oliver."

"Figures."

The two officers and friends, rode in silence for a quarter of a mile.

"Damnit, Colt, the major is probably right. Half a dozen of the men in that detail had a chance to find and steal that gold. Eight thousand dollars is as much cash money as an enlisted man would make in thirty-two years!"

Colt adjusted the two six-guns at his sides and stared hard ahead. "It's a temptation worth a man's time, I'll admit that. But most of these men don't have the ambition or the good sense to try to steal that gold. If we find out who the man is, I can guarantee you it will be a surprise to everyone."

Harding turned, ordered Oliver to bring in the patrol and he and Riddle galloped the last quarter mile into the Fort.

A half hour later, Harding had taken a sponge bath in a bucket of hot water Swenson brought him, had put on a clean uniform and combed out his beard and pasted down his hair.

He asked Swenson to bring the major in.

Major Alexander Zachery was barely five feet five inches tall. He was the shortest major Harding had ever seen. The small man wore a Van Dyke beard that came to a sharp point, and the rest trimmed precisely. Over his left eye he fixed a monocle that draped from a gold chain that circled his neck.

He stared at Harding for a moment, then let the glass fall from his eye on its chain and returned the captain's salute. Zachery stepped forward and held out his hand.

"Nasty business, Captain, I heard about your

loss. My condolences. Did you track down the bastards?"

"No sir, I'm afraid not."

"Pity. We'll find them. Do you know which band it was?"

"No sir. My Tonkawa scouts say it could be one of three different bands in this area. We're working on it."

"Good, good." They both sat down and the major hesitated.

"Major Zachery, I understand you've been conducting an investigation on my post into the missing government property."

"That's right. I have no doubt at all that one or more of your men on that escort greeting party stole the gold, all eight thousand dollars worth."

"You have all the names from those rosters?"

"Yes, the first party, and the men who went back to bring in the wagons. Many of them were with you on your patrol."

"Give the men a day, could you, Major? It was a frustrating and a hard ride."

"I can do that. You had no casualties?"

"No sir. The guilty party must still be in the fort . . . except for messengers. We send out one a week with dispatches heading for Austin."

"I checked. None of the messengers sent so far were involved."

"Good. Now, Major, could I share a drink with you. I need one after that patrol."

"Help yourself, Captain, I don't drink." The major stood, nodded to Harding who had taken a bottle of good whiskey from his desk drawer.

"See you at supper," the major said, his eyes showing his disapproval as he walked to the door.

8

Major Alexander Zachery sat at the first table at the far end of the enlisted men's mess hall. He listened to what the private in front of him said. The major had told the trooper to stand at ease, which the man did, his hands clasped tightly behind his back, his feet eighteen inches apart, his eyes straight ahead.

Kirk MacTavish, private from New York City, was so scared he could hardly breathe. He'd never even *seen a major before,* let alone been talked to by one. He'd always been frightened of officers, they were not like ordinary men. Now he stammered and sweated, and tried to remember.

"Near as I can recall, sir, I never seen no one go near the wagons after we found them. Our lead party of three got there first, made sure nobody was alive and then Corporal Ingles pulled us off fifty yards, told us to stay put. He hightailed it back to the main party."

"And you never approached the wagons

113

yourself?"

"No sir. I ain't that fond of looking at scalped bodies, especially since I knew some of the troopers."

"Did you see the man with you approach the wagons during the time before Corporal Ingles left and the arrival of your captain and Lieutenant Oliver?"

"No sir. He never moved either. We even stayed mounted, case the hostiles came back."

"Fine, now try and relax, MacTavish. You're not on trial here. This is an inquiry, all unofficial. You were in the area for the next six or seven hours, then?"

"No sir, longer. We stayed until morning before we started back with the wagon and the two dead . . . civilians."

"So the part of A company not on the pursuit detail stayed near the wagons overnight, some seventy-five men?"

"Yes sir. It was near dark before we got the troopers buried and our tents set up. It wasn't a good company street, sir, nobody inspected, they weren't lined up right . . ."

"Yes, Private MacTavish, I can imagine. Death has a way of upsetting a routine." The major frowned. This was going to take a lot longer than he figured. He might have to interview all ninety-five men from Company A. One or more of those twenty men who went on the chase could have found the gold before the midnight departure time.

"How much money do you make a month, Private?"

"Twelve dollars, sir. But there's laundry and the tab at the sutler, and . . . usually not much left."

"So eight thousand dollars to you is a fortune?"

"Land sakes yes, sir. More money than I ever hope to see or to own, even to dream about."

"Thank you, Private MacTavish. That will be all."

MacTavish snapped a salute that was far from perfect. The major returned it with a perfunctory wave and Kirk walked quickly from the nearby doorway. As he went out, the next man in line entered, his campaign hat under his arm.

Across the wide parade grounds in his office, Captain Harding listened to his adjutant.

"Second day of the major's inquiry. So far he's talked to forty-three men. He's hearing about the same thing from most of them. He wants to talk to everyone on the trip from A company, regardless of whether they went on the volunteer chase group with you, or came back the next morning, stayed as guards, or went back with mules to drive in the wagons.

"The man has an all summer's job. I'm more interested in the Comanche. Why in hell did they run off to the Staked Plains?"

"Maybe they always do this time of year," Riddle suggested.

"The Tonkawas say usually the Comanches never get that far west, at least not lately."

"Maybe some ritual, some ceremony. You know how tied to nature most of the Indian religious rites are."

"You don't think they were simply running away from my patrol?"

"No. They probably didn't even know you came any farther than the first valley. They would have scouts out watching for you. They knew the minute you turned back."

"The first time."

"That was enough. By now they have a cold trail."

Harding stood and paced across his office. "So you're saying I should just quit? That the trail is so cold I'll never find Sadie?"

Riddle shook his head. "Not at all. But it looks like there isn't going to be a chance to get Sadie back right away. There are sources. The white hunters out there, still a few trappers around who know the Indians, the traders, the comancheros and a few friendly Indians. We put out the word that there is a small blonde blue-eyed girl out there with the Comanches we want back.

"We watch and wait and try to get some information to tie down which band has little Sadie."

"That could be six months or a year from now before we got any information! What will happen to Sadie?"

"Colt, we need a starting point. We can't charge all over Texas and Indian territories looking for Sadie without knowing something about where she is."

"Damnit, John, I have to do something!" Colt bellowed. They glared at each other for a moment without rancor. Each man trying to find a solution to the problem. If they didn't it would tear Colt Harding apart, get him cashiered out of the service and sent on a lonely trek searching for his lost daughter in a harsh and unforgiving land filled with his mortal enemies.

Slowly Colt began to nod. He stared out the small window into the large courtyard parade ground.

"I have an idea. Help me work it out. Every army campaign ever waged was successful or better because of good intelligence, scouting reports, information. Right now that's what I need for my campaign. I need to know which band, and where that band of Comanches is. Right, John?"

"Absolutely, but how . . ."

"So I get the intelligence."

"We can't keep sending out company sized patrols. Division is going to start asking questions, looking for some Indian kill figures or reports of raids . . ."

"Right! John! Exactly right. So we don't send out company sized thrusts. We do it smaller.

"Smaller could mean a whole platoon getting wiped out," John Riddle said.

"Yes, again you're right. How can I do this so I don't get in trouble with Division, and so I protect my men, and still get the job done?"

Captain Harding stared at the big map of western Texas for a long time without saying a word. Then he turned and went to his door. In the outer office he pointed at Corporal Swenson.

"My horse, Corporal. Saddled, canteen and a pair of binoculars. Let me know when you're ready."

John leaned against the door frame.

"You're going out by yourself, alone?"

"I've been called stupid, but I'm not that dumb. I'm going to do some high level planning, and I can do that best in the saddle. With a saddle thumping me on the butt I seem to think better, somehow. Alone. I'll be back before the noon mess call."

A half hour later, Colt Harding rode hard across the prairie for a quarter mile, then eased off and let his big black walk. He had ridden since he was four. His parents had a big country place on Long Island out of the bustle of New York City. They lived there most of the time, and had a stable of six horses.

When he got in trouble, or was lonely, or mad at

everyone, he ran to the stables and rode. Once he was gone two days, riding all the way to the end of Long Island and back. His parents were frantic.

Now he reverted to form. He was angry and mad, he was so damn lonely he could scream. So he rode. He let the big black walk, moving toward the small stream. She drank, then stood in the cool water for a moment before he urged her out to the near bank from the hock deep water.

An hour later he walked the black into the fort just before the noon mess call.

He had worked out the only solution he could. He left his horse with a trooper who hurried up from stable duty and walked into his office, his riding crop slapping steadily on his blue army trousers with the broad yellow stripe down the side.

Lieutenant Riddle looked up from his desk.

"So?"

The captain waved his adjutant into his office and when the door was shut, Harding grinned.

"I'm not taking a company, or a platoon, or even a squad. I'm going out alone, with Big Ear and six of his Tonkawa scouts."

Riddle jolted back a step. "Alone? That's insane, that's . . ." But as he thought about it he began to nod. He laughed softly and then a big grin broke out on his face. "Tricky, but effective. You keep the army out of it. The scouts are on leave, you're on a month's furlough you have coming, and could be in St. Louis, or New Orleans for all we know."

"And I have the best damn protection any soldier ever had. Those Tonks will keep me out of trouble, go around any big band of Comanches, and we will travel light with grass fed Indian ponies. I'll go in buckskins and with my two forty-fours."

"How long, Colt?"

118

"As long as it takes. I've built up two months of furlough. I'll be leaving tomorrow morning."

"What do I tell Major Zachery?"

"That I'm going on leave to recover from losing my family. The goddamn truth."

"He'll want to inspect your gear before you go—due to his inquiry."

"He's free to do so. Send for Big Ear, I think he'll like the proposition I'm going to make him."

That afternoon Major Zachery interviewed Captain Harding about what he knew of the gold theft. Colt told him exactly what he had done that evening and all that he knew. He told the major that he didn't have the gold or know anything about it, and that he was leaving the next morning on a furlough.

"What about this inquiry?"

"You don't need me here, Major. You can inspect my gear before I leave."

"That won't be required. I did want you here when I find the thief. And I will find him."

"I'm sure you will, Major. Is there anything else?"

Zachery stood, shook his head and walked back to his quarters.

A short time later, Big Ear smiled at the Pony Soldier captain.

"We go long ride. Indian pony. Live Indian style?"

"That's right, quietly, without being seen. We ride until we find which Comanche band has Sadie, and figure how to get her back."

"How pay Big Ear?"

Colt was ready for that. "You know how you've been asking to bring your lodges near the fort? I've decided after this trip, after we find Sadie, then you can bring your tipis and your women and horses to a new camp a mile down from the fort on the river in that little valley."

Big Ear grinned. Colt had a deal. They arranged to meet outside the fort a mile upstream the following morning. Big Ear would bring an extra Indian pony for Colt. He would ride out on an army mount, leave it in the brush and Corporal Swenson would bring it back the next day and slip it back in the corral.

"Tell no one anything about this," Colt cautioned the Tonkawa, but he was certain half the fort would know his arrangements before noon the next day.

Just so it didn't get back to the Division of Texas Headquarters in San Antonio.

Across the compound, Garland Oliver sat on his bed cleaning his army issue .44 Remington pistol. He had his sergeant giving the first platoon riding instruction and drill. The rest of the afternoon was free. He heard a knock on the door, then the partition opened a crack.

"Cleaning lady," a woman's voice said.

Oliver, surprised at first, relaxed. He'd been jumpy lately, worried about the gold.

"Yes, Mrs. Unru, come in. I'll stay out of your way."

"I could come back later, Lieutenant Oliver."

"No, now is fine."

She smiled, came in and closed the door. Ellie Unru was not a raving beauty, but out here in the wilds she was a woman and that was enough. She was maybe five feet and three inches, slightly plump and with good breasts. He watched her move around sweeping the plank floor, then dusting and cleaning up some of his equipment that had scattered.

She came toward him and bent to pick up something from the floor. He watched her. As she bent her blouse sagged open and showed both her big breasts hanging free, not encumbered by a wrapper or even a chemise.

She looked up and smiled, but didn't cover herself.

"Well now, I've shown you my . . . my things. Sorry."

"No . . . no, don't move, they are lovely, just beautiful."

She blushed prettily. "Thank you, sir." She hesitated. "Sir, they wouldn't mind getting petted a mite, if you was in the mood and all."

He shot a quick look at her. She was serious. In the six months she'd been cleaning his room, he'd never touched her, even though he'd heard most of the cleaning and laundry women were available with a little persuasion and three dollars.

His hand reached out and pushed inside her blouse, catching one swinging prize.

"I'm in the mood," he said, his voice husky as he hurried to the door and locked it from the inside securely.

A half hour later he lay naked beside Ellie on his bed. She had pulled a blanket up to cover her hips, but her breasts swung free as she sat up.

As he made love to her twice, he had wished he could tell her about the gold. He had made the perfect theft, and now there was no one he could brag about it to! He felt alone and frustrated. He wanted to give Ellie one of the new twenty dollar gold pieces, but knew that would cause him trouble.

Instead he gave her three dollars and she smiled and rubbed her breasts over his face until he chewed on them.

"You're a gentleman, you are," she said. "You make love soft and gentle like the way a woman wants. 'Course I never done nobody on post before, 'cepting my husband. You're a wonder, Lieutenant Oliver, you are.''

He kissed her pink nipples again, figured she was about twenty-two or three and helped her dress.

"Ellie, you come again tomorrow to clean, in the afternoon. I want to show you a new game, and I'll have something special to tell you.''

She rubbed his crotch through his blue pants.

"You best have something loaded and ready to fire as well,'' she said, then picked up her cleaning gear, winked at him and went out to the covered porch area and down to the next room she was supposed to clean.

Oliver sat on the bed for a minute, remembering how good it had been with her. Hell, it was *always good* with a woman, better even than in his hand. Sometimes he wondered why he didn't get married so he could have sex every night until he was too weak to get it up.

He laughed and went over and locked his door. He made sure the curtain was covering the narrow window to the courtyard, then he pushed the washstand aside, and using his knife, pried up the loose floor board next to the wall and looked down at the gold.

By now everyone in the fort knew there was eight thousand dollars in gold missing. *Eight thousand in gold!* He picked up a handful of the coins. They had the new date on them, 1869. He had no idea when new gold coins went into circulation. But it certainly would be easy to identify these before others of the same minting came out.

He stacked them up, counting out a hundred coins. That was two thousand dollars! He'd never thought he'd have that much cash of his very own.

And now he had eight thousand dollars! He must have four hundred of the coins!

Slowly he put the gold back between the two by six joyce below the floor boards. He swung the board back in place and pushed the wash stand so it covered half the four inch wide plank.

He was a rich man!

But he couldn't tell anyone. Perhaps by this time tomorrow he would have a confidant, a woman he could show the gold to, or at least tell her about it, and brag about how he accomplished the feat that had the army brass in convulsions. Yes, tomorrow he would tell Ellie. She would keep his secret. He might even run off with her and the eight thousand dollars.

Oliver stretched out on the bed, daydreaming how pleasant it would be to have Ellie's lush, willing body whenever he wanted to!

9

Captain Colt Harding rode out of the fort's unfinished front gate on an army black, not his usual mount since he was going on furlough. His saddlebags were filled with raisins, nuts and all the dried fruit he could find in the storeroom.

In his blanket roll was enough hardtack to keep him and half the Indians coming with him alive for a week. Big Ear had guaranteed his captain that there would be no problem with food. They would hunt as they needed to, they would live off the land.

Colt Harding had left his uniform in his closet. He was not on official business, so he wore a set of well used buckskins he had picked up two years ago in Wyoming.

He was shedding his army image, his army clothes, and soon his army mount. He rode west along the trail to Austin, then when he was out of sight of the fort, cut sharply north to the small stream and found where Big Ear and his men waited.

He had agreed to ride an Indian pony, but held out for a small, light weight saddle. Three of the Tonkawas had saddles. He held up his hand in greeting, then dismounted and moved the saddle off the army black to the smaller, grass fed Indian pony.

Out here the ponies would expect only dry grass and some greenery to eat. There would be no problem finding oats for them.

Big Ear came up and fingered Colt's buckskins. "From mountains," he said. "You buy far away?"

"Wyoming," Colt said. "Thirty day's long ride west."

That satisfied the leader of the Indian scouts.

Colt had decided to "go Indian." He would take off his buckskin shirt a half hour the first day and let the sun melt into his pale white skin. The second day he would increase the time by fifteen minutes and then fifteen minutes more each day until at the end of the week, he would be able to go all day without the shirt, and he should be a toasted brown. It would let him blend in better with his new detail of fighting men.

His size was a drawback. He knew few Indians who were six feet tall. He would compensate. His only concession to comfort were his army boots, which he hid under the tight legs of his fringed buckskins.

Colt was surprised how fast the Indian ponies moved across the prairie. They had covered more than fifteen miles when they stopped at a small creek. Two of the Indians vanished into a light sprinkling of woods, and returned in ten minutes with two rabbits and a pair of grouse.

They dressed them out at once, started small fires and soon had them roasted. They pulled the cooked meat spart with their fingers and ate.

Colt did the same thing and while he didn't think he was hungry, the roasted rabbit tasted better than anything he had eaten in a long time.

When the meat was gone, they filled up on water, topped off their army issue canvas water bags, and rode again.

There was no stopping two hours before sun set as Colt was used to with an army unit. Big Ear led the riders, and kept pushing ahead along a trail that would take them well north of the hidden valley and toward the Staked Plains.

They stopped an hour after sunset, and ground tied their horses, then hobbled them and rolled out blankets and slept. Before now, Colt had not been able to understand how the Indians could travel so far across the plains so quickly. He was beginning to get the idea.

They simply punished themselves, riding longer and harder than a Cavalry unit could manage with their heavy stock, heavy equipment, and any wheeled rigs they might have. If he wanted to fight the Indians on an even footing, he would have to make some drastic changes in the way he went about it.

It only took them three days to reach the lofty cap rocks that barricaded their way. They stopped half a mile from the small stream where the band of Comanches had disappeared before.

Big Ear led his men on a series of half circles around the area. Each time they moved closer to the mouth of the small stream and made the circle again. The fourth time, they found hoof prints.

"More than two handsful," Big Ear said. "Indian ponies. None with shoes." He sent one man to scout out the trail the horses had taken once they left the concealment of the small stream. Big Ear went part way down the trail that led generally due east. He pointed to lines in the dust.

"Travois track," he said.

"Which means the women, kids and household gear are all on the move. The band has left the Staked Plains, but in small groups and moving to the east so they can join up at a new location," Colt said, reasoning it out as he went.

Big Ear nodded. He grinned and his eyes almost closed.

"Soup, all right?" he asked.

Colt scowled. What the hell, he was buying friendship and loyalty. Slowly Colt bobbed his head. "Okay for you, not for me. First we have to find the bastards."

"Find bastards, two, three days," Big Ear said.

The following day Big Ear and his remaining men scoured the trails, washes and streams that came down from the high plateau eight hundred feet above. Six places they found where more riders had come away from the Staked Plains. All showed signs of Indian ponies as well as shod stock, and the remains of travois track even after the ponies had been driven over the trail behind the litters.

The Comanches were moving back toward the Brazos.

That night two Tonkawa hunters brought in a small buck deer. It would dress out less than a hundred pounds, but that was still about fifty pounds more meat than they could eat.

To Colt's amazement, the seven Tonks ate an average of six pounds each of the venison the first night. The feast went on for more than six hours, and they rolled away from the fire only when they could stuff no more down their throats.

Colt had not tried to keep up with them, but every hour he had eaten more, and by the end of the evening he felt bloated and groggy. He had been introduced to the Indian law of the plains. Eat when there is food to eat—it may be days before there is anything else.

The following morning the braves rose and staggered away to relieve themselves. When they came back, they uncovered the banked coals of the pit fire, and cooked more venison. It would be rancid by noon. They didn't have time to dry it, so they ate the best portions.

Two hours of feasting and almost all of the venison was gone except the larger bones and some of the tougher meat around the lower legs.

"Now we ride," Big Ear said.

Only then did he tell Colt that one of his men had trailed the Comanche and found where the trails had merged. The main body was more than fifty families, with maybe six hundred head of ponies and horses.

"Should be more horses," Big Ear said. "Maybe come later."

Colt and his Indians reached the juncture trail before six that evening. They followed it until dark, then camped.

Big Ear sent a man on ahead to track the hated Comanche in the moonlight.

Colt had no trouble sleeping. He had total trust in Big Ear. The braves knew that their families back near the fort would suffer if anything happened to the white-eye chief.

With morning, Colt talked to Big Ear.

"Scout come back last night. Comanche camped ten miles ahead, two days ago, then move on. Should catch them in two hard days ride."

"Chief, we're not a war party. We want to track them, find out where they are and where they might be in two weeks. Then we go back for our forces. Do you understand?"

"You promise soup," Big Ear snapped.

"Would you rather eat soup or live to be an old man with many grandchildren? We are seven against sixty warriors."

Big Ear looked at Colt with anger for a moment, then he smiled and laughed. "Yes, we find now, then later we eat soup. It is good."

The next two days they put fifteen hours in the saddle. Just before dark on the end of the second day, they saw the smokes of the Comanche.

Big Ear and Colt worked up silently to within two hundred yards of the camp. The tipis of the Comanche spread out along the South Fork of the Wichita River. There were more than sixty lodges showing in the bright moonlight. There were no sentries out, no scouts.

The lodges swung around a gentle curve in the Wichita that ran no more than three feet deep now in summer and less than fifty feet wide. The valley had gentle slopes and was a quarter of a mile wide. At once Captain Harding worked out how he would attack the settlement.

Big Ear wanted to go closer, but Colt ordered him back. They moved to their horses and quietly rode away, south and east toward the Fort Comfort.

When they were in the open, Colt took command of the detail. He said they would ride until midnight, sleep until six and ride until they came to the fort.

He relented the next day when it grew dark. But they were halfway. The second day after that they rode into the fort and Harding began immediate preparations for a company sized patrol to go to the field against the Comanche.

Big Ear had seen enough signs and recognized the large tipi that stood at the center of the Indian camp. There was the head of an eagle painted on the tipi cover. It was the Eagle band, the one led by Walking White Eagle, a brilliant, and much loved leader of the Comanche nation.

10

The sun rose slowly, as if reluctant to start the new day as it warmed the tipis on the South Fork of the Wichita River in Western Texas. The camp came alive slowly. Smoke lifted here and there from the holes in the tops of tipis. Men shuffled into the woods to relieve themselves.

A young boy scampered out of a tipi in his breech-clout, threw a rock at a lodge a few yards away and ran quickly to hide behind a tree.

In front of the large tipi with the eagle head on it, White Eagle sat talking with a young brave. He was fifteen, a man-child who was receiving his last instructions before he went on his vision quest.

Every warrior was obliged go on a vision quest to become a man. He had to talk with Mother Earth alone, live off the bounty of Mother Earth and determine his path in life. It was a pivotal day for Horse Walker, because this was the time he would discover his true medicine and find his warrior name.

It all depended on his vision.

"Horse Walker, you will open your soul to Mother Earth and to all the spirits, you will watch and wait and find your vision before you return. It may only take you a few days, you may be gone for three or four weeks. When you have seen your vision you will know it and you will act as a warrior and say it is time for you to return to your own tipi."

Horse Walker stood, lowered his head in respect, then ran eagerly and vaulted on the back of his war pony still in training. He carried only his personal medicine bag tied between his legs, his breechclout, and his best bow and six arrows. The six arrows indicated he would return before six weeks had passed.

Without looking or speaking to another mortal, Horse Walker rode regally out of camp and into the low hills of the Wichita.

White Eagle smelled the coffee. Of all the gifts of the white-eyes, the coffee bean had been the best, even better than the fire-stick-that-shot-many-times. Always Smiling had roasted the new coffee beans in an iron skillet over a low fire, then mashed them and ground them fine before she scooped them into the copper pot and boiled the coffee.

As he drank the steaming brew, White Eagle toyed with one of the new pistols. He had learned how to take the metal cartridges in and out of the chamber. How to work the hammer. Twice he had fired all six rounds from the weapon.

It had been a thing alive in his hand, and he had to use all of his strength to control it. Not at all like the silent, sturdy feel of a bowstring as it released.

He had taught four of his best warriors how to use the pistol. Had trained them how to shoot it, and how powerful it was. The pistols were to be used only to fight against the Pony Soldiers. It was a condition of his gift and would be absolutely obeyed.

This morning he would train eight more warriors in how to use the pistol. Some of them already had rifles, so it would be easier. The pistols would be the only chance his warriors would have if they were overrun by the blue coats.

The soldiers had fires-many-times pistols, so the Comance must have them too, so they could defend themselves.

It took all morning to teach the warriors how to load the rounds into the chambers and ready the weapon to fire. They fired until each man had shot his weapon twelve times. Then they loaded them again.

"Keep the fires-many-times pistol with your shield and lance. Keep it loaded always. Be sure no one else touches it, and allow no young boys to be near it. The pistol will be our final defense when fighting with the blue shirted Pony Soldiers."

"It would be good to hunt rabbits with," Running Wolf said.

The men laughed. Running Wolf was not the best marksman with his bow.

"Not hunting. With the pistol we hunt the blue shirts only."

When the session ended, White Eagle walked with Running Wolf back to his tipi and watched Laughing Golden Hair.

She looked more Comanche already. Cries In The Morning had made a proper suede dress for her with fringes of trade beads and some elk's teeth. She had on new, tiny moccasins and her long blonde hair was braided, greased and tied to each side to keep it out of her way.

Sadie sat in the dust in front of the tipi trying to scrape a buffalo hide. She watched Cries In The Morning, and tried to do the same thing with a scraper as big as both her hands. She didn't have the strength yet to do the job.

"*Hi, tai,* little friend," Cries In The Morning said gently. "You will learn. You are trying."

"*Toquet?*" Sadie said looking up. She had learned that word well.

"Yes, are you trying, *toquet,*" her Indian mother said.

Sadie turned and stared hard at the tall man. He was the one who hurt Yale and who carried her over his shoulders on the pony. He had hurt her, too. There were still scabs on her wrists where the rawhide had cut into her flesh.

Sadie did not like the tall man. She would never be his friend. She looked back at the hide. The lady beside her with the happy smile, scraped the hide so well. Sadie wanted to do it that good too! She tried again, and again.

White Eagle nodded at the small blonde haired girl and walked back to his tipi. He sat down in front of the big tent, crossed his legs and watched the flow of the life around him.

He had brought the tribal life back into balance. There was a fine edge between two much war and too little, between a band that was falling apart, and one that was growing. The leader had to keep everything in balance, maintain some control, but make the men feel that as a Comanche warrior he was free to join any band he chose.

It had been a mistake to run all the way to the Staked Plains. The presence of the blue shirts so deep into Comanche lands had sent near panic through the whole band. Never before had the Pony Soldiers penetrated so far into the western lands of his ancestors. Times were changing. The white-eyes kept moving westward. There seemed to be nothing to stop them. They bred like rabbits with a dozen children in each lodge.

White Eagle sighed as he watched the flow of the camp around him. They were back in the plains where the willow grew, where the buffalo were plentiful, where they could find nuts and berries to help make their pemmican more tasty. The first hunt was a good one, the rawhide boxes were heavy with jerky which would be pounded into pemmican for their winter food.

They were on the South Fork of the Wichita, well north of where the Pony Soldiers had found them. Now they were free of the probing eyes and the long rifles of the blue shirts. Now they could get back to the Comanche way of life.

He looked up as Laughing Golden Hair skipped by with a new found friend, a girl a year older. They were chattering and giggling as Laughing Golden Hair tried to learn more Indian words. They hurried past the tipi to the edge of the stream.

The Indian girl pulled off her dress and waded into the stream. Laughing Golden Hair hesitated. The older girl called to her and then the small white girl took off her dress and kicked out of her moccasins and stepped into the cool water. Her skin was tanning slowly. She still was white in contrast to the other children, but soon there were a dozen small girls splashing and laughing and playing water games in the shallow, cool mountain stream.

Talks A Lot came from the tipi with a bowl of nuts

and berries for White Eagle. He thanked her and then felt of her swollen belly. She smiled.

"Your son is busy this morning moving to a new camp site I think. He will be a strong son, and will be the new chief when you are eighty winters old!"

White Eagle patted his son again within the womb and sent her on her way. Talks A Lot had been a deliberate effort to sire a son. He must have a son. Talks A Lot had four brothers, and he hoped the idea of males had been strongly rooted in her mind so when her body chose the sex of her child it would be male. He did not understand such things.

The wind and the clouds, the sway of the prairie grass, the way an owl hoots or a crow calls or an eagle screamed all had meaning to White Eagle. He was a man of the land, a fellow user of the bounty that Mother Earth brought forth.

But when it came to understanding women, he was like a babe trying to fight the People Eaters, the hated Tonkawa. He snorted. Perhaps this time he would have a son. If not he would take a fourth wife. He was a chief, it was not only alllowed, but often expected. A son was a necessity for a great chief.

For just a moment he worried about the Pony Soldiers. Who was this blue shirt who worried him? Was he one who had been raided? No, the Comanche never raided a fort or the lodge of a Pony Soldier. They were too strong. An outpost, a small band of the men with yellow stripes up their pants?

Perhaps. Then he remembered the supply train. There had been fifteen blue shirts there. That was where he got the pistols and rifles. The woman and child on the train? Yes, it was possible they had been going to the fort, the family one of the chiefs? It was a chance.

Perhaps he should put out sentries? Warriors disliked sitting on high points watching a back trail. It was not rightful duty for a real warrior. Tomorrow he would find two or three of the older boys not yet warriors and give them the job of being scouts watching to the south and east. That was where the Pony Soldier wagons had been. That was where the army would come from if they still searched.

He watched four young boys charge through the camp on their ponies. They pretended they were attacking an enemy camp, wielding their short lances, pretending to shoot with their bows as they maneuvered their ponies through the crowded camp using only their knees and feet. They were developing the skills they would need as warriors.

For a moment he was at peace, pleased with his band, happy that his son was growing and would be born in a month. Satisfied with the first hunt for their winter's food.

In a month it would be time to go meet the Mexican traders, who had beads and mirrors and all sorts of steel and metal they could fashion into arrow and lance points. They traded for horses and mules. On the next raid he would keep his stolen horses for trading.

White Eagle stood up and went inside his big tipi. He found his second wife Prairie Flower who sat on her raised bed sewing on a pair of heavy winter leggings for him.

Gently he curved his hand around her breast. She glanced up eagerly, dropped her sewing and held his hand to her breast. He sat beside her. Quickly she lay down lifting the soft suede dress she wore.

"Today I think it is right so I can make a fine son for you, White Eagle. I so much want to bear you a son!"

White Eagle rolled on top of her and nibbled at her ear lobe.

A few minutes later, he did the best he could, planting his seed deeply into her. The rest was up to Prairie Flower.

Outside again, he called to the three young boys and gave them their lookout assignments. They accepted them with anticipation. It was a first step to becoming a warrior, and it meant there might be trouble and a chance to prove their valor in battle! They took a few provisions with them, got their bows and arrows, and raced for their ponies. They would not be back for five days, the usual time for a lookout.

They were almost warriors, defending their families, and the whole camp. It would be a wonderful adventure!

White Eagle watched them go, remembering his first call to be a lookout when he was twelve. He had watched for raids by the People Eaters. One had come and he had hurried to warn the camp, then been in the heat of the battle.

That day he had taken his first scalp. He had become a full fledged warrior when he was thirteen.

White Eagle sat near his shield and lance in front

of his tipi and thought about earlier days. Why did
things have to change? Why were the Pony Soldiers
chasing them?

11

Major Zachery was the second man to see Captain Harding after he returned from his long range scouting trip. He scowled with disapproval as Colt signed some forms on his desk and cleaned up the paper work he had missed while he was gone.

"Captain, that was a foolhardy thing you did, chasing off after those savages."

"I found them, Major, that's the important factor."

"No, Harding, the important fact is that we still haven't recovered the eight thousand in gold that belongs to the United States Army. I want the matter settled before you go on this patrol."

"Do you have all of your interviews conducted yet?"

Major Zachery turned away. "No, not all of them."

"Then I'd suggest that would be the most crucial part of the investigation. I'll be glad to leave any men here you need to talk to."

"When are you leaving?"

"In two days at the most. I don't want White Eagle to move his band again."

"I'll give you a list of men I need to talk to."

'Good. Now if you'll excuse me, Major, I have a fight to get ready for. No longer am I chasing Indians. I'm finding them, waiting for them, then attacking them for a goddamn change!"

Ten minutes later Lieutenant Riddle scratched his balding head and looked in wonder at the orders.

"I don't understand. No sabers, no bugle, no wagons, no pocket change, and each man to carry his own rations for fourteen days?"

"You read well, John. Damn well."

"Living off the land?"

"Half the time, until we get beyond a certain point. The Indians will be given the same rations, but will act as hunting providers. We'll make out fine."

John Riddle tossed down his pencil and snorted. "I could fix you up with Indian ponies too, if you want. Then you wouldn't have to carry any oats."

"I'd love that, but we don't have time to train the troops. I'm the only one besides the Tonkawas who'll be on an Indian pony. Those little nags are used to grass feed. They can move sixty miles a day without even breathing hard."

"You're serious?"

"Damn right. Remember I just came back from a long ride on one of those little grass eating wonders." He took a list from his pocket. "We'll take B company this time. Make sure none of the men on that list are used as fillers. Major Zachery still needs to talk to them."

"Easy, compared to what you're going to do. Two weeks with no wagon support?"

144

"We'll turn the Indian tactic against him. We move fast, and as quietly as possible. No gunfire of any kind allowed before contact with the hostiles. All hunting will be by bow and arrow. We'll travel light, push our mounts to their limit, sleep in the open without tents, cut down every pound of weight we can. The less the horses have to carry, the faster and farther we can move every day.

"If the damn Comanches can make sixty miles a day, then Company B and I damn well can too!"

The following day, Company B with six fillers from Company A, mounted up for inspection. They were lean and trim. They carried one blanket per man, ten pounds of oats, no shelter half or ground cloth, no change of boots or uniform, no sabers, and no extra food, just the fourteen days ration.

"Feels like we're going on a damn picnic!" one of the troopers yelped.

Captain Harding himself made the inspection. The troops had been ordered to tie their blanket roll in front of the saddle as usual, and to tie the bag of grain immediately behind their saddle where the tent half usually rested. Their food supply would be in their saddlebags, or tied in back with the grain.

Half way through the inspection, the captain turned it over to Lieutenant Edwards, the B Company Commander.

"You know what I want, Edwards. Any weight we can save will give us that much more advantage.

In his quarters, Garland Oliver relaxed after a day of drilling his company. When their chance came, he wanted them to be experts on horseback and with their weapons.

Now he looked over his "rich" list. He still hadn't decided what he would do, or when with his brand new eight thousand in gold. He had an idea it would be a good practice simply to take the gold and two good horses from the stables, and vanish some night just after taps. In short, to desert. He'd have a good twelve hour head start and with two horses to trade off, he could be well toward Austin before they could send anyone after him.

His plans for escape were interrupted by a knock on the door. Ellie Unru came in with fresh towels and a bucket filled with all sorts of cleaning materials. Once inside she set down the items and flew into Oliver's arms. They fell on the bed and tickled each other and then quickly undressed and began to pet and stroke each other.

Before she let him enter her she smiled sweetly.

"First, promise that you'll show me the gold. You said you would, now I want your promise as an officer and a gentleman." He lunged at her but she moved her hips and they both laughed.

"I promise, I promise, before you go today, I'll show you the gold."

She smiled and opened her knees, accepting him.

They made love furiously, twice, and then she dressed quickly and looked at him. She stood aside while he moved the washstand and lifted the floor board. He gave her two of the gold pieces and watched her expression. As she fondled them he fondled her breasts and she smiled and kissed him.

"We're going to have a wonderful life together, Garland. There's my husband of course, but he won't mind. He's all army anyway. We'll just leave him here when we run away together."

She kissed him again, rubbed his crotch and then slipped out the door with her cleaning gear heading for the next quarters to work on.

The next morning at six A.M., B Company rode

out from Fort Comfort, Texas under the command of Captain Harding, with Lieutenant Edwards and Lieutenant Ned Young and ninety-five enlisted men.

The first day they made a little over fifty miles. The men grumbled as they kept riding into twilight, and didn't stop an hour after dark. Usually a cavalry unit stopped two hours before sunset. They cooked their salt pork, ate it with hardtack and swilled it down with coffee before they fell into their blankets.

It was the usual 4:45 A.M. rising, but there was no bugle. The captain's orderly roused each sergeant who kicked his men out of blankets. They were in the saddle by 5:30, a half hour early, and again the men voiced their displeasure.

The Tonkawas were along in force, twenty-three of them, and all eager to draw some Comanche blood, and if possible eat some Comanche soup. They all knew what they had been promised by the white-eyes captain. For most of the Tonkawas any excuse to kill a Comanche was valid.

The second day the Indians brought in a dozen rabbits and ten grouse. While not enough meat for all the troops, half of them had meat that night, with the other half in line for meat the next day.

The second day Harding and his tough little Indian Pony, with Big Ear at his side, churned up a little more than sixty miles by the captain's calculations. It was an hour and a half after sunset when the first cooking fires blossomed in a stretch of brush along one of the many rivers that run east and west through northwestern Texas.

Neither Harding nor Big Ear knew which one it was. They did know they were half way to the Comanche camp on the South Fork of the Wichita.

That night, Harding and Edwards went over the

layout of the bend in the Wichita where White Eagle had camped.

"We'll put half our troops at each end of the camp, if we can take them by surprise," Harding said. "Then on a gunshot signal, we drive toward the center, and force anyone who runs to go across the water to the other side. The stream will slow them down."

"We shoot just the braves, Captain?"

Harding set his jaw. "Lieutenant, have you ever seen a cabin or a ranch or a wagon train when the Comanche get through with it?"

"No sir."

"They kill everything that breaths, everything! We'll repay them in kind. But—no children. Make it clear to your men that the braves and squaws are targets, but no children. My baby girl is in that camp somewhere, and I'm going to tear every lodge apart until I find her!"

"Yes sir. Understood. Not a single child will be hurt, no exceptions."

Captain Harding walked around the small campfire they had, then stared off into the distance, north and a little west. His Sadie was up there somewhere, and he was coming to take her home!

The third day of the march the men were tired and sore. None of them had ever traveled a hundred and ten miles in two days before. The fact that they were only half way to the battle cut at them as they rode.

But they kept moving. They were heading into a battle! Most of them had never faced an Indian. Some of the men had been on the frontier for three years and chased dozens of Indian Bands but never caught one. Now they would see the sight of blood.

They stopped for a scheduled cold noon break. They rubbed down their horses, watered them and were about to start again when four Tonkawa scouts came into the group with two freshly killed deer.

Captain Harding gave the word and the troops fell to butchering the deer and cooking it. Most of the meat wound up fried in skillets over quickly made fires. Within an hour the two deer had been reduced to a pile of bones as the troopers each had a slap of venison.

Morale was much better the rest of the afternoon and two hours of riding into the night before they made camp. Most of the men still bloated with venison, ignored supper, rolled up in their blankets and slept.

The next day at noon, Big Ear welcomed back two advance Tonk scouts who reported that there were lookouts on the trail ahead. The scouts had caught sight of the lookouts when they flashed mirrors at each other in the bright sunlight.

"Locate them all, then eliminate them quietly," Captain Harding said. "We want to be a total surprise to the main camp."

The main party rested at four that afternoon in a heavy stand of timber at what Big Ear said was three miles from the Comanche lodges.

Big Ear and Captain Harding moved up through the small hills and underbrush until they could look down on the tipis spread along the small river.

"Somewhere down there is my baby girl," Harding whispered half to himself. He would find her. Damned if he wouldn't!

Back at the main party, Harding ordered that there would be no talking above a whisper. The men were to cook their supper and turn in. They would be up at three A.M. to move into attack position.

The grumbling ceased, as men began to sweat. Most faced a battle for the first time in their lives.

The blooded veterans knew the risks, and fell into the habit that they had built up before any battle. Some wrote letters. Some read letters. A few prayed. All of them turned and twisted trying to go to sleep.

At 3:30 A.M., Company B moved silently through the light brush. Half the troop under Lieutenant Edwards, two platoons, swung to the north. Captain Harding and forty-five men of Platoons Three and Four were at the southern end of the half mile long Indian campsite.

Captain Harding kept his troops mounted and a hundred yards behind a low crest. Just over the ridgeline, a gentle slope ran another hundred yards to the first sprinkling of Comanche tents.

The day before the sun had risen at 5:30. Today should be about the same Colt figured. They would attack as soon as it was light enough to see, a few minutes after dawn, maybe 5:10. He checked his six-guns, both were firmly in place.

His signal shot, when it came, would be from his Spencer repeating rifle, and the round would tear into the big tipi with the eagle on it. Big Ear had told the captain that most likely the chief, White Eagle, had brought back the girl child to be adopted by a woman with no child. So Sadie would not be in the chief's tent.

The morning began to lighten.

A bird called its morning song.

Somewhere a coyote wailed its last lonesome plea for a mate.

Captain Harding looked at the tipis below. It was time!

He lifted his rifle over his head and brought it down to the front. The troopers behind him walked their mounts forward, in a platoon front, stretched out in a line forty-five men wide. When they were in position, he raised the Spencer again, and this time sent two rounds into the largest Tipi.

His men surged forward, silently. The hooves made almost no noise on the soft floor of the woodsy slope.

There had been no answering shot from the northern point, there was not supposed to be.

Captain Harding rode silently ahead of the others, then fell back in line, so some eager marksman didn't shoot him instead of a Comanche.

A tent flap flew upward and a surprised Comanche warrior stepped outside his lodge. Two rounds from carbines slammed into his chest, driving him into his own happy hunting ground inside his tent.

A woman screamed.

From the northern part of the camp came more rifle fire.

Here a dozen flaps came up, braves slipped out, doubled over, running toward the horses. Some brought up rifles and returned fire.

The charging troopers fired at anyone who moved, smashed into the tipi area before many of the Indians managed to get outside.

Captain Harding dropped the reins of his Indian pony, brought up both pistols and fired at a brave just leaving a lodge. The round caught him in the throat killing him instantly. The captain flashed past the lodge, came to a second one where most of the Indians were out, the men, women and children running toward the river.

Harding charged foward, knocked down the squaw and shot the brave through the back. He looked anxiously at the three children racing for the stream. None of them was Sadie, too large and too dark haired.

He whirled the Indian pony, saw his men methodically firing into the lodges, chasing anyone who left them.

Directly ahead of Captain Harding a brave ran from a tipi, in his hand an army revolver. Harding bellowed in rage and shot the Indian twice in the chest, then charged over him with the Indian pony and stormed toward the next knot of frightened Indians.

To the north, Edwards' men swept everything in front of them as they worked forward. Half a dozen women and children shied into the river, rushed across and vanished in the brush on the far side.

Two braves darted and stumbled and scurried through the horses and tipis to the fringe of woods and slid in out of sight.

Edwards slashed a warrior with his saber, lopping off his ear and severing the left carotid artery. The brave died before he slid to the ground.

The men of Company B concentrated on the braves, but now and then a squaw would come in their sights and they fired. Nobody tried to kill any children but some fell under the hooves of the prancing, charging mounts.

Two minutes after the first shots were fired the confused mass of men, horses, women and children was unbelievable. The troopers hardly knew who to fire at. Blue shirts were on every side and they reverted to their pistols for quick, sure shots.

Woman and children splashed through the stream and into the safety of the woods on the far side. It quickly became obvious to the Indians that the Pony Soldiers were not following them there. They located children and relatives and hurried farther away to safe hiding places in thick brush.

Only two braves made it to their horses, and both

were dispatched by rifle fire before they could get within fighting range with their lances, the only weapon they had time to snatch up as they ran through the melee.

Warriors concentrated on saving their lives. They had no weapons with which to fight, they were totally surprised, many running around naked from their beds.

Half the warriors who were given pistols caught them up and used them. Running Wolf killed one Pony Soldier and seriously wounded a second before three of the Cavalrymen saw him with the weapon and cut him down with a dozen shots. He fell between tipis and was trampled a dozen times by charging army mounts.

Captain Harding suffered a bullet wound to the left shoulder. He kept riding and firing, reloading his right handed weapon twice before he looked around and saw that the braves who could still fight had been driven away. Those left were so wounded they couldn't move.

For a terrible few moments there were a dozen pistol shots as badly wounded Indians and horses were put out of their misery.

Captain Harding took casualty reports from his officers. They had suffered four dead, twelve wounded. Two of the Tonkawas had been killed, but Edwards was not sure if they were shot by the Comanche or his own men.

As he watched, Harding saw two Tonks slipping off into the brush. Each carried something. The captain was not sure he wanted to know what it was.

He had his men form up and they went through the village tipi by tipi, looking for one small blonde girl. They did not find her. Over the half mile stretch there were more than twenty bodies. When the final count was made of the enemy losses, Captain Harding nodded grimly.

They had found twelve dead braves, six women and two young boys. The Tonkawa scouts had killed three youths on the lookout posts. Twenty-three dead. It was a good start.

Now they would burn everything in the village.

Even as he thought of it, a cold wind sprang up and ten minutes later, a crashing thunderstorm struck, sending lightning flashes by the dozen, thunder rolling almost continually, and a slashing wind driven rain that pushed the Pony Soldiers inside the lodges for shelter.

Most were amazed how well made the tipis were, and how well they turned aside the rain.

"Looks damn like the cabin where I grew up, 'cepting it's round," one rawboned recruit drawled.

When the storm had passed a half hour later, Captain Harding decided everything was too wet to burn. Instead he sent his men in two waves into the brush across the river looking for the Indian women and children, and his daughter.

He led the probes. They discovered two small groups of Indian women and kids, but there was no child there the right age, let alone with blonde hair and blue eyes.

Harding let them go and rode back to the village, where he tied his dead over their saddles, replaced two dead army mounts with Indian ponies and tied two of the dead men on board.

He had twelve men injured. Only one who shouldn't be riding, but there was no other way to get home. For a moment Harding considered using one of the Indian travois, but he quickly rejected the idea. No self respecting Cavalryman would lay on that contraption for two hundred miles. He'd rather be dead.

He put out security and let Corporal Marlin take care of the wounded. He poured some liquid on the captain's shoulder wound, then bound it tightly.

"The slug went right on through, sir. We're lucky there. Got a few that didn't. If we can get home in five days, should be all right." It took two hours to get the wounded ready to travel.

Captain Harding was a mile away from the Eagle band camp when he realized that none of the Tonkawa braves were with him. He had promised them soup, so they were having it. There was no way he could stop them. He was sure by now their soup was boiling and it would be supplemented with fried steaks. The Tonkawa were indeed the People Eaters as the other Indians said. But they were also the best scouts that Captain Harding had.

He guessed that the Tonks would rejoin the line of march sometime the following day.

They did, arriving at noon, sliding into place as if they had never been away. The only difference Harding could notice was a sly smile that Big Ear now carried, and he moved quickly when Harding spoke.

It would be a long ride back to Fort Comfort. Harding knew he had failed. He had ridden the Comanche to ground, he had attacked him on his own territory, in his own village, but he had not found Sadie. The report to the Division of Texas would be one of victory, but in his heart he knew the one victory he wanted had not happened.

He would return. He would find the Eagle band again, and when he did, he would watch and wait. He would make sure where his daughter was being held prisoner, which woman had adopted her, and then he would strike in the night with a swift and sure scalpel, cutting out the one tipi, moving inside quietly and finding his daughter, killing everyone there and slipping away like an avenging angel in the night before anyone knew he had been there.

Yes! That was how he would find his daughter, how he would rescue her. He still owed the damned Comanche more than he could ever repay. Today's fight was simply an interest payment against the principal. He couldn't wait to go after the hostiles again, as soon as possible.

It had to be before winter. Until then he would have to play soldier at the fort. He had to make it all look like a regular Cavalry Post functioning the way it should.

He could play the game. He had to. At least until he found Sadie.

12

Cries In The Morning had been awake that fateful morning, watching her small golden haired daughter sleeping. It was a delight for her to look at the child any time of the day, no matter what she was doing. She got up and made sure the buffalo robe was around the small pale shoulders, then stood and looked at her husband.

At the same moment she heard the report of the rifle and the slugs hitting the big tipi nearby. She knew at once that it meant they were being attacked by the Pony Soldiers. She grabbed Laughing Golden Hair from the buffalo robes, held her tightly and ran to the flap of the tipi.

Cautiously she lifted it a crack and peered out. On the hill across the way she saw a line of blue coated Pony Soldiers riding forward and firing their long guns.

She screamed at her husband. He was on his feet already, searching for his pistol.

Cries In The Morning knew the white-eyes must

never see her golden child or they would take her back. She slipped out the flap, edged around her lodge and ran past two others toward the stream. It was the only way to go. She could hear firing from the other end of the camp. There were Pony Soldiers there was well.

Laughing Golden Girl did not make a sound. Her eyes were as big as the new moon. Her small arms clung to Cries In The Morning as she splashed into the stream, waded up to her waist across the deepest part and then rushed up the far bank and into the fringe of trees and brush.

Cries In The Morning hurried into the deeper woods and found a thorn thicket. She lay down and holding Laughing Golden Hair she slowly worked her way under the thorns a dozen feet into the center of the maze, where she found room enough to sit up.

Gingerly she broke off the dead stalks, and then remembered her knife strapped to her ankle. She used it to cut away more of the thorns until they had an easy place to sit.

Cries In The Morning could hear the screams, the rifle shots, the cries of a horse that was wounded. She told Laughing Golden Hair to stay where she was.

"I must go and help the others," she said, then held out both hands with palms flat and pushed them toward Sadie.

At last Sadie nodded, "*Toquet*," she said softly. Cries In The Morning nodded and wormed her way out the way she had come in. Now she didn't have to hold the child and it was much easier.

She peered from the thorn bush. She saw no one. Cries In The Morning lifted up and ran toward the river. At the edge of the brush she saw a dozen women she knew, some crying, some with children.

She saw one woman floating face down in the water, drifting slowly downstream.

The camp was a mass of terror, battle and confusion. Nowhere did she see the brave warriors putting up a fight. They had been totally surprised. Most had been still in bed. She could not see Running Wolf.

The Pony Soldiers were everywhere, trampling down tipis, riding through drying racks, shooting at both men and women. She saw one warrior leave the place they had the horses, but he was shot and dropped off his mount.

Tears streamed down her face. So many were dying! There must be something she could do! She saw Prairie Flower struggling through the water. There was blood on her chest!

Cries In The Morning leaped up and ran as fast as she could to the edge of the stream, splashed in and waded to Prairie Flower. She caught the young woman's shoulders and urged her through the water to the far bank.

Prairie Flower fell there, and Cries In The Morning talked to her softly, told her they had to move farther, to get out of sight.

"Just a few more steps, help me get you to safety!" Cries In The Morning said. The woman she tried to lift did not respond. She lay as if she were unconscious.

Cries In The Morning lifted her head and turned her over. The stain on her chest had stopped bleeding. The pump that pushed the blood through her veins had stilled. Her eyes stared at the sky without seeing how blue and beautiful it had been moments before.

Cries In The Morning lay Prairie Flower's head down gently, turned and looked for others she could help. She caught a baby from a woman who already had one to carry and they raced into the woods.

Cries In The Morning made a dozen trips into the water. She had seen quickly that the Blue Shirts were not firing at those in the stream. She helped them up the bank and into the woods, and urged them to run deeper into the woods and hide themselves so the Pony Soldiers would not be able to find them.

She lay at the fringe of the woods, her breath coming in ragged gasps. There were no more to come across. The rest were dead or captured. She had recognized the war cries of the Tonkawa. She had not seen any of the hated People Eaters, but she knew they must be in the fighting. The very thought made her shiver. Now, with nothing more to do, she hurried back to the briar growth, found the same spot and wormed her way inside where her Laughing Golden Hair reached for her, holding her tight.

"I didn't think you were ever going to come back!" Sadïe Harding yelped in sudden pain and spoke in English. She cried then, cried because this reminded her of when the guns had fired before and her brother was hurt and her mother was thrown out of the wagon. It all hurt so much. She never wanted to see anything like that again.

When the first bullets struck his lodge, Walking White Eagle came alert at once. The sound of the gun was enough to tell him they were under attack. He uttered a fierce war cry of the eagle, grabbed his bow and six arrows and his pistol and slid out the flap of his tent slowly. His tipi was near the center of the half mile string. He yelled at two or three other braves who joined him.

They could hear the firing now at both ends of the

camp. They all headed away from the river, toward the high ground immediately in front of the tipis, but not yet covered by the Pony Soldiers. Three more warriors joined them so they were seven. They ran like antelope, squirming past the first twenty yards of open ground before the Pony Soldiers worked down to them.

Once in the cover of the trees they moved to the north, in behind the Pony Soldiers and sent a dozen arrows at the attackers. One Pony Soldier went down, but they rapidly moved out of range.

Two of the warriors with White Eagle had pistols, but they were no good at this range. He waved the party of six warriors forward. They crawled on their bellies the last fifty yards, sprang up directly behind the Pony Soldiers and at twenty yards fired into a half dozen men who were racing around a tipi, terrorizing a woman and two children inside.

One of the Pony Soldiers fell dead, a second was wounded before the blue shirts turned their fire at the warriors. Each of the soldiers had a pistol and they all rode hard at the seven warriors, knocking down one and scattering the rest.

White Eagle was out of ammunition. He had shot his last arrow. His attack was over. He could do nothing now but watch his beloved band be ravaged by the Pony Soldiers. Tears crept down his cheeks as he watched. He should charge into the melee with his knife, but he knew he would die quickly. There must be a hundred of the mounted men. Only one or two of his band had made it to a war pony.

White Eagle hung his head in shame. What happened to the lookouts? Why hadn't they been warned the soldiers were coming?

Then he saw a flash of pony soldiers below and three Tonkawa braves rode by as the fighting quickly died to an occasional burst of pistol fire.

The battle was over, the Eagle band had lost. Now all he could hope for was that the officers would not order everything destroyed. He could not even get across the river now and help protect the women and children who were driven that way.

What did this white-eye chief want? Why had he used Comanche tactics against the Comanche? He had used surprise. He had hired Tonkawas to scout and kill the lookouts. He had raided the Comanche in his heartland, his summer camp, the very soul of the Comanche nation.

How was this white-eye chief so smart? He must be part Comanche to think like a Comanche.

White Eagle had to lie in his hiding place as the Pony Soldiers scoured the far bank and into the woods hunting for something. He never did figure out what. When they captured a group of women and children the soldiers simply looked at them, shook their heads and let the captives go free.

So the white-eye chief wasn't quite good enough to be a Comanche, or he would never have let the captives go.

Two hours later the wounded Pony Soldiers were mended, their dead loaded on horses and the troop moved out of the camp. The hard thunder shower may have convinced them that Mother Earth was not pleased with the Pony Soldiers. It also made everything so wet they failed to burn the first tipi they tried to light on fire.

Another half hour and the column moved out of camp, four wide, riding as though they were on a parade, moving away from the destruction, the death. Using rear guards and pickets along the sides.

White Eagle watched and learned. He also noticed

that the People Eaters were not with the Pony Soldiers. His eyes hardened as he realized where the Tonkawas were, and what they were doing.

As soon as it was safe, he sent the four warriors he had around him to round up the rest, to bring everyone still alive to the hill beyond the river, where they could assemble. He rushed to the place where the boys herded the horses.

The stock had not been bothered. He whistled for Flying Wind who came at once. He rode to a high point where he could see the way south. The column of blue shirts was now three miles away and proceeding. He would send out scouts to check their march.

Next he rode to the Street Of Tears, and checked each of the dead.

Already he could hear the keening and the wailing of the mourners. He found two young warriors, told them to go get their war ponies and follow the Pony Soldiers until they stopped for their night camp, then come tell how far away they were.

He assembled the rest of the band. Twenty lay dead in the camp. He feared the three lookouts would be found dead and mutilated. It was a severe blow.

Twelve warriors had been killed. He called the remains of the council around him on the hill and they decided what they must do. First the bodies would be prepared for the burial rites, then the camp would be struck and moved far from this river of death.

Suvate! This place was finished. Never again would a Comanche band camp here winter or summer.

Always Smiling sought out White Eagle and told him of Prairie Flower's death. He walked to where she lay and dropped to his knees and cried. There was nothing he could say. She had been a good wife, she had borne him a daughter. He would always remember her. He could stay near her only a short time. He had the whole camp's welfare to think about.

He carried her across the river and put her on her bed in the tipi. Then he counted the dead and wept.

By midday all of the People still alive had returned to the camp. Six of the tipis were ruined beyond repair. Only parts of the buffalo skins could be used in a new tipi cover. The lodges were taken down, everything that could be salvaged was saved and packed and an hour after high sun, they were on the march, northward. But there was no joy, no laughter, no rambunctious boys tearing around.

It was a journey of tears.

They wound as high into the hills as they could get. Then carried the bodies of their dead to the highest point and wedged them into crevices of rocks where their spirits could be free to float into the heavens.

There was only enough time for the briefest of burial ceremonies. The three lookouts had been found and brought back to the camp by warriors. They were buried in the same ceremony.

Then White Eagle pushed the People northward again. They were nearly out of their traditional territory. It couldn't be avoided. They would push into the fringes of the Kiowa territory and try to go around any Kiowa camps they saw. White Eagle hoped they could find a good camp on one of the forks of the Red River.

He worried about the twelve lodges without warriors. Cries In The Morning lost her husband. How would she live? White Eagle sought her out and soon the arrangement was made. Cries In The Morning and Laughing Golden Hair would come to his lodge. Her tipi would be given to one of the warriors who had lost his in the raid when horses drove their hooves through it in a dozen places and tore and ripped it into pieces.

Cries In The Morning would not be his wife, she would be an aunt, do her share of the work, and White Eagle would hunt for her and the child and support them. In turn she would care for the daughter of Prairie Flower.

All around the line of march, other arrangements were being made. Two of the widows went back to their parents' lodge to live. Two others found a brother who would take them in until they could marry again.

The ruined tipis would be replaced as soon as possible. At least the white-eyes had not burned their robes and lodges, or scattered and burned their jerky ready to be made into pemmican. The raid had been costly, but not shattering. Their lives would go on, but there were wounds that would never heal, dead who would never return, and dreams and plans forever lost.

White Eagle looked at the campsite Always Smiling had picked out for them. They had been on the move for five days. They had crossed one branch of the Red River and moved farther north and west to another one. Again they were in the northern fringes of the traditional lands of the Comanche.

This would be a good camp site. It had water, and graze for the herds. Plenty of firewood. At once he began to think how it could be defended. Where he would want his scouts and lookouts. Never again would he sit in his lodge fat and happy and not worry. He had twenty souls on his conscience.

From now, forever more, he would be at war with the white-eyes. They would not catch him sleeping again. The white-eye Pony Soldier chief who led the raid on his camp would know sorrow, he would know pain.

White Eagle would discover who the Pony Soldier was. He had yellow stripes down his legs as the chiefs did, and he carried two revolvers in holsters around his waist. Once he had seen the man plainly. The two revolvers had white handles. There should be someone among the tribes who had heard of this Pony Soldier chief. White Eagle would find his name and one day they would meet on the field of battle and one of them would die!

13

Captain Colt Harding rode with his men into Fort
Comfort the sixth day away from the hostiles. There
was no rush to get back. He had extracted a heavy
price from the Comanche, but he had paid with the
lives of four of his men.

He took a long hot bath. Had his orderly, Corporal
Swenson, order him a steak dinner with mashed
potatoes and all the trimmings from the cooks, then
he faced Major Zachery. The sour look on the officer
told the captain what he wanted to know.

"No luck yet in finding your gold, I see."

Major Zachery stared at Harding for a moment,
then sat down in the chair beside the desk.

"None. I've got a pair of suspects, but no
evidence." He frowned for a moment. "Captain, the
sooner we get this solved, the quicker you get me off
your post."

"Hell, Major, you're welcome to stay as long as
you want to. Looks like my promotion got hung up
again. Place this size should have a major or two
around."

"I may retire right here. Captain Harding, I've got two of your men who are smart enough, and who had certain opportunity to make the theft. They could have stolen the gold and are just sitting on it. Not a single one of those coins have showed up in the fort sutler's cash box. It takes a special kind of man to hold eight thousand dollars in his hands, and not spend even one of those double eagles."

"Like who?"

"Corporal Ingles, for one. He's an old hand, plenty smart enough, clever and he had more opportunity than anyone else."

"Not a chance on Ingles. He's been in my command for almost three years. Who else?"

"Lieutenant Oliver."

"Now there, you might have something. He's certainly capable, but you do need one little item like evidence. Have you searched his quarters?"

"He's smart enough not to keep the gold there, if he has it. I'm waiting, hoping he'll slip up."

"I wish you luck. He's smart, too smart sometimes. Maybe when I get my reports done on this patrol, I can give you some help?"

Major Zachery waved. "Not much use right now. I'm going to relax and try to beat Dr. Jenkins in our nightly chess game."

When he left Harding leaned back in his chair. His patrol strike at the Comanche had issued his challenge. He would ride the Comanche into the dust if he could. He wasn't sure how many bands there were roaming Western Texas, but it was not a large tribe, maybe seven or eight hundred.

He went to his map and put a spot of red ink on the south fork of the Wichita where he had hit the Eagle band. From now on he would question every scout, every trader, every traveler he could about the Comanche. Soon he hoped he would have another chance at the Eagle band.

In his quarters across the way, Lieutenant Oliver had come back from the officers' mess, feeling full of good food and satisfied with himself. Timing, that's all it was now. He could have taken off when Captain Harding was away on patrol, but it didn't feel right. It would have to be soon.

Ellie was getting to be a pest. Now that she knew about the gold she kept asking him when they were running away. He certainly wasn't going to take her, but that would have to be a surprise for her the day he left.

A knock sounded on the door and the knob turned. He had forgotten to lock it from the inside. Ellie stepped in quickly and closed the door. She had a pair of clean towels over her arm and she dropped them on his bed.

"You locked me out this afternoon. Why you lock me out? Ain't I good enough for you all of a sudden?"

"Ye gods, woman, I was tired. You've been servicing me every day for two weeks. A man gets enough for a time."

"Not you, you're always ready." She did a slow strip tease and soon was naked standing in front of him. She pushed one of her big breasts into his mouth and he groaned and pulled her over on his bed.

After they made love, she asked to see the gold again. He hadn't showed it to her since the first night.

"It's still there, don't worry. It's the best hiding spot I can think of."

"So show me again. I want to touch it, to feel it!"

He opened the floor board and she let the twenty

dollar gold pieces fall through her fingers.

"That feels so good!" She turned to him. Neither of them had dressed yet. "I've been making plans. I'm going to Austin to visit my great aunt next week. It's all planned. I'll ride in the empty wagons going back to Austin. I've got permission and all. That will be a fine time for you to meet me in Austin and we'll ride north as fast as we can heading for St. Louis!"

"I can't go. I have a three day patrol starting tomorrow. I'm taking fifteen men on a scouting patrol. We go out once a month."

"Oh, damn! I had counted on it. Maybe I should cancel my visit to my great aunt."

"I think you should."

He took the gold from her hands, dropped it back in the hole and closed the floor boards.

"I also don't think you should come here again for at least a week. Somebody is bound to notice when you come so often."

"I sell my cunt, everybody on post knows it."

"Still, I'm under suspicion by the major. Just don't come around for a week."

"You dumping me over?"

"Of course not, we've got an arrangement. I just need another two or three weeks."

He kissed her, rubbed her breasts and then between her legs and she lost her pout.

"One more quick one?"

He shook his head. "I've got a chess game down at the sutler's. But it is a nice idea." He got rid of her at last, closed his quarters and locked them this time and did go to the sutler's for a bottle of beer and a chess game if he could find one.

A day later the sweep patrol left the fort with fifteen men under the command of Lieutenant

Oliver. It was not the best duty, and he was still smarting that he had made three of them in a row now, but he went without any obvious rancor.

Ellie Unru watched the troops go, as did a few of the Pony Solders. It was a patrol full of hard riding, no danger but a lot of discomfort.

Ellie gave the patrol four hours to get away from the fort, so she was sure they wouldn't return. She cleaned the two rooms next to Oliver's then tried his door. It was locked. She used a key from her ring, a skeleton key that would open any of the simple door locks, and slipped inside.

She wasted no time. First she threw the bolt on the door behind her, went directly to the washstand and pushed it aside. With a knife, she lifted the floor boards and stared down at the gold.

She had left everything but essentials out of her cleaning bucket. Now she put the gold coins in the bottom of the bucket and lifted it. Yes, she could carry it, but it took both hands.

She made sure she got the last coin, then put the board back and pushed the wash stand over it.

She smiled as she rubbed the gold.

Ellie knew she was the richest woman in sixteen counties!

She put her cleaning things on top of the gold, covering it completely with a cloth, then carried the heavy bucket to the door.

Ellie knew she could not go directly back to her quarters. She had to do the rest of her work. She had two more officer rooms to clean.

She went outside, locked the door behind her, and carried the bucket with both hands fifty feet to the next officer's room. She had trouble getting the job done inside, and she admitted it was not a complete cleaning. She was so excited she could hardly keep from wetting her drawers! She owned eight thousand dollars in gold! It was almost too much to understand. She would have to get used to it a little at a time.

She did one more room, then carried the bucket back to her quarters where the eight married enlisted men were housed. Once inside she tried to think of a spot to hide the gold. Oliver would know who took it at once.

Every hiding place she figured out she later rejected. It had to be outside, she decided at last. And she had to bury it in a bucket, but that meant she had to do it after dark. She had been trying to grow some flowers just outside her door. She could dig there with one wondering about it.

But she waited until it was dark, then dug a hole. The ground was so hard she took the gold from the bucket and put it in an old flower sack and wrapped it with string. Then it was easier to get in the ground and covered. Over the spot she put three colorful rocks she had found in the prairie. It was good enough to fool Garland Oliver.

Inside her quarters she took out the sauce pan from the back of the small cupboard and looked at the gold coins. She had kept out five of them to touch and feel and play with. A hundred dollars! That was more than half a year's pay!

She was humming when her husband, Ira, came in just before supper time. He had been on stable duty today and he hated it.

"Nothing but shoveling out horse turds and dirty straw," he always said. He was a small man, with a drooping moustache, thinning hair and a left arm with rheumatism from too many damp, cold nights in the field.

"What the hell you so happy for? You fuck a

general or something this afternoon?" he bellowed at her.

"I get happy over other things, too, Ira. But no, I didn't lift my skirts this afternoon, I just worked my cunny off."

"And that makes you happy?"

"I'm still thinking about going in to Austin for a week or so."

"Not enough army pricks out here for you, Ellie?" He spat on the wooden floor. "Christ, once a damn whore, always a floozie. I should have known better."

"You loved me, remember."

"Yeah, five years ago when I had peach fuzz on my cheeks. I didn't know any better. You took me for a sucker. I'm not eighteen anymore."

"I am! I'm getting younger and prettier every day."

"Bullshit! You're getting sloppy and fat and in another two years you'll be paying the privates if they'll squeeze your tits."

Ellie flounced away to the back of the one big room. Maybe she would go to Austin anyway. She could sew twenty of the gold coins in the lining of an old coat she had, or maybe forty. A dozen trips and she'd have all the gold in the Austin bank! She was sure that Major Zachery would search everyone leaving the post until the gold was found. But he wouldn't know about linings.

She smiled as she started making their evening meal.

Two days later, Lieutenant Oliver returned with the patrol. They had seen and chased a wandering band of Indians, but could not identify them. The six braves may have been an advance party of some sort, or simply hunters. Oliver reported that one of the hostiles was wounded but the others escaped.

In his quarters he fell on the bed for an hour before he moved. Then he washed up and at once noticed that the washstand was not in the precise location where he had left it. He pushed it aside and checked the hiding place.

"Gone! Be damned, she did it!"

He sat there on the floor, alternately pounding the planks with his fists, and thinking of all the deadly tortures he was going to use on Ellie Unru. When he had calmed down enough to be rational, he stepped outside, grabbed the first trooper he could find and ordered him to go find Ellie Unru, the cleaning woman, and tell her to come to his quarters at once to clean his room.

Oliver stood beside his window to the parade grounds watching the enlisted men's quarters across the way. At last he saw Ellie as she came from her door and walked the long way around under the small porches built out in front of some of the areas, until she got to his door.

She knocked and waited. He let her in and saw she had her bucket and broom.

As soon as she closed the door and set down the bucket he grabbed her around the throat and squeezed hard.

She choked and gagged and tried to talk.

"You bitch! You thieving cunt! You stole my gold! I'm going to have the pleasure of ripping you apart before I kill you. I'll do it the way the Comanches do with prisoners."

She was shaking her head at him. At last he eased up enough to let her talk.

"Didn't steal anything!" she wheezed.

He let go and hit her cheek with his open palm. She staggered across the room. He followed and hit her again, a hard slap on the side of her head that turned her half around.

"Bitch! Bitch! Bitch!"

She recovered enough to be able to talk. Her voice was still wheezing and whiskey rough.

"Didn't steal anything. You hit me again, I'll go right to Major Zachery and tell him you stole the gold and show him where you hid it. He'll believe me. He can find gold shavings and dust in that hiding spot. Now, don't touch me!"

Oliver stopped. He hadn't expected her to react this way. Maybe plead for her life, maybe strip and try to seduce him. He shook his head.

"You won't go to the major, because I'll accuse you of stealing it from me. He'll tear your quarters apart."

"Won't work, Garland. He won't find a thing, cause I didn't take your old gold. Somebody else must have found it."

"Where did you hide it, Ellie? Tell me or I'll kill you yet. Then you won't tell the major anything."

She watched him closely. He meant it. She had to change her tactics just a little. "Maybe we can work together. You help me get both of us out of here, and I'll bring the gold. Agreed?"

He stared at her, then at last nodded.

"First, there's a small item we must dispose of. My husband, Ira."

Oliver never flinched. He'd expected something like this. She needed him to get away.

"Leave him here when we ride out."

"He'd suspect something and find us. You have to kill him, quickly, tonight."

Oliver began to sweat. Shooting somebody on a patrol was easy enough, but to do in a trooper right in the fort, was a lot harder.

"No, we leave him here. Where's the gold?"

"You find out after Ira is dead. Do it tonight, or forget all about the gold, and remember, I'll go straight to the major. I'm just a private's wife, a cleaning woman and ex-whore. You can't hurt me at all, Garland sweetheart. Do it tonight. He'll be drinking at the sutler's until late. Catch him coming home."

Ellie turned and walked around him to the door.

Oliver made no try to stop her.

"Remember, tonight. You kill Ira, then we can get away from here." She paused and laughed. "I might even teach you the right way to make love. God knows you need some basic training in how to please a woman." She whirled and went out the door, carrying her broom and bucket. She never looked back.

Oliver watched her go, then sat down on his bed. How had he let her get the upper hand? Yeah, he showed her where he hid the gold. Dumb! He'd sure as hell never do that again. Now he had to do as she said or he'd never see that eight thousand dollars again, and all of his big dreams were dead and buried.

He went to supper mess as usual. Only three lieutenants ate in the officer room. He didn't remember what he ate or said to the other men.

Back in his quarters he sharpened his knife, a four inch, heavy bladed hunting knife he carried on his belt on patrols. That evening he was in and out of the sutler's combination store and saloon twice. He saw trooper Unru there the second time. He was playing cards for matches and buttons and drinking steadily.

Good. A drunk would be easier to approach and to fool. There was no moon. The middle of the deserted parade grounds might be the best spot to slit his throat. No, he had to make it look like an Indian raid.

Back in his quarters he found the two Indian arrows he had picked up at the Buffalo Creek wagon train massacre, and a tomahawk with a steel blade fitted tightly into the wrappings. He would use the tomahawk, leave it in Unru's skull. That way it would pinpoint the blame and keep any suspicion off him.

It should work.

He made one more trip to the sutler, bought a new deck of cards, made sure Unru was still there and went back to his quarters. He carried the arrows and tomahawk under his shirt, as he slouched in the darkness near the sutler's waiting for Unru.

It was nearly midnight by the Big Dipper clock in the sky, when Unru reeled out the door with a buddy. They sang a bawdy song as they staggered across the parade ground.

Unru stopped and urinated, and they both laughed. The other man headed for the bachelor enlisted quarters and Unru turned toward his end of the barracks.

Oliver caught Unru half way across the one hundred yard wide parade ground. He called softly and the trooper spun around.

"Unru, is that you?" Oliver asked.

Unru squinted at him. Then saw the bars on his shoulders and started to salute.

"Yeah, yes sir. Private Unru, sir."

"No saluting, soldier. I've got a small job I want you to help me with. Ccme along."

The alcohol could not dull Unru's training to follow orders immediately, and without question. He turned and walked back toward the middle of the parade grounds beside the officer.

No one else was about. The interior guards were patrolling the inside of the fort's long rows of buildings. Most of them were not extremely alert either.

The center of the parade grounds was deathly dark.

Oliver pulled out the tomahawk and pointed toward the stables.

"See over there near the stable area, Unru. We've had a report of some Indian activity."

The enlisted man looked where he was told. It was the last act of his life. Oliver slammed the Indian hatchet down with much more force than was necessary. The sharp steel blade drove into Private Unru's skull, penetrated to the handle and pounded the trooper to the ground.

He had died instantly.

Oliver dropped one of the arrows, broke the second in half and left it a short distance away, then walked quickly toward the least busy section of the fort, the area that would be finished soon for guests and the stables. He met no one. That was good.

He shuddered slightly. It had been little harder than shooting that meddling sergeant. He grinned. It had been easy! Now what had been a mountainous problem had been solved. He got to his quarters quickly, went inside and bolted the door, then washed and slipped into his bed.

He wondered how quickly the body would be found. There was no guard post that covered the middle of the parade ground so the body might not be found before sunup.

Oliver lay awake for two hours trying to decide if he should go to Denver or San Francisco to start his new life. There would be more opportunity in either town. New money was not a hindrance there as it would be in New York or Boston. Yes, he would go west, and he was leaning toward San Francisco. He had never been there.

He could ride part way on the new railroad, even though it hadn't made it all the way to the West Coast yet. He had never ridden far on a train. It would be interesting.

Strange about the Indian raid that must have just taken place. None of the sentries saw a thing. Why would the Indians penetrate to the middle of the parade ground and kill one drunk trooper on his way home from a night of drinking? Strange questions, but the Comanches were strange people.

No, they were not people, they were savages. They would never be people, they were hostiles, with no regard for human life, no civilization, no morals, no manners. They were truly savages. The quicker the army could wipe them off the face of the continent, the better.

14

Laughing Golden Hair snuggled deep into the soft warm fur of the buffalo calf. The skin had been taken in December, when the short hair had grown heavy and lush to form the absolutely prime coat. It was the softest, warmest of all the robes the small white girl gathered around her.

She had been with the Comanche now for almost a month. She was beginning to feel at home with them. True, she did miss her other mother, but her Indian mother, Cries In The Morning, had been so kind and gentle, had taught her many words of the People and shown her how to do dozens of things around the tipi.

Laughing Golden Hair was glad the band was not moving again. She had been frightened when the blue shirts had charged into the camp. She remembered little of it except the booming of the guns and the screams of the People.

She didn't understand why she lived in a different lodge now. Running Wolf, her mother's husband had gone away somewhere. Her mother tried to explain it to her, but Cries In The Morning had started crying and Laughing Golden Hair couldn't understand the words.

Now they lived in a bigger lodge, where there were two other women and two girls she could play with, and a warrior. His name was White Eagle, she had learned that. He was the leader of the Eagle band of Comanches, but everyone called them the People.

For a moment before the others in the lodge woke up, she became Sadie Harding again. She thought of her soft, blue-eyed mother with the long golden hair like her own, the gentle way she had held Sadie and sang to her. The exciting times she told them they would have when they got to the fort where her daddy worked.

It seemed like only yesterday, and then again it seemed like a very long time ago. She blinked back tears remembering the gun shots and the screams of the horses and the hollering by the troops and the Indians.

She wondered if Yale was all right. Often they had played "dead" falling down where they were. But after the game was over they got up and went on playing. She never did see Yale get up after he ran at the big Indian who threw their mother out of the covered wagon.

She did not connect the big Indian with White Eagle. That bad man had hurt Yale and her mother. He had hurt her arms too, and tied her over his back. But most of all, he had his face painted all black and he looked ugly.

Cries In The Morning rolled over on the soft buffalo robes that lay around the outer edge of the big tipi. They were on the sides of the covering that came to the ground and inward, so the cold and wetness would stay outside.

Cries In The Morning smiled when she saw her new daughter was awake.

"Hi, tai, you-oh-hobt pa-pi. Toquet?"

Laughing Golden Hair smiled and bobbed her head. She had understood all the words. Her new mother said, Hello friend yellow hair, is everything all right?

"Toquet," Laughing Golden Hair said. She had not yet learned the words for going potty. She stood and put on her small breechclout and pointed to the tent flap.

Cries In The Morning understood, rose and took her small charge out to relieve herself. It was so good to have these small mothering duties again. It had been so long.

White Eagle saw them leave. He smiled. He had not known the small yellow hair would be in his lodge when he brought her back. It was well. She would be a chief's woman someday, perhaps his own son's woman. If he had a son.

Talks A Lot was due anytime. The women were ready, the birth lodge had been prepared.

He watched his two wives sleeping. They had found a new camp that was safe. The council had made sure of it. They had talked about it for two days, and at last they had decided and the pipe had been smoked and all had agreed to abide by the decision.

From now on, all of the warriors would be used as lookouts and sentinels to keep the camp safe. It was part of their regular duty. They would man lookouts for three day's journey in the two most dangerous directions, and one day's journey in the other two.

Never again would the people be surprised in their robes, sleeping while the enemy white-eyes charged into the camp with guns blazing.

White Eagle went out to the horse pasture and whistled for Flying Wind. For two hours he worked with the young war pony, drumming into his quick mind every motion, every movement that White Eagle wanted, using only his knees, his legs and feet to guide the pony. When he was satisfied with the colt's progress, he took him to a patch of thistles the young horse loved and let him eat.

Back at the lodge, Cries In The Morning had spread out the last buffalo skin her late husband had shot on the hunt. She had scraped it once, but now it needed a second scraping to remove more of the fat and bits of flesh from the skinning. It had to be smooth and nearly the same thickness all over.

She used a metal scraper made from the blade of a hoe that Running Wolf had stolen on one of the raids.

Laughing Golden Hair had tired of playing with White Eagle's two daughters in the lodge, and sat near the big hide as her mother scraped. Soon she found another scraper, a smaller one and worked on the side of the skin.

Always Smiling came and watched for a moment, then shook her head and took the scraper and showed Laughing Golden Hair how to do it properly. The small white girl pouted for a minute, but when she saw how the older woman did it and how gently, she took back the tool and smiled.

Sadie realized she had never been scolded once since she came to the People. She had not been spanked or disciplined in any way. She couldn't remember any of the children being spanked or scolded.

When the little boys got too rambunctious their parents simply told them that was not the way the

People acted. It was the sharpest reprimand they received. They seemed to grow up free and happy, but with respect and love for their parents.

Little Sadie wondered again about her mother. She frowned trying to remember exactly how she looked. The long golden hair was easy, but it was becoming harder to remember her mother's soft, pretty face.

Her father was easier, because they had pictures of him to look at. And Yale was easy. She wondered how bad Yale had been hurt when he played dead?

Her two new sisters came and caught her hand. They were going to find berries. She looked at Cries In The Morning who smiled and nodded.

The three girls ran off, each wearing the small breechclouts. Laughing Golden Hair had her hair greased and braided so it wouldn't get in her way. Her skin had taken on a pleasant tan, so she was much darker than when she arrived, but still a shade or two lighter than her sisters.

They ran to the stream, waded in it for a minute, then hurried to some tall bushes that had black colored berries. The other girls ate a few, so Laughing Golden Hair tried one. It was good! Almost like the wild blackberries she used to eat. They had brought small baskets, and picked enough berries to fill two of them, then took them back to the lodge and hurried again to the stream.

"Swimming," the oldest girl who was just past six, said to Laughing Golden Hair in Comanche, but she didn't understand. She caught the smaller girl's hand and they stepped into the water.

Then the two Indian girls took off their breechclouts and dropped naked into the cool water. Sadie felt white again as she watched them. Her mother had told her . . . What had it been about not

taking off her clothes? She shrugged. Her sisters did
it. She loosened her breechclout and dropped it on
the shore and ran into the water, screeching at the
chill, then falling into the coolness and laughing
with the others.

They played until they were chilled, splashing and
dunking their heads under, then rushing out to a
grassy place and lying in the sun to dry themselves
and get warm again.

As she lay there half dozing, she thought about
the Pony Soldiers whom she had seen galloping into
the village. Her real father was a soldier! What if he
had been with the other Pony Soldiers looking for
her? She had not cried out to tell him where she was.

She frowned. She wondered if her daddy would
come and get her? But Cries In The Morning had
run off with her, hid her away from the Pony
Soldiers. As Sadie, she was confused. Didn't Cries
In The Morning know she wanted to find her Daddy
again? She would try to tell her. She would learn
more of the words so they could talk together better.
With the girls she didn't need to know as many
words.

She sat up and suddenly realized she was naked.
She put on her breechclout and felt better.

Soon the three girls were playing tag. When they
tired of that they hit a round leather ball stuffed
with buffalo hair. They used sticks and tried to hit it
past the other team. When they had enough of that,
they went back and picked more of the black berries
and ate them.

Wash her hair! Sadie remembered that her mother
used to wash her hair every Saturday night. She
hadn't thought about the days of the week for a
long, long time. She wondered what day it was? It
didn't matter here.

She wanted to wash her hair.

Laughing Golden Hair began to unbraid her hair. She left the other girls and ran for the stream, taking off her breechclout again she hurried into the water, sat down and ducked her head again with her hair loose and flying. She washed it carefully, using sand from the bottom to wash the buffalo grease from her hair. She washed it three times as the other girls watched.

When she rinsed all of the sand away she felt cleaner than she had been in days and days. She sat on the shore, put on her breechclout and let her hair dry in the sun. She looked in a quiet pool and saw her blonde hair dry into a fluffy halo around her head.

It felt so good that way for a change.

Back at the tipi, Cries In The Morning looked at her new daughter and laughed, then combed out the long blonde hair, greased it and braided it again, talking all the time, laughing and letting Laughing Golden Hair know she had not done a bad thing. It was simply better braided this way.

That was when Sadie let the tears roll down her cheeks as she cried softly. She wanted to go home. She wanted to see her Mother and Father, and even Yale.

She wanted to go home!

The tears came freely then and Cries In The Morning looked surprised, then hugged her gently and crooned a soft lullaby.

15

At 7:15 A.M. Major Zachery stormed into Captain Harding's office. His shirt was buttoned crooked, his hair still rumpled and there was a snarl on his face.

"Harding, what the hell is going on this morning? What's this about an Indian attack?"

Captain Harding leaned back in his chair, slowly locked his fingers together behind his neck and stared at the only man on the post who outranked him.

"And a good morning to you, too, Major. I've been up since a little after three A.M. when the body was found. I've been trying to figure it out myself ever since.

"About three this morning a guard cut across the parade ground and stumbled over the body of Private Ira Unru. Killed with a tomahawk. Two Indian arrows were found in the vicinity. We can find no other loss, damage or sign of any Indian intrusion. How would you call it?"

"Just one body? Doesn't sound like Comanches. Any horses stolen?"

"Not a one, not a bridal, not a round of ammunition. I don't think it was an Indian attack either. But someone wants us to think it was."

"Maybe it's tied in with the stolen gold?"

"Maybe. More likely Unru said the wrong thing to the wrong trooper last night at his regular drinking bout and that person more than evened the score. We're searching out just who was in the sutler's saloon last night, and if there were any fights."

"Sounds like work. I'm going to have my breakfast."

"I had mine. Take your time. This probably has nothing to do with your missing gold."

"Unru did you say? The name sounds familiar."

"Been here almost a year, first hitch, but an average trooper these days."

Major Zachery waved and left for the officer's mess. As he did, the sutler came in. His name was Hans Altzanger, a German immigrant who ran a fine store on the post and a small saloon area for the drinkers. Hans held his cloth cap in his hands, twisting it nervously.

"You wanted see me, sir?"

"Hans, yes, come in and sit down. You heard about the problem?"

"Unru, yes, good customer. But he drink too much. I tell him. Last night I not sell him more."

"You cut him off? Did that make him angry?"

"No, he had others buy for him."

"Did he get in any brawls, any fights last night?"

"No fights. I not allow."

"Did Unru argue with anybody, yell and scream?"

"No. Others, not Unru. He a quiet drinker. Even cry sometimes. Not fighter when drunk."

Captain Harding scowled. He had been afraid of that. No good suspects. "Hans, do you remember who was in your store last night? Could you give me the names?"

"Some. Not know all names. Maybe Corporal could help. Hans describe, Corporal know name?"

"Yes, Hans. Good idea. You talk to Corporal Swenson. I want the names as soon as you can remember them."

The store man went to the outer office. Captain Harding marched to his small window and looked at the parade grounds. Why would a private, a married private, be murdered?

He knew the stories about Mrs. Unru, Ellie. She was what some commanders called an "available" woman on post. Some isolated forts and posts with no wives on board, even brought in two or three fancy ladies for the entertainment of the troops.

Often the wives of enlisted men did laundry and housecleaning for the men and for officers. Quite naturally some of the women were not offended by making a few dollars extra to help with the family budget.

Mrs. Unru had been mainly an "officers' woman. Two of the enlisted men's wives had a clientele among the enlisted swains.

He rubbed his chin. Unru didn't seem to mind that his wife whored around. Why would somebody get mad at him for his wife's loose living? Not reasonable. Maybe the other way? Unru objected to someone laying his wife and . . . no not likely. He was right back where he began.

Corporal Swenson came in the door.

"Captain, sir. We have a list of ten names. The others will be harder. Thought you might want to start to talk to some of the ones we have."

Harding nodded and took the sheet of paper. He looked down the list and stopped at the bottom one, Lieutenant Oliver's name was on the list. He went to the outer office and up to Altzanger.

"Hans, Lieutenant Oliver was drinking last night?"

"Oh, no sir. He bought new deck cards. Said had heard about new solitaire. His desk missing card."

"I see. So he didn't stay very long?"

"Just few minutes. He look around, leave."

"Thanks, Hans. You keep working on that list."

Five minutes later Major Zachery opened Colt Harding's office door and stepped inside.

"Got something to show you, Captain. You might remember I said I had some suspicions about two men. I've been keeping watch on the two. So far I have a record of twelve days in a row when Lieutenant Oliver was visited by a young lady in the afternoon, in the evening, once after taps."

"Some men are younger than we are, Major. Been a good long time that I've had a woman every day for twelve days."

"True, but the name of this woman is what makes it interesting. Her name is Ellie Unru."

Captain Harding turned quickly. "Damn interesting. Here's a list of some of the men who were in the sutler's saloon last night. Look at the bottom name."

"Oliver!" the major roared. "Let's arrest the bastard."

"On what charges, buying a deck of cards or fucking the post officers' whore?"

"He wanted to get rid of Unru so he could take over the woman."

"Major, you've seen Ellie Unru. She isn't the kind to drive men to murder. And Oliver isn't the kind to go overboard for a cheap whore like Ellie Unru. We need some proof."

"It still could tie in with the missing gold."

"Legally 'could' is the weakest word in the book. We still need evidence."

"I want your permission to search the quarters of Lieutenant Oliver and Mrs. Unru. That's where we'll find enough proof to scare them into confessing."

"Some commanders might operate that way, Major, but I never have, especially with my officers. Out here we put our lives on the line for each other a dozen times a year. I don't want any mistrust between my officers. We do it another way."

"What other way?"

"I don't know. We trap them somehow, trick them. We need some kind of a plan."

"When you get one, let me know," the major said sarcastically. "I'm fresh out of clever plans."

"Oliver is still just a suspect. I'm waiting for the full list of men in the saloon last night. We might find a much better suspect."

"Try this story," Major Zachery said. "Oliver steals the gold, hides it in his quarters. His regular cleaning lady finds it and confronts him. He says he'll marry her and run away. She beds him for two weeks, then changes her mind, steals the gold from Oliver and hides it. Now, she says kill my husband and run away with me with the gold, or I'll go to the captain and tell him you stole the gold. Over a barrel, Oliver does in her husband. Which brings us up to now."

"Work good in a dime novel, Major, but I'm still looking for the facts. Even if we arrested Oliver, we don't have a shred of evidence to use in a court martial."

"He'll confess, and we won't need evidence."

"Oliver would confess only to save his neck from a noose."

"So what the hell can we do now?"

"I'll conduct an investigation, talk to the men at the saloon, not let on to Oliver he's even a suspect, and maybe we'll get lucky. He might head out of the fort some dark night. If he does, I'll have a man watching his door and we'll know. Then we'll grab him. Otherwise, we watch and wait."

By noon Captain Harding was hard at questioning the men individually who had been at the sutler's last night. He got no help in his quest. There had been no fights, almost no arguments, and the two people who really argued were not involved with Unru at all. He sat in a corner nursing one beer after another, until he left with a friend who had no reason at all to kill the slight private.

By supper call, Captain Harding had discovered no new facts, and nothing to help him. He called in Major Zachery.

"I have a suggestion. I'm asking Ellie Unru to come to my office in about fifteen minutes. I'll keep her here for half an hour. That will give you plenty of time to search her quarters. I won't know anything about it. Deal?"

The major grinned and left the room at once.

Ellie Unru was nervous as she sat in the outer office waiting for the captain to talk to her. He kept her waiting for twenty minutes, then asked her in.

"Mrs. Unru, first let me tell you how sorry we all are here at Camp Comfort about your loss. It's a tragic murder. No Indians were involved, and we're trying the best we can to discover who killed your husband."

She wept silently into a handkerchief clutched in

her left hand.

"Mrs. Unru, would you have any idea who might have hated your husband, who might have wanted to do him harm? Did he owe anyone a gambling debt, for instance?"

"No sir. Mr. Ira never gambled. He drank some, but he said he needed it for his rheumatiz. He was a kind man. Not really educated or smart, but kind."

They talked for another five minutes, then Captain Harding gave her the list of men from the saloon to check over. She looked at each one and shook her head.

"None of these men would want to harm my Ira. I just don't know who it was."

"What are your plans now, Mrs. Unru? You won't be able to stay in the married enlisted quarters."

"I . . . I thought of that. I guess I'll go into Austin. I have a friend living there. I really haven't planned much."

"No hurry. But within a month we need to know what you'll be doing."

They talked a few more minutes, then Captain Harding stood and escorted her out of his office.

Ten minutes later Major Zachery came in, a smile on his face. He closed the office door, and held his closed hand out to Harding.

"Never guess what I found in the poor widow's quarters." He opened his hand.

A bright, shining double eagle lay there. Harding looked at the mint date. It was 1869, a coin that had not been issued yet and was not due out until the following month. It must have come from the box of stolen coins.

Captain Harding smiled. "So we have a good suspect. That's still not enough evidence to arrest her. Where did you find it?"

"It was under a small couch, as if it had fallen and rolled under there and she didn't miss it. Not to miss two months pay for an enlisted man's wife is not normal. She must have had three hundred and ninety eight other coins like it to play with."

"Maybe," Harding said. "How did she get them? That's what we have to prove. Also we'll need those other coins. If she's hidden them, we could play old billy hell in convincing her to show us where they are."

"That will be the job of the court martial," Major Zachery insisted. "I still say Oliver stole it, she used her body to sex him up and get a look at the gold, then she stole it. Now she's got him doing her dirty work for her . . . like murder. That makes her guilty of murder, too. I say we arrest them right now, before either one can make a run for it."

16

When Ellie Unru stepped out of the captain's office, she felt a slight shiver go down her back bone. The Fort Commander knew more than he was letting on. Somehow she was suspect in Ira's murder and probably the stolen gold as well.

She walked stiffly and slowly, befitting a new widow. Ira's burial would be the next afternoon. There was no way to put it off another day with the warm weather. Just as well.

When she came toward her quarters, she looked at the three colored rocks she had placed over the spot where she buried the gold. All were in precisely the place she had put them. If they had been moved, nobody could have put them back the same way.

She walked past the spot and went in her door. She never locked it. There was nothing to steal inside. Most of the enlisted men left their doors unlocked.

At once she sensed movement behind her and whirled to find Garland Oliver standing behind the door as she closed it.

His face was red with anger. She had never seen him so worked up, not even when they made love. For a moment more he couldn't speak, then he flew at her and she jumped aside to get out of his way.

"What did you tell the captain?"

She watched him for a moment. His panic/fear attack had passed. He was gaining control of himself.

"Calm down, Garland. I told him what he wanted to hear, that I had no idea who could have killed a wonderful man like Ira. That he had no enemies, owed no one money, didn't gamble and was as pure as the driven snow. You shouldn't be here."

"Why?"

"Because everyone knows I've been sleeping with you. Now my husband is murdered. Not too hard to make a connection, even though it ain't true."

He frowned and bobbed his head. "Damned if you aren't right. But I have some news for you. The minute you stepped inside the captain's office, Major Zachery came into your quarters. He was here for twenty minutes. Has anything been moved? Did he search the place?"

She gasped and looked around. The furniture, what there was of it, was in about the same position. She looked in her dresser drawer. Yes, it had been searched. Things were the same, but a little different. As if a hand had crept through them looking for gold coins.

"Did he find any gold coins?" Oliver asked her, his voice shrill, tight.

"No, it isn't in here. I just had a couple and I . . . I sewed them in the lining of my coat." She looked in the closet and came out with it, showing the round lumps where the coins nestled in thick seams along the buttons.

"He must have found one coin. That damned major looked pleased as a pussycat eating cream when he left your door. He went directly to the captain's office."

"Oh, Lord! I did drop some one night, but I picked them all up. I think."

"You think! God, woman, I could be facing a hanging here, you too! Don't you realize . . . ?" He stopped, took a long, deep breath and looked out the front wide window into the parade ground.

"All right. It's time. We'll leave tonight as soon as it gets dark. You get the gold wherever you hid it, and I'll walk by and we'll stroll to the gate. I'll have two horses there and we'll bribe the sentry, telling him we're going to the stream to make love in the water. He'll believe it."

"And we won't come back," she added smiling.

"True, we won't. All you have to do is get the gold and put on about two sets of clothes so you'll be warm enough to ride through the night for Austin."

She hesitated. Was there any other way? She searched her mind. If the major had found that one gold coin she lost, the whole thing would come crashing down quickly.

"Oh, put the gold in some kind of a picnic basket, and put food on the top. We'll tell the sentry it's a late supper as well."

"Yes, it should work. I can't think of any other way."

"Believe me, Ellie, I've been trying to come up with a better plan ever since I saw Major Zachery slip into your quarters here. Believe me, this is best.

Now, you go out and water your flowers or something, so I can ease out and get away without making a big announcement of my visit."

She did, leaving the door open. She was careful not to get the rocks wet covering the gold sack. When she turned around she saw Oliver walking casually down the side of the quadrangle toward the officer's quarters. She turned and went back inside for more water, then shook her head at the daisies. She didn't think they were going to bloom after all.

Oliver figured he was being watched. There was no way that Major Zachery had not pegged him as the prime suspect in the gold robbery. And now the "coincidence" of the woman he was bedding getting her husband killed, would make the suspicion that much tighter.

He stopped in at Lieutenant Edwards' quarters and found the officer alone. His wife was playing cards in another part of the fort.

"Dan, need a small favor," Oliver said when he was invited in. He and Dan had got along fine recently.

"Yeah, figures. Anybody but my wife."

They both laughed.

"Along those lines. I got a wild one set for tonight. I told you I poke Ellie now and then. Tonight I want to surprise her and take her down by the stream and get her bare ass in the grass in the moonlight."

"You'll have to talk to Ellie about that, I'd say."

"Not the problem. I need somebody to set up two horses and saddles out by the front fence of the paddock. Just down from the front gate. Won't be any trouble with the gate sentry. I'll tell him we're off on a moonlight walk and slip him a silver dollar."

Dan Edwards laughed. "Garland, why don't you just get married and you can have it every night? No more wild schemes."

"The schemes are what keep it fun. Can you do it?"

"Hell yes. Do I want to?"

"So I'll owe you a favor. Come on. I got big plans for her tonight."

"Okay, why not. Just don't get me in trouble."

"Not a chance. Now, I've got to put my first platoon through its paces."

He did. For the next three hours, Oliver drilled his first platoon relentlessly. Major Zachery watched them in the parade ground, then saw them go on a half mile ride outside the fort and return. This line officer knew men, could get them to do what he needed them to do. Too bad he was also a thief, and probably a cold blooded murderer as well.

Oliver had supper in the mess and went back to his quarters. There he stripped to his waist and in the washbowl took a sponge bath from the waist up. Then he put on a clean uniform, and slid his service revolver in his shirt. Yes, it would work in the dark.

Now, if that damned woman would dig up the gold he would be ready. She had bought the story. She wanted to believe him. Once they were two miles down the trail to Austin, the poor lady would suffer a serious and fatal accident.

The secret was for her to believe him enough to bring out the gold from wherever she had hidden it. He'd make damn sure by looking in the bag before they left. They would meet at the gate. By the time they were out, and the private who had been watching him reported back to Major Zachery, they would have enough of a head start. Not even Colt

Harding could track him in the dark!

He had drilled his troops that afternoon to throw the good major off the scent. It also gave him something to do to stay busy. Now it was a half hour to dark. He stepped outside and looked across the corner of the buildings where he could see Ellie's door. He went back inside and concentrated on the small window, but he didn't see her come out of her door.

When it was full dark, he turned up his shirt collar, pulled his hat down over his face and walked past her door. He could hear her humming inside. He wanted to knock, but knew he shouldn't.

Twenty minutes later from the darkness of the parade ground, he saw her door open. There was no lamp burning inside. He saw her shadowy figure bend over the flower bed and start to dig.

Yes! he should have guessed it. He gave her time to get the gold, then walked up quickly as she stepped inside her darkened door.

She yelped as he pushed her inside and went with her. Then saw it was him. Inside she showed him the picnic basket. She lit a lamp and kept it low. He unrolled the sack and found the gold coins and saw them glint in the low lamplight.

There was no reason to leave with her. He had the gold. He had what he wanted.

He slipped his .44 from his shirt and held it by the barrel. When she turned he slammed the butt of the heavy gun down hard on Ellie's skull. He heard it crack. She sighed and fell.

He saw the blood gushing from her skull, staining her hair, then her blouse. He had to finish it. He gritted his teeth and hit her twice more, then again. Each time the bloody handle of his pistol sank deeper into her skull. It fascinated him. He took one last look at all that was left of Ellie before he blew out the lamp.

Oliver put the sack of gold coins inside his shirt, knowing that they made an obscene bulge.

But it was the best he could do. He pushed the .44 on top of the sack, moved a box of shells in his front pocket and slipped out the door.

It was a short way down to the entrance to the paddock through the fort wall. When the square was finished, it would be only one of two openings.

At the paddock gate he talked with the private on guard duty.

"Need to check on my mount. She seemed to have a bad foot this afternoon. I'll look her over and if it's bad, I'll bring her back up here where you have a lantern."

"Yes, sir Lieutenant Oliver. Your mount should be down near the gate end of the paddock."

Oliver thanked the private and walked into the dark corral that was fenced on three sides and walled in by the fort on the fourth. He walked along the building to the fence near the front of the fort and saw the two horses waiting for him outside the barrier. Quickly he stepped through the wire, and led the two saddled mounts slowly and quietly away from the fort toward Auston. No one could see him in the darkness.

With any luck he would be half way to Austin before they knew he was gone. He walked out five hundred yards, then tied the reins of the second horse onto his saddle in a lead line, mounted the first horse and rode away at a walk down the dark trail toward Austin. He knew the route by heart. A hundred and twenty miles.

He remembered he had no food or supplies. But he had his pistol. Perhaps he could shoot a rabbit.

A half mile away from the fort, he lifted the mount to a canter and moved out swiftly. He would ride one horse until it was tired out, then transfer to the other one. That way he could easily outdistance any mounted pursuit that had only one horse each.

Oliver grinned in the soft moonlight. *Mister Oliver,* that was! He was a rich civilian who would discard his army duds just as quick as he could!

Back at Fort Comfort, Private Freddy Daniels followed Oliver as far as the enlisted barracks. He had no idea why the officer had stood in the dark parade ground for so long. Then he slipped into one of the enlisted men's dependent quarters and was there for a short time.

He came out and went to the paddock, and talked with the stable sentry. That was when Daniels went to see Major Zachery.

"You said he went to the dependent's quarters and stayed a time, then went to the paddock?"

"Yes sir. He talked with the sentry. Something about checking his mount."

"I don't like that, Daniels. Was it Ellie Unru's quarters he visited?"

"Yes sir. Maybe three or four minutes."

"Then the light came on, went out and he left?"

"Yes sir."

"I'll check the paddocks, Daniels. I want you to go to the front gate and remind the sentries there they are not to allow Oliver to leave the area."

"Yes sir."

Major Zachery put on his gunbelt and checked his issue .44 pistol, then walked across the parade grounds from his quarters to the paddock. Instead of going straight there, he went to the dependents' quarters and located the Unru door. The room was dark. He knocked.

There was no response. He knocked again. The door had not been locked or latched and it edged open. Major Zachery pushed it inward. A strange odor touched his senses.

He found matches in his pocket and struck one on the door and held it high.

On the floor almost at his feet lay Ellie Unru. Blood oozed and matted in her hair. The whole top and side of her skull had been smashed in. There was no chance she could be alive.

He rushed outside.

"Corporal of the Guard!" he bellowed. "Corporal of the Guard. Dependents' quarters, on the double!"

He raced along the doorways to the opening where the paddock was. The sentry there was alert and saluted smartly.

"Challenge me, damnit, don't salute!" the major shouted. "Did Lieutenant Oliver come in here a few minutes ago?"

"Yes sir. He's in the paddock, checking his horse."

"That's what he said he was going to do. Get me a lantern, quickly!"

The private started to leave.

"Idiot, you can't leave your post. Stay here."

"Corporal of the Guard, the paddock!" Major Zachery bellowed. He heard it repeated down the line. Somebody bolted from the guard room with a pair of lanterns.

"When they get here, send them into the paddock." Major Zachery ran in among the free horses. They moved grudgingly where they slept standing up. He ran to the fence and patrolled around it. He fully expected to find it cut where Oliver had taken a horse and ridden off.

The fence was not cut. He grabbed a lantern from the Corporal of the Guard and ordered him to go tell Captain Harding his presence was requested by the major.

By the time Captain Harding got his boots and pants on, and went out to the paddock, Major Zachery had it figured out.

He pointed to the horse droppings outside the fence.

"Two mounts! They must have been here for at least two hours. Oliver got the gold, killed Ellie Unru, came through the paddock, went through the fence and rode away with his gold and an extra horse."

"For once, I think you're right, Major Zachery," Harding said. He turned and spoke to his orderly.

"Swenson, dig out Sergeant Casemore. Tell him to get dressed for a ride."

Back at the sentry post at the paddock gate, he ordered another trooper to get four of the best horses out of the paddock and saddle all four.

"I want rations for four days and blanket rolls for two riders. Make it as fast as you can, soldier."

"We going after him?" Major Zachery asked.

"No, Major, Sgt. Casemore and I are going after him. We'll take two horses the same way he has. Now we damn well have the evidence we need."

Harding ran back to his quarters, dug out his best pair of pistols, took his Spencer repeating rifle and two hundred rounds of ammunition and went to the front porch. The four saddled horses were ready.

Casemore came running up. He had borrowed

a Spencer and shoved it in the saddle boot.

"Ready when you are, sir," Casemore said.

They stepped on board the army mounts and galloped for the main gate, their relief horses on short lead lines behind them.

17

Captain Harding and Sergeant Casemore rode through the front gate at a gallop and turned toward Austin.

"Only way he could have gone," Harding shouted. "He didn't have any provisions, or damn few. He could make Austin in two days of hard riding. A man can live for two days without food."

They continued the gallop for a quarter of a mile, then walked the horses for a quarter of a mile and galloped again. Three miles from the fort, in a section of the trail that went through a soft dirt spot they got off and used torches of dry weeds to search for hoof prints. They found them quickly.

"First horse is loaded with a rider and four hundred ounces of gold," Casemore said. "That's another twenty-five pounds. The trail horse is not nearly as loaded, like only a saddle. He was walking the nags through here."

"He knows somebody will be after him, but he probably hoped it wouldn't be until morning,"

Captain Harding said. "What we've got to do is punish our horses more than he does. Let's ride."

They galloped their horses for a half hour, then shifted to the second mounts and galloped them for a mile and walked. The horses were both lathering, but they couldn't stop and rub them down.

Six miles from the fort they checked the trail again. By the spring back of some grass in the hoof prints, Harding decided they were less than two hours behind him.

"Just depends how hard his pushes," Casemore said. "I'd bet a dollar that he's counting on us being single mounted when we come after him. On that basis we never would catch him.

"By dawn we look for a little rise in the trail. By that time we should be close enough to see him or catch his dust trail."

"He's going to fight," Casemore said.

"True, and he's a good shot. The bastard is a marksman with a rifle and pistol, so when we get near him we play it easy. We take no chances, but we nail the bastard."

"He won't have a chance in a court martial."

"Oliver will know that. He'll be hard to bring back alive."

"Either way is fine with me," Casemore said. "He's already killed two people, and I've got suspicions about a third."

"Corporal Pendleton on that wood detail?"

"The same. Pendleton was a little bit of a schemer, but he was a damn good soldier. Not a chance he would poke his head up when some Indians could nail him. My guess is that Pendleton knew something about the gold, confronted Oliver about it, and the wood detail proved a convenient way to murder Pendleton and blame it on the Comanches."

"Figures," Captain Harding said, his face etching even grimmer as he lifted the pace to a gallop again.

They traded horses three more times before it got light. Once, about four A.M. they stopped and rubbed down both pair of mounts, fed them, watered both good, then rode again.

Daybreak found them coming out of some brushy lowlands into a slight rise. The land ahead was open and covered with buffalo grass.

Captain Harding hesitated, squinted, then growled.

"There he is, just moving toward the top of that rise. See the two horses riding slow?"

"Got to be him. Out of range."

"We don't shoot at him until we've got him in our sights at a hundred yards or less. I don't want him getting away."

Colt tested the wind. It blew in their faces, away from their quarry.

"Let's have some coffee and bacon or whatever we have for chow," Harding said. "We want him on that down slope so we can get closer."

Casemore made a small cooking fire with nearly smokeless dry branches, and Harding fried bacon and boiled coffee. With hardtack and some apples they made a quick breakfast.

They were riding twenty minutes after they stopped.

"Only way I can figure is that Oliver discovered the gold when he came up fast with me right after our lead scouts found the wagons. I saw him checking the wagons, but I was . . . was busy at the time. He could have taken the gold right then, or later when the detail dug the graves. He could even have got it the next morning when they came back for the wagons. Damn him!"

"Don't worry, sir. This won't get that far to reflect on your career. I'm sure all the major wants is the gold back in government hands. He can work up some explanation about the gold being lost or misplaced or covered up by the Indians. He seems like a reasonable man. He can get the credit, and nobody gets the blame."

"Fine by me, Sergeant Casemore. All we have to do is get the gold back, and convince the major."

They galloped up the hill and at the top eased ahead to look over. The Texas landscape spread out in front of them for a ten mile stretch in a long flat plain with hardly a lift or break.

"We go around him," Colt said. "We drift to the left, swing over half a mile and get around him fast and wait for him just about where the dark line of trees shows up there, maybe eight miles."

"He's a half mile ahead now," Casemore judged. "With any luck we should be able to go around him easy."

They angled to the left, put a half mile to one side under their hooves, then turned due east again. They galloped ten yards apart so they wouldn't create a double dust trail. There was little dust at all here in the grassy plain.

Twice they changed mounts, working the horses harder than any Cavalry officer would except on a flat out charge. But both men knew the horses could take it, and it was the only way to outdistance the man ahead with two horses.

They hit the creek a little less than an hour later, and worked along behind the thin screen of wild almonds and a few wild cherry trees scattered through the willow. They came to the spot the wagons had forded the creek. The water level was coming down, but still ran a foot deep and twenty feet wide.

Casemore slid off his horse and checked the dust of the trail where it had been worn bare.

"He hasn't been past here yet," Casemore said. They tied their horses a hundred yards back on one side, then worked up silently through the brush until they could see the trail toward the fort.

"Got him!" Captain Harding said softly. "There, just beyond that rock off the main trail to the left. Looks like he's heading for the shade upstream a ways."

They both lifted up and faded through the brush on foot without making a sound.

Oliver shifted his angle and rode straight for the water now, ignoring the trail. He got into the brush before his trackers got to that point.

They stopped, gave him time to dismount and look around.

Both Cavalrymen had their Spencer repeaters.

"Careful," Harding whispered. "Not a sound." He motioned Casemore across the shallow stream, then they moved forward.

Ten minutes later, Captain Harding edged around a small wild pecan tree and saw the two army mounts. They had been staked out and hobbled. Both munched on fresh spring grass near the water.

On this side of them, Oliver lay on the grass, his head on his blanket roll, a canteen to his lips as he drank again and again.

It was an old Cavalry trick. If you didn't have enough to eat, drink plenty to keep your belly from screaming at you. Oliver was using the idea while he had the water.

Captain Harding had lost sight of Casemore. Right now, he didn't need him. He lifted the Spencer, aimed carefully, and sent a .56 caliber slug thunking into the tree trunk just over Oliver's head.

Oliver started to jolt away.

"Don't move, or you're dead meat!" Harding bellowed. We've got six men around you. More than one party can use relief horses, or didn't you think of that?"

Before Harding could finish the sentence, Oliver's hidden hand triggered a pistol sending three slugs in the captain's direction. One crashed into his left arm, spinning him away from the tree, and bringing a scream of pain and frustration from the captain.

Even as Colt slammed backwards, he heard another Spencer fire and a second scream stabbed through the quiet Texas prairie.

"Sonsofbitches!" Oliver screamed. "I should have killed you all!"

By the time Harding had pushed himself around so he could see where Oliver was, the man had moved.

A six-gun blasted again, one shot, then a spaced second shot and across the stream there came a howl of pain.

Harding braced himself with the Spencer and pushed upright beside the tree. He stared around the trunk, ignoring the throbbing in his left arm. So he was losing some blood, he had lots. This had to be finished now.

He watched the small brush and plants around the grassy area where Oliver had been. If he had rolled away, he would have stayed low. There. He would have gone that way. A small tree, two feet high was bent to the left and now slowly began straightening itself.

Harding worked the lever on his Spencer and sent three rounds smashing into the thicker brush behind the young tree. He had the lever coming back up when he saw a form lift up and surge toward a foot-thick tree.

Harding lifted the Spencer and fired without aiming, rather he pointed the weapon the way he would a finger when he had to indicate a direction or an individual quickly.

The .56 caliber slug bored from the rifle barrel, spun through the air and caught Oliver just under the heart, slicing through important body parts before it powered out his back an inch from his spinal column taking half a rib with it.

Oliver lay on his back when Captain Colt Harding eased up beside him and kicked the pistol out of his hand. His eyes were angry and tired at the same time. His left hand covered the small purple hole in his chest and he coughed, spitting up blood.

"Casemore!" Harding yelled.

"Yeah. You nail the bastard? I developed a severe case of a broken leg. Lucky round from Oliver's .44."

"Hold on, I'll be over." He turned back to Oliver. "You look a little worse for the wear. Is all the stolen gold in your four saddlebags?"

"Yes."

"You killed Private Unru, and then his widow?"

"Yes, she stole . . ." he went into a violent coughing seizure and screamed as he vomited blood. Wearily he wiped the blood from his lips and turned his eyes toward Captain Harding. The blood now drenched his chest.

"She stole the gold, made me kill her husband before she'd tell me where she hid it."

"Then you arranged to ride out with her, after she

dug up the gold?''

Oliver nodded.

"And Corporal Pendleton. You murdered him, too?''

"Yes. He saw me take the gold.''

"Why all of this, Oliver? You were a good soldier, a good officer. You could have had a fine career.''

"Temptation, too much of a temptation. Haven't you ever wanted to be rich?''

"Not that bad, Oliver.''

Captain Harding stood and went over to the creek to Casemore. The non-com had his leg half splinted. The break was below the knee.

Colt helped tie the branches in place using his own kerchief and then his belt to tighten it solidly.

Casemore screeched in pain as they stood.

Harding lifted him on his back and carried him across the creek. He helped him sit down against a tree without hurting the leg again.

The commanding officer went back to look at Oliver. His face was ashen.

"Lost too much blood. Hole in my back big as my fist. Family going to be embarrassed. They were the end of old money. Couldn't you clean up this whole matter a little for them?''

"Comanche raid?'' Captain Harding asked.

"Why not? You've got the gold. I'll be dead in five minutes. Why should my family suffer?''

Colt Harding looked at him. The man had a point.

Oliver gasped, his eyes went wide, then he screamed and blood spewed from his mouth. He lifted half way to a sitting position, then fell on his side, a long, soft gush of air escaping from his lungs that would never breathe again.

Casemore spat on the ground and shook his head.

"Captain, sir. You're not going to let the

murdering bastard get away with it, are you?"

Captain Harding reached over and took the man's shoulders and eased him back to the ground. It had been a long time since he had dug a soldier's grave. He watched Lieutenant Garland Oliver's face now in repose but still looked to be suffering.

"He paid for what he did, Casemore. Paid about as much as any man can pay. Why should his parents and brothers suffer? They live in Boston. That can be a ridiculously straight laced group back there."

That was when Captain Harding realized that they didn't have a shovel. Casemore tied up the Captain's wounded arm.

"Let's think about it on the way back. We can't bury him here. If the gold is in those two saddle bags, I think I can convince the major to scratch this all out smooth and even. Hell, the Comanches have been known to raid in this close, they even hit Austin once a couple of years ago. Nobody can swear they weren't in here again."

Casemore shrugged. He'd been in the army long enough to ride with the punches.

"Captain, you get me back to the fort where Doc can set my leg, and I'll go along with any report you want to write up." Casemore grinned. "Course, you might have to play my orderly for the next couple of days—help me mount my horse, cook my meals for me, simple thinks like that."

Captain Harding grinned. "I'd thought of leaving you out here with Oliver, but you're so damn mean you'd probably hop all the way back to the fort alone and on one foot. I guess I can be your orderly for a couple of days."

He went to Oliver's two army mounts and checked the gold. The bags were stuffed with gold double eagles. He freed the mount and lifted into the saddle of one, then rode slowly over to where Casemore lay.

"I'll go get our horses. We might as well get half a day's ride in before it gets dark. You up to moving a few miles down the trail?"

An hour later they were riding slowly back down the trail toward Fort Comfort. Every step of the trip bounced Casemore's leg and sent rivers of pain into his brain, but he wasn't about to complain. He was alive. Behind him on the third lead horse, Oliver was spread face down over his saddle, his hands and feet tied together under the mount's belly.

Harding grimaced at the hot sun as he moved along the trail. They would drop off Oliver two hour's ride from Fort Comfort and send out a burial detail. Then he would tackle Major Zachery and the gold problem. He thought he could win it and let Oliver's people live in peace.

He looked northwest.

Up there somewhere his baby girl was a captive of the Comanche. He would not rest until he found the right combination of information and troop movement to have another chance to attack the Eagle Band of the Comanches. This time he would do it right. He would slip in on the Indians quietly, and alone. He would find his daughter and slip away before they knew he was there!

It had to work.

It was his dream, it was his very reason for living. He would get his daughter back from the Comanches or he would die trying!

COMANCHE MASSACRE

1

Captain Colt Harding kicked the big black army gelding in the flanks and drove him forward through the darkness of the gently flowing West Texas prairie. A night hawk screamed somewhere to the right. His scouts told him they were getting close. Another hour of riding and they would leave their horses and move up.

Colt Harding's moonlit face showed tough and stern. He had been watching this band of Comanches for a week. They had found a small herd of buffalo and stopped for an early hunt. Now the Second Cavalry out of Fort Comfort moved in to rout the hostiles. The Daily Report showed that the date was August 14, 1867.

Captain Harding rode at the front of his forty man "Lightning" company, a fast strike force he had put together that could cover as much ground in a day as any Comanche. His troopers were ready to fight at the end of a sixteen-hour, sixty-five mile ride.

His selected men were tough, hardened, the best shots from all the troopers at Fort Comfort, and they had earned the right to be members of this elite group. They were the best in this section of the famous Second Cavalry. He had hand selected them from the four companies at the fort and created a new unit. Some men didn't want to leave their old company, but the lure of something new and good caught their imagination.

For years the Indians had ridiculed the Pony Soldier for his slow footed mounts, his bugles announcing to the enemy that he was having mess, or going to bed, or getting ready to move, and then the lumbering, slow wagons they always brought along. The Indian traveled light and fast, living off the land.

Now Captain Harding's Lightning force did much the same. No supply wagons trailed his troop. No sabers were allowed, no bugles, no tents for officers or enlisted, and every man carried his own food supply for six, eight or ten days. He took another page from the Indian warfare book.

He brought along five Tonkawa Indians as scouts and hunters. Two of the braves worked ahead, tracking the enemy and picking out the best route for the troop. The other three Indians were free to use their own ponies and only bow and arrow to hunt for food for the company as it rode forward.

On one long trip the Lightning Company had covered seventy-five miles in one day. Few Indian ponies could do better.

Captain Colt Harding was not sure if this was the specific Comanche band he wanted, but any Comanche was fair game. He had been hunting Walking White Eagle and his band for three months now, ever since the chief and a raiding party had caught an army supply wagon train and wiped out all but one on board. The only life spared was that of Sadie Harding, age four, who had been captured and taken away.

Colt Harding wanted his daughter back. The same band had raped and killed his wife, Milly, and cut down his son Yale, who was only six. His family had been on the way from Austin to live on the post with him. Their covered wagon had been attached to the army train with an escort for safety.

Captain Harding had more than a score to settle with the Comanche, and especially the chief called White Eagle!

Captain Harding pulled up sharply as the lead scout materialized out of the darkness ahead. He held one hand high, palm toward the riders.

They stopped and Colt walked his black up to the Indain scout who spoke some English.

"Dismount, walk," the small Tonkawa said. His tribe had "gone to the blanket" on an informal reservation. About ten families lived near the fort and the braves served as guides and scouts for the army.

Captain Harding gave a soft command and the men behind him dismounted. They left three horse guards who tied the mounts together and picketed them by sixes.

The Cavalrymen, more used to fighting from horseback than the ground, grouped around their captain in the dimness. Colt lifted his big pocket watch to catch the moonlight. He checked the location of the Big Dipper and grunted.

"Damn near two A.M.," he said to the men. "We're on schedule. It's about a mile to the Comanche camp. We don't want to take any chances waking them up. We'll spread out when we find the camp and each man pick a tipi and do the job. Remember, check for a five-year-old girl with long yellow hair. If Sadie is in there, I don't want her scratched. We get her out first!"

Captain Harding stared at them a moment in the dim light. "I just pray to God that this is the band that has Sadie. Let's go do it!"

They moved out quietly, hiking the mile in a column of fours much the way they would ride. There was no grumbling in the ranks. They had been trained to move without a sound. No jangling spurs, no coins clinking, no metal clanking on metal. They moved Indian quiet, as Capt. Harding called it.

Every trooper had a Spencer seven-shot rifle. The Spencers didn't have the range some of the longer rifles did, but they could throw out a hail of lead better than any weapon on the market.

A hundred and forty rounds was standard ammunition issue for each trooper to carry. The Lightning members carried two hundred and eighty, and twice the ration, or sixty rounds, for their pistols. About half of them had fourteen inch bayonets on the end of their long gun, and a good fighting knife on their cartridge belt. They were ready.

The lead scout held up his hand and the men stopped behind him. It was still dark, the moon coming in and out behind scattered clouds that scudded to the east.

When they were within five hundred yards of the camp, they came over a small hill and saw the village with a few thin streams of smoke coming from twelve tipis below along a small stream.

The scouts signaled to wait and they moved

forward to check for lookouts or guards. Five minutes later they were back.

"No guards," the lead scout said.

Captain Harding gave the signal for the men to spread out in a line of skirmishers. They were five yards apart as they moved silently down the slope toward the sleeping Indians.

Sgt. Richard Casemore watched his end of the line and motioned three men to move up quicker. There was no talking as the men marched Indian-quiet down the hill.

They had instructions. It was to be a "silent attack" as long as possible. They would use knife and bayonet. Not until the Indians raised a war cry or they fired the first shot were the troopers allowed to use their firearms.

Sgt. Casemore and a private slipped into the tipi at the far end of the camp. A smoldering fire blazed up with the gust of air from the entry flap. A brave lifted up still half asleep. Sgt. Casemore bayonetted him in the chest, yanked the blade out and hit him in the face with a butt stroke of his 47-inch-long Spencer repeater.

A woman darted at him. He slashed her with his knife, then plunged it into her chest through a breast.

Pvt. Vorhees caught up a pair of buffalo robes on a low bed against the wall of the tipi. A ten-year-old boy lay there sleeping. Vorhees slit his throat with his fighting knife and moved to the next pile of buffalo robes. There were no more Indians in the tipi.

Sgt. Casemore motioned outside and they ran to the next tipi only to find two troopers coming out of it, one laughing softly, the other, a recruit who was on his first action with the Lightning troop, looked sickly green even in the dim light. He rushed to one side and threw up.

A piercing Indian war cry shattered the silence of the Texas creek bottom. The cry was repeated again and again from other parts of the camp as the Indians came alert.

Rifles and pistols thundered inside and outside the tipis. A brave ran from the next tipi toward the horses. Sgt. Casemore led him with his pistol and hit him in the side. The Comanche went down and tried to get up once, then flopped down and didn't move.

Everyone was screaming and shooting. Sgt. Casemore figured it would be a miracle if at least two of the troop were not killed by friendly fire. He rushed from one tipi to the next. Most were deathly silent.

He came out of one and looked back at the Indian he had shot on the run. The brave was not there. The savage must have been faking his wound. He was gone.

Sergeant Casemore pointed at three privates.

"You three, over there beyond that brush. Go find their horses and don't let them get away. Go now!"

The three trotted away.

At the other end of the camp, just as the attack began, Captain Harding and a private slipped into the farthest tipi. They let their eyes adjust to the dark interior. The gust of outside air brought two adults upright among their buffalo robes.

Captain Harding grunted with pent-up hatred as he drove his bayonet toward the Comanche brave. The man twisted but the bayonet struck him in the side, daggering under his arm directly into his heart. The brave gave a small cry and fell dead.

The private slashed at a small Indian woman who brandished a knife. He jumped back and then slammed ahead with the butt of his rifle, crushing her skull.

Two children whimpered to one side. Captain Harding ran to them, threw off the robes, but found only a pair of Indian children under five.

"Kill them!" he spat at the private and ran out of the tipi flap. He charged the next tipi just as Corporal Nellington ran inside. A brave had started to come out. His knife caught the corporal in the side.

Before the trooper could react, Captain Harding's knife drove four inches into the brave's neck. A geyser of blood sprayed from the wound, painting all three of them. Slowly the brave sagged, then fell away.

Corporal Nellington staggered. Harding caught him and looked at the blade in his side.

"Easy boy, take it easy. Sit down over here." He eased the trooper to the ground. "Take your kerchief off and fold it into a pad. I'm going to pull that blade out and you put the pad over the wound and press it tight. You do that and you'll be just fine. You hear?"

There was no shooting yet. All was quiet in the camp except for a grunt and a gush of the final breath as another Comanche died.

Corporal Nellington nodded. Harding pulled the knife free. It had penetrated only two inches. The Captain saw the compress held in place, then he ran on inside the tipi.

A woman fitted an arrow in a bow and started to draw the string. Captain Harding charged, batted away the bow and bayonetted her in the chest.

"Your people killed my wife!" he hissed at her.

13

A second woman came from the side with a knife before he could jerk out the bayonet. He ducked under her charge, slammed his fist into her belly, then jolted the knife from her right hand by grabbing her wrist and elbow and breaking her arm over his thrust up knee.

She cried out and he smashed a backhanded blow against her face, driving her to the side.

The piercing Comanche war cry came then and was repeated again and again. The woman with the broken arm below him screamed the cry. Shots thundered around the camp.

Captain Harding pulled his service pistol and shot the woman once in the chest, then hurried around the tipi. He found three children, one only a baby. He shook his head, holstered his weapon and hurried out.

He saw only a few Indians running. They were quickly cut down by the sharpshooters.

Suddenly there were no more targets. The clouds shifted off the moon and they could all see better.

Sgt. Casemore sent teams into the tipis to check each one. The men were to look for wounded and living and dispatch all quickly, and count the dead.

A half dozen shots slammed through the early morning quietness as the troopers went about their grim task.

Captain Harding ran from tipi to tipi. Nowhere did he find one with the giant eagle's head painted on it, the symbol of Walking White Eagle. He found the largest tipi—it would be the chief's—the leader's.

Inside he saw only the dead. One brave and three women, and four children. All the small ones were Indian. He shuddered, then left the place.

Sgt. Casemore waited for him outside.

"We've checked every tipi, Captain. Sadie just isn't here. My men report that one brave got away. The rest of the Comanche will know you mean business now. They'll know we can fight the same way they can and show no mercy."

Captain Harding nodded. The rush of emotion was gone. The killing lust had been washed away with blood. His vengeance was dulled.

So much killing!

But the Comanche had asked for it!

So many dead!

Not a fraction of the number the Comanche kill!

The children!

Comanche love to swing white babies by the heels, bashing their brains out!

He turned away. "Very good, Sergeant Casemore. Destroy everything here. Start by burning down each of the tipis. It works best to start the fire inside along the walls."

Captain Harding walked back up the hill thirty yards away from the nearest tipi and sat down.

Why did he feel so old? He was thirty-two and felt right now like he was a hundred. Sgt. Casemore would take a body count without being told. He was a veteran.

He watched as the nearest tipi began to smoke out the smoke hole at the top, then one whole wall burst into flames. The carefully-stitched-together tanned buffalo hides made a crackling, hot fire. They burned the tipi poles in half and soon the whole structure fell in on itself.

Any bodies inside would be cremated.

Just as well.

The sons of bitches had asked for it!

He watched another and then another tipi surge into flames until all twelve of them were blazing. Captain Harding called his orderly, Corporal Swenson. They had become separated in the fighting. Swenson had to pass the riding and shooting tests the same as the other troopers to win his place in the unit.

"Lance, see that Marlin takes care of our wounded. Then bring me a count of the casualties. I didn't see any of our men killed, did you?"

"No, sir, but several were wounded." He saluted smartly to a half hearted wave, and left at once.

Colt Harding stared at the burning tipis. Leave them nothing to live in—no tipis, no robes, no food, no horses. Destroy them utterly! They had asked for it! The fires below burned together, some tipis falling sideways onto others.

In the firelight he could see the drying racks where fresh buffalo meat had been cut into strips and hung in the sun to dry. They must have had a good hunt yesterday. Everyone hunts and butchers in a tribe. Everyone was tired this night.

Everyone died, all but one.

He shook his head to clear it. That was his job, killing the hostiles. He would report the attack, detail his methods and wait for any criticism from the brass. He did not follow procedures, but he wiped out an entire band of Comanche—did not just kill two bucks and chase the rest for a hundred miles and never see them again.

He had not followed procedures. He knew he was supposed to do it the way the army had been doing things for a hundred years.

16

Maybe that's why the Indian was making fools of the army.

No, he couldn't say that. He had found a way to beat the Indians without massive sweeps and thousands of troopers, cannons, wagons, and long supply lines.

He put his chin on his hands that rested on his knees. Perhaps if he closed his eyes for just a few minutes.

"Sir!"

Captain Harding stirred, his chin came off his hands and he looked at his orderly. He saw him silhouetted against an almost daylight sky.

"Sir, Sergeant Casemore has a report."

The First Sergeant of the Lightning troop came up the last ten yards and saluted his commander.

"Sir, we have five wounded. One trooper is dead, Private Ben Zedicher. He was surprised by three braves when he entered a tipi just after the first war cry."

"Enemy dead?"

"We counted forty-nine bodies, sir, before the fires began. That was thirty-one . . . ."

"I don't want a breakdown, Sergeant. Make the report read that forty-nine Comanche were killed in the attack, twelve tipis destroyed and the rest of the village. How many horses?"

"We've captured a hundred and twelve horses, sir, and fifteen mules. Included in that figure are seven branded U.S. army remounts."

"Noted, Sergeant." Captain Harding looked down at the smoking ruins of the camp. "I want everything destroyed. Don't leave one stick another Indian can use. The drying racks should be burned, the meat thrown in the river.

"Save a bale of the jerky. We'll test it on the

17

way home. The rest of it burn or dump in the stream. Crush every cooking pot, kettle and clay dish you find. Nothing is to be left!"

"Yes, sir."

Captain Harding looked up.

"Sir, I've taken the liberty of sending for our mounts. The men could use a day of rest if it's all right with the captain?"

"Yes, right. When we're done here, pick out a camp upstream half a mile and we'll catch up on our sleep. Tomorrow morning we'll head back to the fort."

Cpl. Marlin came by a short time later with a medical report. Only one man was in serious condition, but he could ride.

"We had one dead, sir."

"Yes, we'll have to bury him here. I'll read a service at sundown. Have two men dig a grave. I want it six feet deep."

"Yes, sir."

Captain Colt Harding watched the final destruction of the camp as it grew light. Nothing remained. Tipi poles not burned completely were set on fire to help burn the bales of jerky and more robes that were found.

Bastards gonna find out we can fight as dirty as they do!

He looked the other way, down the small stream, along the little valley to the rolling hills. Texas.

Goddamn Texas! It had stolen away his family! It had killed Milly and Yale. It had kidnapped little Sadie!

He looked north and west. Up there somewhere must be his little baby girl. Somewhere, and with the savages. He prayed that she had not been harmed. Comanches did terrible things to slaves sometimes.

I'm coming, baby! I'm going to rescue you!

He looked down at his hands. His hands and arms, even his face was still red with the savages' blood. He went to the stream to wash away the blood and came back for a clean shirt. It was one of the few luxuries he allowed himself on his ride. It would soon be time for the men to eat their breakfast.

He wondered if any of them would be hungry. For just a moment he thought of how furious he had been when he killed that last Indian woman. Then he turned away. He couldn't think about that. They had brought it on themselves.

2

Captain Colt Harding did let the men rest
upstream from the site of the ruined Indian camp.
As usual after a deadly battle, the five Tonkawa
scouts were nowhere to be seen. Captain Harding
did not even think about what they were doing.

The other Indians on the plains called the
Tonkawas the People Eaters. They were. Right
now they were up in the hills somewhere having a
feast, steaks or a stew or at least soup made from
parts of one of their mortal enemies, the
Comanche.

They would be back in a day or two, happy,
eyes sparkling, making small jokes among themselves. They would ride in and assume their
duties as if they hadn't been away. A curious
mixture of savage and civilized man.

At first Captain Harding had forbidden the
Tonks from any "soup." But soon he realized it
was an impossible order to enforce. Now he tried
to ignore them.

The morning after the attack on the Comanche
camp, the Lightning troop began the homeward

journey. There was no great rush going this direction and they moved about thirty miles a day.

Three days later, Captain Harding had the report he was going to write on the attack well in mind. All he had to do was put it down on paper. The tough part would be what the people over at the headquarters of the Department of Texas in San Antonio had to say about it.

Colt Harding was not a huge man. He stood just a little over six feet tall and weighed one hundred and eighty-five pounds. He was lean and fit, with short cropped brown hair, brown eyes under heavy brows. Lately he had gone to wearing a thick, full moustache. He liked it.

Colt had been in the military all his life. Just out of high school in New York, he had won an appointment to West Point. He graduated in 1860, just in time to get a year of experience before the onslaught of the Civil War. He had been a company commander and quickly rose to bird colonel rank before the war was over, getting in on some of the bloodiest battles in that epic struggle.

Because of his West Point background he was reduced in rank only to captain at the end of the war. He saw many of his friends cut down to lieutenant and even master sergeant as the war machine with over two million men was reduced to about twenty-five thousand. His record was part of the reason he held his rank. The army wanted him to stay in. They would need good officers with experience.

Now after eight years in the army he was still a captain, but he knew he was on the new promotion list. He could only wait for the middle of December and pray.

Captain Harding led the troopers into Fort Comfort after the three day march. Their guideon with the special lightning bolt and the Second Cavalry emblem flew smartly. The men were not tired and made a grand entrance. The rest of the troopers were there to greet them.

Fort Comfort was still being built, but it was already a substantial anchor for the defense of Western Texas. The fort stood near the White River a hundred and twenty miles west of Austin.

It was officially a "wilderness" fort, since there were no settlers or ranchers within sixty or seventy miles of the place. It was not near any trails west, but the army decided there should be a defensive fort there to help ward off the active Comanche war and raiding parties, so the fort went up.

Usually there were about two hundred men stationed at the fort. They had four companies, including the newly formed Lightning troop, and not all were full. As usual they were short on officers, and greatly short on officers with experience fighting Indians.

Fort Comfort was built in the form of a square. Three of the sides were finished, made of tough, practical native Texas clay and straw that the Texans called adobe. It was formed in boxes and set out to harden in the hot Texas sun. When baked dry the large brown slabs were almost as tough as red bricks.

The adobe bricks were eighteen inches long and four thick. They were laid up with adobe mortar into a wall two feet thick that would stop any rifle bullet, and probably a five inch cannonball.

Inside walls of Fort Comfort were a foot thick

with timbers spanning a 24-foot wide reach to the outer wall. This formed large rooms around the whole square.

Each side of the fort was about 300 feet long. Roofs consisted of tar paper over roofing lumber, and then a foot thick layer of soil on top of the paper and that covered with native wood.

The outside fort wall was three feet higher than the roof to afford troopers a parapet to fire over if they needed to.

One of the corners of the quad was not finished yet. It would eventually be home for the tack room, the fort smithy, inside stables, and the future sutler's store. The south side of the wall had the stable entrance that let the horses into the paddock that extended the full 300 feet along the fort's south wall.

Four strands of barbed wire and sturdy posts kept the stock controlled in the paddock.

Now Captain Harding rode through the main gate, took the sentry's salute and turned the troop over to Sgt. Casemore. He rode directly across the parade ground and past the tall flag pole in the center to the west side of the compound which was "officer country."

Harding stepped down from his black, gave the reins to Cpl. Swenson and walked into his Fort Comfort Officer's quarters.

The whole west side of the fort was assigned to officers, their quarters and their families. Married and single officers lived here. There had been only three married officers on the post when he left.

The north side of the fort was enlisted men's quarters with the barracks, a day room and the mess in the far corner. Around the corner on the east side of the fort stood the kitchen, the ordinance shops, guardhouse and quartermaster and his supplies. On the roof over the quartermaster stood the guard lookout tower.

Beyond the gate was the partly finished area of the sutler's store. When the rest of the southeast corner of the fort was finished it would hold the new sutler's store and the inside stables and additional quarters for married enlisted men and guests.

Captain Harding dropped his cartridge belt on the desk in his office room, and continued on into his private quarters. For a moment he expected to hear Milly's sweet voice and the strident young voices of his children . . . .

He slumped in his chair, his hands over his face for a moment.

"Damnit, damnit, damnit!" he said, each word with more force and more anger. Then he gave a long sigh. One day at a time. That was all he could count on now. Slowly he settled down. He would go out to the office, check for dispatches and new orders, then have a long hot bath and a big dinner and a long night's sleep.

Two packets had come from Austin while he had been gone. Lt. Riddle, his adjutant, had laid them out neatly on his desk. On top of them was a single sheet of paper.

"Finally got that new captain for A Company. Arrived three days after you left. His name is Morse Kenny. He came from artillery, and just did two years in San Antonio at our department headquarters. Guess I'm going to have to go to San Antonio to get my promotion."

That was another job Colt knew he had to do, get John his captain bars. He was long overdue. A fort this size needed a captain to be adjutant.

Of course it also needed at least a major to be commander.

He sorted through the dispatches. Mostly routine. Nothing that couldn't wait. Cpl. Swenson came in. He had washed up and changed his shirt, ready for work. He was a good man. As soon as there was approval for another sergeant on the post, Swenson got the stripe.

"Lance, look these things over and sort them out for me, would you? I'm heading for a long bath."

"Yes sir. Oh, I have a message for you from Doc, er Captain Jenkins." He handed Colt a folded piece of paper. "I'll get some bath water hot for you, sir."

Colt Harding opened the hand written note.

"Colt: Lt. Young and I invite you to supper at the Youngs tonight at six. The new captain, his wife and daughter will be on hand for introductions. Hear you provided me with some work on five troopers. See you tonight."

Colt nodded. Just as well meet them now and then get back to work. He had to whip the whole fort into shape for a visit by Colonel Sparkman, their Texas Department Commander. He was coming in October and already it was September 14, 1868. Damn, the time slid past so quickly!

He had a few minutes until the wood fire heated the copper boiler on top of the kitchen stove. Someday he wanted one of those stoves that had the water pipes running through the firebox! That heated water faster than you would think possible.

Two hours later, he stepped up to the Youngs' door and knocked.

Second Lt. Ned Young opened the barrier.

"Captain Harding, glad you could come. Right this way. We were about to have a taste of sherry before dinner."

Harding stepped into the all too familiar officer's quarters. Each of the ten provided was identical except for his own.

A tall thin man across the room stood stiffly at attention. He had a short haircut, the briefest of a thin moustache, and steely gray eyes. Colt liked the man at once.

"Captain Harding, permit me to introduce you to Captain Morse Kenny," Lt. Young said. "Captain Kenny, our Fort Commander, Captain Harding."

Kenny unfroze, smiled and stepped forward and took the hand that Colt offered. The handshake was firm, honest. Colt liked that about him, too.

"Captain Kenny, good to have you with us, finally. I understand you know something about artillery."

"Afraid so. That won't help much here. But I've had a good basic background in cavalry. Commanding a cavalry company is at least my second favorite job in the army. As you know if a man can get even his third choice he's lucky."

The men all laughed. To the side stood the women. Now Captain Kenny motioned that way.

"Captain, may I introduce you to the best army wife this side of Chicago, my wife, Ruth. Ruth, this is Captain Harding."

Colt saw a plain woman, on the small and short side, with a shy smile that helped brighten her face. She nodded and curtsied but did not offer her hand.

"Mrs. Kenny, good to meet you. We've been

waiting three months for the army to decide to send us someone and we are delighted. About time this post had some pretty ladies about."

She nodded again but said nothing.

"The young lady next to Ruth is our daughter, just turned eighteen, Pamela. She'll be with us only a few months before she goes to her aunt's home in Boston where she'll be attending college, of all things. Pamela, this is our commander, Captain Harding."

Pamela was slender with a tight fitting dress that showed her off well. She stared straight at Colt and he found her gaze slightly disturbing, challenging. Then she smiled and her face softened into beauty.

"Captain Harding, we've heard so much about you. Is it true you're developing a whole new tactic for Indian fighting? This Lightning unit of yours sounds fascinating."

She stepped forward and held out her hand.

"It's good to meet you, Miss Kenny. However, I'm afraid that I never talk tactics at a social occasion."

He took her hand and shook it gently then let go. But even as he did there was a spark of electricity that jolted through him. This was a most unusual girl.

"That's my Pamela," Captain Kenny said, steering Colt toward the sherry. "I guess all my army talk over the past eighteen years has had an effect on her."

Soon they had dinner, prepared by Mrs. Young. She was a fine cook, and what she did with the issue rations was remarkable. She had used some of her precious canned goods, Captain Harding was sure. He would see that her supply was replaced from the mess.

It was an enjoyable meal. The men talked over cigars after supper, and Colt further discovered things about Morse Kenny that he liked. He was sure that A Company was in good hands. Now all he had to do was get four more officers and he would be nearly up to strength.

Each of his three companies had only one officer each. The regulations called for "one or two" and he always liked two. He had no officer for his Lightning troop, which he commanded himself. He might keep it that way, at least until he got some response from San Antonio about his highly unusual methods of Indian fighting.

Colt begged off early after dinner, and Doc walked him back toward his quarters.

"I like this Kenny," Captain Dr. Jim Jenkins said. He was forty-one years old, had a grown family and his wife was with a sister in the east. Doc liked it that way.

Colt nodded. "Seems to be a good man. I like the way he sits his saddle. We'll get along well together." He paused. "That girl of his is going to be another matter. I'd guess she's a bit on the wild side."

"You noticed. She isn't subtle at all, is she?" Doc rubbed his jaw. "Yes, Colt. I'd say within two weeks we'll be having some kind of problem with Miss Pamela." He hurried on. "Not with me. I'm a married man. Young and Edwards are, too. Lieutenant Riddle is as well. Doesn't leave her much of a field."

"A girl like Pamela will find a way," Colt said, realizing it was true.

Pamela Kenny had been bored at the dinner. Not a man in sight she could talk to, or flirt with.

She smiled as she slipped out of her knee length drawers and stood in her bedroom for a moment absolutely naked. It was a glorious feeling.

Gently she let her hands rub up from her flat little belly to her large breasts. Oh yes! It wouldn't be long before she would have someone help her do that. Just rub and pet her breasts until she almost exploded!

She slipped into her nightgown. A week. She would give herself a week to pick out a target. Once she had selected the man, she would begin to court him, without him or her parents or anyone on the post knowing!

She giggled when she thought about all the fiddle faddle her mother and father spouted about the difference between the enlisted men and the officers.

After spending all her life on army posts, she still couldn't find a bit of difference. Well there was one. There always were a lot more enlisted, and almost none of them were married! This was going to be an interesting assignment for her father—and for her!

The next morning, Pamela dressed carefully. She chose her brown calico with buttons up the front. It was so tight it almost hurt, but it showed off her breasts delightfully. She pinched in the waist and pinned it in back so the small safety pins wouldn't show. It gave her a curvy figure she knew would bring stares. Pamela just loved to be looked at.

By ten o'clock she had found her way around to her father's A Company office. It was a small room where the company records were kept, and a corporal sat helping with the army paperwork. Her father and Cpl. Vic Gregory were going over the rosters and assignments.

"Daddy, you could at least introduce me," Pamela said after she walked in and Victor stood up, but her father only waved and went back to work.

"Oh, sorry. Corporal Gregory, this is my daughter Pamela, Corporal Victor Gregory, our company clerk.

He stood and nodded, but when she held out her hand, he took it and held it a bit too long.

"Yes, now, Corporal, we have a lot of work to do. Pamela, nice of you to visit. You should be helping your mother with the unpacking."

"She wanted me to tell you dinner will be promptly at 12:15."

He ushered her out, but not before Pamela had managed to wink at the corporal when her father couldn't see her. All the way back to her quarters, Pamela memorized Cpl. Gregory's features, the shy little way he grinned, his soft blue eyes and brown hair. He was tall, not as tall as her father, but plenty tall. He was a little on the slight side.

For one quick hot moment she wondered how he would look naked. She put her hand over her face for a second, giggled and hurried on to her quarters, where she flew into the unpacking.

Dr. Jim Jenkins checked the last of his five patients. He had no real infirmary, only two unused visitors' quarters he had commandeered. Two of the wounded would be released as fit for duty tomorrow, but the other two were more serious.

Cpl. Nellington had taken a deep stab wound. He was lucky the savage's blade missed all vital parts, only grazed his small intestine and slid a millimeter past his lung. He would need two weeks of rest.

Jenkins put his feet up on an ammo box and stared at the wall. His wife, Etta, would be going to some tea this afternoon. Then perhaps a bridge or whist game tonight. He had spent enough time at both to last him forever. When he got this Texas assignment out of San Antonio, he had urged Etta to go back to Philadelphia and stay with her sister.

He was glad he did. Yes, he missed her, but his sexual needs were muted now. A once a month romp with one of the laundry women kept him in line, and helped out her finances.

He had tried to talk to Etta about this side of him, but it was simply not the sort of thing he could do, nor would Etta have understood. To her, sex was something done in the dark, in their bedroom, only at night, preferably with her eyes closed and flat on her back with a grimace on her face. A duty not a pleasure.

Poor Etta.

He grinned, but not so poor him. He sobered, thinking about Pamela. She was a pretty girl, ripe for picking, and from what he saw tonight eager to get on with learning about sex. She was going to be trouble, he knew it.

At least it wouldn't affect him. He walked over to his wards and checked the men in the beds. Three of them were sleeping. Nellington still had a lot of pain. Doc dug out a pair of sugar pills and had Nellington take them with a glass of water. The water would do more than the pills to settle him down. Amazing sometimes how a placebo would help.

He watched the ward for ten minutes and when he left, Nellington had dropped off to sleep.

Back at his quarters, Colt Harding lit the lamp on his big desk and looked over the roster. One more officer, that would help. He needed at least two more good officers. And he wanted John Riddle to get his captain's bars. He was due.

He would put another promotion request through tomorrow. He stood in front of a big map of Western Texas and put a red topped pin at the approximate location where they had wiped out the small band of Comanches.

Others pins showed on the map. One was the Wagon Wheel Massacre where his wife and son had died. He had thirteen blue pins there for the troopers who had also died. Large, yellow headed thumbtacks showed frequent sightings of Comanche bands. There were a dozen yellow tacks indicating hunting grounds, hunting camps, summer camps and two for winter camps where the Comanche felt the most safe.

He searched the area, wondering where White Eagle and his band were camped. He'd give six months' pay to know for sure where they were. At least he was learning a lot about Indians on this campaign. He had talked at length to Hatchet, one of the lead scouts from the Tonkawa who could speak some English.

Most of the plains Indians did little during the winter except try to stay warm and have enough to eat. They found safe winter camps with plenty of wood and water in a faraway spot and nearly hibernated for the winter. There was no fighting, no raids, no attacks during winter.

In the spring they left their winter camps to find fresh grazing for their herds of horses and to find new hunting areas. They nourished themselves and their horses into the best of health, and by

May or June were ready to make war on an enemy tribe, to raid another tribe to capture women and children, or to raid the white eyes for women and horses.

Early summer was the time for raiding and war. This period was the glory time for the braves and lasted all summer. Most of the Comanche bands moved often, sometimes twice a week, searching for grazing and new hunting grounds.

When fall came the plains Indians suddenly called a stop to inter-tribal warfare. Their warriors did not kill white eye settlers or ride for women and horses.

Almost by agreement the Indians said, enough war, it is time to go hunting and lay in our winter's food supply. Sometimes, mortal enemies in the spring and summer would battle the mighty buffalo side by side without a harsh word spoken.

Hunting continued as long as the winter food supply was not adequate, or until the shaggy buffalo wandered too far out of the reach of the tribe.

Then the tribe went to a new winter camp, snuggled down in their tipis, found wood for their fires and hoped that the food lasted until spring.

Winter! The ideal time to attack the Indian! Catch him when all of the warriors were at their ease on winter camp. Hit them in all their winter camps and wipe out the whole Comanche nation!

Eventually he would find the White Eagle band, and Sadie, and he would have his little girl home again!

3

Walking White Eagle stood looking across the land that had been Comanche hunting grounds for as long as the old men and their fathers' fathers could remember. He had brought his Eagle band high in the Texas plains, even above the Red River, where the white eye and the Pony Soldiers never came.

He needed peace and a resting time. Time for his band to get back to the old ways and to live as their fathers did, fearing no one, ready to ride and battle with any other Indian tribe.

White Eagle wanted a few months without worry of the white eye captain and his Pony Soldiers in blue shirts.

Even after the surprise attack by the Pony Soldiers, his band was strong and had grown again until now he had more than forty tipis scattered along the tributary of the Red River. He had found a small, virgin valley, where he figured that no Comanche band had made camp in for two men's lives.

The grass was lush and nourishing for the

ponies. The stream bright, chattering and pure.
The sky was so blue he knew it was coming to the
crisp fall days. There were still many berries,
some crab apples and even a few wild walnut
trees someone had planted long ago. And there
was more game than they had seen in months.

His band had been grievously wounded by the
attack by the Pony Soldiers and the captain who
wore two pearl handled shoot-many-times-short-
guns. They had lost twelve warriors, and several
women and children in the attack by Pony
Soldiers two months ago.

It had been a terrible defeat. Only the softness
of the victors had prevented the losses from being
shattering. If the Pony Soldiers had killed the
women and children they captured and then had
destroyed the tipis, robes and all the food
supplies, it would have been a true disaster.

But the Pony Soldiers had not learned to fight
the way a Comanche fights. The women and
children were spared as was the camp. Now they
were rebuilding their strength.

The winter hunt would be coming soon, the last
hunt before the demons of winter whistled down
out of the hills and tried to bury their tipis in
Mother Earth's blanket of new snow.

Another week and they would start their hunt.
The buffalo were plentiful in this region, more so
than farther south. It would be a good hunt and
he prayed to the gods for a short and a mild
winter.

Sadie Harding, who now thought of herself
more as Laughing Golden Hair, her Comanche
name, sat in the soft grass outside the big tipi
with the head of an eagle painted on the side.

The sun was warm on her bare back here in

White Eagle's camp. She had two sisters to play with now that she and her mother, Cries In The Morning, had moved into the big lodge with the chief and his family. It was the way of The People. Everyone helped take care of everyone else.

Their old tipi had been given to a warrior and his family who had theirs destroyed by the Pony Soldiers in the surprise raid. For a moment Sadie felt a twinge of doubt. Should she have run to meet the Pony Soldiers when they came? Were they trying to find her to take her back to her beautiful mother and her father who was also a Pony Soldier?

She was confused. Cries In The Morning had been good and kind to her these last three months. She realized that she had never been spanked or scolded since she came to the Comanche camp. The Indian children seemed to do almost anything they wanted to. There was no problem with them.

The Indian children she knew enjoyed their days, played, learned to do what they needed to do to help support the band, but had fun all the time.

How long had she been here now? She thought it had been about three months. She had been through at least three full moons. She remembered that because Cries In The Morning was fascinated with the full moon. She sat outside one night watching it from moonrise until it set early the next morning.

In three months she had learned many Comanche words. She had to just to survive. Now she felt hot and sticky, and ran to the stream and sat with her feet in the cool water.

The September days were still warm, but there was a touch of winter in the air nights and mornings. Soon the snow would come and Laughing Golden Hair wondered what she would do then. How would she stay warm? How did you stay warm in only a tent?

Every time they moved, she had been surprised how much work her mother and the other women did. They did *all the work*! White Eagle explained to her one day that the warriors must be ready at all times to defend and protect the village.

Tradition had built up that the warriors stood at the outer circle of the tipis, with their bows and lances, and now their guns, as the move began.

The women packed up everything in rawhide boxes, and bundles, took down the tipi and formed the travois and packed everything on board. It was simply the way of The People.

Young boys were in charge of the horses. They brought the riding mounts to the women and girls, then drove the spare horses and mules up to the line of march. They were the drovers for the trip, when they weren't playing at being warriors, raiding the village as the women finished their packing, or making a nuisance of themselves.

But the women did not complain when a pretend raid by six teenage boys knocked down meat drying racks, scattered children or disrupted the camp's routine. The young boys were developing the skills and talents they needed before they could become warriors. In a few years the same boisterous boys would be defending the whole camp!

Sadie fingered her braided hair. Soon she would wash it again, let it fly into a blonde halo around her head. She loved her hair loose and blowing in the wind. But Cries In The Morning silently shook her head, chattered about how hair was made to be combed, oiled and braided. Besides, it was less bother braided, and did not get in the way of the many duties of a woman.

A half dozen other small girls ran up and urged Laughing Golden Hair to come with them. They were going down by the bend in the stream where the spring runoffs had gouged out a deeper pool where they could sit neck deep in the cool water.

She went with them, thought nothing of dropping her breechclout and jumping naked into the water. Everyone did it. She splashed and dunked the girls and enjoyed herself. Then they ran shivering to the grass and lay in the bright sun letting the rays dry and warm them.

"*Hi, tai,*" one of the girls called. "Hello, friends, there are berries just over there. Let's go eat some!"

They all slipped on their breechclouts and scampered to the bushes that had a berry much like the blackberries Golden Hair had seen before. They were good.

They tired of eating the berries and drifted off. Laughing Golden Hair hurried back to the big tipi, wondering what her mother was doing. She found the small Indian woman hanging out strips of venison to dry in the sun. It was cut thin and would dry quickly. Some venison would not be pounded into pemmican for the winter, but kept in a rawhide box by itself as a treat.

The juicy meat was cut into strips eight to ten inches long, then sliced thin. The strip hung was two inches wide, ten inches long and not more than an eighth of an inch thick. This winter it would be delicious to chew on, that's what Cries

In The Morning told her.

There should be stores, Sadie thought. When her mother had run out of food, she went to the store and brought some home. She looked around. Sadie knew there were no stores here, but there should be. She would ask White Eagle where the stores were.

Before she could, her mother came and motioned for her to follow her.

"*Keemah,*" come, Cries In The Morning said, and they went outside to where the small skin of a deer lay. Together they staked it out, stretching it on the ground, then they did the final scraping on it with a sharp blade of steel that was as big as both of Sadie's hands.

Cries In The Morning carefully showed Sadie how to scrape, so she would not go through the skin, but still remove the last traces of the fat and some flesh that remained.

Then the skin would stand for a day before the tanning process began. Sadie wasn't sure what they used to tan the hides, but the mixture smelled terrible. One of the girls said that they used buffalo brains in a paste that was smeared on. Yuck!

Later Sadie brought water from the clear stream and watched her Indian mother pour some of it into a large copper pot hanging over the fire in the middle of the tipi. Already there were slabs of venison in the pot, and several leaves to flavor it.

Now Cries In The Morning asked Sadie to wash off some wild onions and take off the dried tops. When she had done so, her mother cut them in half and dropped them in the stew.

Sadie hoped there would be carrots and

potatoes as well, but she knew there would not be. The Comanche did not believe in digging in Mother Earth to plant things.

Laughing Golden Hair sat outside in the grass wondering what to do next. She had made friends with her sisters. One was called Black Bird. She was a year older than Sadie, smaller and quick, and with dancing black eyes and loved to play tricks on anyone. But she was a good friend, and they enjoyed teaching each other words.

Her other sister was Something Pretty. She was about Sadie's age and usually they were together. It had been only three months since the Pony Soldiers' raid, but already they were best friends. The other two girls were off doing something for their mothers, and Sadie was alone for a while.

She wondered if her family would ever come and find her. For a moment she relived the terrible day when the bad Indians had attacked the supply train that she, her mother and brother had been with as it drove from Austin out to Fort Comfort.

The noise had been loud, with guns and war whoops. Then an Indian had cut a hole through their wagon and her mother shot him with a pistol. But a minute later another Indian stormed into the wagon and threw her mother out, then he hurt Yale.

The tall Indian had picked up Sadie and carried her under one arm as he went through their goods in the wagon looking for something to steal. He found ribbons and cloth and jumped down from the wagon, satisfied.

Later he had tied her hands and feet together, strapping her across his back like a blanket roll.

That way he could use both hands to loot the train.

By the time the raiding Indians left, Sadie had not seen any of the soldiers alive. Her mother lay on the ground without moving. When was her father going to come and rescue her?

Just as tears began to come, a tall Indian man sat down beside her. White Eagle. He was a most important person in the group and the leader of the Eagle Band. He wore only a breechclout and moccasins. His hair was shiny black, much longer than her father's ever had been.

His face was long and narrow and frowning just a little now.

"Laughing Golden Hair, are you unhappy with The People?"

"I would like to go home," she said softly.

"Your new mother is kind to you, you live in my lodge. You have all to eat you want. What more could you ask?"

She didn't understand all of the words, but she got the idea. She had learned Comanche words as quickly as she could.

"I have a favor to ask you," White Eagle said when she did not reply to his question. "Will you teach me to speak the *tosi-tivo* words?"

"White man's words? Why?"

"Soon the day will come when there will be many white eyes here in Comanche hunting grounds. The white eye and the Comanche will have to learn to live in peace near one another. I have heard how it was with other bands of The People far to the east toward the great waters."

"If I teach you *tosi-tivo* words, will you take me to Austin and let me go free?"

White Eagle laughed. "Your mother would

never let you go. How could Cries In The Morning be happy if she lost you? She has lost her husband. If you left, too, she would sit in the dust and build her last fire and when the small fire went out, she would die with the flames."

"No, no!" Laughing Golden Hair said quickly.

"First the *tosi-tivo* words." He brought out an army pistol from his side. *"Hakai tosi-tivo?"*

"Revolver," Laughing Golden Hair said. She knew about guns. Her father always had guns in the house. Even her mother had one in the covered wagon.

He asked her other questions about the revolver. Soon he knew it had six shots, that the bullets were called shells.

"Pistol shoot six shells," he said in English and beamed. He moved on quickly asking the English words for horse, mule, Cavalry, soldier. They talked about numbers, and she taught him to count in English from one to ten.

"How many horses does White Eagle have?" she asked in English. He frowned, looked at his hands.

"Ten hands many," he said.

She giggled and told him that would be a hundred. She had been good with numbers and could count before she was three.

"You have a hundred horses? You are rich."

Then Something Pretty came and the girls raced off to play hoop ball and chase a buckskin stuffed ball.

White Eagle watched her go. Someday soon she would grow up and become the wife of a great Comanche chief. He hoped it even could be his son, only he had no son. Perhaps Talks A Lot would bear him a son. She would be due soon.

White Eagle arranged for a new set of warriors to go up to the lookouts as scouts. The importance of lookouts had been raised equal to that of warriors, war and raiding. A camp must be safe or the band could be wiped out.

That afternoon he went to the spot his horses grazed on the rich grass and whistled for Flying Wind. His new war pony ran to him quickly, nuzzled his shoulder and accepted having his ears scratched.

There should be one more raid for horses before the Comancheros came for trading. He looked at the herd. He had in his string swift paints, duns, whites, bays, claybanks, and two black Pony Soldier mounts. He could have a good trading, but he would demand rifles and pistols.

The last fight with the Pony Soldiers showed him that the old ways were good, but they could not stand up against an enemy armed with rifles and pistols. The revolvers, as he called them now. could shoot six times as fast as a brave could pull the trigger. They were a tremendous weapon.

He would bargain for more.

Now he put a loose halter on his war pony. Flying Wind was the son of his former war pony, and would be a fine replacement. But first he had more training to do.

When he rode into battle or on a raid, White Eagle wanted both hands free to attack or shoot an arrow or a rifle under Flying Wind's neck while hanging off the side. To do that he had to be able to direct the war pony only with his knees, legs and toes.

It took hours and hours of training. Two other braves worked with new ponies as well in the meadow that afternoon.

White Eagle rode his pony again and again at a good sized pecan tree next to the stream, waiting until the last moment before stopping him with only knee pressure. Then he directed the young horse to turn left or right by knee pressure on one or the other side.

Flying Wind had remembered his previous lessons well. At last White Eagle was satisfied with the colt's progress and took him to a deep growth of special grass where he munched away for half an hour.

When White Eagle came back to his tipi, there was a scurrying around like he hadn't seen in months. Always Smiling was not there. Talks A Lot did not sit in her usual place near the flap. Cries In The Morning was screeching at the three girls. There was no food cooking on the fire. A tanning project had been stopped in the middle.

Cries In The Morning shushed the girls and walked up to him.

"Talks A Lot is ready. She has gone to the birthing hut. You should be a new father shortly." Then she scurried away.

White Eagle stood a moment looking at the dying fire. Then he grinned. Before the sun went down, he just might have a son!

Cries In The Morning hurried up the new path to a quickly made hut barely six feet wide. It was made of sticks and poles, covered with leafy branches woven in. There was a roof of newly cut pecan branches. It had been built only that afternoon when the pains began. It had a kettle of water, a soft cloth, and a matt of branches covered with buffalo robes.

In the center of the hut was the birthing hole, where the newborn would drop. The hole was lined with the softest buffalo calf robe Always Smiling could find.

Only Always Smiling was inside the hut with Talks A Lot. They laughed and cried softly and talked of babies and how much trouble they were and how treasured they were by The People.

"The white eye women breed like field mice," Always Smiling said. "Why can't we have babies the way they do? I've seen their lodges with eight or ten young children in families. That's with just one wife for each man!"

"I don't care how many more children I have," Talks A Lot said. She had passed her seventeenth birthday last week. "Just so this child is a boy! If I can give White Eagle a son he will be so proud!"

Always Smiling sobered. She nodded. That was a problem she had gone through with two other women. They all had hoped for sons.

The pains came again. Talks A Lot bobbed her head. It was time. She straddled the birth hole, squatting so the newborn could come into the world straight down and into the soft fur like robe.

Always Smiling had driven a two-inch stake into the ground beside the hole. It reached up three feet and gave the new mother a firm place to grab hold for balance and to use to help her bear down.

"Sometimes the first child is slow in coming into our world," Always Smiling said. Talks A Lot wiped sweat from her forehead and moved back and sat down on the robes again.

Twice more she waddled over to the birth hole. Then the fourth time, the pains brought forth a scream and she gripped the pole hard and bore down.

A moment later her first born dropped into the birth hole. Always Smiling gathered up the infant, tended to it carefully. She held it bundled in the small robe so Talks A Lot could not see the sex of her child. She rushed the baby out to the stream where a small pool had been diverted so the water would warm in the sun.

There she bathed the perfect, screaming girl baby, and wrapped her in another robe, one of the softest fox fur, and took her back to her mother.

Cries In The Morning had hurried into the birthing hut and tended to Talks A Lot. She lay on the robes over the branches and watched the door.

"I have born a girl child," Talks A Lot said, when Always Smiling came in the door. "Otherwise there would have been much shouting and cheering. The next time I will have a son for White Eagle."

White Eagle did not rush to the birth lodge. Word spread quickly that it was a girl. A girl was of little consequence to a chief, especially to a chief who wanted a son. White Eagle sat on the grass in front of his tipi, near his shield and lance where they could be grabbed up at a moment's notice.

He was young. He would have six sons before he was too old. That's when he decided. He only had two wives after Prairie Flower had been killed in the Pony Soldier raid. He could support another. He would select a new bride soon, one who had two or more brothers. He must have a son!

4

The drums beat a steady rhythm.

The entire camp of the Eagle Band listened and the old women and young men smiled. The young girls hurried through their chores and began deciding which of their prettiest dresses they would wear. Would the soft doeskin fringed with trade beads be best, or the slightly tighter dress with two hundred elk's teeth sewn on it so they rattled with the slighest movement?

The warriors sharpened their lance points, tested their bows and wished they could make new bowstrings from spine sinew of a freshly killed buffalo. Old bowstrings could snap under stress.

A steady stream of warriors came to White Eagle's tipi. They had decided the night before that it was time to go on one more raid for ponies, white women and children before the fall hunting began. Their band could use new blood.

The ponies and horses would be for trade with the Comancheros. White Eagle would take thirty warriors with him. That left twelve warriors to guard the camp, and ten or fifteen teenagers almost ready to be warriors. It would be enough.

The dance would be good for the band. It had been months since they had something to dance about. Now they would all come together around a large campfire, and the dancers and singers would do the ceremonial steps and words to insure a productive raid and safety for all the warriors.

Just after dark the dancing began. Everyone from the band who could get to the big campfire was there—the lame, the injured even the sick. It was an event in the life of the band not to be missed.

The drums had been beating all afternoon and now the special ceremonial rhythm began and quickly the men and women dressed in their finest, formed a large circle around the leaping fire. The men stomped and danced one way around the fire; the women went the other direction.

At times the drum beat changed and then the lines stopped circling and slowly moved toward each other, barely touching whoever was opposite, then moved away and began circling again.

This slow, hypnotic dance continued for more than an hour, then a brave charged toward the fire on his war pony. He shouted a Comanche war cry, and the dancers melted back into the crowd at the edge of the firelight.

The warrior skidded his war pony to a stop at the very edge of the log where members of the council sat facing the fire. The young warrior was Elk Wound, a twenty-three-year-old man who had fought with White Eagle against the Pony

Soldiers in the last skirmish.

He reared his horse up on its back feet and when they came down he shouted the Comanche war cry again. He jumped up and stood on his pony's back, arms crossed.

"We will ride tomorrow as the wind sweeps across the plains. We will strike with the cunning of a fox, and the bravery of a rattlesnake. We will strike our enemies before they know we are there and return home with wonderful presents for everyone!"

Elk Wound went on for aother two or three minutes, explaining in detail how they would slip up on the unsuspecting ranches and even small villages. When he finished, he drove his fourteen foot long lance with a sharp steel point into a circle drawn in the dirt three feet in front of the council.

The lance stuck, quivered in place, and remained upright.

Elk wound dropped to his war pony's back and without touchng the hackamore, charged out of the firelight, screaming another Comanche war cry as he went.

There was much cheering and shouting and stamping of feet. Then the dance began once more.

They danced until after the Big Dipper had fallen out of the sky to the north, then went to their buffalo robes for one last lovemaking with each of their wives before the dangerous mission to come.

Two days later they found a small settlement well down the Red River. They were still far from any other white eyes. These white eyes were challenging them, building lodges and putting up poles to keep their horses in out here deep in the traditional Comanche territory. It was a slap in the face of every Comanche warrior on the raid.

They waited until darkness, then slipped up within hearing distance of the five wooden lodges. They had been made by stacking logs on the side and notching the ends so they stayed in place. Smoke came from the chimneys even though it was still warm outside.

Four members of the council on the raid talked. They had seen eight men among the cabins, many women and children. The council decided they would rest now and attack at dawn. Two of the younger warriors protested.

"We can attack now, rout them in the dark. Kill the men, take the women and children and all of their horses and six of the small buffalo type cows and head back for our camp."

The council argued with the warrior, but he could not be convinced. That was when White Eagle remembered the control that the Pony Soldier captain had over his men. If he gave the order to cease fire, they stopped. If he said go, they went. If he told one group to attack, or to cross the river, there was no discussion, the Pony Soldiers went as ordered.

It was not so with the Comanche warriors. Each man was a force unto himself. His vision quest had told him to be. But it made group operations harder. Most of the warriors knew that a group attack was best, that it needed some form, some strategy. But all too often one or a pair or a group of warriors would become impatient and attack early, or would ignore the plan of the council.

He watched the warriors and most seemed

content to wait to attack until dawn. Many warriors believed that night attacks were dangerous. If they were killed at night, their spirit would forever have to wander in darkness, never being able to find the light and to pass on into the glorious afterlife with their parents and friends.

Most of the younger warriors laughed at such talk. They said there was little danger of even being wounded by the unskilled farmers and rancher white eyes. Most of them could not even fire their weapon accurately.

An hour before sunrise two warriors left their ponies and slipped up to the closest cabin. The five small houses were built in a rough circle, with not more than fifty yards between them across the circle.

White Eagle had been awake for an hour watching the site. When he saw the two warriors leave, he roused the rest and they worked up as close as they could to the cabins. They were in the side of a small valley, and three of the cabins were in the edge of the woods of live oaks and pecan trees.

A scream stabbed through the night.

All was quiet for a moment, then a pistol fired in the nearest cabin, and White Eagle lifted his voice in the Comanche war cry that signalled his warriors forward. Half a dozen had already charged into the darkness, now all of them surged forward.

A white eye staggered out his front door, pistol in hand. White Eagle shot him with an arrow through his heart and leaped to the man's side in time to grab the pistol before he dropped it.

Comanches darted into all except one of the

houses. In that one the people inside had been quick enough to close the door and bolt it in place. Window shutters slammed into place as well over the two windows and for a moment the attackers were stopped.

Limping Crow ran from one of the cabins with a woman. He stopped in the better light and stared at her. She was young, with dark hair and wore a long white nightgown. With his knife he slit the cloth from neck to hem and threw it aside. The woman tried to cover herself.

Limping Crow slapped her and she shrieked, but let him pull the ruined garmet away. Limping Crow nodded, tied her hands and feet with rawhide and dumped her on top of her ruined nightdress. Then he laid one of his arrows across her. The arrow was specially marked with a dotted red line around the shaft near the feathers. It was the Comanche way of marking his goods.

Limping Crow screeched a war cry and raced back into the house. Just inside he saw the man he thought he had killed. The seriously wounded German settler threw a hatchet with deadly aim. The blade of the heavy instrument sliced through Limping Crow's chin, splitting the bone and continuing downward. The blade chopped through his neck, severing his spinal column and stopping at last buried in his chest.

Limping Crow died in seconds.

A second warrior in the cabin lit a fire inside so he could see. He dragged Limping Crow out of the burning cabin, then rushed back in, slit the German's throat and hurried out with a bolt of cloth for his wife.

White Eagle charged into another cabin, saw a man lift a long gun, but before the man could fire,

White Eagle shot an arrow into his chest. When the white eye's finger pulled the trigger, the weapon was aimed at his wife. Her face and chest dissolved in a frothy mass of blood and pulped flesh as she slammed against the wall and fell across the cold stove.

Light began to tinge the east.

White Eagle checked the white eye man. He was dead. He had been clutching a rawhide sack. White Eagle pried it from the stiffening fingers and looked inside. Past the drawstring he found a tumbled group of the same round golden discs he had seen before. Always Smiling had liked them.

The man protected them with his life. How were they so valuable? Did they possess good magic? Were they favored by the gods for their beauty? He shrugged. It was more *tosi-tivo*, more white man's ways he had to learn. He would take the woman's clay and find out about it.

For a few minutes he searched the cabin. He found the shotgun, which he threw aside. It was too big, he had no bullets to fit it. He had never seen a shotgun before.

Beside the man he found two pistols. He took both, tying them to his surcingle. There was a rifle on the wall that the man had no chance to reach. White Eagle took it down and was about to leave the cabin when he heard a small voice.

On the bed platform against the far wall he saw movement in the dim light. He jumped to the bed and pulled off the blanket. A small boy lay there. He was no more than three years. A boy, a son! He scooped the boy up, carried him outside and put him down where other warriors had set loot.

One of the cabins was already burning. He heard a wild scream and then a warrior pulled a woman into the firelight of the cabin. She had been stripped naked. The warrior looked at her for a moment, seemed fascinated by her large white breasts. Then he threw her to the ground and shouted with delight as he pulled loose his breech-clout and mounted the white eye.

There were none left alive in the four cabins. They looked at the last one. Gun barrels came out firing slots. As it grew lighter the warriors would become the targets.

Quickly they left, taking their treasures with them. White Eagle looked at the white woman near Limping Crow's body. The arrow across her chest was his. He picked her up and ran with her and the small boy into the pecan brush out of sight of the last cabin, then sat them down.

"Stay," he told them in English. The woman looked up, her tears dry on her cheeks. She nodded and held the small boy in her arms.

The last cabin was a problem. The weapons coming out of the firing slots were shooting now. No one could creep up near enough to it to set it on fire.

Several fire arrows were shot at the roof, but it would not catch on fire.

White Eagle solved the problem. He went upwind of the cabin, cut green pecan branches and carried them to a fire just inside the fringe of woods. They were twenty yards from the back of the cabin.

Soon the smoldering green pecan leaves produced a thick white smoke that drifted against the cabin rear wall. When the shooters inside were blinded by the smoke, White Eagle and four others rushed the wall, set fire to the brush they had carried with them, and soon the smaller logs on the wall caught fire. More and more brush and small limbs and then larger chunks of wood were piled against the burning wall.

When the entire back wall was burning well, the Indians moved to the side and the front to wait for the victims inside to come out.

None ever did. They heard several shots, but did not know why. When the rear wall burned through and fell inside, they got the front door open. A farmer and his wife and two children lay dead on the floor, all dead of gunshot wounds.

By that time it was full light. The warriors delighted in searching the remaining cabins for treasures to take back to their lodges.

Some took hoes, one a spade, another two new leather halters that could be reworked into war bridles. When everyone was satisfied with the plunder, the cabins were burned down. There was no barn, but in the corral and a small pasture nearby, they found twenty-five horses and six mules. All were rounded up and two young boys brought along for the purpose were assigned to drive the horses back to the Comanche camp. It was too early for the whole party to head back yet.

White Eagle looked at the woman Limping Crow had claimed before he died. White Eagle had rescued her from the exposed position. By rights she was his. He had no need for a slave. She was of child bearing age. He could use her as a brood mare. Yes, a son from her would still be his son!

He caught a horse for her, told her with signs and his few English words that she must care for the boy. She nodded.

Then she pointed at her body. "Clothes?" she asked. He didn't understand. She caught the small boy's nightgown and shook it. "Clothes."

"Clothes," he said, then understood. He went with her back to the ashes and the scattered belongings. She wept as she looked at what had been her home. Her husband was dead somewhere in the ashes.

Quietly she searched and soon found two pair of men's pants that were not too big. They were overalls. She found a woman's blouse. With an effort she put it on. She knew who owned it and a sob caught in her throat. All dead but two of them! She ran back to the big Indian who now "owned" her and stepped on board the pony. No saddle, not even a saddle blanket.

They were several miles down the river before she realized that she had no shoes.

White Eagle pushed the band hard. They found a small farm and bypassed it. Another ten miles down the Red River they found what they wanted, a cattle ranch. White Eagle had eaten beef, but he was not impressed by it. The beasts were too small, and they were not as available as the buffalo.

Still in an emergency a few beef would be handy. And they did not run off.

They attacked the ranch as soon as they arrived. The woman and boy were left to the rear. The battle was over in two minutes. Only three men and two women lived at the small ranch. All were killed and scalped in the fight.

The warriors swarmed over the barns and corrals. There were fifty horses in the corrals. From the looks of them all had been ridden.

The horses were rounded up and after the house

and barn burned to the ground and the corral torn apart, the raiding party headed for home, with fifty more horses and ten of the cantankerous Texas longhorn beef cattle.

It took them four days of hard riding to get back to their hidden valley. White Eagle had allotted the horses to the warriors, then split them into four groups and they took off in different directions, but all headed generally to the west.

Twice White Eagle sent scouts to check their back trail. No one was following them.

The four groups met a day's ride from the camp and moved on together. A mile outside the summer place, they stopped and each man put on his best bit of loot. Some wore fancy jackets, some top hats, some war paint. They sent one man into camp to let them know the raid was over.

At noon they made their grand entrance into camp. White Eagle came first with his captives. The woman told him her name was Doris. She had braided her hair on each side, and since she had not tried to get away, White Eagle untied her hands so she could hold the small boy.

Each night when they stopped, White Eagle had talked to the boy, told him what a bright future he had, how proud he would be to be a Comanche chief. All he had to do was grow and learn and be better at everything than any of the other boys. It would be easy!

The women, old men and warriors left in camp came out to greet the raiders. The girls wore their prettiest dresses, the women danced as they waited, small boys threw sticks at the girls and chased the dogs.

The parade of warriors and their herd of horses and ten steers went through the half mile long stretch of tipis. Flying from proud lances were a dozen scalps. They would be treated before the dance that night. The parade turned at the far end and came back, with each warrior dropping off at his own tipi. The horses were sent to the pasture where boys tended and protected them.

That night the traditional victory dance was held. Again the drummers announced the festivities. When darkness came the dancers assembled and soon the first warrior rode into the circle. A fresh buffalo hide had been spread on the ground near the council.

As the rider charged into the circle scattering the dancers, he drove his lance deep into the buffalo robe, then recounted to all listeners how he excelled in war and raiding, and especially how he had taken his scalp and stolen many horses.

When he finished, he rode out and the next warrior rode in, drove his lance into the buffalo robe beside the previous one and recounted his bravery over the challenges of the enemy.

When the last warrior had given his talk, White Eagle rose from the council log, and told of the death of Limping Crow. The crowd was silent for a moment, then the dancing continued. The name of Limping Crow would never be spoken again in the camp. It would be bad medicine, and bad for his spirit trying to climb out of the small hill where they had given him his above ground burial on the return trip.

There was a new family in camp. A warrior who had been with Bear Claw's band. Any Comanche could live wherever he wanted to. No one could deny a warrior of a family the right to attach himself to one clan or another. It was his right.

When Running Thunder came into the White Eagle band camp, he was greeted as any warrior. As he sat and talked with White Eagle, he asked if the chief knew of a Pony Soldier captain who rode at the head of his column with a pair of white handled pistols.

White Eagle passed the pipe to the warrior, thought for a moment, then nodded.

"I know him. I have seen him. He is different from the other Pony Soldiers. He attacked our camp two months ago. I think the man is half Comanche, the way he moves."

"He has been talking to everyone he finds who travels through our Comanche lands. He tells all he is giving a large reward for the person who brings back to him his small golden haired daughter called Sadie."

"I have heard the same story."

"It is reported that this Pony Soldier has said he will give a hundred horses or two hundred dollars in woman's clay, the gold coins the white eyes treasure so highly."

"I will remember the story," White Eagle said. They rose and he went into his tipi. Usually White Eagle would arrange to sell a slave or a captive at once if it would be profitable.

But not for Laughing Golden Hair. She was a special one. She was the delight of Cries In The Morning. More important, some day Laughing Golden Hair would grow up to marry a Comanche chief and be a great leader of her adopted people.

He watched the small girl for a moment, then went outside. It was not proper for a warrior to pay so much attention to a girl child.

He found the woman, Doris, who was also

staying in his lodge. He told her it was her job to protect and take care of the small white boy.

"Are those my only duties?" she asked. He saw the rise of her breasts, the flare of her thigh, but he nodded.

"For now, your only duties."

5

Captain Colt Harding moved another pin on his wall map showing where a traveler had seen a group of Comanches moving across the rolling Texas prairie. That could put the band anywhere beyond the Colorado River and to the north. He pushed the pin into the map where the last tributary of the Texas Colorado showed on his map.

The three foot square map had become a patchwork of pins where different travelers had seen Comanches. Some of the sightings he believed in but many were probably fanciful imaginations. But which ones were which?

He had been making reward offers to everyone. He could get up two hundred dollars if he had to, but a hundred horses would be harder. It didn't matter.

Anything, he would do *anything* to get Sadie back from those savages! He'd even leave the army if it came to that. Colt thought of the sweet young face, the darting blue eyes, and the long blonde hair that was a perfect match for her mother's. He blinked rapidly and turned away.

He couldn't dwell on that line of thought for more than about thirty seconds.

A double knock sounded on the door and Cpl. Swenson came in.

"Captain Kenny of A company is here to see you, sir."

"Right, send him in, Swenson."

Captain Harding had recovered his composure and his face was set and formal when the A Company commander came through the door.

"Morning, Captain Kenny. You seem to be settling in rather well here at Fort Comfort."

Across the parade grounds, Pamela Kenny had waited patiently for her father to leave the A Company headquarters room. When he went into the fort commander's office, she hurried down from where she had been talking to Lt. Edward's wife. Pamela watched as Mrs. Edwards turned into her own quarters.

Pamela marched into the Company A office and closed the door gently. Cpt. Victor Gregory bent over his desk.

"You might at least invite a lady to be seated," Pamela said with an annoyed lilt in her voice.

Gregory scrambled to his feet, bracing at attention.

"I'm sorry, Miss Kenny. I—I didn't see you come in."

"So where may I sit down?" Pamela asked.

"Sit down?—oh, yes, here, I'll bring a chair." He did, holding it for her. Instead of sitting down she caught his hand and held it. He looked at the door.

"Miss Kenny. Your father is at the fort commander's office. He just went over there."

"I know, silly. I waited until he left. I came to

talk to you. I've only seen you twice since we first met a week ago."

"That's as it should be, Miss. You're officer people."

"That doesn't make a bit of difference to me. I like you, Victor Gregory. I don't care if you're an important general or a private."

She moved around the chair until she stood directly in front of him. "I said I like you. Do you like me? Just a little?"

He lifted his eyes in exasperation. "Land sakes, yes, Pamela Kenny. I think of almost nothing but you. I've been making mistakes, getting into trouble. You're about the prettiest little thing I've ever seen!"

Pamela glowed with the praise, the compliment. She looked up at him, openly, watching his face. "Then why don't you do something to show me?"

"I just told you."

"You might even be so bold as to ask if you could hold my hand, maybe. . . ."

She stopped as she reached over and put her hand around his and gripped it tightly.

"Your daddy walks in here right now and I'm busted back to private!" he said through clenched teeth.

"Oh, poo. I can talk him out of anything." She leaned closer to him, then stepped forward so her breasts touched his chest. He looked down, his eyes wide as sunflowers. Then she put her arms around him, pushed tightly against him from hips to chest and hugged him.

"I been wanting to do that for more than a week now, Victor Gregory!"

His ears were red, he could feel the blush

creeping down his neck. He was aware that there was a hardness crawling rapidly from his crotch and he had no power at all to stop it.

She still held him.

"Do you like this?" she asked.

"Oh—damn!"

Pamela giggled. She reached up and caught his neck and bent his head down. Pamela Kenny stretched up on tiptoes and pressed her lips to his in a quick kiss.

She finished the kiss, touched his chest and stepped back. "I hope you liked that, too, Victor Gregory. If you did, see what you can do about arranging so we can meet sometime, alone, so maybe we can kiss again."

She smiled, twirled around so her long skirt lifted enough to show a flash of leg all the way to her knee, then she went to the door and looked out quickly to see if anyone was watching. There was no one nearby, so she waved to him, winked and slipped out to the walkway.

Pamela continued on around the square to the sutler's store where she had been instructed by her mother to go for some cinnamon.

She walked along, pleased with herself. Victor had been absolutely *purple* when she kissed him. He evidently was totally inexperienced with women. That was fine. She had felt the sudden swelling at his crotch! At least with him things wouldn't get out of hand.

Pamela wondered if he had hair on his chest. Bill, back in San Antonio had lots of black hair. He had let her play with it while he was . . . She smiled and hurried into the suttler's store. It was so small and had little merchandise except staples. It was nothing like the big stores in

Washington D.C. and in Philadelphia. Maybe someday soon she would be back there.

"You must be the new girl," Hans Altzanger, the sutler, said as she came to the small counter.

"Yes, sir. Pamela Kenny. My mother wants some powdered cinnamon."

"Just have one left, Miss Pamela. Anything else today?" That question brought all sorts of strange, wild, crazy ideas to her head, but she shook her long blonde hair.

"Only the cinnamon, thank you. How much is that?"

She paid him seven cents from a small coin purse and walked quickly back to her quarters. This was the night her mother was "repaying" the welcome dinner they had been given. All the officers on the post were invited, and of course, they all would come. It would not be seemly to refuse, partly because there were so few officers.

Captain Kenny was home early that afternoon to help his wife, Ruth, with the dinner. He was quite a cook in his own right when he had the time.

He came into the main room where the table had been expanded with three extra leaves and stared at his only child for a moment.

"Pamela, you could do a lot worse than stay right here at Fort Comfort and set your cap for the fort commander. He's a vital, young man, with good sense and should be a major soon. Do you like him?"

Pamela shorted and stood, so her father could know what a good figure she really had. "Father, Captain Harding is well over thirty."

"He's thirty-two."

"All right, he's thirty-two, which is nearly

twice as old as I am. He's too old for me. Besides, if you haven't noticed, the man is in deep pain and in mourning for his murdered wife and son and his kidnapped daughter. Give the man some breathing room."

Morse Kenny nodded. "Just wanted to see if you noticed. You probably also know which officers on the post are married, and which have wives back east."

"Oh, Daddy. With only seven officers in the whole fort, it isn't hard to figure out. They're all married except the captain. Of course you are four officers short on the roster."

Captain Kenny chuckled. "Is there anything you haven't missed? I guess it will be good for you to go to college. You seem to have more of a head on your shoulders than some junior second lieutenant could handle."

Pamela smiled. "I think you are quite right about that, Father, and the same applies right up to most majors who I have known. Now I should be helping Mother with the dinner."

There were ten for dinner that evening at seven-thirty. Mrs. Kenny had done the cooking. One of the enlisted men's wives, Mrs. Ida Barlow, did the serving.

Captain Harding was there, as well as Dr. Jenkins, and Captain Kenny and his wife. Lt. Edwards and his wife, Olive, sat together as did Lt. Young and his wife, Grace. Lt. Riddle was slightly late arriving. A dressed up and pretty Pamela rounded out the ten. Even if she did think so herself, Pamela knew she was the prettiest lady there. She was also the youngest.

She had arranged so she could sit next to Captain Dr. Jenkins. He would talk the whole time with Pamela's mother since they both hailed from Boston.

On her left was Lt. Young. She had decided to see how much she could tease him that evening without getting angry looks from her mother.

She drew out the twenty-four year old lieutenant, getting him to talk about himself. In the low buzz of conversation no one paid much attention to what the others around the table were saying.

Pamela had been asking more and more personal questions of Lt. Young. Now and then she saw Grace Young bend around her husband and scowl at her, but Pamela ignored it.

She moved and her leg brushed the officer's leg under the table. His gaze darted to her and she touched her mouth with her hand.

"Sorry," she said and continued talking about how she was looking forward to going to Boston. A short time later her leg brushed his again and this time held the contact. She glanced at him and saw color rising up his neck.

Mrs. Young looked around her husband. Her face was flushed with anger, she could barely speak. At last she got the words out.

"Miss Kenny, would you please leave my husband alone!"

There was a moment of shocked silence around the table. Grace Young's strident voice had cut through the talk and everyone heard the words clearly. Quickly Lt. Young rose, took his wife by the hand and led her to the small entranceway near the front door.

He mumbled his apologies to Mrs. Kenny that his wife had not been feeling well all day, and hurried her outside and down the walk toward their quarters.

Pamela had not let the movement affect what she was doing. She had a delicate bite of the roast beef and looked at Dr. Jenkins.

"Doctor, I understand in Boston you had some interesting methods for helping women deliver their babies without pain. Can you explain the procedure to me?"

Doctor Jenkins chuckled, then shook his head. "I'll be glad to when you're at least eight months pregnant, and when we're not eating this fantastic supper that your mother cooked for us."

"Fine, I'll wait," Pamela said.

Her father shot her one of his sternest looks. She had seen it many times before at a company dinner. It was the last warning before he removed her from the table. "Excused!" would be his word for it.

She settled down. No use wasting a good dinner. She especially enjoyed the mashed potatoes and the beef gravy. It was one of the most satisfying evenings she could remember in a long time. If Lt. Young had not reacted the way he did, she would have put her hand on his leg next. That always brought results at the stuffy dinner table gathering.

Captain Kenny had given her a stern lecture after the guests left about her responsibilities as his daughter.

"Somehow you were teasing Lt. Young. I don't know how and I'm not interested in knowing. But, if it happens again, you will never again have dinner with us when we have guests. Do I make that point particularly clear, Pamela?"

"Yes, Father. Clear." She lowered her gaze, as she knew he would expect her to. She could play the obedient child for a few more weeks.

The next morning, Captain Kenny had to hurry off to train his troops. No one brought up the problem she had created at the dinner the night before. After breakfast, Pamela sat near the window and watched her father march across the parade grounds. He was all army officer and always would be.

That same morning, Captain Harding had called out his Lightning Company to train. Their regimen was slightly different than the other troops. Captain Harding was buying ten dollars worth of ammunition a month to use in training.

Most of the army did little or no target practice. It was considered a waste of time, and too expensive to allow. Captain Harding went against the practice, and listed much of the ammunition expended as being used in "patrols and clashes with hostiles, mostly Comanches."

This morning he had taken the forty men of Lightning Company two miles beyond the fort to the east where there was a slight draw where the land leveled out to meet the White River. There he brought them into a company front in ranks of four, ten long and then rode to the long side of them.

"Left turn, Hoooooooo!" Captain Harding called. The men turned their horses toward him so he faced ten men on horseback, four deep.

He signalled the two Tonkawa scouts he had brought with him. The two were the best riders from the Tonkawa camp. One of the Indians jumped off his horse, left it and ran thirty yards ahead. He stopped and looked behind him.

The second scout, still mounted, pounded toward the man on foot at a flat out gallop.

Without losing speed or stride the Tonkawa on the horse scooped up the Indian on the ground, and a moment later he was mounted behind the first Tonkawa and the two rode away.

The members of the Lightning Company shouted and cheered as the successful pickup was made.

The Indians circled and came back. The Tonkawas traded places, with the man who had been on the ground, now riding the horse. They looked at Captain Harding.

"Men, you've just seen a dandy little maneuver that could save your scalplock one of these days. How many of you can pick up a man who's on foot?"

One man lifted his hand. He was a recruit who had been on the post only a short time.

"At least one. You'll have a chance to prove it. Every man in the company is going to learn how to do this before we go in for chow. Is that understood?"

Some of the men grumbled, others grinned. This *was* a maneuver that could save lives in an attack.

The Indians did the pickup again and again, doing it slowly, so the troopers could get the idea. Then the Tonkawas picked up a trooper, told each man how to do it, when to jump, what part of the horse or saddle or the other man to grab.

The first few tries resulted in the Pony Soldiers falling off the horse. One man hit hard and sprained his wrist.

When the first man made it up, everyone cheered. Three hours later each man had been picked up by one of the Indians. Then the troopers began to do the picking up.

Again they followed the example of the Indians, who showed them slowly how to do the job.

The man who said he could pick up a downed man was Pvt. Oxford. Riding at a good gallop, Oxford picked up one of the Tonkawas. Then he explained to the now eager troopers how to do it.

It took an hour before another trooper successfully hauled a downed rider onto his horse. It was not pretty, but it worked.

Captain Harding moved that man with Pvt. Oxford to one side and worked with the rest.

Lightning Company dragged into the fort that night a half hour after dark. But every man was grinning. They had done it! Every man, even Sgt. Casemore and Capt. Harding had both picked up a man and been picked up.

Captain Harding brought them to a company front and rode up and down the line.

"I'm proud of you men! You're proving me right. With good training and the right tactics, we can beat any Indian tribe they try to send against us. Sergeant Casemore, see to it that special chow is served up for your company. You deserve it. Carry on."

Sgt. Casemore snapped a salute to his captain, bellowed out the orders and moments later the men took their tired mounts to the stables where they spent three quarters of an hour rubbing them down with dry straw, and then feeding them a full ration of oats.

"In the cavalry, your mount comes first," Sgt. Casemore bellowed as they began to growl. "That animal is more important than your rifle or your balls! He can save your damned hide." He grinned and slapped a black army mount on the rump.

"Chow is fifteen minutes, just in case anybody is interested."

Captain Harding ate the cold supper Cpl. Swenson brought him, fell into bed and slept without waking until five A.M. He rolled over and tried to go back to sleep. He ached in every bone. His arms felt like they would drop out of their sockets.

He groaned as his feet hit the rough floor boards. Then he grinned. At least he knew how the rest of the Lightning Company felt. He had fallen twice before he learned how to help to be picked up on a charging army mount.

When he tried to pick up a man he nearly lost his saddle again. It took him four tries to pick up a trooper. Then he did it four times in a row to prove to himself that he really knew how.

Today they would learn how to shoot from a horse, Comanche style. For that he needed a hot breakfast.

He went to the mess hall and to the small officers mess at one end where he ate half a dozen eggs, sunny side up, six thick slabs of bacon, a stack of hot cakes and three cups of coffee.

The troop sat in the sun waiting for him at six-thirty when he came out of his quarters.

"Lightning Company all present and accounted for, sir and ready for training," Sgt. Casemore bellowed.

They rode smartly out the gate and toward the same draw they had used before. This time the Tonkawa Indian scouts demonstrated how to hang off one side of a pony and shoot a rifle under the horse's neck. After years of riding with both boots in both stirrups, it took a lot of practice to ride with one.

At last one of the men hooked his left knee around the saddle horn, then he had the balance to lean down and fire under the horse's neck with one hand on the Spencer.

The men rode by single file, five yards apart on dry runs, trying to get their balance.

Captain Harding called them together. When he organized the Lightning Company, he had broken the company down into four squads of ten men each. A corporal was leader of each squad.

He glared at them. "I hope to hell you men have a little more respect for the Indians when they ride at you off their mounts so all you can see is a foot and an elbow. It's damn tough. Our problem is that the Comanches are way ahead of us. They have been learning how to ride this way since they were five years old.

"They ride without either hand, and can draw a bow and arrow and hit what they aim at, under the damn pony's neck." He walked his big black around in a circle for a moment.

"All right. We're not going to learn how to do this today. For the next three days, I'm leaving each corporal in charge of practice of his squad. Four days from now we'll have a live firing test, to see how many of you can pass it. Every man of every squad will pass, or he's out of the company. The squad that shoots the best score on the target will get a hundred extra rounds for target practice."

"Any questions?"

Sgt. Casemore lifted his hand. Captain Harding nodded.

"Sir, can we have one of the Tonks for each squad as an instructor?"

"Done." Harding looked around. Already the men were talking it up, making side bets. He grinned. Sometimes there was more than the field manual way to get a job done.

He led the company back to the fort just in time for the midday meal of salt pork, potatoes, and beans.

Captain Harding slumped in his chair in his office and stared at the map of West Texas on his wall.

Where was she? Where in hell and in Texas was his little girl, Sadie?

6

The man had to be at least sixty, Captain Harding thought as he looked at him across the desk. His hair hung around his shoulders in dirty strings, his beard scraggly, uneven. A sore on his cheek had not healed and his face was burned dark from the sun and the wind. His eyes squinted almost shut from long experience in self preservation, but he chuckled as he looked up at the cavalry officer.

"Yeah, I know what yer about to say. But don't bother me a twit. Sure, I know I'll probably never find that one big strike, or even a little one. Still, could be some silver in these washes and the low bluffs. Man's got a right to try. Too damn cold out there in the real mountains.

"Had my fill of Californi and Nevader. Nuff of them places. Warmer come a summer in Texas." He took a bite off a plug of dark chewing tobacco and nodded.

"Thankee for the chew, been nigh on to a month since I had some. Finally used some cactus skin offen some of them big wide parts. Tough as all

77

hell it was, but didn't taste none too bad."

Captain Harding poured another two fingers of his best Kentucky bourbon into a glass and handed it to the prospector. He sipped at it as if it were a great luxury he wanted to last as long as possible.

"Getting back to the Comanche, Mr. Thayer. They don't bother you, you say. You can ride right past their camp, or even stop by for a smoke on their pipe."

"Right as rain, sonny. They know I ain't gonna move them out of their lands. Know I ain't gonna start farming or use up all the game. I'm no threat."

"Can you show me where you've been lately, and where you've seen any Comanche camps?"

"Reckon. You the feller hunting the little white girl captive?"

"That's right. She's my daughter. Her name is Sadie Harding, she's five years old by now and has been gone over three months."

"Mmmm. Reckon she's safe. Comanche like to steal kids to adopt to some squaw with no youngens. Done all the time. Treat them like bone china. Never seen a Comanche hit a kid, or scold one bad even. Kids are damn important to the Comanche. The squaws don't drop many kids of their own, you see—"

"Where have you been prospecting, Mr. Thayer?"

The old man stood with a bit of a hitch, then went to the wall map slowly.

"Well, now I came back down the Colorado here, the Texas Colorado that is, not the big one over in Colorado and Utah and Arizona and Californi. Didn't see but maybe one band in there.

Don't know for sure who it was. Tipis was up when I went by."

"Did the biggest tipi have an eagle head painted on it?"

"Nope, sure didn't. That'd be White Eagle's band. Met him once or twice. Big son of a bitch."

"Where did you go from there, Mr. Thayer?"

"Hit the hills for a while, then down to the White River and here I am."

"Before the Colorado?"

"Yeah, I went up Beaver Creek off the Wichita, then the North Fork of the Wichita all the way to the Caprock that protects the Staked Plains. Saw two or three Comanche bands up in there." He frowned for a minute, his eyes almost closing. "Nope, don't remember no eagle tipi up in there neither."

"Mr. Thayer, I would be grateful if you would keep an eye out for the Eagle Band. I'm sure that's the group that stole Sadie. I'm not sure they still have her, but it's likely." He stood and went to the map and then back to his desk.

"I'm offering two hundred dollars in gold eagles to the man who helps me rescue Sadie. If the Indians want to make the arrangements to ransom her, the price is a hundred horses to the warrior."

The old prospector whistled. "Great damn! That's enough to make any brave change bands and be a rich man."

"I just hope it works. How are your supplies, Mr. Thayer? Could you use some army hardtack, beans and salt pork? We have no tinned goods, but we'll set up your grub pack."

"That'd be more than welcome, Major," Thayer said with a twinkle in his eye. He always promoted these soldier boys at least one rank. They loved it.

"I'll have Corporal Swenson take care of you, Mr. Thayer. Stop by anytime. And remember those two hundred dollars. I want my little girl back."

The old prospector took Colt's offered hand with surprising grip and went out to see Cpl. Swenson who already was making out a list to go to the supply quartermaster.

Captain Harding stood on his small porch watching the prospector and the corporal heading for the quartermaster. He looked to the north. Sadie was up there somewhere!

Ten troopers rode by heading for the gate. He recognized them as members of his Lightning Company. They were going out to practice shooting under their mount's neck, Indian fashion. He would love to see the surprise on the Indian's faces when they found the cavalry attacking with some of the Comanche's own tricks and tactics.

He would use every strategy, every device, every method he could to defeat the Comanche. He was not too proud to use Comanche techniques. If they worked for the hostiles, they damn sure would work for a more disciplined unit. True, it had to be a tough, bone hard, mentally strong Cavalry outfit. But that's what the Lightning Company would be after another month of training.

By then the Comanche would be getting ready to go into their winter camps. Often several bands came together for the long winter, to gossip, trade lies, meet relatives separated during the summer and to pool their resources. He would love to catch two hundred braves hunkered down and feeling safe in some snow clogged small river valley and move in on them with every gun blazing!

Across the parade grounds Pamela Kenny smiled. It had been two days since the dinner at the Kenny's quarters, and Pamela hadn't seen Corporal Gregory since. So, she simply took matters in her own capable hands. Now she sat in the small A Company headquarters office as Victor Gregory sweated behind his desk.

"Miss Kenny, your father said he'd only be gone a few minutes. I'd appreciate it if you stay right there in the chair until he gets back. I worked three years to get my stripes. I ain't gonna risk losing them now for a kiss or two."

"Three or four or five warm, wonderful kisses, Victor. Wouldn't that feel good!" Pamela stood and walked with hips swaying and breasts bouncing as she moved up to him. She went around his desk. He stood suddenly. She pushed her chest against him and saw his nostrils flare and his breath catch.

Pamela pushed her hips hard against his and felt the bulge. He was excited, too!

Her arms went around him tightly. "Now kiss me proper or I won't let you go."

"Miss Kenny!"

"Call me Pamela, sweetheart. Now kiss me."

Victor hesitated, knew what it could cost him, but this feeling of wanting her so much was just as bad. He bent and kissed her. Tried to pull away but she held him. She nibbled at his lips, licked them with her tongue, then kissed him again so hard it made his teeth hurt.

Slowly she ground her hips against his. He was

getting bigger and bigger! Oh, yes!

The door opened and Captain Kenny stalked in. Cpl. Gregory jerked away and pushed at her, but her arms held him fast.

"Cpl. Gregory! Pamela! What in hell . . . ."

Captain Kenny charged across the room, pulled Pamela away and punched Cpl. Gregory in the mouth, slamming him backwards where he tripped over a chair and crashed to the floor. He looked up dazed and surprised.

"Keep your hands off my daughter, you little bastard!"

Pamela had been pushed to one side, now she went to Victor and helped him stand up, then turned toward her father.

"Daddy, you stop that! You touch him again and I'll report you to Captain Harding!" She walked around the small room a moment as she tried to hold onto her own temper. "Now everyone just calm down. It was just a little kiss, for goodness sakes. Daddy, don't tell me you never kissed a girl before you married mama."

"Young lady, I'll deal with you later. Now you get out of here, go home and stay in your room until I get there. You and I are going to have a long talk."

"Oh, Daddy. I know where babies come from and how they are made. I'm a grown woman!"

"Maybe in some ways. In other ways you're still a little girl. One thing for sure, you're still an unmarried young lady, and you'll get yourself straight home to your room. Now!"

"Oh. . . ."

"Not another word, Pamela Jean!"

When he used that tone and her middle name, he was near the point of exploding. She sighed, smiled at Cpl. Gregory, who stood ramrod stiffly at attention, and walked out the door.

"Damn!" Captain Kenny said. "At ease, Victor, relax. You're not in trouble, Pamela is. My daughter is spoiled and grew up without even asking me, and she's an outrageous flirt." Captain Kenny scowled.

He could be in trouble. It was a court martial offense for an officer to strike an enlisted man. He'd done so in front of a witness. Damn stupid of him. He had to tread delicately here.

"Corporal Gregory, my apologies to you. I shouldn't have struck you. It was a spur of the moment thing. I saw my little girl being assaulted by a man. Of course, now when I have a moment to think, I know that wasn't the case. I can see how she had you trapped. It's happened before, I'm afraid, on another post."

"I'm sorry, sir."

Kenny looked up in surprise. "I bet you don't mean that, Corporal. You mean you didn't enjoy getting kissed by my beautiful daughter?"

"It wasn't that, sir—I mean—I guess I did—but I didn't encourage. Oh, damn!"

Captain Kenny laughed now. The surprise of the tangle was over. He reasoned that the enlisted man would not report the blow to anyone. He was happy in his clerk's assignment so he was not in the field so much. Kenny was thankful that he'd come back when he did, before this romance situation got any more complicated. It was impossible. He was an enlisted. Not a chance he could marry a captain's daughter. The code just wouldn't allow it.

"Victor, don't worry about this situation. You're a good clerk, I'm not going to bust you for kissing my daughter. I'd also expect that you would understand my sudden fury when I caught her with you. That was why I struck out at you. For that I apologize."

"No apology needed, sir. It was still my fault. I should have pushed her away."

"Takes a strong man to do that to a pretty girl. I've had a problem or two like that when I was young." He walked around the small office. "Damn. I just wish it hadn't happened. Relax. I'll put this office off limits to my romantic little girl, and restrict her to her room for a week. That should help. Maybe by then she'll pick out somebody else to bedevil."

"Yes, sir. She sure is a right pretty girl."

"I know. The trouble is, she knows it, too. But we'll all survive until December. That's when she leaves for Austin and Boston. So, Corporal, is the little problem all forgotten? I'll forget you were kissing my daughter, and you'll forget that my fist somehow grazed your jaw."

"Yes, sir; that seems like a good trade."

Captain Kenny held out his hand and they shook.

"Now, Corporal, let's look over that list of weapons. We've got to get men in the same squad with the same type of rifle, or at least the same size of ammunition. We'll trade around within the company as much as we can. We may need to make some trades with other companies as well."

The next day Captain Kenny led twenty of his men on a scouting patrol. He had been assigned to it a week before. They would be gone for three days and two nights. Sgt. Zach Upland would remain at the fort in charge of the rest of the company and the company clerk would remain behind as well for administration.

It was a routine patrol, a way of showing the flag to the hostiles if they were in the area, to remind them that the U.S. Cavalry was on duty and would challenge them.

The first day of the patrol, Cpl. Gregory winced each time the door opened to his small A Company office, but he was relieved at the end of the day when Pamela had not come in. She was supposed to be restricted to her room. But he figured Pamela would work some dodge to get around that.

Gregory was from Iowa, had been working on his father's farm until one day he decided he had been looking at the rear end of a plow mule long enough. He enlisted. He had been in his share of Indian fights, came in just at the end of the fighting in Sixty-five so missed the Civil War.

Now he was concentrating on getting into a position where he could strike for his sergeant's stripes. Once he got them he was set up for the rest of his life in the army. A sergeant had the best spot in the Cavalry!

The second day went by without incident as well. He and Sgt. Zach Upland kept the company going on an even keel with some extra duty for those left behind.

He had to get the roster set for the next day and before Cpl. Gregory realized it, the afternoon was gone. He lit a lamp to take care of the last page he had to check.

He was concentrating on the papers and didn't even look up when the door opened and closed.

"Yeah?" he asked.

When no one responded, he looked up to find Pamela Kenny a foot from his face. She kissed him at once, sitting in his lap on the chair, pulling his face up to hers.

"No!" he said forcefully when he tugged his lips away. "Your dad would kill us both. Stop it!"

"Victor, you don't mean that. I've wanted to kiss you again for just days and days!" She kissed him quickly and this time he couldn't protest. He had thought of her every waking moment, but knew she was unattainable. She was officer people.

When she let his lips go, she nuzzled against him.

"We can't do this. You know the army rules about enlisted and officers. You're an officer's daughter. I'd get rawhided out of here on a rail, I touch you."

"I won't let them." She stood, caught his hand and pulled him toward the outside door. She pushed the locking bolt in firmly, then led him to the small back room, the captain's office. She left the door open so some of the lamp light would come into the room, then she kissed him again, pressing her sleek body against him from toe to chest.

He growled and put his arms around her pulling her tighter against him.

When the kiss broke at last she pushed away slightly and began unbuttoning the four fasteners on the top of her dress. It snuggled against her chin and came to her wrists and swept the floor as most dresses did.

He watched with fascination. Then she spread the top of the dress wide and to his surprise there was no other garments under it. Her breasts glowed, pink and white, erect red nipples pulsating as he watched them.

Victor Gregory had never been with a woman before. She lifted his hands to her breasts and held them there. Then she kissed him tenderly and they sat down on the rough boards of the floor.

Her hands rubbed his crotch, then fumbled at the buttons.

"Darling Vic, don't worry. I'll show you exactly what to do. No one will come. Father is gone for another day, and I told Mother I wanted to talk to Mrs. Edwards. We have two hours to love each other!"

Quickly she wiggled out of her clothes until she was naked, then she pulled off his clothes.

He sat there staring at her completely nude form. He had never seen a woman like that before. She was better than any of his sexy dreams. He reached for her and soon discovered that making love was not as hard as he thought it might be.

Three times they brought each other to the heights and Vic Gregory could never remember being so delighted, so thrilled, so much in love.

As they pulled on their clothes, he was full of plans.

"My enlistment is up in two months. I was going to reenlist, but I don't have to. My dad needs help with the farm back in Iowa. It's plenty big enough for two families. We'll get married here, of course, or in Austin. I'll be a civilian again."

She kissed him and let him pet her again, then they slipped into the other room.

"Darling Victor, don't make a lot of plans. Things can change. Let's just enjoy what we have now, and see what happens." She kissed him, then brazenly rubbed his crotch. He reached for her hungrily, but she pushed him away and stepped into the night. She was full of talk about Mrs. Edwards when she got back to her quarters. Her mother was working on piecing a quilt, and barely noticed when Pamela came in.

The next morning, after their three days of practice, Lightning Company assembled in the sandy draw and stacked up four cardboard boxes so they were about the size of a man. They anchored the bottom box with heavy rocks, and wired them together so they would stay upright.

Captain Harding watched as the squads came past on their shooting test. He had the fourth squad lead out. The first two men had learned their lesson well. Most of the men wrapped one leg around the saddlehorn, leaned down and with both hands fired their Spencers under the horse's neck. They were each allowed two shots.

After each man passed the target, markers ran in and circled any holes in the "man" sized cardboard boxes and called out the hits. There was a drawn bullseye on the "chest" of the boxes. A chest hit counted five points, a hit anywhere else counted one.

Only one man fell off his mount during the test. He was given three hours extra riding training to perfect his under-neck firing.

Captain Harding looked at the results that Cpl. Swenson had tallied.

Three men in each of the squads had scored one or more chest hits. The top point producer was the second squad which had six chest hits and eight other hits for a total of thirty-eight points.

Captain Harding nodded. "Well done, men. Now when the chance comes, we can give the bloody Comanche nobody to shoot at the way they do to us."

Next on the training were ambush attacks. Captain Harding led the men in a march through the prairie in the usual four abreast formation, then suddenly he would pull one of his ivory handled pistols and fire twice in the air.

"Ambush! From the left," he shouted. "Dismount and take cover!"

At once the men dismounted, one trooper in each squad was assigned the job of leading the horses away to safety and protecting them. The rest of the men flattened behind any cover they could find, and on a given signal began firing their allotted four rounds to the left.

Captain Harding sat above it all with his pocket-watch out watching the second hand tick around. He noted times as the horses were led away, the men found protection, and the command by Sgt. Casemore to fire was given.

Four times they went through the exercise, then Captain Harding led them back to Fort Comfort. He decided there was enough heat in the sun to dry another series of adobe bricks, and assigned C Company the next day to go to the draw with the exposed adobe clay deposits and make one hundred adobe blocks.

Their own masons would lay up the blocks when they were dry. He had forgotten about working on the rest of the fort. Now he knew it was time. Soon the snow would be flying.

Back at the fort, he sat in his office chair and stared out the small window for a moment. His Lightning Company was progressing nicely. He wished he had some kind of cold weather gear for the men. If he took them out into three foot deep snow in their standard blue uniforms half of them would freeze to death.

He would write to San Antonio about what equipment he could requisition for winter patrols. He didn't think he would have any problems getting what they had. The real worry was that the army had little equipment for the really cold winter weather.

His eyes strayed across the map of West Texas. No one had been by the fort since Mr. Thayer, the prospector. Someone must be out there in the Comanche country. Soon, perhaps soon there would be a break.

7

The next morning, Captain Harding was in the middle of a letter to San Antonio headquarters asking what cold weather gear the army had developed for winter patrolling.

Cpl. Swenson knocked and came into his office.

"Sir, there's a man outside who says he knows where Sadie was ten days ago."

"Bring him in!" Colt snapped, jumping to his feet, the letter forgotten. He was almost to the door when the man came in. He looked more Indian than white. He had long black hair, coppery skin, a hawk nose and he wore buckskin with fringes more common in the mountains of the far West. Dark eyes took in the office in a sweeping glance, then settled on Colt.

"Captain Harding," he said formally. "My name is Wesley Tallpine. I know where White Eagle's tipis were ten days ago. Your daughter is with him."

Harding stepped forward, held out his hand. The man took it and shook. His face was blank, unreadable.

"I hope to God you do, Wesley Tallpine. I'm Colt Harding. Are you sure it was my daughter?"

"Can't be absolutely sure. But they called her Laughing Golden Hair. She was four, maybe five years old. She has been adopted by a woman called Cries In The Morning. Both live in White Eagle's big tent with an Eagle head painted on the side."

"I've seen the tipi up on the Wichita," Colt said.

"They're near that now, on part of what I think is Croton Creek, that runs into the Wichita. To hell and gone up there, Captain."

"Two hundred miles?"

"Closer to two hundred and twenty. Lost my trading wagon first day out from there. Left me with my riding horse and I came down here in ten days, easy twenty mile a day."

"Excuse me, Mr. Tallpine, but are you Indian?"

"Most folks don't wait so long, Captain. They just call me Breed and have it done. My mother is white, my father is Comanche. I was the result of a raid on a white settlement where I was later born. But I also know the Comanche lingo and the people. Lived with Trailing Bear's band for three years. I can also read and write."

"Good man to have around. The girl was brown-eyed, right?"

"No, sir, Captain. Eyes blue like a mountain lake in morning."

"You're sure it was Walking White Eagle's band?"

"I sold him some goods. Curious, he paid for them in gold double eagles. Never seen a Comanche do that before."

"Curious is right. Will you lead me back to his

camp?"

"The two hundred still waiting?"

"In gold, as soon as we get little Sadie out of there."

Tallpine hesitated. "Can't right guarantee you'll get her out. Comanches don't like giving up adopted children. I'll guarantee to guide you to the camp for a hundred dollars."

"Done!" Colt thundered holding out his hand. Wesley took it and grinned.

"See the quartermaster for some dinner and gear if you'll need any. Is your horse good? We'll be covering sixty to sixty-five miles a day. Show him to Corporal Swenson. We'll be leaving at five-thirty A.M. We travel hard and fast, no wagons."

"I'll be damned. Sixty-five miles? I figured you'd do sixteen maybe eighteen."

"Not with this kind of information." He led Tallpine to the outer office.

"Swenson, get Sergeant Casemore in here on the double. We'll be leaving on a patrol early in the morning. Take care of Mr. Tallpine here, the best we have to offer. Send Casemore in when he arrives."

Captain Harding went back into his office and studied his map of Texas. They would be traveling almost due north past a sometimes camp ground the Comanche used to use. Then on north to the very edge of the caprock below the Staked Plains. They would not be quite as far north as when they whipped White Eagle before, but they would be farther west.

Harding had no thoughts that this would be a simple walk up attack. He was sure that after his lesson, White Eagle would have seasoned warriors out about three deep as lookouts and scouts to protect his south and west flanks. The band might have left and be in a hunting camp. If so the Tonkawas could track them. An attack during a hunt would be to the Pony Soldier's advantage.

Colt went to a corner wooden file case bolted to the floor and unlocked the bottom drawer. He took the drawer all the way out. Below it was a floor safe dug through a hole in the boards and into the dry Texas soil.

After working a combination, Colt opened the lid and took out a thick leather bag with a drawstring. From it he counted out five double eagle gold coins. He closed the bag and put it back.

Five minutes later Sgt. Casemore stopped in front of his desk and saluted.

"Sergeant Casemore reporting as ordered, sir!"

"At ease, Casemore. Let's look at the map." The two men went to the large scale wall map. "We're here in Fort Comfort. Tomorrow morning we leave for a ride north, about two hundred and twenty miles. Four days of riding. We attack the next day. A man came in with positive identification on Sadie. She's with White Eagle, for sure."

"We're ready sir. The usual double ration of ammunition?"

Colt nodded.

"Rations for what, four days, and Tonkawa meat for the rest, Captain?"

"Sounds good. Have your men get their gear ready and get them bedded down as soon as it gets dark. We'll move out at five-thirty A.M."

"Yes, sir!"

When Cpl. Swenson came in to tell him the trader was being fed and would bunk down in the barracks, Captain Harding told his clerk to notify six Tonkawa scouts they would be needed for a patrol.

"Have the top six men we usually take. We'll use four as scouts instead of two, and two for hunters."

"Yes, sir."

The first day on the trail was uneventful. The Tonkawa scouts brought down a two point buck deer the first afternoon and they roasted venison as soon as they stopped for the night. They had covered sixty miles, Colt figured.

He chewed through the seared part of a section of ribs and tore off the juicy venison underneath. It wasn't a neat way to eat but the mule deer meat was delicious. As soon as they ate, the tired men fell into their blankets.

The second day went about the same, but no big hunting success. Three rabbits and a pair of ducks. Colt passed and ate hardtack and drank his coffee.

By the end of the fourth day they had covered another 200 miles. They had slowed down when the scouts reported some signal fires ahead. Whenever possible they traveled through draws and valleys and in woodsy fringes along streams.

But now and then there was an expanse of open country they had to cross.

The Tonkawa soon read the smokes.

"They know we come," War Hatchet, the head Tonkawa scout, said after riding back from the point a mile ahead. "Smoke say forty Pony Soldiers."

"Damn. There goes our surprise. How far ahead of us is the camp, Tallpine?"

The Breed stared at the darkening country

around him. "Not more than five miles," he said.

"Will the Comanche move their camp?" Captain Harding asked the Tonkawa.

"Yes, no?" he asked.

Tallpine shook his head. "No, White Eagle won't move. By now he knows how fast we're traveling. He knows we could run him down with the heavy travois and the women and kids. He'll find a defensive spot and fight. He'll also try to ambush us as we move up."

When the men had eaten and rested for an hour, Colt called them out of their blankets.

"We'll move up to within rifle range of them in the darkness," Colt ordered. "That will spoil any surprises they have planned for us tomorrow morning."

Tallpine grinned. "You would make a good Comanche chief," the halfbreed trader said.

The scouts pulled back to a hundred yards and the men walked their mounts forward silently. Nothing jangled, there was no talk, only the soft walking hoofbeats and the occasional blow of the army geldings.

They moved a mile with no problems. Then an owl hooted in front of them, and War Hatchet appeared out of the gloom beside Colt.

"Not owl, Comanche," War Hatchet said softly.

Tallpine agreed. "Damn poor owl call," he said. "Sounds like a boy."

Another mile forward a better owl called into the night. It was answered by a call farther ahead. Colt grinned. The Comanches knew forty Pony Soldiers were moving up through the night toward their camp. They had no way of knowing when an attack might come. The Comanche warriors would be awake all night waiting. Colt would let his men get some sleep when they were closer.

There were no more owl calls.

"The Comanche scouts know we're here," Tallpine told Captain Harding. "They will follow us as far as we go, and report to White Eagle."

"So no one surprises anyone else," Colt said. "It will be a matter of who can fight the best."

"And who has the best rifles," Tallpine said.

Colt looked at him in the dim moonlight.

"Rifles? White Eagle has rifles?"

"He had them when you attacked him before, you told me. When I was in his camp, I saw several warriors with rifles. They seemed to know how to use them."

"He steals them from everywhere that he raids. He picked up twelve rifles and twelve pistols when he attacked our supply train four months ago."

The scouts came back and halted the troop. They reported they wanted to work forward carefully and check the lay of the hills just this side of the camp.

An hour later War Hatchet came back and motioned them forward. They walked their animals, still in a column of fours, for two more miles, then dismounted, left them in control of the designated wrangler for each squad, and moved forward on foot.

They went up a rolling hill, through light brush and stunted live oaks. At the top of the hill they stopped. They were less than a hundred feet above a silvery strip of a river below them some three hundred yards away.

In the moonlight they could see the tops of the

tipis where they were pitched protected by a twenty foot deep gorge the stream had cut through the land.

They would not be able to fire directly into the camp or the tipis. Colt frowned.

"Didn't seem this protected when I was down in there," Tallpine said. "But then I came in from the other way."

"Too damn late to come at them from the north!" Colt brayed.

He sat down and stared at the tops of the tipis. Too late to go around. The other side might be equally protected. The hostiles knew they were here and had not attacked them. They must feel their camp was well protected. And the damn savages had a good supply of rifles and probably plenty of stolen ammunition.

Colt listened to a night hawk, the shrill cry of the bird as it made a kill. He doubted if that was an Indian. He tried to think how he would defend the gorge if he occupied it.

He would cut notches in the edge of the cliff and put his riflemen there with a foot high parapet of earth to fire over. He would have an excellent field of fire up the hill aimed at anyone attempting to come over the top. A brutal advantage.

He needed a five inch gun to blast those snipers off the hill and to drop exploding rounds into the gorge.

Next best thing were the hand bombs he had prepared for an attack several months ago but did not have a chance to use. They were dynamite sticks cut in half, taped together along with thirty to fifty large headed roofing nails. The nails were taped tightly to the dynamite. When the dynamite exploded the short nails screamed out in all directions like deadly shrapnel. He had brought tabout twenty of the bombs which were distributed through the troop.

Tomorrow he could send two men to crawl down the hill with rifle fire protection and get close enough to lob the bombs into the village.

No! One of the bombs could kill Sadie!

He would be limited in using the bombs against the snipers along the rim, if indeed White Eagle put men there.

Colt moved below the ridgeline on the reverse slope and lit a match to check the time. Three A.M.

A night attack!

That would let his men work down the three hundred yards to the edge of the gorge under protection of darkness. Even if the Redskins had rifles at the lip of the gorge, the shooters would have no targets!

He alerted the men, told Sgt. Casemore and the squad leader his plans.

"We'll work down to the lip of the gorge as silently as possible. None of the hand bombs will be thrown without my explicit permission. My daughter is down there. Her safety is my primary concern.

"No one is permitted to fire at or near the tallest tipi with the eagle head painted on it. We move out in five minutes. Absolute silence and no firing until I give the command."

The troopers spread out at five yard intervals and moved down the slope on whispered command. Halfway down the night hawk screamed in protest, and Colt knew then that it was not a hawk but a Comanche within fifty feet of them, pacing them to the side. He sent two

Tonkawas that direction and a few minutes later heard a scream.

One less Comanche.

They made it to the lip of the gorge and looked over. None of the troopers found any firing positions on the lip. They looked down at the campsite and saw that everything appeared normal.

No people were in evidence, but there would be none this time of the night.

Tallpine edged up to Captain Harding.

"There should be some smoke from the tipis," he whispered. Some banked fires. My guess is the camp is deserted, that there is not a Comanche there. They have scattered across the hills to the far side, and down the gorge both ways."

Captain Harding looked over the situation. He sent one squad back to the top of the hill and told them to dig in on the reverse slope to give them covering fire. He put two men on each side to cover their flanks. Then he passed the word that the men should find cover from the slope across the way. The other side of the gorge was little more than fifty yards away.

One small, folding shovel had been issued to each squad, and now the men used the tool, their bayonets, and carried larger rocks to build protection from direct fire across the gorge. An hour later the activity was over and the troopers settled down to wait for daylight.

Captain Harding talked with Tallpine. "What will White Eagle do when it's light?"

Tallpine looked at the situation. He had quickly brought up rocks and fashioned protection for himself and Captain Harding.

"White Eagle will look over the situation. If he

thinks he can attack and win, he will. He has protected his women and children and the old men. He will provide rifles to protect the tipis. There will be no chance to burn them this time. They will storm back in a direct battle to protect their tipis. Without them they all would die this winter."

"We can throw our hand bombs into the tipis, damage them as much as possible," Captain Harding said.

"This is not the camp site where the tipis were when I was here before," Tallpine said. "I knew it was different. White Eagle must have been moving from one spot to another to find the perfect site that he could protect."

"When did he take his women and children out?" Colt asked.

"Probably when his scouts reported that you were moving forward under darkness to get into position to attack the village. He had no choice then."

Each squad appointed a guard and the rest dozed. They got two hours of sleep before daylight.

With the first streaks of dawn, Colt Harding was alert and watchful. There had been no sounds, no movement from the village below. Not a horse, not a dog was present. It indeed was deserted by its people.

Captain Harding scanned the edge of the ravine on the far side. It slanted upward slightly as the land did on this side, but he could find no sign of new earth moved, no feathers, no lances, no Indians.

An owl hooted across the ravine, then one far to the right.

Tallpine came awake at once. "The Comanche are ready to attack us," he said softly.

Captain Harding passed the word to his right and left. "Alert. Be ready. Do not fire without my command."

Down the line a trooper hunched up to change position, lifting his backside a foot above his parapet.

A rifle snarled from across the gorge, the round burning a quarter inch gouge out of the trooper's rear end, dropping him into his hole with a screech.

"Two rounds per rifle. Fire!" Captain Harding bellowed. Sixty rounds of hot lead drilled across the gorge into every shrub, rock and hump that might be providing concealment for a Comanche.

When the sound died down, Colt checked the village below. It strung out a quarter of a mile along the gorge, but still he saw no Comanches. He took one of the hand bombs from his shoulder bag, checked the four inch dynamite fuse and made sure the detonator was pressed securely into the dynamite.

He lit the fuse and when he was sure it was burning well, threw it over the side toward the closet tipi, maybe thirty yards away across the small stream and fifty feet below.

The bomb landed three feet short of the tipi, jolted forward another foot, then exploded with a shattering roar that echoed up and down the gorge. The nails slashed through the tipi, gouging holes a foot long in places, snarling through a small hole in others.

When the sound quieted, Colt turned to the left, then the right, at last he looked up the hill. There was a flurry of rifle fire from the top aimed the other way. Sgt. Casemore was more than earning his keep. The Comanches had tried a rear attack.

Captain Harding passed the word for the grenadiers in each squad to throw two hand bombs each. Soon the eight bombs sailed into the air, blasting in and among the tipis below. One of the buffalo skin covered tipis burst into flames and burned brightly in the soft morning light. Half a dozen others were riddled by the roofing nail shrapnel.

The answer came from across the gorge at once. A shower of fifty arrows arched into the sky so they would fall on the dug in troopers as artillery shells would.

A pair of screeches down the line gave evidence that some of the arrows had cut white flesh.

To the left flank a rifle fired once, then again and again.

Another probe.

Captain Harding motioned to Tallpine. "Call to White Eagle. Tell him if he sends out Laughing Golden Hair, his band may live in peace without the Pony Soldiers hounding them."

The halfbreed called out the message in Comanche, and waited for a reply. It came a moment later.

"White eyes attack Comanche. Comanche lives in peace. Pony Soldiers must leave."

"Tell him we will not leave without the small golden haired girl," Captain Harding said.

The message was called across the gap.

"We have only our own children. You must leave now."

"Tell him if he does not give up Laughing Golden Hair, a thousand Pony Soldiers will come and overwhelm him, and kill everyone in his band,

and destroy his tipis and his winter food supply and the name of White Eagle will be known throughout the Comanche nation as a fool who died and let his whole band die as well because he was stupid and without honor and because he refused to let a captured white girl go free."

It was a long speech, and when he finished, Tallpine lifted his brows.

"Now you've made him mad," the Breed predicted.

White Eagle shouted back at once and Tallpine translated.

"White Eagle and his band can defend themselves. But they will not kill all of the Pony Soldiers if they leave at once and never return. If they don't there is no way they will live to see another sunrise."

Captain Harding replied: "If White Eagle does not give up Laughing Golden Hair, two thousand Pony Soldiers will track his band forever, and punish them and pursue them all the way west to the smoking waters and north to the Big Muddy. The White Eagle band will never know a day of peace again!"

White Eagle replied: "If the Pony Soldiers don't leave before the sun is at the top of the sky, he will deliver Laughing Golden Hair to the Pony Soldiers fort one pound at a time until the Pony Soldier captain has all of the child in a hundred pieces. The blue shirts must go, or the small girl will die when the sun is on top of the sky."

Tallpine translated it quickly as it was spoken. When the last words were given he nodded to Colt.

"I'd say we go. Chiefs do this all the time, use hostages and captives as poker chips. Captives have no value to a chief. And shouting this threat to you, so all his people could hear it, means he must carry out the threat or lose much of his good medicine and his power to lead his people."

Colt stared at the other side of the gully for a full minute, then nodded. "Pass the word. Squad one move up the hill smartly, the other two squads be ready with covering fire if the enemy fires. Go!"

They got all three squads up the hill without a shot being fired. Sgt. Casemore called in the flankers and they waited for the next command.

Captain Harding watched the Indians across the way move skillfully back out of the line of fire into pecan and live oak trees across the way. They had won again. Damnit!

He nodded to Sgt. Casemore and motioned to move back toward the horses. The men tending the mounts had taken the usual precautions but walked the animals forward as close to the troops as was safe.

Ten minutes later, Captain Harding and his forty men with only three slightly wounded, moved down the valley to the south, heading back to the fort. It would be a long ride home, and an uhappy one.

Colt Harding stared back at the hilltop again. There had to be a way to get Sadie back from that savage, but how? He had to devise a plan that would not fail. He had to rescue Sadie before the Comanches turned her into a savage!

8

Half a dozen Comanche warriors followed the
march of Lightning Company as it headed home.
When the troop was ten miles south of the Indian
camp, all but two Indian lookouts went back to
Croton Creek to spread the word. Only a few
warriors had returned to the campsite to check on
the damage.

The bombs the Pony Soldiers had thrown
caused severe damage. It would take many hours
of splicing and patching by the women to get the
tipi covers back in shape for the winter cold.

When the scout braves returned, the call was
given and from everywhere around the village the
People appeared and returned to their tipis. The
fire started by one of the bombs had burned only
one tipi. It was a total loss. At once new skins
were given to the Elk Wound family so a new
cover could be made.

Always Smiling went into the woods to find
strong poles to form the tipi frame. They were
hard to find in this area. She wished they were in
the fringes of a pine forest. It took her the rest of

the day and then she found only three of the seven needed.

Warrior's Woman had begun the task of laying out the skins, matching and shifting and then cutting them to fit to form the cover. It was all done on a clear spot on the ground near the stream. When Warrior's Woman had each section ready, she waved and three or four women came in and stitched the heavy pieces of buffalo hide together with tough buffalo sinew.

The women worked until darkness, then went to their own lodges to cook food and do the rest of their daily chores.

For an hour after they got back to camp a search was made. At last the warriors had found Rabbit Lair. He had been one of the scouts shadowing the Pony Soldiers when they arrived last night. Even before his body came back to camp over his war pony, the wailing and keening came from the whole village.

They had suffered their last loss in several months, but it made it no easier for Rabbit Lair's family. He would be prepared and then properly buried sitting upright in the highest peak they could find among the low hills.

There his spirit would be free to soar into the sky and to fly with the eagles and to reach the great hunting grounds where every shot was sure and every stomach was full.

Sadie did not know of the attack until she returned from a long horseback ride with her mother. The two had been instructed by White Eagle to go upstream, a two hour ride, and stay over night. That had been when it was still light the previous evening. White Eagle knew the Pony Soldiers were coming. He would take no chances of them finding Laughing Golden Hair.

Sadie had enjoyed the ride, eating a new kind of blueberry, and playing in the stream. Then they slept on the side of a hill under a huge live oak tree. It was like an overnight picnic!

Cries In The Morning did not tell her about the Pony Soldiers. She had taken Sadie three hours upstream rather than two just to be sure. When they came back that morning it had been slowly, carefully, watching every direction. When she heard the faint call of the cry that the enemy had been defeated and it was now safe, Cries In The Morning smiled and hurried with Laughing Golden Hair to White Eagle's tipi.

By that time Talks A Lot had repaired most of the damage in the big tipi with the eagle painted on the side. The worst of the bomb explosion had missed the chief's tent. It had two slashes and two of the nails had punched through the hides with their points but been stopped by the flat heads.

The strange nails were pulled out and saved.

"Soldiers here?" Sadie asked her mother.

Cries In The Morning nodded. "*Toquet,*" all is well. She explained that they had come and thew bombs but then White Eagle talked them into going back to their house of many walls.

"Why did they come?" Sadie asked.

"Who knows what the *tosi-tivo* think or why they do it. They came but they are gone. That is good. See if you can find some wild onions for me along the creek."

Sadie and two small friends hunted for wild onions, found one small patch and dug up half of them, leaving the rest for whoever found them the next day and so they would grow and multiply in Mother Earth.

The talk was only of the raid, and how they had outsmarted the Pony Soldiers. The women chattered while they repaired the tipis and sewed on the new one. The warriors gathered in small groups talking about the raid, and how they could have performed better.

White Eagle sat in his tipi with the flap closed staring into a small fire and smoking his pipe which he had filled with fresh tobacco from the trader.

He was troubled more than he would say. How had the voice speaking in the People's language known the name of Laughing Golden Hair? How had the Pony Soldiers come directly to the Comanche camp even in the dead of night?

There were a dozen hard questions for which he had no answers. There was no one to ask. His people looked to him for answers, not to bring him answers. There were no old men he could talk to.

Runs Plenty was so old his mind wandered. If he was still not the best arrow maker among the Comanches, he would have been left behind to push his nose into the dust and die with dignity. Two other former members of the council had lost all interest in the band, or how it functioned. All they wanted was a pipe and one good meal a day. They rocked their days away sitting in the sun and making up lies about their youth.

Captain Two Pistols had found him again. How could White Eagle fight against this Pony Soldier? Some of the warriors wanted to track the Pony Soldiers, catch them in the open and attack, holding them there until their bullets ran out, then cut them into small pieces and bring back many guns and scalps.

But this Captain Two Pistols was too smart for that. He would never wait for them to catch him. His men could ride as far a day as the best Comanche pony could. It would be hard to catch them before they found their fort.

An hour after sunset, the twelve members of the council sat around a small fire where the shadows bounced off the thick wall behind them, and the stream chattered at their feet. At the council each of the members could talk, no one outranked anyone else.

"I was sad when we let the Pony Soldiers walk away without a fight," Running Thunder said. "We should have attacked, followed them, chased them all the way back to their little fort."

"And we would have lost a dozen warriors!" another man said. "We stopped the white eye's attack. We turned him back, we defeated him, and at the cost of only one warrior. It was a great victory for Comanche warriors!"

"No!" Fox Paw bellowed. The young warrior was only nineteen, but already one of the best in the band. "We were like old women. We did not fight, we defended. We were not warriors; we were rocks stopping bullets from the puny rifles. A Comanche lives to fight, to make war on the Pony Soldiers."

He stopped and looked around and saw enough nods to encourage him.

"We should fight the Pony Soldier whenever we find him, and especially when he chases us down to our own village. Such a thing must never happen again! We had six hours warning that the Pony Soldiers were coming. Six hours of daylight. We could have dropped our tipis and scattered in

111

twenty different directions and left the Pony Soldiers chasing their own horses' tails!"

"The council decided we should stand and confront the Pony Soldiers with our camp so easy to defend," White Eagle said. "Where was Fox Paw when the council decided? He was sitting with the pipe in his hand. Will he not now take the responsibility of his own decisions?"

"In my heart I protested the plan even as I accepted it," Fox Paw said.

"My ears can't hear what your heart says unless your heart uses your mouth to tell me," Elk Wound said. "We have council so we may speak our hearts and our minds."

"Captain Two Guns must be punished!" Fox Paw shouted. "We must seek him out and slaughter his troops and take his scalp as a warning to all other Pony Soldiers!"

"Fox Paw demonstrates his nineteen years of lack of wisdom," White Eagle said softly. "To seek out a Pony Soldier captain is to ride into his fort. The Captain Two Guns can bring four times as many riders as he had today. He can bring as many guns as we have horses and ponies. We must think clearly, talk straight, and decide where to move now that the Pony Soldiers know where we are."

"We should move toward the Pony Soldier fort so we may launch a raid on it," Fox Paw screeched.

The council was still for a moment.

"We should move north, past the Peace River, high on the tributaries of the Red, perhaps to Mulberry Creek where we made camp one summer," Thunder Dog said. "A hundred miles to the north, but still in front of the caprock."

"I will not run away from Captain Two Guns!" Fox Paw thundered. He jumped up, his feet spread wide, his hand on the knife at his hip where it hung from his surcingle. "I am not afraid of the Captain Two Guns!"

"We must stand and fight somewhere," Proud Buck said softly. He was old, nearly fifty. "We have been driven back and back from our lands. We must stand and fight somewhere or we will be forced up to the Staked Plains and then off the far side of that."

White Eagle stood and walked around the fire. He turned at the far side and faced the council.

"We are Comanche. Many bands are moving. We can not battle the whole two thousand Pony Soldiers alone. There are ten times two thousand of the white eye soldiers. Not even all of the Comanche bands together can battle a forest of white eyes like that."

He went back to his place around the fire and sat.

"Some of the old ways are fading away. The white eyes are limiting us in some areas. It is like trying to push against the spring flood of a mighty river. We will never win. But we can live as the Comanche always has, for as long as possible. We can promote the old ways, we can move and hunt and winter and be Comanche to the very last. It would be foolish to throw ourselves into the whistling bombs and the long guns of two thousand white eye Pony Soldiers."

He loked around the council. Fox Paw still stood defiantly.

"It is my suggestion that we move north, as Thunder Dog suggested. We may go all the way to Mulberry Creek. Always Smiling will find a good camp. What is the feeling of the members of the council?"

"Wait!" Fox Paw moved closer to the council members. "It was easy to see today that White Eagle is protecting the band, but he is spending more time to protect the one who is causing us the trouble. Without the white eye girl, Laughing Golden Hair, we would not be Captain Two Guns' target. He is not after us. He is searching for his child. We spend too much time worrying about her safety rather than that of the band as a whole."

"Let each man speak his heart and his mouth," White Eagle said.

Each warrior talked briefly about his feelings about moving, when White Eagle lit the pipe and it went around. Each man smoked it except Fox Paw. He was free to move with the band or not. Each Comanche could go his own way whenever he wanted to.

They would move in two days. It gave everyone time enough to do things in an efficient organized way. They had a few more racks of meat to get dried, the packs to make.

The next morning, just as the sun came up, Fox Paw waited outside White Eagle's tipi. He wore only his breechclout and moccasins. In his right hand he carried his knife. In the left a three-foot-long piece of rawhide two inches wide.

Two warriors going to train their war ponies passed and spoke to him, but he ignored them, staring at the still closed flap of White Eagle's tent.

A half hour later the flap came open and White Eagle stepped outside. He saw Fox Paw, saw the knife, saw the stripe of rawhide. White Eagle sighed. "Fox Paw, there is no need for this."

"I have a need. The whole band has a need. We have a great need for a new leader."

"Is he to be only a boy such as you, Fox Paw?"

Anger flared in the youth's face. "I am a Comanche warrior. I have made coup many times. My scalp pole is as full as any warrior in our camp, as full as your own."

"Still, you are only a boy. Take your young family. Go with no anger, find a band that fits your beliefs, your temperament."

"No. I like this band. I just don't like its leader." He threw down the strip of rawhide at White Eagle's feet.

"You don't have to do this, Fox Paw. Your pride is hurt. Forget it. Take your family and find a new band."

"Pick up the fighting rawhide!" Fox Paw screamed. By then half a dozen braves had gathered. Women and children peeked out through tipi flaps.

"There is no other way, Fox Paw?"

"None. Soon you will be the ex-leader of this band!"

White Eagle bent and picked up the rawhide strip. He looked at it for a moment, then glanced at Fox Paw. "When?"

"When the sun is at the top of the sky. At the ceremonial fire."

"I'll be there."

Word spread through the camp like a prairie fire. Seldom did a dispute between members of a band become so heated that it could not be talked out by the old men or at least by the war leader.

Now and then it happened that neither of the parties would leave the band. If the problem was serious enough it could be settled only with a *muerto* strip of rawhide.

As White Eagle sat in his lodge preparing himself for the fight, he could remember seeing only one *muerto* fight before. One of the warriors had been killed, and the other one so badly cut up that he never rode into battle again.

White Eagle seriously considered packing his tipi and leaving the band. He knew that almost all of the fifty tipis would also come down and go with him. But that would not settle the problem.

Fox Paw was young, strong, agile. White Eagle knew that he faced the reality that he could be dead before nightfall. He took a deep breath and looked around the tipi. It had been a good life. He had tasted leadership, victory, a good woman, he had seen his children born, he had defeated the Pony Soldiers. It was a good day to die.

Every activity stopped in the village as the sun climbed to the highest point in the sky. Fox Paw waited at the ceremonial fire ring. The council sat in its place minus two members. Everyone in the camp who could walk there, sat or stood around a large circle that had been drawn on the bare earth.

White Eagle walked through the group looking at no one. When he saw Fox Paw he riveted his stare on the young warrior. White Eagle carried the *muerto* strip of rawhide. Sometimes a knot was fashioned in each end, but not this time.

He walked to within six feet of Fox Paw. White Eagle looked up at the sun.

"It is time," the eldest in the council said.

White Eagle threw the strip of rawhide at Fox Paw's feet. His sullen expression changed to a smile. He grabbed the rawhide and held one end, walked up to White Eagle and handed him the other end.

Thunder Dog stood from his position in the council and nodded to each of the men. They took the rawhide strip and each man put one end of it in his mouth. White teeth clamped down hard on the strip.

The rawhide strip had to remain in the mouths of both men. That was the only rule. If one man dropped the strip—he lost—he died.

The men faced each other. Each had his favorite fighting knife. Both of these were about twelve inches overall, with an eight inch blade that would cut on either side of the three inch tip.

They each wore only their breechclout and moccasins.

Thunder Dog lifted a lance and held it. The two fighters watched him. Then suddenly he hurled the lance into the ground beside his feet and the fight began.

When the three foot strip of rawhide was taut, only the tips of the fighting knives could reach the other man. But when they surged together all parts of the other man's body were open to attack.

The two men crouched, knees bent, arms wide for balance and attack. Both men were experts at knife fighting. They held the knives the way one would a saber to slash or stab. Slowly they circled each other, the rawhide tight.

Fox Paw jolted inward, his left hand out to ward off any blow at a vital area, his own knife thrusting forward at White Eagle's chest. White Eagle was slightly taller than the other man. He lunged to one side to avoid the blow, pulling Fox Paw with him on the leash.

White Eagle's knife slashed out at the unprotected left arm, and drew a quarter of an inch deep blood line three inches long.

Fox Paw pulled back and they feinted and circled.

Both men tried to be patient. The strategy in any kind of knife fight, White Eagle knew, was to be patient and wait for an opening. If you had to attack, be sure that you had a hand or shoulder to take a minor cut or stab as a sacrifice to get inside the opponent's blade and give him a deadly wound.

There were no rules. Kicking, biting, hitting, anything was allowed when a man fought for his life!

The two circled each other again, then White Eagle dodged to one side, reversed himself and slashed out with his knife in a roundhouse swing of his right arm. The sudden tactic caught Fox Paw off guard and the long blade slashed a shallow gash across Fox Paw's belly.

He pretended not to notice it, charged himself and drew blood from White Eagle's shoulder but the wound was minor. White Eagle was not in a position to counterattack.

Fox Paw bent low, grabbed a handful of dirt and threw it at White Eagle's face and at the same time drove in slashing viciously with the eight inch blade.

White Eagle got his hand over his eyes just in time to ward off the dirt, but he couldn't recover in time to avoid the blade. It drove into White Eagle's left forearm, scraping the bone. The searing pain jolted through his system making him gasp.

His own knife answered, slashing hard across

Fox Paw's right forearm, bringing a wince and a howl of pain.

At once Fox Paw shifted the blade to his left hand. During the movement White Eagle saw his chance and kicked upward hard with his right foot. The top of his foot caught Fox Paw's left wrist, snapped the bones and spun the big knife into the dirt.

White Eagle drove forward, slammed his body against the weaponless Fox Paw, throwing him to the ground on his back. White Eagle sat on the other warrior's belly and poised the big knife over Fox Paw's throat.

Both men were panting from the struggle.

"Kill me!" Fox Paw shouted. "Kill me now!"

White Eagle shook his head. "I will not. The blade is there, use your right hand and drive it into your throat if you wish. I would rather have you as a member of my band."

Fox Paw's right hand grabbed the hilt of the knife. He looked at White Eagle. His eyes went wide and bulged for a moment, then looked down at the knife. He screamed, but his hand did not move. Tears leaped to his eyes and he turned his head.

White Eagle stood, took the rawhide and slashed it in half.

The argument was over.

The fight was over.

It was forgotten.

By cutting the *muerto* rawhide strip, White Eagle had given Fox Paw permission to remain in the Eagle band.

His wife hurried up and stopped the blood from his belly and arm, then pulled his left hand forward. Fox Paw yelled in pain as she felt the broken wrist bones, meshing them together. Then she put a pair of white buffalo ribs on both sides of his wrist and bound them firmly in place with thin strips of wet rawhide. When the rawhide dried, it would tighten and hold the wrist firmly in place between the bone splints until the bones mended.

The next day when the band got ready to leave, Fox Paw and his wife and two small daughters turned away to the south. They would search out another band and join them.

White Eagle watched them go with sadness. His band needed every fighting man it could get. He wished the warrior well and reminded him of his great victories in war and raiding. Fox Paw nodded, the pain still great in his arm. But the praise from White Eagle made him sit taller on his war pony as he and his small herd of horses angled south toward the Colorado.

9

The trip north toward Mulberry Creek took the
Eagle Band nearly three weeks. The third day out
on a leisurely trek with the whole band, they came
upon a large herd of buffalo. Since there was
water nearby and plenty of graze, they made a
quick hunting camp and launched one of the three
or four fall hunts they would need to provide
enough pemmican for the winter.

Again and again the Comanche broad-tipped
buffalo arrows brought down the shaggy beasts.
The women ran up and the butchering process
began.

The Comanche used almost every part of the
shaggy beast, from the hide to the hair, to sinews,
to brains to the hooves. Each part had a
dedicated plan in the Comanche way of life.
Without the buffalo the Comanche nation would
die quickly.

For a week, the buffalo strips hung in the hot
sun. When they were dried, they were stored by
each family in large rawhide boxes and tended
and protected. The jerky would soon be pounded

into a powder and mixed with buffalo fat and some kind of flavoring such as blueberry, blackberry, persimmon or even pecan or walnut to make pemmican. Then it would be stored for the winter needs.

Pemmican was the winter staple. With enough the band could winter over without pain. Without enough pemmican it would be known as the winter the babies cried—just before they began starving to death.

A week after the hunt began, the Eagle band moved on north toward the Peace and the tributaries of the mighty Red River. Three days later they stopped again in a sheltered grove and launched a second major hunt. The buffalo had not moved far and feared nothing, right up to the moment a Comanche arrow pierced their hearts, and they stumbled, then tumbled to the Texas high plains in a rolling jumble of fur and dust.

Then sharp knives slashed, the giant creatures, some weighing as much as a thousand pounds, were skinned out on one side, the flesh was cut from the bones and sent to the drying racks. When one half of the creature had been cut up, a pony was used to turn the carcass over so the rest of the skin could be carefully removed and the meat taken off.

Bones were saved to be formed into tools. The brains would be used later in the tanning process. Stomach liners became bags to hold small items, and water bottles. Nothing went to waste.

Through the three weeks that Doris had been a captive of White Eagle she had been treated well. She knew she was not a slave, but neither was she wife to White Eagle. Already there were three women in his tipi, but it was not crowded.

At night, when no one could hear, she sobbed for her dead husband and her small daughter, and the lives of the twenty-eight others who had lived in the small cluster of buildings. They thought that five cabins together would be safe from Comanche raids. They had been wrong, dead wrong.

Her days were filled learning what the other women did, trying to help them. She always had been good at making herself useful, and she adapted quickly to the Indian ways. The food made her ill for the first week, but soon she learned to tolerate it and eat it as a matter of course.

Most of her time was taken up caring for Daniel. The small white boy had been Bill and Barbara's son. Now he was orphaned. White Eagle delighted in the boy. When the flap was down on their tipi, he played with the small bundle for hours. Quickly White Eagle taught him to fight and wrestle, and he named the white boy, Charging Bear, because he pretended to be so ferocious when he played with the giant Indian. He was not afraid.

It had been the second week of Doris' captivity that White Eagle came to her bed. He sat on the edge of it and talked softly to her. She understand none of it, except for an English word now and then.

At last he lay beside her, and she knew what he had been trying to tell her. She had always enjoyed making love with her husband, even though she had the idea nice ladies weren't supposed to. Now she discovered new and tantalizing lovemaking with this tall Indian.

She tried to figure it out. Nothing was that

much different, but perhaps it was just the thought of being caressed and then entered by a *savage* that set her on fire. She responded with such fire and desire that their lovemaking often turned into noisy, laughing, yelling affairs that surprised the other women in the tipi.

For ten nights in a row, White Eagle planted his seed deep within her. He had made her understand the second night that he wanted her to get pregnant.

Doris knew she was not pregnant by her husband when she was captured. After the first shock wore off, she realized that she *wanted to get pregnant* by this tall, darkly handsome Comanche, even though she knew she couldn't. She knew she was being disloyal to her dead husband and all of her friends, but this was reality, here and now. She had to live and this was the way right now to make sure of it. White Eagle would not sell her to another band, or let anyone harm her if he thought she were pregnant with his child!

When White Eagle left her that night, she found Daniel and checked him where he slept in the softest buffalo robe. He was a tough little one. He had adapted much already and was learning Comanche words. If he stayed there for two years, he would be a Comanche forever!

Doris had made friends at once with Laughing Golden Hair. They talked English with each other, and both helped White Eagle learn more English words. Laughing Golden Hair was so pretty that Doris wondered about her own looks. Her hair was still braided. She hadn't washed it since she was captured. She'd do that tomorrow.

Later that same day, Laughing Golden Hair

caught Doris's hand and pulled her toward the creek. She wanted to show her a new patch of berries she had found.

White Eagle watched them go. His face showed no emotion. But he was pleased. His last two captives were working out well. Soon the tall white Doris would be pregnant and growing a son for him. Then he would have two sons!

Already he had started teaching Charging Bear how to shoot the small bow and arrow he had made for him. The boy was quick to learn. He would make a fine chief.

White Eagle took out the soft leather pouch with a drawstring of rawhide lacing and fingered the *tosi-tivo* gold. It was called gold money, and Doris had told him it was greatly valuable.

He remembered the trader who had come in a broken wagon with goods for sale. The wandering half white man knew no Comanche tongue, but drove a hard bargain.

At first White Eagle had bargained with horses. The trader had four rifles, and White Eagle wanted them. Instead of twenty horses for each rifle, White Eagle offered the trader one of the gold coins for each rifle.

The trader had been so surprised to see the gold he couldn't cover up his eagerness. He demanded three coins for each rifle, but at last took one. For one more of the coins, the trader sold the Comanche the rest of his stock of beads and trinkets and ends of cloth. The Comanche women were delighted.

Now White Eagle stared at the sack of gold coins. He had counted them. There were more than fifty. How had one small rancher found so much of the woman's clay? White Eagle shook his head in amazement, then put the gold away where it was safe from prying eyes. No one except Doris knew that he had the gold coins. Some day he would need them.

Sadie was happier than she had been in weeks. Having another "mother" in the tipi was a joy, especially since she could speak English. Sadie had cried when she told Doris about the raid by the Indians on the supply train and how so many had died.

She wasn't sure what happened to her mother and brother.

"When will my father come to get us?" Sadie asked.

Doris held her tightly. There was no way she could tell the small child that her father had come with the Pony Soldiers when they were at the Croton Creek camp. Her father and his soldiers had not been able to defeat the Comanche.

Now they were going north again, away from the Pony Soldiers. Doris felt hot tears creep down her cheeks. She realized that this was not just a vacation, or a pleasant outing. She suddenly understood that she could be here with the Comanche for the rest of her life!

At once she hardened her mind, she would accept the kindness and the loving of the Comanche, but she would from this day forward wait and watch, and look for a way to escape. When she found it she would take Daniel and Sadie and they would slip away and find their way to the nearest settlement. It would have to be a good plan. Just walking away would not work. Even with good fast ponies the Comanche would catch them quickly.

It had to be an excellent plan, and it had to be

the next time the Pony Soldiers found them. Yes, that was it. She had to plan and watch and wait. When the Pony Soldiers came she would escape with her two small charges!

Sadie had wondered about all the talk about the Pony Soldiers after the raid, but she did not connect it with her father. If her father had been that close he would have come and taken her away to the fort. She was sure of that. So it must have been some other Pony Soldiers who didn't know she was there.

She had found a bow one of the older boys had outgrown, and she was learning to shoot arrows. It was a lot harder than she thought. One of her tipi sisters helped her. Black Bird was more than seven years old and could use a bow and arrow well. She was White Eagle's daughter and patiently showed Laughing Golden Hair how to shoot with the bow. She helped her again and again, and after a while, the white girl got the idea. Then it was a matter of practice. She would learn to shoot a bow as well as Black Bird and Something Pretty, her other tipi sister who was also five.

The three girls ran to the stream but it was too cold to go swimming. They splashed a minute, then sat on the bank letting the growing colder sun warm them.

For an hour they took out the curved buffalo bones the older women used for sticks to hit the buffalo hair-stuffed ball. They knocked it up and down a grassy field until they were all exhausted. A cold drink from the stream and a handful of berries refreshed them, and they walked back to the big tipi arm in arm.

Laughing Golden Hair had tanned well these

last three months. She was almost the same copper color as her tipi sisters. All of the small rope burns had healed and each day it seemed her hair grew longer. Cries In The Morning loved to grease and then braid it in proper Indian fashion.

Some days Sadie thought about home a lot. On those days she ran to find Doris and they talked about their homes and what the other white people were doing. They always went off by themselves to say these things, so no one would hear them.

Today, Sadie wandered around the tipis watching people. She was about to check in one of the other tipis for a friend when an Indian boy ran between the tipis shouting and waving his bow and arrows at everyone he saw.

White Eagle stepped from his tipi and scowled at the boy for a minute, then he pulled his lance from where it stood beside his buffalo shield in front of his tipi and ran to where the boy stood threatening one of the old men.

White Eagle stopped eight feet from the youth. "Lame Beaver, put down your bow. We are your friends here. This is your band."

Lame Beaver turned toward White Eagle. His eyes were wide and wild. There was a strange expression on his face, and as he breathed through his mouth, flecks of foam came out.

The youth yelled. It was not a Comanche war cry. They were not words, but a terrible cry of an animal who had been wounded. As he screamed, Lame Beaver notched an arrow and lifted the bow with the arrow aimed at the band's leader.

White Eagle swung his lance—the butt end of it jolted into Lame Beaver's bow before he could draw, slammed it out of his hands and then the lance thrust again. The second time it struck Lame Beaver in the back, over his kidney just above his hip bone and he sank slowly to his knees, then fell to one side, the screams still spilling from his mouth.

Quickly White Eagle ran to the boy, turned him on his back and tied his hands behind him with a piece of rawhide thong. Now Lame Beaver was spitting the white bubbles from his mouth. He tried to talk, but couldn't. His eyes were like a caged animal's now.

His screams came again and again.

Three women ran up, but White Eagle motioned them back. Lame Beaver's mother came rushing through the group but she stopped when she saw him. He lay on his side, his legs drawn up to his chest, his face a froth of foam.

His mother took a step back and looked at White Eagle.

"Yes, you're right. Somehow Lame Beaver has caught the Foaming Dog Mouth. Every dog in camp must be tied up so it can touch no one and no other dog or animal. We must do it now or more of us will be struck down by this disease."

Doris came around a tipi, caught Laughing Golden Hair's hand and led her away from the place.

"We don't want to see any more of that," Doris said. She knelt in front of Sadie. "Do you know what he has?"

Sadie shook her head.

"It's called a lot of things, but our people used the word rabies. Just terrible. It can get in a pack of wolves and bats and cats and dogs and kill just everything. If a rabid dog bites a man he can get it, too. He always—" She stopped. "Let's go back to the tipi and see if they find what bit the boy."

Doris kept Sadie inside the tipi the rest of the afternoon.

White Eagle had talked with the council. Lame Beaver had been on his vision quest, he had been on two raids. He was almost a warrior. But it had to be done.

Two warriors had been watching Lame Beaver, not letting him move from where he had fallen. Two other warriors had gone to Lame Beaver's mother's tipi and looked for his dog. Lame Beaver had two dogs he was proud of. They went everywhere with him, hunted with him. Only one was at the tipi.

They reported that Lame Beaver's one dog was tied inside the tipi. Every warrior in camp now searched the area for Lame Beaver's second dog. It took them an hour to find it. The dog had dug a hole and crawled under the back of a tipi, burrowing almost out of sight.

It snarled and snapped at them, foam flickering around its mouth. The warrior who found the dog called White Eagle. He took a club and coaxed the snarling animal half out of the hole, then smashed its skull with one blow from the heavy club.

"Do not touch it!" White Eagle bellowed. He found a strong stick and cut a sharp point on the end. With the point he stabbed into the dog's carcass and carried it far up on the hill. He had brought a spade taken on a raid. Quickly the dog's body was buried deep in the ground and covered.

Back at the camp, the council had decided another important step. Three of the women were told to build a lean-to shelter a hundred yards up the hill. They were to make it rainproof and wind-proof. A pole of dead wood was found. They cut it off three feet long and made a point on the end.

When the lean-to was completed of brush and boughs from the pecan trees and the live oaks, White Eagle went to Lame Beaver. He did not try to talk to him. Lame Beaver's soul was not willing to talk with anyone.

White Eagle lifted him by the arms, and staying behind him, walked Lame Beaver up the hill. At the shelter the heavy stake was pounded into the ground using a large rock. When it remained only a foot out of the soil, a dozen stout pieces of rawhide were tied to the stake, then Lame Beaver was tied to the stake by his ankles, and by his wrists.

His hands were moved in front of him. When White Eagle was sure that Lame Beaver could not get away, the warriors left him. One warrior stood twenty yards away. Someone would guard him day and night.

All the rest of the day, Lame Beaver screamed and howled and cried. Those in the camp below tried not to listen. Every dog in camp was eyed with suspicion. They would stay tied up for fifteen days, then if none showed signs of the foaming dog mouth disease, the camp could get back to normal.

The second day, Lame Beaver stopped screaming. He had yelled so much that his voice would no longer function. No one went near him. The Comanche had seen rabies before. They had found it in bats and wolves and coyotes and rabbits.

Only once before could White Eagle remember one of the People having it. The warrior had killed three women and a child before he had been killed. The sickness had turned him into a raging animal.

"Crazy Mouth" some of the People called it. Hopefully they had stopped it before anyone else had caught the disease. White Eagle was not sure how Lame Beaver caught it, but it usually came from a dog. Now they would watch and hope.

Lame Beaver went into convulsions the third day. His body shook and jolted and he wailed in misery. No one was allowed to approach his lean-to.

The fourth day Lame Beaver died. When no sound came from the lean-to for three hours, White Eagle went up to the hill. The boy was dead. The sickness had died with him. White Eagle made his family leave him there for two more days, then his body was carried in a buffalo robe to the highest peak within a days ride and given the traditional burial, so his spirit could lift into the clouds.

White Eagle made them leave the robe there with the body. They came back wailing and crying. His mother slashed her arms to show her grief, and let blood spread down the horse she rode. Only when she was back at the camp did she close up her wounds.

White Eagle visited every tipi the next day. Nowhere did he find anyone sick. None of the dogs were showing any signs of the rabies. They had stopped Lame Beaver in time. He went back to his tipi and played with little Charging Bear. In two or three days they would have to go to a hunting camp. It was time. The leaves were falling. Winter was coming. Two more hunting times and they would be ready for their winter camp.

Then White Eagle would have endless days to play with Charging Bear, teach him to become a chief, and to watch Doris's belly swell with the growth of his own son. She must have a son!

10

Red Hawk had watched Lame Beaver die. They had been good friends. Red Hawk did not understand why his friend was gone, why he would never seen him again. The gods struck down a promising young warrior for no reason. It only made him all the more ready to go and confront the gods. He was ready now. Perhaps that was part of Lame Beaver's reason for dying—to help show Red Hawk his path in life.

Red Hawk sat in front of his father's tipi for an hour after Lame Beaver died. Then he went to two of the Old Men and talked to them about a vision quest. Each told him something different. Each gave him some idea of what he should do and how to do it. Then he went and sat outside White Eagle's tipi waiting until he was asked to speak.

White Eagle came back from the lean-to on the side of the hill, he saw Red Hawk but did not acknowledge him. He went into his tipi and a half hour later came out and motioned Red Hawk to follow him. They went to the council fire logs where White Eagle sat and indicated that Red Hawk should stand and speak.

"Great Chief White Eagle, I am ready to begin my vision quest. I have spoken with the Old Men, learning from them what I can. Now I wish your instruction, advice and counsel."

White Eagle had done this service many times before for young men as they went on their vision quests. It was a time when each new warrior-to-be must purify himself, prostrate himself to the gods, and ask their direction. Each one hoped for a vision to lead him on his journey through life. At the same time he might learn his new name through some natural happening during his quest.

"Red Hawk, you have prepared yourself for this quest. You know the rituals of obedience to the gods. You know you must be pure in spirit to have a vision, and your quest for that vision is one of the most important acts of your life."

"Yes, White Eagle. I understand all of this."

"You know that you may take enough jerky or pemmican for only two days. If your quest lasts longer you must live off the strength of your body and your spirit."

"I understand all of this."

"Who created Mother Earth upon which we all live?"

"The council of the gods made the land and all that is in and on it. The gods of the council are the gods of the wind, of the thunder, of rain, of the trees and of the buffalo and horses. The gods all join together, and I seek their guidance through a vision of my destiny in life, of my work, of my duties as a Comanche warrior!"

"Then begin your quest. Take only your knife,

breechclout and moccasins. Treat every rock, every tree, every hill and valley as one of the gods of the People. May you be successful, Red Hawk, in your vision quest!''

White Eagle stood and stared at the youth for a moment, then Red Hawk spun on his foot and walked slowly out of camp toward the north and the highest mountain he could see. He wanted to find his vision high in the sky overlooking as much of Mother Earth as possible.

Red Hawk did not run, nor jog. He knew he had to conserve his energies for the ritual ordeal that was to come. He did not understand all of it. Other boys who had been on their vision quest had told him parts of it. He knew he must find a favorite place and plead with the gods to grant him a vision. Then he must sit and meditate until it happened.

It might take a day, it might take a week or even two weeks. He would have to know how long he could wait and pray for the quest, before he had to leave to get back to the camp.

Once in a great while a young man came back without receiving a vision. He was allowed one more chance. Failing that, he would have to go through life never becoming a warrior, never able to take a wife. He would do menial jobs for the band for the rest of his life.

Red Hawk walked until it grew dark. He was about half way to the peak he had selected. It was not much of a mountain, but it was the best he could find in this part of the high Texas plains.

He had heard the less water you drank, the quicker you would have the vision. He drank sparingly as he went across small streams, then not at all as he climbed up the low hills in front of the higher ridge.

When night came he sat against a rock and watched the stars. There were dozens of star gods, but he couldn't remember their names. Names weren't as important as listening for them to speak to you. Red Hawk sat very still listening, watching the scudding clouds block out the moon and the stars.

But none of them spoke to him.

He ate a little of the jerky, chewing it for as long as he could before he had to swallow it. Sometime before the Big Dipper fell from the sky, he slept.

Morning came and the warm glow of the fall sun shone on him. He had not felt cold. Often he felt cold even under his buffalo robes in his parent's tipi.

Good! It was the first sign that he would have a successful vision quest!

He hiked up the hill again, went over one ridge, then another and about noon came to the top of the ridge. He could see for many days walk in each direction. He had brought along some of the sacred powder from the Medicine Man and now pinched it with his thumb and finger and tossed a pinch in each of the four directions, imploring the gods to see and hear him, and to grant him a vision and a serious task for his life.

After he scattered the sacred powder, he sat down on a large slab of rock, crossed his legs, and put his hands on his thighs. He sat that way for two hours, but no one spoke to him. Nothing happened.

Once a curious Eagle circled high overhead, dove to within twenty feet of him, then retreated with a call of rage because his hoped-for prey turned out to be his greatest enemy, man.

For the next two days Red Hawk sat on the slab of rock. He was warm in the day and cold at night. He slept sometimes, but tried to stay awake. He had eaten nothing the last two days, hoping to save his meager food for the walk home.

The third day he had trouble sitting up. A film seemed to come down over his eyes and he blinked to get rid of it. He began to sing his song of life, making it up as he went along. The wonders of his life, the glories of the People, the marvels of the Eagle Band. But he didn't feel inspired, the songs came out dull and routine.

He put sharp stones between his toes so the pain would keep him alert. His stomach began to hurt and then he vomited. He was dizzy most of the afternoon. At last he moved to a stone with sharp edges, and put small rocks to sit on to help him keep awake.

He wanted to sleep.

He feared if he slept he would never awake.

The dizziness came again and he fell to the rocks, gashing his forehead. Blood ran down his face.

He had not noticed the storm clouds rushing toward him. Lightning snarled from the clouds to the ground. Lightning was a sign of the gods' anger. Then to reinforce the anger came the roaring thunder as the gods banged the earth against the clouds to show their continuing unhappiness.

Rain drenched Red Hawk. It revived him. He sat up straight again on the sharp rocks. He put a round pebble in his mouth and sucked on it. For a moment his stomach felt better.

With the rain came a cold wind, and flakes of

snow dropped, then they were replaced with hail the size of pheasant eggs. The hailstones were not hard, but soft and broke when they hit him.

He laughed at them. He could crush hail stones! The hail stones hit his face and came away red with his blood. He laughed again and welcomed the gods' testing him.

Then the dizziness came back and he fell forward, protecting himself with his hands and lay there as the rain and hail pounded down on him.

From far off he saw a large black stallion racing toward him. The stallion had eyes of green anger, and smoke and flames blazed from his nostrils. Steam issued from the great horse's mouth as he raced up the mountain and stood panting and heaving at Red Hawk's side.

"Get on my back," the horse said to him.

Red Hawk was not surprised to hear the horse speak. At once he jumped up and leaped on the bare back of the black stallion and they raced away, only they were no longer on the ground. They sailed in the air. Below he saw the Eagle Band camp on Mulberry Creek. He watched as they flew over the rolling plains and into the desert and the sparse growth and over the high snow covered mountains he had heard about that were two moons journey to the west.

These mountains always had snow, even in the hottest summer, and they were covered with huge forests of trees so tall it would take all day to walk around one that had fallen to the ground.

Red Hawk saw men and machines he didn't understand. He saw long strings of wagons with white covers on them, and white eyes plodding along beside the wagons or driving cattle along behind them.

He saw a huge steam belching horse made of iron that was ten horses long, and clattered along on shining ribbons of metal that extended so far into the distance that they at last came together into a single point.

He found a company of Pony Soldiers ride against him and his black stallion, and he was a mighty warrior and crushed the whole company, killing each one and racing back to show White Eagle the forty rifles and forty pistols that he alone had captured. His scalp pole was bending so it broke when he hung all forty scalps on it.

He kept asking the black horse what it meant, but the stallion pretended that he couldn't talk, merely flew around and let Red Hawk see all the parts of his vision.

Then slowly the big horse settled back down on the same ledge they had left from. As Red Hawk dismounted he asked the stallion again what it all meant.

The stallion snorted and pawed the ground with his front hooves. "I only bring you to the vision, I am not allowed to tell you what it means. That is up to you to figure out."

Then, as Red Hawk began to ask him another question, the black stallion vanished in a wisp of mist. The mist too was gone and Red Hawk slumped to the ground and fainted.

When he woke, the warm sun was up high. The ground looked as if the snow and rain had never come.

He had his vision!

Red Hawk remembered it all perfectly. He would determine its meaning as he went back down the mountain. He found the rest of his food in the small rawhide bag he brought with him and ate. Then he was strong enough to start down.

He had discovered no new name signs. Nothing had approached him. He would keep his name since none other was ordered. He would be Red Hawk, and soon a warrior!

As he walked down the slope he began to evaluate his quest and to translate each of the symbolic events into day-by-day duties he must undertake for the tribe. He was far from finished by the time he hiked back to the camp on Mulberry Creek the second day.

His heart stopped a moment when he saw the bare banks of the creek. Only a few indications were left that a band had camped there. At once he knew what he had to do. He searched the woods near where the horses were kept. After half an hour he found his pony with a long tether in fresh grass.

All he had to do was look for the tracks of the band and follow them to the hunting camp they would establish. Again they had headed north and some to the west.

The caprock could almost be seen from here. Perhaps some day they would go all the way to the Staked Plains!

Red Hawk mounted the pony and rode to the far end of the camp where he saw the most tracks. Soon he had found the travois pole marks in the dust. He rode out at a natural canter. He would find the band within a day or two at the most.

Red Hawk smiled. He had found his vision, he would soon be a warrior! It was a good day to be alive!

11

After the standoff with White Eagle at Croton Creek, Captain Colt Harding pushed his men hard. They arrived back at Fort Comfort after a little over two days riding.

The men were frustrated that they had not had a chance to close with the Comanche in battle. The Tonkawas were furious that they were not given the one Comanche killed so they could enjoy some of their special "soup."

Most bothered of all was Captain Harding. He had a strong feeling that his daughter was so close that day that he could have almost touched her, yet she was a continent away. White Eagle possessed one bargaining chip in this poker game that Captain Harding could not top.

If the army kept pressuring him to release Sadie, or of the Pony Soldiers moved in too close, White Eagle could kill his captive. The savages held that advantage that the white men would never have.

So Captain Harding had to develop a whole new plan to rescue Sadie. He would still use his

Lightning Company as an example of how the army should be fighting the hostiles. He had received one favorable letter about the plan from Colonel Sparkman in San Antonio, headquarters of the Division of Texas.

But for Sadie it would have to be something else. Perhaps a surprise raid by him and the Tonkawas. Another leave of absence. Move so the Comanche scouts never knew they were within a hundred miles. Creep into their camp at night, grab Sadie from the big tipi and be gone in the darkness before the Comanche knew anything had happened.

He had threatened to do it that way before, but it involved tremendous risks. His whole career, his very life was in the worst kind of jeopardy. The Tonks might even decide to use him for their stews and steaks and barbequed ribs! They could say the Comanche had killed him.

At the fort the returning company was met by a six man escort. The three wounded were moved in first, then the rest came in as smartly as they could.

In his quarters, Captain Harding looked over the dispatches which Lt. Riddle had sorted through. There had been only one come in.

Lt. Riddle watched his commander. He poured them each a shot glass of whiskey and handed one to the Captain.

"You contacted White Eagle?"

Captain Harding lifted the shot glass and drank it down in one blast. He coughed and put the glass on the desk.

"Hell yes. The Breed talked to him like a cousin. The only problem was White Eagle threatened Sadie if we didn't vamoose. He had us blackjacked. We left."

"Damn." Lt. Riddle pointed to the dispatches. "Nothing important in there. Routine. We're getting in some more rifle rounds, and twenty new Spencer repeaters. Maybe someday every man will have the same make and caliber of weapon."

Lt. Riddle walked to the window and came back. His face was strained, he seemed uncomfortable. Harding noticed it at once.

"All right, John. Tell me what the hell went wrong. You've been acting like you were heading into battle for the first time. Tell me."

"Yeah, hard man to fool. We've got a little bit of a problem. Day after you left, we had some visitors. Five covered wagons pulled up to the gate. We've got five families who want to homestead nearby. The men are out riding, looking around for the best spots. Three of them want to be cattle ranchers, as I recall, and the other two will be dirt farmers, sod busters."

"Homesteaders! Way out here? Christ! I thought the folks at Austin said nobody was to come out this far."

"Did. But Austin isn't the authority on government land. Nobody told them not to come, so here they are. They say they figured to locate nearby so the fort can protect them."

"Where are they camped? We'll go pay them a social call tomorrow."

"Downstream on the White, maybe a half mile. They settled in just above the Indian camp."

"Exactly what I need, five homestead families to worry about. They said we were supposed to protect them?"

"True. They've been here for five days now,

getting impatient to drive in some stakes."

Captain Harding swore in a whisper for two minutes, never repeating himself. He unbuttoned his blue uniform shirt. "See if I've got a clean shirt in the bureau, we better get out there right now and send them back to Austin."

Lt. Riddle, Captain Harding and six men from B Company rode out a half hour later. The wagons could be seen from just outside the fort at their downstream location.

As they rode up, the officers saw that the wagons had been pulled into a defensive circle. Three cooking fires were going, and twenty or thirty civilians wandered around inside and outside the wagon ring. To the left was a rope corral filled with horses, mules and a few steers. It was an unholy grouping.

A man came forward. He was one of the ranchers. Cowboy hat, boots, and a gunbelt with a new looking hogleg.

"Evening, Captain, heard you and your men just got back. Sorry to hear you didn't rescue your little girl, Sadie. Oh, I'm Josh Wilson."

Captain Harding swung down off his horse and shook hands with Wilson.

"Pleased to meet you, Mr. Wilson. I hope you've reconsidered homesteading this far from the safety of other settlers. It's absolutely far too dangerous out here. We're a hundred and twenty miles from Austin, and two years ago some Comanches raided farms not two miles from Austin."

"Know that, Captain. We're here. We know where it is. We're setting out stakes in the morning to claim our homesteads. Afraid that decision is made, not one you have any authority over."

"But you'll want me to risk my troopers and officers to defend you when the Comanche find out you're here. They hate four-wallers worse than anything. You'll be throwing a life and death challenge right in their teeth."

"Progress, I guess you'd call it, Captain Harding. Sorry, but we're here to stay."

Wilson was a tall, stringy man, who moved with an easy stride and had a casual relaxed appearance that probably belied his quickness and ability with his six-gun. Captain Harding had seen a man or two like him before. Gambler. Wilson had been a gambler at one time or another.

"Captain, the five of us worked it out. For the first few years we'll all live in a compound of five houses, built close together and inside a solid wall. We figure we can make the houses and the wall out of this adobe clay blocks like you made your fort of. We got our carpenter building us the form boxes now and we found a new deposit of clay. We'll be on the White River here about another mile down, where the valley spreads out and there's plenty of grass and the trees are still standing along the creeks."

"Wilson. There isn't any chance that I can let you stay here. I do have authority over undeveloped areas."

"True Captain, but once we get our stakes down, this area becomes developed. Talked to the State Attorney General in Austin, and to the army's liaison man there. He gave me a letter for you."

Captain Harding took the letter and held it. "I know what it's going to say, Mr. Wilson. But do you know what a man looks like after the Comanches scalp him and then mutilate the body?"

"That I do, Captain. Not a pretty sight."

"And have you seen a ranch or farm after a Comanche raid? You know what they do to the women and children?"

"I do, Captain. I fought with the cavalry for two years back in fifty-seven. We did a mite of Comanche work ourselves with the Second Cavalry."

"Then I shouldn't have to tell you the danger."

"You don't. We didn't come here for your permission, your approval, or for your anger. We're here, and we're going to stay here. We'll have three cattle ranches and two farms all picked out. In a year or two we should be able to provide you most of your beef, vegetables, beans, potatoes, and wheat and oats for your stock. We can save the army the cost of transport from Austin. I've already put in a bid with the District of Texas Army Headquarters Quartermaster to supply you."

"Thought of everything, haven't you, Wilson?"

"I hope so. We're risking the lives of thirty-two human beings out here. We're going to see that the plan works. For our first herds we'll gather up the strays we've been spotting. I figure there are at least fifty thousand head of cattle running wild in this part of Texas. Most of them were cut loose during the war, and just never rounded up."

"Mr. Wilson, I'll see that target practice is conducted away from your compound, and that your homestead and buildings will be off limits to my troopers and officers. You're welcome to the fort at any time."

"Well, that's mighty neighborly of you, Captain Harding and Lieutenant Riddle. Now that the formalities are over, would you like to meet the rest of our people?"

"Sorry, Mr. Wilson, I'm just back from a sixty-five mile ride and I'm wanting a bath. Perhaps at a later time." Captain Harding stepped up on his horse and Lieutenant Edwards followed. They said goodbye and cantered back to the fort.

"Two of the girls in the group are over sixteen," Lt. Riddle said. "They could present us with some problems."

"Off limits," Captain Harding growled. "Any man who touches those civilians gets twenty years pounding rocks!"

They rode a hundred yards.

"How is our eighteen-year-old trouble maker doing?"

"Pamela. She hasn't caused any more explosions that I know of. She has been causing her father some gray hairs, though I'd say. Captain Kenny will be leaving tomorrow morning on a three day sweep patrol. He requested a second one to get a feel of the country."

"Good. He's going to be a fine addition to our staff."

Back at Captain Harding's quarters, Cpl. Swenson had two boilers of hot water waiting on the stove. Colt Harding tried to soak away some of his anger and his mounting problems.

Farther down the officer country side of Fort Comfort, Captain Morse Kenny stood in front of his daughter, Pamela. Both were angry. Both had already said things that they shouldn't have, but a stubborn streak common to both refused to let them recant.

Pamela set her fists on her hips and glared at her father. "Yes! I said I love him. I want to marry him. I don't care if he's *only a corporal* as you said. A man is a man, and he's as good as any officer on this post!"

"He hasn't even been to school past the fourth grade. He doesn't know who his father was." Captain Kenny threw up his hands and sat down in his chair. "I don't understand you, Pamela."

"Obviously, Father. I'm not a little girl. I'm a woman. I have the desires and needs of a woman. That's why we get married. I will marry Victor whether you want me to or not. And just to make certain, I'm warning you. If you try to interfere, I'll go straight to Captain Harding and tell him how you beat up on Victor when he hadn't done a damn thing!"

Kenny jumped up. "Stop swearing, Pamela. And I'm sure you wouldn't tell Captain Harding!"

"I would, I will! Now just settle down and get used to the idea of having a grandchild. I want maybe six kids."

"You couldn't turn in your own father?"

"If you try to stop Vic and me, I most certainly will. His enlistment is up in two months. We'll go to Austin and be married there. Write to auntie and tell her I won't be coming to Boston."

"This is insane!"

Captain Kenny still thought the whole idea of his long protected daughter falling into the clutches of a lowly corporal was disgusting. He led his patrol out the next morning, and for the first time he had included Cpl. Victor Gregory in the roster. He could at least see how the man functioned in the field.

Even so, the idea of an enlisted man for a son-in-law was ridiculous, totally unacceptable. It would be awkward even having them over for supper some night. No other officers could be present, that would be for certain.

He sighed, led the twenty man patrol out the gate and sighted in on his compass, then headed into the sector he needed to sweep to be sure there was no Comanche activity. It was about twenty miles west of the fort. They would be on the site before midday.

The patrol moved along well toward the objective, a small hill called Rooster's Knob. They covered the twenty miles and took a break. At this point the usual procedure was to split the patrol in half. One unit would sweep around the west side of the knob and down a long valley often used by Comanches.

The second element would take the eastern side, move up a different low valley and they would meet some ten miles north.

Captain Kenny had never liked the idea of splitting up a force of any size when there were hostiles around. But it was the only way to cover the ground they had to in three days. He sent Sgt. Dean Franklin with the first squad and he took the second. He made sure that Cpl. Gregory remained with him. He wanted to keep an eye on the young man.

Captain Kenny talked with his sergeant.

"Do the sweep and stay out of trouble," Kenny cautioned. "I don't like splitting up. Don't start a fight with any Comanche you see. They'll probably run if they see you first. We'll meet at the head of the two valleys sometime around two hours from now."

"Yes, sir. Should be no problem. We've all done this before."

"Except me, Sergeant. I'll try to measure up. Move out."

Captain Kenny had felt his face flush at the unintentional slap in the face Sergeant Franklin gave him. He was the new kid on the block even if he was a captain. Another few months and he'd have his garrison duty tag shaken off.

He moved out his men at a ground-eating canter. It was the roughest way for a man to sit a horse, but it was a natural pace for most horses, and they could maintain it for hours without tiring.

For this operation they were in a two abreast formation, with Captain Kenny at the head of the small column. He watched behind them and saw that they were sending up a thin cloud of dust. If there were Comanche in the area, they would know someone was coming.

The patrol flushed through the dry course of a small stream. It probably had run during the spring and halfway into summer. It had watered a half dozen pecan trees and a few live oak. They rode through the trees and brush, found no evidence of an Indian camp and moved on up the flat, dry valley.

A hawk circled high over the landscape. They saw no game. To the far left Captain Kenny thought he saw a moving brown mass which could be a herd of slowly grazing buffalo. He had never actually seen buffalo up close. He was anxious to put that small problem behind him.

Cpl. Gregory rode up beside him.

"Sir. To the left ahead there's a dust trail. About two fingers off north, sir."

Kenny looked in that direction and saw the trail. It was a much larger trail than their own, which meant more horses. He held up his hand and the patrol stopped.

"If it's a raiding party, they'll want to check us out and see if we're a wagon train or settlers," Gregory said.

Captain Kenny remembered that Gregory had won his stripes in the field before he went to the clerk's job.

"Corporal, how many riders would you guess are out there?"

Gregory looked at them again, then at the sun. He paused. "Hate to say it, sir, but I'd figure twenty or twenty-five. They're turned and are coming directly at us."

"Not shy, are they?"

"Not the Comanche, sir, in what he considers his own front yard."

They were a mile from the closest cover of any kind. Even the pecan trees had deserted them.

"That grove about a mile to the left," Capt. Kenny said quickly. "We'll head for that and see if they want to fight."

'Ho-oooooooooo," Captain Kenny called and swung his arm forward. The patrol galloped half way to the trees, then cantered the rest of the way. The dust of the riders came closer. By the time they were in the cover of the trees, the hostiles could be seen. They were Comanche.

"At least twenty-five," Kenny said. "Move the horses back, tie them and get the wrangler back up here," Kenny barked at Cpl. Gregory.

Five minutes later the men of the first squad of B Company lay behind downed logs and hastily pulled up rock barricades as a Comanche raiding party held a small council just out of the best rifle range.

They ended the pow-wow and fanned out in a long line, then the center of it broke for the trees, charging in the form of a wide "V" of Comanche warriors.

"Hold your fire until I give the command to fire!" Kenny shouted. The men held. At three hundred yards they looked at the new captain. At two hundred yards they began to sweat.

When the Indians reached a hundred yards the Comanches began firing rifles.

"Fire!" Captain Kenny shouted.

The officer aimed his new Spencer and squeezed off a round. One of the lead ponies took his round in its head and stumbled and fell. One down.

The ragged volley that came from the brush killed two of the frontal charging Comanches, and put down three horses. The raiders never came within more than fifty yards of the cavalrymen.

They wheeled and raced back to a safer range.

"They'll be back, Captain," Cpl. Gregory said.

"Casualties?" Kenny bellowed. Only one man was hit. He had a crease along one shoulder.

"The next time they come, shoot for their ponies. Head shots on the horses. Without their war ponies they are helpless. You hear me? No sentimental slobs here. Gun down their mounts and we'll save our scalps."

The men acknowledged his command.

For a moment, Captain Kenny thought of sending someone to bring back the rest of their patrol. With another ten guns here the Comanche would turn tail and ride off.

Gregory. He could send the corporal on the mission and he might be spotted by the

Comanche and captured. For just a fraction of a second Captain Kenny realized that would be a good way to get rid of a major problem with Pamela.

He rejected it out of hand. Cpl. Gregory was the highest non-com he had in his group.

"Be coming back soon, sir. This time I'd guess they'll put half their men behind us. Usual Indians ain't too good at tactics, but this bunch seems to be following orders pretty damn good."

"Suggestions, Corporal Gregory?"

"Yeah, but it better wait a minute. We got visitors again."

This time the Comanche attacked in a long line riding past the clot of gunmen in the pecans and live oaks. They hung on the off side of their mounts offering no target to the cavalrymen. The squad followed its orders and fired at the horses. Two went down dead, two more were wounded and turned out of the line limping back out of range.

"Next time they'll split up, try to get two or three savages into the brush," Cpl. Gregory said. "Can't let them penetrate or we'll be in trouble."

Captain Kenny filled one of the magazine tubes with .52 caliber rounds and watched Gregory.

"You said you might have a suggestion, Corporal."

"Yes sir. This bunch ain't gonna go away. They took dead and they'll want to take our scalps. I'd say it's a raiding party heading toward Austin. We better get Sgt. Franklin and his men. Wind's blowing away from him, so chances are he won't hear the gunfire. There's a cut across country this side of the knob. I could catch him and get him back here in about an hour."

"Risky. Won't the Comanche chase you?"

"Not if you give me that big gray you're riding. It can outdistance anything they've got."

"You could get killed, Gregory."

"Yes, sir. But the odds are better if we get some help. We didn't bring that much extra ammo."

"Go, Gregory. Now, before they attack again. Get out of the back side of the brush and you can be a half mile away before they see you. Good luck."

Gregory gave him a half smile, filled another empty magazine tube and put it through the stock of his Spencer. Then he saluted and crawled back toward the horses.

Captain Kenny watched him go, then looked out front again. "Casualties?" he called.

"Yeah, Captain. Ingles down here is hit bad. Took a round in one lung I'd guess. He's out of it for now, leastwise."

"We've got help coming, Franklin. So we just hold out. If you can't get an Indian target, kill his god damned pony. They won't fight without their horses. They value those war ponies much more than they do their wives. So shoot for the horses!"

"Here they come again," someone said.

They rode past in a line again, hanging off the far side of their horses. By this time there were only four rifles firing from the Indian ranks. Captain Kenny listened for the shots from the riders and tried to hit the horses where he thought the rifle shot came from.

The charge was closer, and half of the braves used bows and arrows now. They moved in closer yet.

Another Indian pony went down. Captain

Kenny waited for the rider to kick free. As soon as the warrior stood up he hesitated. Kenny fired and the brave went down with a .52 caliber slug through his heart.

The Indians turned at the far end and came back, hanging on the other side of their mount this time.

"God help us!" Captain Kenny breathed and aimed at another Indian pony.

12

Cpl. Victor Gregory slid through the brush and trees to the back of the small fringe of woods along the small creek, caught the big sturdy gray the captain rode and mounted.

If he galloped due north out of the brush the trees would screen him from the Comanche out front for a while. Then it would be up to the horse and a flat out gallop for as long as he could take it.

Gregory thought of nothing else but the troops as he cantered north until he looked back and could see the Indians in another attack. He kicked the big gray into a gallop. He responded at once, pounding north and now to the west toward the other valley past the knob of a peak.

As he watched behind he could see no pursuit. But even with the Comanches that could be misleading. They might have sent two men charging along gullies and behind ribbons of brush just out of sight.

He rode hard for a half mile, then eased off and let the gray blow as he walked him. Then he galloped again. He had been right, the gray was powerful and strong. Again after another walk Gregory pushed the big horse across a wide flat area. At the far side he looked back.

If the Comanche had sent anyone after him, they had to cross this treeless flat. No one showed up. He would need another half hour, perhaps more to find Sgt. Franklin. He hoped the sergeant stopped at the small water hole about halfway to the meeting spot.

Back at the fringe of trees that protected the first squad, Captain Kenny cautioned his men.

"Let's start conserving our ammunition. Don't fire unless you have a good target, either a Comanche or a horse. I mean a head shot on the horse. A slug in his rump won't hurt an Indian pony much."

The Pony Soldiers had beaten off the last ride by, and now the Comanche bunched just out of range and talked things over. Once more they streamed past at about fifty yards. When fewer shots came from the brush and logs, the Comanche surged closer. They were met at thirty yards with a barrage of hot army lead. Two more braves were picked off their horses and fell dead to the ground. Three more horses died in their charge.

The Comanche hurriedly pulled back.

"Seven," Captain Kenny said softly. They had killed seven of the Comanche and put at least ten of their ponies out of action.

As he watched the gathering of savages, two of them broke away and rode toward the creek. They entered the area of tall dry grass two hundred yards upstream and a moment later rode out of the grass.

Smoke sifted up, then billowed in a black cloud as the wind pushed the just set fire toward the hidden cavalrymen along the stream. The fire ran before the wind, jumped the creek and raced down the far side. For a while it looked at if the fire would go around them, then it turned with the wind and raced toward them.

"Into the creek!" Captain Kenny bellowed. "Lie down, get wet all over. If the fire gets to us, we run out the other side and get our horses!"

The men moved to the foot deep creek and lay down, soaking their pants and shirts, spilling hatfulls of water over their heads.

The fire boiled toward them, but when it was twenty yards away, the crazy Texas wind shifted again and blew the flames back on themselves into the charred grass. The fire went out.

"Back to the logs!" Kenny yelled. "Here they come again."

The fire had blackened a large area to the left of the cavalrymen and prevented the Comanches from sneaking up on them through the grass that had been there.

It was a frontal attack again, riding by, screaming and firing from under the pony's neck. Two more ponies were killed and the men on foot were quickly picked up by the charging horsemen and ridden to the rear out of danger.

Two more of his men had been hit, one seriously. Captain Kenny watched the hostiles. They seemed to be arguing among themselves. Two riders rushed forward on their mounts, picked up the two dead or wounded braves and hurried away. Captain Kenny ordered his men not to shoot at the mercy mission.

He could see one of the braves being tied onto a

pony, his hands and feet bound together under the horse's belly.

When the Comanche came toward them the next time, only half rode the circle firing at them. Three or four slid into the brush above and below their position and dismounted. The Indians were coming at them through the brush as well! They would have to defend three sides and at the same time protect their horses.

Captain Kenny yelled at the men, told them of the danger and they hurriedly formed themsleves into a small circle, each man facing outward, so they could defend every point of the compass.

Ten minutes later a shot sounded from the brush upstream. Private Ingles who had been wounded on the first charge took another Comanche bullet. He had been hurting so badly that they couldn't move him. He lay ten feet from the circle.

At once two rifles blasted six rounds into the brushy area where the soft blue smoke rose from the shot. They heard no response.

Captain Kenny scanned the woods in front of him. He put his most experienced men to cover the woods, the two recruits to fire at the horsemen in the open.

Another single shot sounded from downstream. One of the cavalrymen swore.

"Missed me, you bastard!" he shouted and fired six rounds into the brush. A scream billowed from the brush and they could hear someone rushing away.

This time the charge from the mounted savages came within ten yards of the woods before all eight guns left firing cut into the attackers and drove them back.

One more charge like that and we won't be able to fight them off, Kenny thought. He wondered how the ammunition was holding out.

"Conserve your rounds," he barked. "Make every shot count." Captain Kenny counted his rounds. He loaded another magazine tube with the .52 caliber cartridges and lay it beside his Spencer. He had fourteen rounds left. Enough for two more charges, if he was careful. Then he would use his pistol. He should have sixty rounds for the six shooter, but he desperately hoped that the savages didn't get so close he could use the revolver.

A half hour later they had. Four more charges had cut down the captain's effective cavalrymen to four. One had an arrow wound in his left shoulder. The tip had gone all the way through and one of the men had broken the arrow and pulled the shaft out.

Now four of the savages were in the brush to their left close enough for pistol use. He had sent ten rounds at them. There were at least four or five more in the brush on their right, and the mounted Comanches kept riding at them, trying to overrun the position.

"Here they come again!" one of the wounded men shouted. He lay on his back, with an arrow in his upper chest. He hadn't been spitting blood so they figured it had missed his lung.

The devils slashed in on their ponies. Ten of the animals were dead just beyond the brush now. Captain Kenny had no idea why these Comanche were willing to pay such a high price for this one stretch of creek bed.

"One more time!" the captain bellowed. "Let's beat the bastards back once more!"

The dozen mounted Comanche came at them again.

Captain Kenny saw another of his men go down. God! He wasn't sure they could hold out this time.

Just before the Comanche riders charged into the woods to try to overrun them, a cavalry bugle sounded loud and clear from close by blowing the attack call!

To the left and slightly upstream Captain Kenny saw the blue shirts coming. It had to be Sgt. Franklin's squad. The twelve mounted men surged forward, rifles spitting lead. The dozen Comanche raiders stopped, yelled among themselves for a moment, then turned and raced back to where their wounded and dead were on horses.

They paused briefly to exchange rounds with the new detail of yellow legs, then mounted up and charged away into the rolling hills.

The Indians still in the woods, faded away through the brush, both up and downstream. They evidently found where they had left their ponies, mounted and rode after their brothers.

Sgt. Franklin did not make the mistake of splitting his own force and sending half of them chasing the Redskins. He would have ridden into a trap if he had, Captain Kenny figured.

The first squad rode into the woods, dismounted and quickly began to tend to the wounded. Captain Kenny put out guards, then checked his men.

Pvt. English and two other troopers lay dead of arrow and ball. Five more were wounded, but they all could ride. Only three men of the second squad were not casualties.

The sun was fast fading. It would be dark in a half hour.

"We'll camp just upstream tonight," Captain Kenny said. "We'll ride for the fort with first light. These wounded men need to be treated."

Just after dark the three cavalrymen were buried in shallow graves. First squad had an issue small folding shovel that the men took turns using. When the graves were three feet deep, Captain Kenny read a page from his well worn officer's manual. He used the order of burial in the field.

Three men from the first squad stood guard during the night in three hour watches. No Comanche raiders bothered them.

The next morning Captain Kenny counted dead war ponies. There were twelve of them down and dead or dying. He put two out of their misery, picked up two Comanche bows with their strange sinew strings, and half a dozen Comanche war arrows, with their broad metal points, feathers, and the different painted markings on the shafts. He marveled how they could get the shafts so straight without woodworking tools.

They rode for Fort Comfort at six A.M. and arrived shortly before noon. The doctor tended to the wounded at once. Captain Kenny insisted that his men be treated before he was, and watched the doctor work.

That evening as he sat in his favorite chair and smoked his pipe, Pamela came in, her eyes wide in wonder as she looked at the Indian bows and arrows.

"They actually shot you with one of these, Father?"

"Afraid so, I forgot to duck once."

"Savages, they simply are savages."

"Gregory is quite a man, Pamela. He rode to get the other half of our patrol and saved all of our skins. If it hadn't been for him, you'd be going to my funeral tomorrow."

"Oh? Really."

"Yes, really. What I'm saying is that I'm giving him permission to court you."

"That's nice."

"Nice? Before you threatened to tell Captain Harding about my little fight with Gregory if I didn't say he could court you."

"Yes, but now it doesn't seem so important. I was talking to Lieutenant Edwards today. Did you know that he had two years of Harvard before the war? He's really an extremely interesting man."

Captain Kenny frowned, they started to jump up. The pain in his shoulder stopped his quick movement.

"Pamela Kenny, Edwards is also a *married man.* I absolutely refuse to let you see him again, even socially. You forget any silly romantic ideas you might have had about him, do I make this all clear, Pamela?"

"Yes, Father. Of course. You're a wounded army hero. How could I possibly go against what you say? Is there anything I can get for you? Anything I can bring you?"

Captain Kenny frowned at such unusual behavior. She was up to something, just what he would have to find out. Nothing would sink his chances on this base as quickly as his daughter getting mixed up with a married officer.

He sent her for a cold bottle of beer from the sutler's store. Captain Kenny shook his head.

No, it couldn't be. She wasn't crazy enough to become involved with a married officer. It must be something else.

13

Captain Colt Harding and Lt. Riddle sat in the office looking through the dispatches that just came in by two riders from Austin. Since the Wagon Wheel Massacre four months ago, all of the dispatch riders traveled in pairs from Austin.

None had been lost since they doubled up.

"Be damned, look at this," Colt said, flipping a dispatch to Lt. Riddle. He read it.

"From: Col. Phil Sparkman, commanding, Texas Department, San Antonio Texas, Military Division of the Missouri.

"To: Captain Colt Harding, commanding, Fort Comfort, Texas.

"Captain. Reread your suggestion about cold weather gear for winter operations against the Comanche. I have passed your suggestions on to General Phil Sheridan at his headquarters at Chicago of the Military Division of the Missouri.

"Trust he will appreciate them as much as I do.

"While a fort commander has a certain amount of discretionary use of his troops, you are expected to carry out the routine patrols and escort and other duties expected of you.

"Outside of that, I'll be interested in this Lightning Company you have established, and will watch your dispatches for its successes.

"Winter gear. We have almost none. Suggest you issue double blouses and trousers, three times as many socks and obtain any available great coats for your operations. Will inquire further for special cold weather outer garments at once.

Keep me informed."

It was signed: Sparkman.

"I'll be damned. You got some attention from the old man in San Antonio."

"For a minute at least. He'll forget about it before he sends the dispatch. Anything else I need to see?"

"No. At least not until I go through them again."

"How are the homesteaders doing?"

"We send a patrol out past their places every day now, no contact, just to let them know we're in the area. They seem to appreciate it."

"Wilson been in?"

"Nope. Hard at work on his house. Winter is coming fast."

"They won't make it before the freeze. They'll have to do soddies for this winter. Either that or we'll have to house them here. Let's ride out and see Wilson."

They left just after the midday meal. It was a fine little valley, big enough for the five homesteaders if nobody got greedy. They had laid it out well, with the five houses within thirty yards of one another in a rough circle.

The first row of adobe blocks was up but that

was about all. Captain Harding and Lt. Riddle rode into the circle of foundations and found the five men talking near one wagon. Josh Wilson looked up and waved.

"Is there a problem?" Captain Harding asked as he walked his big black over to the gathering.

"Considerable," one man snapped. "The sun ain't warm enough to dry out the damned mud bricks."

"Captain, meet Dominic Franchette, farmer by trade," Wilson said. "Dom is not a bricklayer. Dominic, this is Captain Colt Harding."

They nodded.

"Mr. Franchetti is right. The weather has turned. We might not see more than six or eight more drying days until the first good freeze."

"About decided the same thing, Captain," Wilson admitted. "What the hell are we supposed to do now?"

"Soddy. Build yourselves soddy houses for the winter. Get a good start on your adobe blocks next spring and have your houses finished before midsummer."

"You want us to live in a hole in the ground?" Franchetti asked, anger tingeing his words.

"Not exactly a hole in the ground, Mr. Franchetti. The idea is to start it against a small hill or a bank. Dig into the bank say three feet down. Then cut sod about the size of your adobe blocks and stack them up like bricks. Go into the bank three feet and up three feet and you have a six-foot-high structure.

"Then put the logs across the top, add anything you have to make it waterproof and then put sod on top and a foot of dirt, then more sod and you have a place you can keep warm. I've seen some soddies that would be hard to tell from a frame house once you're inside them."

"Don't want to live in a damned hole," Franchetti said, scowling.

"Mr. Franchetti, I don't know where you come from, but this is Texas. It gets freezing cold here in the winter, and living in that covered wagon is going to mean you'll lose half of your family to pneumonia or maybe just freeze to death. What do the rest of you think about soddies?"

Wilson introduced the other three men.

Harding got down from the saddle and shook hands.

Henry Zigler was about forty, had a wife and seven kids. He was a plodder, a follower. He was the second farmer in the group.

Bert Banning was a rancher. He was a raw-boned Texan by his accent, not over twenty-five or six, had a wife and one child.

Juan Martinez was about the same age as Banning and they appeared to be good friends. He said he was starting a cattle ranch too, and had four sons and a daughter to help him.

Banning took off a low-crowned brown cowboy hat and scratched his light colored hair. "Hell, sounds good to me. Get us out of the damned wind and the cold. Maybe even snow. Can't do nothing else until spring nohow."

The other two men nodded their agreement. To the left a quarter of a mile a series of small hills and ravines and some washes funneled into the valley.

"What about the spot?" Harding asked. "You want to go over to them breaks, or do it right here? You've got plenty of sod around here to build a hundred soddies."

"Let's do it here," Wilson decided. "I'm gonna dig down about two feet, then start stacking up the sod. We can get poles from the creek brush to cover over a twelve-foot span no trouble. Make a twelve by twelve should be big enough."

"Too big," Martinez said. "Lots of work. I'm making mine eight by twelve."

The other men began talking, figuring out how to make windows, where to put the doors, which way to face the house. They soon decided to make the dugout soddy next to their permanent house.

Wilson held out his hand to Captain Harding.

"Thanks for the help. We'd be freezing our balls off out here in another two months."

"Just covering my area of responsibility for civilians," Harding said formally. Then he laughed. "You get started and need help on the sod, you give me a call."

Wilson looked up, pleased. "Obliged, Captain, I'll do that."

"What outfit in the Second were you with, Wilson?"

"Second Battalion, A Company."

"You were an officer?" Riddle asked.

Wilson grinned. "Yeah. Strange times. From corporal to Brevet Captain in six months. We had some powerful bad fights with the Comanches about then, lost most of Company A in two quick battles with the Comanche." He shrugged. "I better get to marking out my new house and digging my basement. Thanks again, Captain."

As they rode back to the fort, Captain Harding nodded. "I think they'll make it. In two days check to see that they have a good start, then send out two squads to help them cut out sod. If they don't get those soddies up, we'll have thirty-two more mouths to feed and bodies to house inside the fort."

Lt. Riddle looked at his captain. "Right. We've got enough problems with our own. Speaking of trouble, has our Miss Pamela been behaving herself lately?"

"Far as I know. October can't come too quickly for me when she'll be gone."

The same time the captain rode back from his talk with the homesteaders, Pamela was thinking about Second Lieutenant Ned Young. She had been trying for three days to get him alone, and at last she figured out how to do it.

There were two unoccupied officer quarters along the officer's country side of the fort. One of the doors had been left unlocked and Pamela discovered it.

Twice she had met Lt. Young on the fort. She had smiled sweetly and made some excuse to talk to him. Each time she had told him she thought he was the very finest officer at the fort, and that he was dashing and handsome in his uniform. She had promised a lot with her eyes when she left.

Now she had the spot where they could talk, alone, if only she could find Lt. Young. She had figured out how she could do it. She combed out her hair, put on a bonnet and asked her mother if she could go to the sutler's store for some blue thread. Her mother frowned but nodded.

"You come right back and don't be talking to anybody, you hear?"

Pamela hurried out the door, walked the long way around the square past the barracks and enjoyed the men staring at her. Nobody knew about her kissing Cpl. Gregory, and they never would. At the sutler's store she bought some blue thread. Lt. Young was not there. She went home past the unfinished section of the fort and saw a work party there. Lt. Young was directing them.

He saw her and came to the edge of the new building.

"Miss Kenny. Afternoon. It's warmed up a little."

"Yes, Ned, it has. Could you help me. I have a problem."

He looked at her quickly.

"I know, we can't talk here. The second officers quarters down from ours are vacant, the door is unlocked. Could I see you there at four-thirty? I would be just ever so grateful."

Lt. Young watched her with critical blue eyes. He was five feet nine inches tall, about average for the day, with soft brown hair he kept cut short. He had a closely trimmed moustache.

"Is this something really important, Pamela?"

"Yes! Oh, yes! It's military, officer-enlisted man thing, and I need an officer's advice."

He half turned away. "Yes, I'll be there. Just don't let anyone see you go in." He walked away as if they hadn't been talking at all.

Pamela grinned. She felt a little stirring way down deep between her legs and her face blossomed into a big smile. Two enlisted men walking by, noticed, and turned to watch her.

At twenty minutes after four, Pamela convinced her mother she had the wrong shade of blue thread and left for the sutler's store to exchange it. She knew this was a busy time around the fort. Men were working with their horses after exercises or training. The enlisted men were still under orders and busy.

She walked slowly along the path under the awnings along officer row. At the vacant quarters she simply turned the knob and went inside. Anyone seeing her would mistakenly suppose that was her father's quarters.

The inside was chilly, the government issued furniture stark and some covered with sheets. She pulled the sheet off a couch and sat down to wait. For a moment her hand rubbed her left breast and she smiled. There would be no problem with Lt. Young, she was sure. She remembered pressing against his leg at supper at her father's quarters. He hadn't really removed her leg. Somehow his wife had known what she was doing. The bitch!

The door opened and Lt. Young stepped inside. He pushed the locking bolt in softly and turned to her.

"I don't want anybody surprising us and getting the wrong idea. This is strictly officer advice, friendly, impersonal. You know I'm married. There can never be anything—"

When he turned around, Pamela had the top of her dress open and spread apart. She wore no chemise or wrapper under it. Lt. Young had taken two steps toward her before he saw her. Her big breasts glowed with their youth, all milky white with soft pink areolas and deep red, large nipples.

Ned Young took another step and stopped. She jumped up and threw her arms around him, pressing her bare breasts against him.

"Darling Ned! I've wanted you to make love to me since the moment I saw you! You're the handsomest man I've ever seen." She leaned back. "Do you like my titties?"

Lt. Young groaned. His wife had been cold as

an icicle lately. He always had been fascinated by breasts. His hand came up and covered one. They were so big, so beautiful!

"Yes, darling! Pet them. They want you to pet them. Oh, that is marvelous. You can do just *anything* you want to me, lover. Anything, but we've got to hurry."

Fifteen minutes later, Lt. Young pulled up blue pants with the yellow stripe down the leg. Christ, twice in fifteen minutes! He still didn't believe it. She was so young, and beautiful, and she'd let him do anything. She had let him make love to her the one way he'd always wanted to try.

Neither of them had fully undressed. She pulled her dress together and buttoned it. When she stood Lt. Young couldn't tell she wore nothing under it. Not a damn thing!

He went to the door and cracked it open and looked out. "You go first. I'll wait awhile. I can always say I'm thinking about changing quarters."

Pamela slipped out to the walk in front of the rooms and went quickly back toward her parent's quarters. In her pocket was the same spool of thread, but she'd convince her mother it was a different shade.

The flush had faded from her cheeks. What a lover! Lt. Young was going to be the best serviced officer in the army. Now she knew it would be easy to be with him again. Her whole body warmed as she thought about their love-making.

Then she pushed it out of her mind as she went through the door and into her parent's place. She had to play the dutiful daughter again—for awhile!

* * *

At the homesteader's site, the five men were digging. Each one had laid down chalk lines for the inside measurements of his soddy house. The more they worked the smaller the temporary house became. At last they all decided to build soddies that were ten feet square.

Josh Wilson had spaded down a foot deep around his ten foot perimeter. It was hard work. He dug methodically. None of them came out here expecting sudden riches and luxury. They just hadn't thought about housing for the first winter. Josh realized they had started too late in the summer. But they all had the land they wanted, and had a start on their houses.

They talked about all working on one soddy at a time, but first they had to get started. There were no hired hands available. Josh's wife, Mary, came out of their covered wagon, and smiled, the edges of weariness showing through. She had been a city girl in St. Louis. He'd warned her about marrying him, but she wouldn't let him go.

She was of sturdy German stock, and larger than most women at five feet five. She took a round pointed shovel from near the wagon and stepped over the chalk line.

"Welcome to my living room," she said, then began to throw dirt out of the hole and far enough to the side to leave space for the twelve-inch-wide sod strips they would be laying down the walls.

By sundown, Mary had blisters on her right hand.

"Darn, I forgot to give you gloves," Josh said. They paused and looked at their new home. They were down a foot and a half in one corner, over a foot around the rest of it. They put down their tools and went to check on the Martinez soddy.

Juan grinned up at them. Juan, Carmelita and their two oldest boys all were throwing dirt out of the hole. Juan had a square pointed shovel and leveled out the bottom two feet down. Half of the ten foot square was down to depth, the rest nearly so.

"We'll come help you as soon as we get ours dug," Juan said. "We help each other, just like we planned in Austin."

"Damn right, Juan!" Josh said quickly. "You've got some mighty good dirt diggers there."

Carmelita looked at the sun. "Supper!" she said and dropped her shovel.

"Me, too," Mary Wilson said and hurried back to her wagon to light a cooking fire and get some food ready. She wasn't sure what to have tonight. There were leftover baked beans from dinner, and she would boil some potatoes. She also boiled some beef jerky they had brought with them. It wasn't bad when it was boiled up and then fried.

Josh grabbed Carmelita's shovel and began digging. He and Juan talked about how they would start their roundups in the spring. They would bring the cattle into a small valley just downstream about two miles. They could herd them in the small valley until they got used to staying together.

All three of the men had registered brands with the state at Austin before they left. They even had a blacksmith make up two branding irons each for them. Josh had his brand the JW. He was getting anxious to brand his first cow, but that would not be until spring.

After they got their soddies up, the men

planned to ride south and east looking for cattle. They could rope a dozen or so and drive them back to their ranches. The beef would be their main staple of food during the winter. Any of the cows that survived would be the start of their herd.

"Figure we can round up about twenty, maybe twenty-five before the snow flies," Juan said.

As they finished cleaning up the bottom of the square, it was dusk.

"Be over to help you tomorrow," Juan said as the men waved and went to their wagons and the warmth of their campfires.

Josh took a cup of coffee Mary handed him and sat down next to the larger fire away from the cooking fire that glowed with hot coals but little flame.

"Yes, Mary, we were right in coming. I'm glad we did. We have a chance to build something good out here. If the damn Comanches stay their distance until we get established and can afford some ranch hands who will be guards too, we should be all right."

Mary watched their three children, ages five to one, playing in the covered wagon.

"I know it's going to work out, Josh. We'll work hard and hope for the best. What else can we do? I know it's going to be just fine."

14

Pamela Kenny sat in her room on the big bed patiently working on a cross stitch napkin. It was supposed to be a set of four, a Christmas present for her aunt in Boston, but that had been for last Christmas. Maybe next Christmas.

She smiled to herself, glowing at the gentle way Lt. Ned Young had made love to her. She was a woman! She could take care of a man's needs just as well as any woman. Probably a lot better. Ned said they did it a way he had never done before! She was so thrilled and delighted! Maybe she should marry Ned after all.

He was an officer. She giggled. She didn't care a twit about whether a man was an officer or enlisted. She thought the whole army thing was just stupid and silly and loved it when she and her mother could live off a post in the city. Like in San Antonio, even. It had been better in Washington. Now she would give her girdle to live in Washington D.C.!

She laughed softly. There were plans to be made. She would carry on her affair with Ned for another month, then insist that he divorce his wife and marry her. It was the only right thing he could do, the proper thing.

Pamela laughed again. Men were so ridiculous. Didn't they think women enjoyed sex as much as they did? They were silly fools, but women had to put up with them. They were needed around a bedroom.

"Pamela." Her mother called. "I need you to help me get dinner ready. Come on out here."

Pamela checked with a hand mirror to make sure she was not flushed, then she went out and peeled potatoes and carrots to go in the beef stew her mother had cooking.

It was a little after noon the next day when Pamela made another trip to the sutler's for a bright red yarn for the cross stitchery work. She had some but her mother didn't know it. There was a chance she might run into Lt. Young.

He wasn't in the store, but the minute Pamela entered the roughly set out establishment, she realized that Grace Young, Lt. Young's wife, was there.

The woman who had cried and yelped and hurried away at the dinner a few weeks before, did not run away this time. She marched up to Pamela and without warning slapped her face.

Pamela jumped back a foot, her eyes wide, a startled yelp sputtering from her mouth.

"What in the world?" Pamela said.

"You know precisely what that was for. Should I do it again?"

Pamela looked at Grace Young, and this time spoke softly so no one else could hear.

"If you can't hold your husband, that's your problem."

Grace Young surged forwrd, her eyes furious, her mouth open in a yell of hatred, her fingernails clawing at Pamela's face. The younger girl tried to jump away, but Mrs. Young was determined.

She grabbed Pamela with one hand and her fingernails raked down across Pamela's face, digging four deep grooves in her cheeks, which filled with blood.

Pamela screamed. But she didn't retreat. She lashed out with her reticule, banging Grace on the side of the head. Then Pamela rushed forward her fist doubled up, her right arm stiff. It was more of a battering ram than a punch, but it connected with Grace Young's jaw and knocked her down.

Grace sat down with a plop, and Pamela fell on top of her, screeching and clawing and pulling her hair. The two rolled over in the aisle, dumping a stack of galvanized buckets.

Mr. Altzanger, the store manager, rushed up.

"Stop that! Ladies, stop that at once!" he shouted.

The two women on the floor rolled over again. Grace Young hit Pamela with her closed fist and Pamela's nose spouted a red flood.

Pamela kicked Grace off and sat up, clawed at Grace's face. This time her fingers found flesh and drew two bloody trails down the woman's cheeks. Grace screamed and dove forward, her head hitting Pamela's chest and driving her to the floor.

A pair of enlisted men looked on with glee, cheering on the two fighters.

Sgt. Casemore happened in the store and he ran up, grabbed Pamela and shouted for Altzanger to hold Mrs. Young. A moment later the women were parted, both still on the floor. Their skirts hiked up over their knees, exposing legs encased in stockings and white drawers.

"Ladies, cover yourselves!" Altzanger said in a hushed whisper. The six enlisted men watching cheered, then booed when the skirts covered up the women.

"You two better get back to your quarters," Altzanger said, mopping his suddenly sweaty brow. A captain's daughter and a lieutenant's woman! It would be all over the fort in ten minutes.

Sgt. Casemore looked sternly at Pamela. "Your father is going to be unhappy about this," he said. "I better see that you get back to your quarters." He reached down to help Pamela up. Instead of reaching for his hand, she swung her fist once more, catching Grace on the right eye.

Sgt. Casemore grabbed her hand, pulled her to her feet and propelled her out the door to the sidewalk. Mrs. Young would have a beaut of a shiner come morning.

"You shouldn't be fighting," Sgt. Casemore said as he held her arm and walked her quickly toward her quarters.

"The bitch insulted me!" Pamela snorted. "And she hit me first."

"I don't know how your father is going to react, but I do know what Captain Harding will do. You could even wind up in the stockade."

"He wouldn't!"

"Matter of discipline. Be surprised what can happen." He knocked on the door and waited until Mrs. Kenny opened it. She took one look at Pamela and thrust her fists to her hips.

"Now you've done it, girl. You'll be in Austin within two days if I know the army and your father. Then to Boston with you. My poor sister doesn't know what she's asking for."

"Then don't tell her, Mama. Sergeant, would you ask the fort doctor to come treat my wounds? I might catch rabies from that mad animal that attacked me."

Sgt. Casemore touched his hat in a salute. "Yes, Miss, I'll be glad too. She's all yours, Mrs. Kenny. Fracas took place down at the store with Mrs. Young."

Ruth Kenny nodded and pulled Pamela inside. The door closed promptly and there was a loud wail through it as Sgt. Casemore walked across the parade toward the fort medical office.

Captain Kenny heard about the fight within fifteen minutes of the last round. He left his small company office and marched straight across the parade grounds to his quarters. Doc Jenkins had just finished tending to Pamela. He had put some antiseptic on the scratches and applied a cold cloth to her nose to stop the bleeding. Then he put salve on the scrapes.

"Captain. Got the wounded all tended to. Broke up my day something fine. The scratches aren't deep enough to leave scars, but there will be a thin mark there for six months or so."

"Thanks, Captain, I appreciate your professional ministrations." He pointed to Pamela and motioned her into the kitchen.

Ruth Kenny let the doctor out and he rubbed his jaw as he left, paused a minute looking at the closed door, and then chuckled as he walked back across the parade to his small dispensary.

He should retire from the army, set himself up in a nice little practice for rich old ladies in Chicago, and live out his days with fine food, fine music and drama, and get waited on hand and foot by his wife. Should do it, probably never would.

Inside the Kenny quarters, Captain Kenny stared in frustration at his only offspring.

"How could you do something like this, Pamela?"

"Me do it? She slapped me first, right there in the store. I just came in to get some yarn and she walked right up to me and slapped me and started hitting and scratching me, and—"

Captain Kenny held up his hand stopping her.

"There's more to it than that. Why did she hit you?"

"I don't have the slightest idea. The woman must be unstable, a real crazy."

"No, she isn't. What did you do, Pamela?"

"I didn't do anything! I don't know why she hit me. I didn't do a blamed thing!" She ran out of the room to her big bed and slammed the door.

A half hour later, Captain Kenny was back in his quarters after a frank talk with Lt. Young and his wife. He went to see Pamela in her room.

"You'll be leaving the fort day after tomorrow, Pamela. I've checked with Captain Harding. You and your mother will go on the supply wagon to Austin. There will be a twenty man escort. From there you and your mother will go to Boston. Your mother will explain in detail the trouble you've been in here, with Lieutenant Young and with Corporal Gregory.

"Your aunt is a strict woman. You won't have a chance to stray from the straight and narrow there. The matter is closed."

At seven-thirty the next morning, Captain Harding rode out of Fort Comfort with his forty man Lightning Company. They were rigged for the field, three days rations, one blanket, one change of shirt and socks, their rifle and pistol.

They rode past the homesteaders and found two squads of men from C Company under Lt. Young's direction, cutting sod from the prairie and hauling it in flat bed wagons to the five soddy houses which were progressing nicely. One was up to window level, a second one up to head height and a dozen poles had been stretched across to start the roof.

Captain Harding turned the men into the next valley over where he called them around him.

"You're in advanced training now, men. First our review. We'll have a competition on the pickup of a downed rider." He laid out the course. The squads competed against each other. All of the squads except one man dismounted. The contest was to pick up a downed rider, and bring him back to the starting line, where a second rider would leave, go out and pick up the next downed man until the entire squad had picked up a rider and been picked up himself.

Second squad won the match.

They moved on to shooting at a dummy target by firing under the horse's neck. One man fell off, and was teased by every other man in the company. When each man had fired five rounds at the target under the mount's neck, Captain Harding called them together again.

"You all have knives. Some we issue, some you buy. Just how well you can use that weapon could save your hide. The Comanche are expert knife fighters. And the Tonkawas aren't slouches. We have four Tonks to give us some pointers. Break up into squads and do the knife training."

The men grumbled. Captain Harding bristled.

"You'd rather sit on your ass back at the fort and get your fat ass shot off the next time we go out on patrol? If not, sharpen up! You'll be using sticks instead of knives so nobody gets killed. Watch these Tonks, they know knives. Let's do it!"

The Tonkawa Indians called out one man at a time, and gave him a stick for a knife. Then they invited the tropper to attack them. Nine times out of ten, the Tonkawa would disarm the trooper and have his stick knife at the blue shirt's throat.

Patiently the Tonkawas drilled into men the basics of fighting with a knife: Stay low, use it to slash or stab. Never let the other man know what you will do in advance. Protect yourself. Always be ready to take a wound on your arm or shoulder to get inside and give a fatal thrust or slash of your own.

Sgt. Casemore growled and charged his Tonkawa. He had done some knife fighting for real, but the Tonk sidestepped his charge, tripped him, kicked away his stick knife and held his own stick across Sgt. Casemore's throat.

Sgt. Casemore worked for twenty minutes before he was sure he had a better method of knife fighting. He just prayed to God that he never would have to rely on his knife.

Captain called the men together again and they took a dinner break. It was cold and fast. The sun was directly overhead and the only warm thing around. After twenty minutes, Captain Harding told them the next project.

"Designate one man from each squad as the runner. That man will ride out in any direction he wants to go, and have fifteen minutes to get to a hiding spot.

"Then your Tonkawa scout will teach you how to track that man. Once the runner has gone for fifteen minutes he must stay in place until he's found. Don't just follow the scout. He'll make you do most of the work. Look for hoofprints, bent grass, listen for noises, watch for sudden flights of birds or movements of animals. I want every man in this troop to be able to track a midget through a patch of cactus and never get scratched."

Captain Harding made the men face away from the direction the runners took. When they had ridden out of sight, he turned the men around and the tracking lesson began.

The Tonkawas were all good trackers. Captain Harding had learned as much as he could from them on his ten day junket three months ago to find out where Sadie was. Now he wanted his men to know the same things.

The scouts made the men take turns finding the trail. They corrected when the trail was lost, showed why they got off it. When an unusual problem came up, they explained mostly by signs what went wrong, or how to find the way over sheet rock, or down a stream.

All four of the runners were tracked down in an hour. Captain Harding nodded, told Sgt. Casemore to head the men back to camp. They rode in tired, but somehow more pleased with their army duty, and their new found skills, than any of them would have thought possible six months ago.

Captain Harding had his dinner brought to him that night, read a magazine for two hours, then went over his master plan. His troop was ready for the Comanche. He hadn't heard from any travelers lately about where the White Eagle band could be. There had been no more trouble with raiding Comanches since Captain Kenny's attack.

But where was Sadie?

The trader, the halfbreed, who had led them straight to White Eagle's camp, had stayed at the fort for a week. Then he headed for Austin and new supplies. He wouldn't trade with the Indians again until next spring and summer. Nobody else had come through from Indian country.

The Pamela Kenny problem was resolving itself. He didn't have to take a hand in it. Captain Kenny knew what had to be done. Colt fully expected that the girl had bedded Lt. Young somehow, and his wife found out. Young probably would stay at the Fort. The gossip would die down quickly.

Even the homesteaders were shaping up. With another week of good weather, the soddies should be done and the families moved inside. Then they could concentrate on making rock and concrete fireplaces in each soddy. There weren't enough pot bellied heating stoves for all the soddies.

Stoves could be moved out of unused officer quarters, but Captain Harding hoped for the fireplaces.

Sadie, Sadie, Sadie! He took out a bottle of whiskey he had been saving. A knock sounded on his door. He opened it and found Doc Jenkins there.

"Figured it was 'bout time we had another game of chess. What do you say, Captain?"

"You ready to get your ass whipped again, Jenkins?"

"Mmmmmm. Never ready for that, but has happened. Can't rightly remember when. Back in twenty-eight as I recall."

They both laughed and the doctor came in and set up the board he carried under his arm.

They played four games of chess, each winning two. By the time the doctor went home, the bottle of whiskey had been reduced by nearly half.

"Good night, sweet prince," Doc Jenkins said and weaved into the night.

Captain Harding was sober as a Comanche tee-totaler. That bothered him a little. He was still trying to come up with an absolutely unstoppable way to rescue Sadie as he fell asleep.

15

The lookout in the fort's tower near the front gate saw him first. There was only a thin trail of dust followed by a larger dust trail. The sergeant of the guard reported to the officer of the day, Lt. Edwards, who sent out a six man patrol to investigate.

'Yes sir, Captain," Lt. Edwards reported minutes after the patrol went out. "It looked damn like a small force, maybe six or eight, chasing one rider."

Both officers went to the lookout and used their field glasses. By then the dust trails were closer. The Pony Soldiers were a mile out and riding hard.

"Damn, I think you're right, Edwards. Looks like one rider with about six Comanches riding hell to leather behind him. The Indians only have one pony each, which is probably why the rider in front still has his scalp."

They heard rifle fire then. At a half mile the patrol began firing in the direction of the chasers. There was little chance to hit them, but the pursuit group hesitated, came on another hundred yards, then turned and rode off.

"I gave Sergeant Barlow instructions not to chase the hostiles if they were Comanche," Lt. Edwards said. They watched the patrol meet with the lone rider, turn and escort him back toward the fort at a walk.

"I want to talk to that man when he gets in and recuperates a little," Captain Harding said as he went down the ladder to the fort roof, then to the ground. "Wonder where in hell those Comanches came from?"

An hour later Lt. Edwards brought a man into Captain Harding's office. He was short, stocky and looked tough as saddle leather. He had a full beard, at least six months worth, and his brown eyes glittered from under bushy eyebrows. The man wore store bought jeans and a homemade fringed buckskin shirt. He stepped forward briskly and held out his hand. Colt guessed he was not thirty yet.

"Want to thank you and your men, Captain. Damn hostiles was againing on me at the last there."

"I'm Captain Harding, glad we could help."

"Oh, my moniker is Lars Chaney. Guide covered wagon trains over the Oregon trail. Thought I'd take a look a little farther south coming back this time. Traveling alone."

"How many Comanches chase you?"

"Started with about twenty, I'd say. But they didn't have no spare ponies to switch to, so I figured Sioux Chief and me could outlast them. That is one hell of a horse I got."

"Comanches probably wanted the horse more than they did you," Lt. Edwards said.

"About the size of it. Mighty obliged for the help out there. Nothing like half dozen Pony Soldiers to put the Comanches on the run."

"I wish that were true. How far did they chase you, Mr. Chaney?"

"Well, let's see. They spotted me about ten o'clock yesterday morning. I'd say that was about a hundred and twenty miles out mostly north and a little to the west."

"Your horse ran for a hundred and twenty miles?" Captain Harding asked, incredulous.

"Well, no. I knew Sioux Chief could outlast them little Indian ponies. All I had to do was stay alive. Had this blanket that I doubled over so it was three inches thick and I tied that to my back and so it covered my neck.

"Then I rode. I'd charge along and outdistance the heathens, then old Sioux Chief and me would walk, resting up. When the Indian ponies started catching up within arrow shot distance, Sioux Chief and me would ride hard again and get a big lead."

"And you did that for twenty-four hours?" Lt. Edwards asked.

"Peers as how. Once they knew a short cut I didn't and they damn near got me. But I figured something like that was sprouting, so I didn't walk that time, just kept riding and came out about a quarter of a mile ahead of them. You never seen such a bunch of mad Indians in your whole damn life!"

"Did that blanket stop any arrows?" Lt. Edwards asked. "We found several arrow wounds on your horse."

"Deed it did, Lieutenant. I felt at least a dozen good solid hits. When I'd get ahead I'd reach around and clean them off. I guess six or eight stuck in the blanket."

"You're welcome to stay and rest up, Mr. Chaney," Colt Harding said. "Glad we could be of service. I do want to ask you some questions about your route, when you first saw the savages, if you saw a camp, where it was, then your route here."

"Yep, more than happy. That map will help." He went to the wall map of western Texas and studied it for a minute.

"I go mostly by rivers. I came down around that helluva big caprock out there, this side of it and went mostly south then. Let's see, rivers. Streams." He stared at the map for a minute.

"What are all of these pins and tacks?"

"Those are locations where Comanche bands have camped or hunted," Captain Harding said. "We're trying to keep track of them."

"Oh, well I sure came through a batch of them. Traveled mostly by night and thought I'd slipped through. Then just about here, they spotted me, and the chase began."

"That's at the headwaters of the North Concho River," Captain Harding said. "We've never been in there much. Was it a hunting camp, or set up for winter?"

"Damned if I know. I kept away from their camps as much as I could. Did see a hunt going on at one place."

"Were they big camps or smaller ones?"

"Hunting camps, maybe forty or fifty tipis, in the ones I saw. Half a dozen camps strung between there and the big cap rocks."

"Could you take us back to the spot you last saw the Comanche camps?" Colt Harding asked.

"Sure, for a scout's pay. What can you offer?"

"Pay you a dollar a day. More than a second lieutenant makes in this man's army."

"Done. I get to bring my own horse."

"Done," Colt said and reached out his hand. "We'll be riding in the morning, so rest up." He looked at him. "And eat something, I don't want you falling off your horse half way there."

Cpl. Swenson took the scout out to get him some quarters and food.

Colt looked at Lt. Edwards. "I'll be riding the Lightning Company fast tomorrow. I want your company to follow us at forty miles a day. We've got about a hundred and ten miles to do. You'll be there in three, and we'll be there in two. No wagons. Expect to be in the field for about eight days. Take six Tonkawa scouts. Two for scouts and four to hunt for the troop. We'll move out at six-thirty as usual."

"Yes, sir, I can put forty-eight of my fifty men into the field."

"Good, make it double issue of ammo, and food for eight days issued to each man. Your scouts will know the general area, but have them follow our trail. See you at supper."

Two days later, Captain Harding trailed his column of fours into a sparse growth of live oak on a dry hillside. They had been seeing fragments of a herd of buffalo most of the afternoon. Now just before sunset they came on a herd that stretched more than a mile in front of them.

"I've never seen so many buffalo in one place," Captain Harding told Sgt. Casemore as they stopped and looked out across the shaggy brown mass of animals.

"I'd guess maybe fifty thousand," Sgt. Case-

197

more said. "Damn, they just keep showing up down beyond that hill!"

"Bring up the scouts, let's do some calculating," Captain Harding told his sergeant.

A few minutes later the lead scout, Hatchet, Captain Harding and Sgt. Casemore looked over the top of the small rise to the north. The buffalo herd was only a scattering of brown splotches on that side of the hill. Not more than two miles ahead they could see smoke from a dozen Indian tipis drifting into the windless sky.

"Hunting camp," Hatchet said.

"How many Comanches?" Harding asked.

"Three hands warriors."

"Fifteen," Lt. Edwards said to the scout. He shrugged.

"No chance to slip up on the place in the daylight across all that open land. We'll wait for darkness and be ready to hit them in the morning. I want to know for sure if it's White Eagle's band or not."

They dismounted in the shade of the evergreen leaves of the live oak and waited.

The Lightning Company had quickly left the regular troops behind the first day as they moved away from the fort at a smart canter and with the scout Lars Chaney leading the way. By now they were a day ahead of Company B and Lt. Edwards.

As darkness settled over the high plains, the mass of brown buffalo blended together into a sea, then faded to blackness. They had heard no shots from the hunting camp. Evidently this band used only arrows to kill the big buffalo.

When it was full dark, the troop mounted and rode at a walk down the far side of the small hill and toward the brush lined stream where the

Indians had their hunt camp.

The brush would cover their approach from the down wind side. Captain Harding remembered seeing a small wooden hill slightly north and behind the hunting camp. This was their objective. They circled well around the camp, passed shaggy mounds of buffalo bedded down and sleeping, and at last came to the point where they could ride up the slope into more live oak. A few pecan trees lined the stream course.

Once under cover with his troops, Captain Harding took Sgt. Casemore and Hatchet and worked through the woods as close to the Indians as they thought safe. There were several camp-fires among the tipis but none was large enough to shed much light on the size of the place or the number of people.

Captain Harding could not determine if any of the tipis had a large eagle head painted on it.

Back with the rest of the troop, Captain Harding gave the men four hours of sleep. They put out double guards. Then Colt Harding settled against a tree. They had left their horses saddled to be ready to move or fight at a moment's warning. Colt thought about the upcoming battle. If they were only a small band, he would kill all of the men and destroy the camp, sending the women and children chasing away to a different band. They always seemed to know where the other groups were.

He would not slaughter the women and children. As he dreamed he wondered where Sadie was and how he could rescue her.

Cpl. Swenson touched his shoulder and he came awake, his hand on one of the ivory handled pistols at his hip.

"Yes?"

"Four-thirty, sir, silent reveille," Swenson said.

"Thanks, Swenson, get Sgt. Casemore over here."

Captain Harding wanted to order Hatchet and his Tonkawa scouts to the rear and not engage in the fight, but by the time he sent for them, they had already vanished into the night. They would join the fight when it was won, and escape with some of the loot they prized highest, Comanche steaks.

The Lighting troop mounted up and paused at the fringe of woods along the small creek less than a hundred yards from the sleeping Indian hunting camp.

Faint streaks of light stabbed through the darkness, bursting it apart as dawn came slowly, irreversibly.

With the light, Captain Harding rode up and down the line of troopers staring at the various tipi tops. Nowhere could he find an eagle head. This was not White Eagle's band.

The Pony Soldiers had their orders. They would kill every Indian man they could find. They would not harm the women and children unless one of them fought back with deady force by bow or firearm. Then the trooper would defend himself with deadly force.

As the night gave way to dawn, Colt Harding could see that the tipis were surrounded with racks and racks of meat that would finish drying in the sun. He had seen the racks up close. They had sharpened pegs to stab the meat on. The rows of pegs bound to a bipod on each end and laced across with crossbars. Simple to make, to take down and carry along.

All at once it was fully daylight. A dog barked in the village. A brave lifted a flap and walked towards the brush behind the tipis to relieve himself. Before Colt could designate a man to shoot the warrior, a bowstring twanged and just as the brave looked up, a Tonkawa arrow drove through his chest, killing him without a sound.

Captain Harding lifted one of his ivory handled pistols and waved the men forward. Sgt. Casemore at the far end of the line of forty men spaced five yards apart did the same. When they were out of the brush, Captain Harding doubled his fist and pumped it up and down over his head and the line of men began to run forward.

A pistol shot slammed through the brisk Texas morning jolting the troopers out of their sense of unreality. One of the Pony Soldiers screeched in pain and fell with a round in his shoulder.

The Indian who shot the captured pistol, bellowed a Comanche war cry and was cut down by five .52 caliber Spencer rifle bullets. But the camp was alerted.

Warriors fled their tents with pistols and rifles and bows and arrows. Four of the braves were blasted into Comanche heaven before they could turn and fight. Three more ducked behind other tipis and resisted.

The line of troops kept running, swept through the first line of tipis and caught two braves nocking arrows. They surged around the tents, and when the firing was over outside, two man teams searched each tipi, but found no more men, only women and children.

A young boy of about twelve caught up his dead father's fourteen-foot-long lance with the razor sharp point and rammed it forward at a soldier's broad back. Before he got there two Spencer slugs hit him, knocking him down. The lance missed, and the Indian boy died.

After a brief talk with the captain, Sgt. Casemore told his men to herd all of the people to the far end of the camp and make them sit down on the grass.

When that was done six men went through the village with torches, setting everything on fire that would burn. The rest of the drying racks were knocked down, and thrown on the burning tipis.

The wranglers brought up the horses where they had been kept safe, and half the troops mounted while the other half pushed over tipis so they would burn faster, and piled unburned poles into the flames to be sure they were destroyed.

Rawhide boxes of jerky were thrown into the flames. Everything they could find that would burn was destroyed. Just as they were about to mount up the rest of the troop, a single war pony thundered into the camp from the woods. The brave on the horse saw the devastation, wheeled his horse and amid a dozen shots, fled back into the brush.

"Two men! Follow him! Don't let him get away alive!" Sgt. Casemore had bellowed the command without asking his captain. Two men closest to the man surged after him on their black army mounts.

"Let's get out of here to some defensible spot, Sergeant," Captain Harding called. The troop mounted up, rode into the bush and back to the small knoll where they had spent the night.

On the long flat land extending from the small hill, they could see three horses racing north. One of the horses faded and soon stopped. The second man fired a full magazine of rounds at the Indian ahead of him, but he was soon a quarter of a mile ahead and out of effective range.

Slowly the last pursuer turned and rode back. A messenger had escaped.

When the two riders returned, Sgt. Casemore and Captain Harding had decided.

"No sense waiting for whoever he's going to tell what he saw and bring them back. We've finished our mission, let's move toward the fort on our trail coming out so we'll meet Lieutenant Edwards."

They rode at their usual sixty-five mile pace, and it was just before noon that they saw the first hostiles. A lone Indian brave silhouetted himself on a small hill to the left of the line of march and waited until he was sure the Pony Soldiers saw him. Then he slid down out of site behind the hill.

"Trouble," Sgt. Casemore said, riding up to his captain.

"I saw him. What do we have around here for a defensive position if we need one?"

"Not a damn thing, Captain."

"Pull in our outriders. Those damn Tonks back from their feast yet?"

"Not a chance. That's a two day pig-out for them," Sgt. Casemore said.

"Look up there, Sergeant."

Then men both looked ahead. A small valley opened up and from it rode thirty Comanche warriors, painted, armed and ready to do battle.

"Thirty of them, forty of us, not bad odds," Casemore said. "None of that last bunch had many rifles. If all they got is bows and arrows, we won't have any trouble."

They heard a scream behind them, and racing toward them a quarter of a mile away came a cloud of Indians.

"Christ! Must be a hundred of them!" Colt bellowed. He looked around again. The small stream was wider here. Just ahead he saw an island where the water swept around each side. It was twenty yards wide and three times that long. More important, it was thick with wild pecan trees and a few live oak. It might be just enough of an advantage.

"To the island!" Captain Harding bellowed. The troops saw it and galloped fifty yards to it, splashing through two-foot-deep water to get to the dry land in the middle. The wrangler grabbed the horses and moved them to the center of the little island and tied them individually to trees.

Quickly the troopers dropped behind trees and a few logs. Some began piling up rocks at the very front of the "V" where the water parted to go around the island.

"How many of them would you guess?" Sgt. Casemore asked, his voice calm.

"At least a hundred and fifty," Colt said. "I should have figured it. Such a large herd of buffalo would pull in the Comanche from all over the surrounding area this time of the year. They're having their last hunt before their winter camp."

The rushing Comanches from the rear had stopped two hundred yards away. They had not expected a pitched battle. They wanted to ride down the yellow legs horse to horse, lance against pistol. This was not an expected move by a cavalry unit.

The Indians from the front of them swept

around one side, out of effective rifle range and teamed with the hostiles upstream.

"Keep your heads down men, and let's find out what they have. My guess they are short on rifles. They wanted to get in close where their lances and bows and arrows are more deadly. We'll find out soon."

Sgt. Casemore had moved half way down on one side of the double line of troopers. He had stretched them at four yard intervals from the point down each side, then put two men in the middle.

"Make yourselves any kind of barricade you can," Casemore bellowed. "Old logs, rocks. Use your cup to dig up rocks and dirt. You beat that cup up enough right here saving your scalp, you'll be glad to drink from it all scratched and bent."

As the soldiers waited, the Indians milled around. Now and then one or two would gallop flat out toward the Pony Soldiers, only to pull up and spin around and race away.

There seemed to be some kind of discussion going on at the Indian meeting. Scout Chaney watched them.

"Looks like they got two or three bands together for the hunt and now nobody can figure out who's in charge. No war chief, or more likely four or five war chiefs. But they are damn upset. They wanted to ride us down."

"Figures," Captain Harding said. "They'll decide. They only have six more hours before dusk."

Ten minutes later the Indians broke into a wide front, then half a dozen men rode faster to form a wide "V" so each warrior had a clear shot at the enemy.

They rode forward slowly at first, then as the "V" formed, they came faster and charged straight at the point of the stream where it parted and went down both sides.

"Hold your fire until my command!" Captain Harding shouted. The Comanche war cries shrieked through the afternoon Texas stillness.

One rifle from somewhere in the Indian ranks fired. The savages came closer and closer. When they were fifty yards from the point of the creek, Capt. Harding bellowed: "Fire!"

Forty rifles belched black powder smoke and forty .52 caliber lead slugs snarled toward the Indians. Four of the five Indians riding the point of the "V" either lost their lives or their horses in the first volley.

From then on it was ragged firing as the men pounded out the seven rounds in their Spencer repeaters.

The Indians kept coming, surging into the water and heading straight for the point of the defenses.

Captain Harding lifted his Spencer and sighted in on the jolting form of a Comanche warrior. He fired. The man fell off his horse but the mass of Comanche warriors kept coming. They were only twenty yards away from the point of the island!

16

Sadie Harding sat under a big pecan tree near a stream and pounded the dried buffalo jerky into powder using a hand sized rock to beat against the hard jerky that lay on another rock. When she had the copper bowl filled, she carried it to Cries In The Morning, who was mixing the jerky with buffalo fat and pecans. When it was all mixed and pounded together it became pemmican, the staple of the Indian diet during the winter months.

Sadie emptied her bowl and watched Doris, the only white eye woman in the camp. She and Doris and little white boy called Daniel, had become good friends. They could speak English when the Comanches weren't listening.

Doris pounded jerky, too, and they talked about where they used to live. Doris never talked about the settlement where she was captured. She talked about St. Louis, and Austin.

"We've been pounding this stuff for hours," Doris said. "Don't they ever get enough?"

"This is what we'll eat this winter, when we can't hunt," Sadie said.

"Sweetheart, we won't be here this winter. We have to find a way to get away from the Comanche or we'll both wind up being Indian squaws the rest of our lives. Little Dan thinks he's an Indian already."

They had ridden away from the Croton Creek standoff with the Pony Soldiers. Doris had been taken up the river and tied to a tree until the Pony Soldiers had left. Then she was brought back. For a week they had traveled north and now were on Mulberry Creek, a tributary of the mighty Red River. They were far to the north, almost past the long and massive cap rock that protected the Staked Plains.

They had not seen a white eye since they left Crotin Creek. Not a settler, not a wagon, not a soldier. For the moment they felt safe. But again, White Eagle had posted some of his best warriors as guards. They would not be surprised by the hated Tonkawas again. They were protected, they had found a small herd of buffalo for their last hunt, and the butchering had gone on now for three days.

They had so much buffalo meat to dry that they had to make new racks. Families that had already filled their rawhide boxes with pemmican helped someone else. This was a time of harvest and even the warriors helped the women provide the winter's food supply.

With the mulberries nearly gone from the trees, the band could harvest few of them to flavor their pemmican, but they found every remaining berry. Some late fruiting blackberries were used as well along with the ever present pecans from the wild pecan trees that lined many of the streams.

"Do you think my daddy will ever find us?"

Sadie asked.

Doris stopped pounding the jerky and nodded.

"Oh, yes, darling girl, he will, and he'll rescue us and carry us back to the fort and I want to take care of you just like you were my very own little girl, just forever and ever." Tears brimmed her eyes as she thought about her own little girl she had seen the Comanches kill without mercy. "I'll always take care of you, Sadie!"

White Eagle rode in with another horse packed heavily with meat ready to be sliced and hung. He watched Doris a moment as Always Smiling and Talks A Lot unloaded the meat, he walked over to the white woman. She wore a buckskin dress with only a few beads on it. Her dark hair braided on each side.

White Eagle patted her belly and used one of the words he had learned in English.

"Baby?" he asked.

She watched him a moment, then nodded. He grunted and walked away. He had been asking her that question every day now for a month. She would not tell him that she was pregnant before, but now she realized it must be important to him. He must want a son of his own. Doris could not tell him that she could never have any more children. Her last child had messed up the works too much, the doctor told her.

But she would not let White Eagle know. Even that small hold over him might be used to her advantage. She watched the country as they rode north. She knew they must be far to the north in Texas, up in the Panhandle somewhere. Indian Territories were not too far away to the east. But that wouldn't be much help. They would have to get horses and ride east and then south. But how?

No, she would have to wait until the Pony Soldiers came again. But then the Comanches would probably tie her up again, and take Sadie away into the hills so even if the camp were attacked, Sadie would not be there. There had to be a way. There simply had to be! Doris would go crazy if she had to be an Indian squaw the rest of her life.

Four more days of drying the buffalo meat and the rawhide boxes were filled. Now everyone worked at pounding the jerky into pemmican. When the baskets were filled and the boxes overflowing, the whole camp took on a feeling of expectancy. They would soon be going to a winter camp. They were so far north they had no idea where it might be.

That evening White Eagle came to Doris's bed and sat on the edge of it as she fed Daniel. When she finished White Eagle played with the little boy for a while, then settled down to his lesson in English. He was a quick learner. He remembered many more English words than she remembered Comanche.

"Talk English," White Eagle said.

"Good morning, sir," Doris said.

He repeated the words, not sure what they meant. She explained to him with signs and other words. He nodded.

"We must talk about my people," Doris instructed. Day by day she tried to teach him words that he would need if he ever met face to face with white men in some kind of a treaty or bargaining conference. It was happening more and more. Before White Eagle had lived his life out, she was sure he would be pleading with the white men for the good of his people. She could

210

help that much at least.

Deep down she hated him for being part of the savage mob that had tortured and killed her family and friends. But she also realized he had chosen to spare her. She really owed her life to him, and so did small Daniel. It was a strange and discomforting position.

For an hour they talked English. He told her how to say the same thing in Comanche. Sadie sat listening, her quick mind picking up most of the words. She had a natural talent for languages, Doris decided.

White Eagle permitted the instruction for about a half hour more, then he stood.

"I must go now," he said in English, grinned at his own ability and stalked out of the tipi.

He took four of his best ponies, but not his war pony, and tied them in front of another tipi.

A warrior came out of the tipi and stared at the ponies, then at White Eagle.

"These beautiful ponies are for Slender Pecan, your oldest daughter."

The warrior nodded and went back into his tipi. For three hours White Eagle sat in the grass beside the horses. He waited patiently. It was part of the ritual. When a man wanted a girl as a wife, he made an offering of horses to her father. If the father or the girl herself unfastened the horses and walked away with them to her father's herd, the marriage was approved.

After another hour White Eagle was losing hope. Then a slender girl of fifteen came out of the tipi. She wore her finest dress with more than a hundred elk's teeth clicking and making small noises as she walked. She had a round, pretty face, with eyes that never missed a thing. She had already turned down two offers of marriage. This time she walked to White Eagle, smiled at him, then unfastened the horses and led them to her father's string of ponies where the young boys herded them.

That night Slender Pecan came to White Eagle's tipi. There was a bed made ready for her. She was his third wife, and Always Smiling and Talks A Lot were pleased. A war chief should have at least three wives. His white woman and Cries In The Morning did not count, even though he did use the white captive as a wife. Now there would be a boy child in the chief's tipi! It was the fondest wish of the Indian women.

Slender Pecan shivered as she lay under the buffalo robes waiting for her husband. He came to her bed quickly. The fire had died down to a soft glow and no one built it up. Always Smiling and Talks A Lot moved outside into the moonlight to sit beside a small fire and let the new bride have some privacy.

White Eagle slipped in beside her. He had dropped his breechclout and now felt her bare legs against his. His hands found her breasts and her pretty face and he played with her a moment, then pushed her over.

"You must make for us a boy child," he told her sternly. She looked up and nodded. Then he repeated the words over and over again as he thrust deep into her to plant his seed into this new and fertile field. Slender Pecan had two brothers, she knew about males and would be male oriented and would surely bear the chief a male heir.

That day White Eagle had thrown the magic mix of herbs and sacred powders to the four corners of the sky in the ritual appeasement of all the gods he worshipped. He had called on his special god to make him virile and to make his new wife ready to produce a male son.

It would happen. This time it would happen, White Eagle had no doubt.

The next morning the council met. It was time to move to their winter quarters.

"We will winter with our cousins the Mesquite band as usual," Elk Wound said. "But we are not sure where they have made their last hunt."

"They usually work along the Peace River," another warrior said. "We can send a scout to find them."

White Eagle listened to the talk, but always he was thinking that they must stay well away from Captain Two Guns. The man must be half Comanche. He was a worthy opponent. White Eagle knew that he could never go below the Wichita River again. The White Captain must be made to travel many days rides to find the White Eagle band.

But when they made winter camp there would be four, perhaps five bands staying together. No Pony Soldier would dare to challenge two hundred warriors in their winter camp.

He listened to the ideas of the warriors around the council. Soon it was decided to send a rider to find the Mesquite band. Then they would make their plans. They had two or three weeks before the other bands would be moving to winter quarters.

In the tipi Doris sat holding Daniel as he ate pemmican and chewed on buffalo jerky. There had been no fresh meat since the hunt. Everyone was full of red meat for awhile.

Sadie sat near Doris and leaned against her.

"Will we die in the snow this winter?" Sadie asked. She looked up and Doris wanted to hug her.

"No, of course not. The Comanche live through the winter, how else to you suppose they grow so old? We will be snug and safe and warm inside the tipi. You know how the sides come in and we put our beds and buffalo robes on them to shut out the cold. The tipi cover is thick and will keep the fire's warmth inside."

"I would rather be in a house, or at Fort Comfort. That's where my mother was taking us when the bad Indians hurt us."

"Fort Comfort? I'm not sure where that is, but we'll find it someday."

"Then is my daddy really coming to get us?"

Doris blinked back tears. How could she tell her? There was little chance of any large scale cavalry action during the winter. It just had never been done. Which meant she and her two small charges surely would have to stay until the spring or summer before they could get away.

Doris frowned. Within a month or two, White Eagle would know that she wasn't pregant. She had no idea what he would do to her then. She would probably lose her favored status and become a slave. She might even have to sleep outside. No! She would kill herself first!

No! Then what would happen to little Dan and to Sadie? She had to survive, she had to help the children get away from these savages. It was the only course she could take.

17

What now looked like two hundred painted, mounted Comanche warriors stormed the front of the small island in the North Concho River where the forty men of Lightning Company hunkered down firing their Spencer seven-shot rifles as fast as they could.

At twenty yards the toll on the attacking Comanche braves was awesome. Horses went down, others fell over them.

Comanche braves fell from the saddle wounded or dead.

Horses screamed and rushed down both sides of the island without riders.

Suddenly the crush of Comanche at the point broke and the warriors splashed down the shallow stream on both sides, taking more killing shots from the cavalrymen.

"Broke them, by damn!" Captain Harding shouted. Fifty to seventy five of the mounted warriors never came close to the island. When they saw the deadly fire of the guns-that-fire-many-times, they turned and pulled back out of range.

"Let the wounded leave if they can," Captain Harding bellowed.

In front of the island it looked like a slaughterhouse.

Twenty braves lay dead. A dozen more crawled slowly back toward the north. Fifteen horses sprawled in the shallow water, half of them dead, the rest with broken legs or serious bullet wounds.

Captain Harding sent two men with pistols out into the water to put the last of the Comanche ponies out of their misery with head shots.

After the mercy blasts the Texas countryside was quiet.

"Load all the magazine tubes you have, men. They'll be back. Let's have a casualty report to Sgt. Casemore by squads."

Captain Harding loaded the three tubes he had that held the six shots of .52 caliber rounds for the Spencer. He hadn't realized he'd used three on the attack.

Now he looked around. He had no memory of the Comanche firing arrows, but there were fifty or sixty arrows he could see stuck in the ground behind the troops, broken on the rocks, and some in tree trunks.

A lot of them must have been shot by riders behind the first wave. They would send them up like a mortar shell hoping the arrows would land on the troops.

Captain Harding picked up an arrow two feet from where he lay and examined it. Straight and smooth, as though it had been turned on a good wood lathe. How did they get them so straight working with shoots of willow?

Sgt. Casemore came up with a casualty report. He had a bandanna wrapped around his left arm. Blood seeped through it and stained his blue shirt sleeve black.

"Sir, we have one man dead, Private Barlow. He took an arrow through the throat and died in seconds. He was on the point. We have eight men with minor wounds, all arrows. All of the eight, including myself, are fit for duty and on line ready for the next charge."

"Damn! Sorry to lose Barlow. He was a good man. Tell the men I'm proud of them, they fought just like we trained to do. Christ, I thought they were going to charge right over us for a few seconds there."

"It was close. I think we put down two or three of their war chiefs. That's going to cause holy hell in the ranks."

Lars Chaney, the free lance scout, pushed up from behind the log he had been using to shoot over. He loaded a tube with rounds.

"Hell, the Comanche ain't done yet. Don't count on no more head on charges, though. Think the hostiles out there discovered the Spencer repeating rifle this afternoon. Probably the first time they seen what it can do." Chaney chuckled. "Give a keg of whiskey to be a mouse in somebody's pocket out there listening to what the Comanches are talking about."

"What do you think they'll do now?" Harding asked.

"Palaver for another half hour. Then they'll wait us out. Once we get out of here and start moving, the odds even up. Fact is they'll have the advantage. Yep. Reckon that's what they'll plan."

In front of them thirty yards, one Comanche lifted up from the water and looked at the island. At last he began crawling through the water to the shore fifteen feet away. On shore he rested a minute, then tried to stand but couldn't. He looked back at the island and the forty guns there, then crawled toward the cluster of Comanche warriors three hundred yards away.

Another Comanche lifted up, and ran flat out for the shore.

Colt Harding brought up his Spencer and knocked him down with his second shot.

"I said the wounded could leave, not some son-of-a-bitch playing dead," Colt shouted to his men. "Now he can leave."

The man hooted and cheered.

Sgt. Casemore looked at the pow-wow. "They might give us one more charge, I don't know, Captain. They sure as hell won't be as confident of overrunning us this time. We took a lot of the fight out of them. I counted twenty-one Redskins out there who ain't moving. That hurts this bunch."

A rifle shot slammed into the island. Missed everyone.

"First squad, one round per man, drive that bunch back a ways. Three hundred yards."

The ten Spencers spoke in a ragged volley. The Comanches reacted at once, galloping out of sight over a small rise.

"Everyone stay down," Sgt. Casemore bellowed. "They are still there and we're still pinned down. We'll be here a while so get comfortable, or work on your barricade. Now's a good time to move some dirt."

Captain Harding looked at his guide. The

Tonkawas had not returned. "Mr. Chaney. How far behind us should our B Company be by now?"

"Sir, at forty miles a day, they should arrive about dusk. A messenger from us to go after B Company would be picked up by the Comanche at once, so we better not try to hurry up B Company any."

"My thoughts. Casemore. Pick out your best man and send him to the back of the island. Keep him in the brush and tell him to watch for B Company. When he spots them he should fire three times in the air."

"Yes sir." Casemore crawled down along the line keeping under cover as much as he could.

"So now we wait," Captain Harding said.

"Think I'll do a little yard work case them Comanches decide to come back," the scout said and moved back to his log. He used a big knife and began digging a shallow trench in back of the log so he could protect himself better.

Captain Harding never saw the man leave for the brush. Good. Probably the Comanche lookouts didn't either.

A half hour later a twenty warrior band of Comanche showed briefly on the rise ahead, then galloped to the west. Ten minutes later another band showed themselves and rode to the east.

"Just letting us know that they're still with us," Captain Harding said.

"About all they can do," Chaney agreed. "Once it gets dark we could pull out. Most of these Comanches don't like to fight at night."

"First we wait and team up with Edwards and Company B. I like the numbers better with fifty more men."

A Comanche rider bolted over the hill and

stormed straight at the island. He stayed on the grass and when he was fifty yards away he wheeled and charged back to the rise and out of sight.

A trooper along the line leaned over the stub of a log to secure it better. He was totally exposed to the Comanche.

Before he could pull back, a Comanche warrior lifted up from behind a dead horse twenty yards away and shot an arrow. Five Spencers blasted the warrior before he could reach for another arrow. He went down in a froth of bloody water and then lay still.

The trooper caught the arrow in his side. He fell back over the log and lay there swearing. The cavalryman next to him checked the arrow. It was in past the barbs and didn't extend through the flesh.

Captain Harding crawled along the troopers to the hit man and looked at the wound.

"Private Fisher, isn't it?"

"Yes, sir. Sorry."

"Don't worry about it. We won't be able to do much about that arrowhead until we get out of here." He drew his knife and notched the shaft on both sides two inches above the flesh. Then before Fisher knew what his captain was doing, Harding broke off the shaft. Fisher groaned and almost passed out.

Captain Harding took a metal flask from his inside pocket and opened the top.

"Take a shot of this now and then, Fisher. Don't give these other troopers any. You'll need all that's there."

"Whiskey?" Fisher asked.

Captain Harding nodded. "All of you, keep

your heads down. B Company should be showing up in an hour or two. Then we'll decide what to do."

For an hour things were quiet. Then a rifle from a hidden position sent six rounds into the small island over a period of five minutes.

The quiet after that was strained. Then the men felt something unusual and at the same time heard it.

"Oh damn! I heard that sound before," Scout Chaney said. "Sir, I suggest we mount up damn fast and get out of here!"

"Why, Chaney?"

"Buffs! That's a buffalo stampede heading this way!"

"To the horses!" Colt bellowed. "Mount up and move out. Buffalo stampede coming!"

The men ran for their horses. Cpl. Swenson had the captain's mount to him in thirty seconds. They mounted and rode to the rear where the other men were mounting.

"There they come!" somebody yelled.

The men looked through the brush and trees upstream and saw a shaggy, brown river as wide as the small valley and every one of the beasts charging downstream. They blanketed the valley and the water, making great geysers of splashes.

"Downstream, to the south," Captain Harding roared again and the troops galloped out of the trees, across the shallow stream and to the banks on both sides, racing forward.

The buffalo thundered on. Slowly the riders began to outdistance the shaggy bison.

Captain Harding fired his pistol twice and waved the men to the left up and across a small hill in an effort to get out of the way of the creatures.

Just as they topped the rise they saw below them fifty Comanche warriors who shouted their war cries and stormed up the hill.

There was no other place for the cavalry company to go.

"Charge!" Captain Harding bellowed. "Pistols, Up!" They were a hundred yards from the hostiles when over the same ridge, a quarter of a mile down appeared a blue ribbon of riders.

The familiar bugle call of "attack" echoed through the small hills, and the Comanches looked up in surprise and anger. The two forces were still fifty yards apart when the Comanche turned with no apparent order and rode away.

Half the troop got in rifle shots at the retreating backs of the Comanche before they vanished over a slight rise.

Three minutes later Company B rode up in a flurry of flapping guideon and shouts of welcome.

Captain Harding rode back up to the brow of the rise and looked down at the small North Concho River. A thundering mass of shaggy brown beasts still poured down the narrow little valley. They smashed flat brush and tore around trees, tipping over many of the smaller ones and trampling them into kindling.

He rode back to his command, checked to be sure he had all of his Lightning men. Private Fisher was grinning, half drunk but able to sit on his horse. He sang a song softly, but nobody minded. Sgt. Casemore reported all men present or accounted for, including the dead trooper, Barlow, tied over his horse which was on a lead line.

Captain Harding shook hands with Lt. Edwards and they both decided it was time to put some distance between themselves and the last hunt of the season for the Comanche.

They rode until it was dark, saw no more sign of Comanches, and only a few straggling knots of buffalo. They camped that night on the highest hillock they could find and kept out double guards.

It was an uneventful night.

Two days later they rode into Fort Comfort. Lt. Riddle met them at the gate.

"Everything's been quiet here. Got the Kenny women off with an escort heading for Austin two days ago. Dispatch rider came in. You have a three pager from Col. Sparkman about your Lightning unit. I get the idea he'll want to come take a look at your men in action before long. He says General Phil Sheridan is interested."

"The hell you say? He'll have to get in line and wait until I'm ready to see him. First I get a bath."

A half hour later, Captain Colt Harding relaxed in his hot bathtub in his quarters. One more mission against the Comanches that did not result in rescuing Sadie. She wasn't at this site, but she had been with White Eagle. He knew it. But the damned Comanche was a good tactician. There was only one way to get Sadie out of that camp before the snow began, and it had to be before the Comanche settled down in a winter camp with as many as three hundred other tipis.

He had to concentrate now on going in with a dozen or so Tonkawas, going in quietly, without an army unit trailing him. Going in and beating White Eagle at his own tricks. That was the only way he would ever see his little girl again. He had three weeks to a month to do it. Now was the time! He had to do it, and he had to do it right now! He'd get started first thing in the morning setting it up.

For the first time in four months, Captain Colt Harding felt he was on the right track. Now he had a chance. He might never return from this probe, this mission, but he would know that he had done every goddamned thing he could to get Sadie back where she belonged, and out of the clutches of Walking White Eagle!

Tomorrow! Just wait until tomorrow!

PONY SOLDIERS

They were a dirty, undisciplined rabble, but they were the only chance a thousand settlers had to see another sunrise. Killing was their profession and they took pride in their work—they were too fierce to live, too damn mean to die.

_____2620-1   #5: SIOUX SHOWDOWN
                     $2.75 US/$3.75 CAN

_____2598-1   #4: CHEYENNE BLOOD STORM
                     $2.75US/$3.75CAN

_____2565-5   #3: COMANCHE MOON
                     $2.75US/$3.75CAN

_____2518-3   #1: SLAUGHTER AT BUFFALO
                     CREEK $2.75US/$3.75CAN

BUCKSKIN

The hard-riding, hard-bitten Adult Western series that's hotter'n a blazing pistol and as tough as the men who tamed the frontier.

#18: REMINGTON RIDGE   by Kit Dalton
___2509-4 $2.95US/$3.95CAN

#17: GUNSMOKE GORGE   by Kit Dalton
___2484-5 $2.50US/$3.25CAN

#16: WINCHESTER VALLEY   by Kit Dalton
___2463-2 $2.50US/$3.25CAN

#15: SCATTERGUN   by Kit Dalton
___2439-X $2.50US/$3.25CAN

#10: BOLT ACTION   by Roy LeBeau
___2315-6 $2.50US/$2.95CAN

#5: GUNSIGHT GAP   by Roy LeBeau
___2189-7 $2.75US/$2.95CAN

LEISURE BOOKS
ATTN: Customer Service Dept.
276 5th Avenue, New York, NY 10001

Please send me the book(s) checked above. I have enclosed $ _____
Add $1.25 for shipping and handling for the first book; $ .30 for each book thereafter. No cash, stamps, or C.O.D.s. All orders shipped within 6 weeks. Canadian orders please add $1.00 extra postage.

Name _____

Address _____

City _____ State _____ Zip _____
Canadian orders must be paid in U.S. dollars payable through a New York banking facility.   ☐ Please send a free catalogue.

The hard-riding, hard-bitten Adult Western series that's hotter'n a blazing pistol and as tough as the men who tamed the frontier.

#26: LARAMIE SHOWDOWN by Kit Dalton
____2806-9 $2.95

#25: POWDER CHARGE by Kit Dalton
____2754-2 $2.95

#24: COLT CROSSING by Kit Dalton
____2728-3 $2.95US/$3.95CAN

#23: CALIFORNIA CROSSFIRE by Kit Dalton
____2674-0 $2.95US/$3.95CAN

#22: SILVER CITY CARBINE by Kit Dalton
____2649-X $2.95US/$3.95CAN

#21: PEACEMAKER PASS by Kit Dalton
____2619-8 $2.95US/$3.95CAN

#20: PISTOL GRIP by Kit Dalton
____2551-5 $2.95US/$3.95CAN

#19: SHOTGUN STATION by Kit Dalton
____2529-9 $2.95US/$3.95CAN

DOUBLE-BARREL WESTERNS
Twice the Action—
Twice the Adventure—
Only a Fraction of the Price!

Two Complete and unabridged novels in each book!

The Sure-Fire Kid and **Wildcats of Tonto Basin**
by Nelson Nye.

_____2474-8 $3.95 US/$4.95 CAN

Gunslick Mountain and **Born to Trouble**
by Nelson Nye.

_____2497-7 $3.95 US/$4.95 CAN

The Bushwackers and **Ride the Wild Country**
by Lee Floren.

_____2610-4 $3.95 US/$4.95 CAN